Luca Veste is a w⸺ ith two
young daughters ⸺iversity
in Liverpool. He is the author of four novels, *Dead Gone*, *The Dying Place*, *Bloodstream* and *Then She Was Gone*.

Find out more at www.LucaVeste.com or follow @LucaVeste on Twitter and Facebook.

Praise for *Then She Was Gone*

'A page-turner'   ***Sunday Times Crime Club***

'Veste's Italian and ⸺duced an intriguing hothouse flower'   ***Financial Times***

'I loved it – I was gripp⸺ e end I couldn't leave it alone! A chilling stor⸺t made my blood run cold'   **Jenny Blackhurst**

'Luca Veste's Murphy⸺ pinnacle of modern crime fiction. Totally c⸺   **Steve Cavanagh**

'Socially incisive, emot⸺y gripping, *Then She Was Gone* is another t⸺nd marks the coming of age of the Murphy⸺   **Eva Dolan**

'Four books in and Murphy and Rossi's Liverpool is as dark as the Mersey. With missing children and dodgy politicians proving Veste's grip on social issues remains bang on the money, it's all tied up in a breathtaking and satisfying plot'   **Nick Quantrill**

Praise for *Bloodstream*

'This is a twisty, psychological crime debut in a gritty setting: a new favourite for police procedural lovers'   **Clare Mackintosh**

'Luca Veste is leading the new wave in British crime fiction'
                                                              Jay Stringer

LUCA VESTE
THEN SHE WAS GONE

SIMON &
SCHUSTER

London · New York · Sydney · Toronto · New Delhi

A CBS COMPANY

First published in Great Britain by Simon & Schuster UK Ltd, 2016
A CBS COMPANY

1 3 5 7 9 10 8 6 4 2

Simon & Schuster UK Ltd
1st Floor
222 Gray's Inn Road
London WC1X 8HB

www.simonandschuster.co.uk

Simon & Schuster Australia, Sydney
Simon & Schuster India, New Delhi

A CIP catalogue for this book
is available from the British Library.

Hardback ISBN: 978-1-4711-4755-5
Paperback ISBN: 978-1-4711-4139-3
eBook ISBN: 978-1-4711-4140-9

Printed a̲   Typeset by Hewer Text UK Ltd, Edinburgh
                                    K) Ltd, Croydon, CR0   Y

Simo̲   urcing pap[]
that is made f   od grown in sustai   and support e Forest
Stewardship C   the leading interna   est certification o   anisation.
Our books   the FSC logo re printed on FSC certifie   aper.

THEN
SHE WAS
GONE

For Uncle John "Murphy" Kirkham
Thank you for the inspiration
and for everything else over the years

ONE YEAR AGO

Tuesday 1 September

He had no final memory of her. Only a single image. One last moment, trapped in an interminable loop, playing over and over in his mind. There, every time he closed his eyes, mocking him.

Tim Johnson was beginning to accept that there was nothing else about his daughter he would ever remember.

People will tell you that love at first sight doesn't exist. That it takes time to feel all the emotions that make up the L word. Comfort, familiarity, yearning. They don't just appear overnight.

Those people are wrong.

Have a child and feel that bolt of lightning when you hold them for the first time. A little face looking up at you, completely at your mercy and dependence. That's love at first sight. When his daughter had been placed in his arms, he had fallen in love instantly. Head over heels, flat on his back in love. His whole life had led to that point. Every mistake, every misstep, it had all been worth it.

It had taken him a couple of days to find the best route to walk around the park. The area was new to him and full of hidden surprises, nooks and crannies to discover. He had seen it only in pictures before now, the large pavilion-type structure taking up most of results when he searched for it on Google. A circular building with glass windows making up the outside structure.

There was, of course, more to Sefton Park than that building. The park itself covered at least two hundred acres; a piece of tranquillity in the heart of the city of Liverpool, its vast green spaces surrounded by trees. He had found a cafe in the middle of the park, an old fountain nearby. The whole area undisturbed and well-kept, despite the reputation of the local youths. There were closer parks, but it was worth taking the extra time to visit this one.

The days had seemed much longer recently. It had become more difficult to fill the quiet moments.

'Feed the ducks, Molly? That's what we'll do today, hey, baby? Daddy take you to feed the ducks?'

The four-week-old child he pushed around the park in front of him didn't open her eyes, having fallen asleep before they'd even reached the park. The motion of the pushchair sending her straight off.

'When you're a bit older, we'll find some swings in this place. You'll like that.'

A balding man, desperately hanging onto the last remnants of his thirties, jogged past them, his heavy breathing and the tinny dance music filtering through headphones breaking the silence.

The jogger didn't seem to notice him, lost in the effort of running just a little further.

A cool breeze whistled through trees to the side of them, disturbing birds perched in the treetops. He looked up as they took flight, circled and settled once more. Autumn was drawing in. The last remnants of summer already forgotten.

'We'll have to wrap you up warmer soon, Molly. It'll be cold this winter, I think.'

He'd lived in the north of England for almost a decade and still wasn't used to the subtle differences compared with the south where he'd grown up. They passed another large open space of field. A bare patch of land sitting unused. Just a vastness, opening up and then encircled by a line of trees in the distance. A small inlet of water ran beside the path, broken twigs and leaves floating on the surface.

Silence settled back in. A contrast, he imagined, with the weekends and school holidays when the park would be bustling with life. Children of all ages being let loose by harried parents, taken for a walk to use up some energy. Football and cricket matches being organised on the spacious green land. Jumpers for goalposts and all that nostalgia.

He imagined sitting there, a blanket underneath him and the sun on his face, hearing the sounds of laughter and raised voices. Pictured Molly running off, never too far, but enough for her to learn a little independence. Meeting friends, discovering new things and new pleasures.

He imagined a life there. The thought of it made him smile.

When he heard the footsteps behind him, he thought it was the jogger again, back for another lap. The hurried slaps of soles hitting the path as they headed in his direction didn't make him flinch or turn around.

Maybe if he had, things would have been different.

In the pram, Molly fussed a little, so he slowed his pace and tried to soothe her. He moved the dummy closer to her face, the suckling increasing as she finally found it again and began to calm once more.

The first blow didn't register at first. The surprise of it, a dull thud at the back of his head, his vision blurring for an instant, was so unexpected in the peace of the surroundings.

The second blow buckled his legs. He tried to steady himself, clutching the pushchair's handles as his balance went. A third blow sent him to the ground.

Not like this. Not like this.

He crumbled to the ground, the fall not registering as his weight hit the floor. The sound of the pushchair falling with him became muffled as the blurriness returned with vigour. He tried to reach out towards it, but his hands didn't obey. As he shifted onto his side, he saw a black boot scrape towards him. He tried to shake his head, but that just sent waves of pain through his temples. A feeling of nausea swept through him, the edges of his vision growing darker by the millisecond.

That single image, just before he lost consciousness. The wheel of the pram, holding Molly, his life, spinning round and round.

Not an image of his daughter. The pushchair couldn't have fallen beside him with her facing him. No, she was facing the other way, so all he saw was a wheel. Spinning and spinning.

As he lost her.

*   *   *

He didn't know how long he was out for, but the sun was still beaming down when he rubbed his eyes and got to his haunches. The memory of what had happened came back slowly to him, making him rise to his feet, before falling back down onto his knees and dry heaving onto the grass beside him.

'Molly,' he tried to shout, though his throat betrayed him. He swallowed back bile and tried again. 'Molly.'

He turned to where he'd seen the last image. Saw only an empty path. No spinning wheel. No overturned pram.

No Molly.

No daughter.

No life.

Wednesday 2 September

Twenty-four hours she'd been gone. Out there, without him. Scared, confused. If a four-week-old could feel those things. Wondering where he was. She knew his face. That was how it worked, he was sure of it. It didn't matter if it was twenty-four hours, or twenty-four days. She would remember him.

Please don't let it be twenty-four days.

'Do you not have a photo of . . . Molly, did you say?'

He sighed for what seemed the thousandth time since the detectives had reappeared at the house. 'I've told you again and again, no I haven't. She's only a few weeks old and I have been too busy to print any yet. I had some on my phone, but that's been stolen, along with my daughter. What are you doing here? Shouldn't you be out there, finding her?'

'Mr Johnson, I can assure you we have officers out there doing exactly that. The best way to help us is to give us as much information as possible, OK? Now, let's start at the beginning again. Think we can do that?'

He nodded, tiredness washing over him. He had been awake all night, unable to sleep. Once the police had arrived at the park, everything had begun to pass in a blur of questions and offers of tea.

'We've only just moved here,' Tim said, a sigh escaping from his mouth. 'We were over on the Wirral before here.'

'And why the move? Where's Molly's mother . . . Lauren was it? Yes . . . where is she?'

He hesitated, again, as he had every time he'd told the story. 'I don't know. I haven't spoken to her since we had to leave. I tried calling her, but there's no answer. She hadn't been well for a while . . .'

'In what way?'

He pointed to his head, his hand moving upwards slowly. 'Mentally. During the pregnancy she was saying very strange things. She'd put on a show of being fine for the midwives, nurses, things like that. Not that she'd let me in for the appointments.'

The detective looked up from her notepad at that. 'Why do you think that was?'

He bristled a little at the accusatory tone. He didn't trust her. The headscarf wasn't right, not with the Scouse accent alongside it. It made him wary of her. 'She wasn't thinking straight. She thought I was going to bring bad luck in. She wanted only women around her. Even for the birth. I wasn't allowed anywhere near the place. Couldn't even hand out cigars in the waiting room like a nineteen fifties dad. Had to wait at home by the phone for her to call me.'

'That can't have been easy.'

He relaxed a little as the detective's voice became less accusatory. Maybe it didn't matter so much that she was one of those Muslims. Or a woman. 'No, it wasn't. I wanted to be there for her and Molly. To cut the umbilical cord and all that stuff. It wasn't exactly what I had been expecting.'

The detective leaned towards him, her coat brushing against the edge of the couch. 'Then what happened?'

He took a breath. 'The first few days were fine, a struggle, of course, with a newborn, but it seemed like all the weird stuff had been forgotten. Then, I came home from doing a shop to find her setting things on fire in the backyard.'

'What sort of things?'

He looked around for the glass of water he'd had earlier, but couldn't see it. 'All of the clothes we'd bought Molly. Photographs she'd brought home from the hospital. Molly's moses basket and all her bedding. It was like she was trying to erase any trace of our daughter's life.'

The detective glanced towards her partner quickly before turning back to him. 'Where was Molly when this happened?'

'She was inside the house. She'd been left on the living-room floor. I picked her up and made sure she was OK. Lauren was still outside, just staring at the flames.'

His mouth was dry, his whole body itching to stand up and go across to the kitchen and satiate his thirst. He waited instead.

'This was two weeks ago,' he said after a few seconds' silence. 'I gave her a few more days, just to see if it was a one-off. She just got worse. I couldn't leave the house without Molly. I was scared of what would happen while I wasn't there. I didn't sleep much, not that you can anyway with a newborn, but it wasn't because of that. I was worried about what she would do.'

The detective shifted back on the couch. 'What led you over here, to Liverpool?'

He swallowed back dryness. 'I had to go out and get a few bits. Molly had been crying for a while and I'd finally got her down to sleep. I didn't want to disturb her, so I didn't take her with me. Lauren had been in a good mood that day, so I thought it would be OK if I just went to the shop quickly and came back . . .'

Every time he had got to this part of the story, he had begun to shake. Imperceptibly at first, before it became more noticeable.

'I came back home and she was on the doorstep with Molly in the pram. They were about to leave, but she wouldn't tell me where they were going. I . . . I persuaded her to go back inside. That's when I saw the note on the coffee table in the living room. She tried to hide it, but I got to it first.'

He remembered the fear on Lauren's face, the way she shrank back from him. She was like a stranger.

He left that part out.

'It said she was taking Molly away. That she had to take her away from me. I tried to speak to her about it, but she was just babbling. It read like she was . . . she was going to do something stupid.'

The Muslim detective didn't speak, waiting for him to continue.

'I knew I had this place waiting for me if I needed it. So, once Lauren had fallen asleep that night, I packed a few things and came over here. I thought giving her some time might be best. My aunt passed away a few months ago and my cousins are still trying to sell the place. I had a key from when she was still alive.'

'We talked to your new neighbours . . .'

He shook his head, trying to work out why the conversation hadn't gone the same way as it had done previously. Before, when he'd reached this part of the story, there had been sympathy and concern. This was different.

'We spoke to a number of them. None of them remember you arriving here, let alone with a child in your company. No one heard a baby crying, which seems odd. Why do you think that would be?'

He opened his mouth and closed it again. Considered his answer first. 'I don't know. The average age around here isn't exactly on the young side. Maybe they didn't have their hearing aids in or something.'

'Mr Johnson,' the detective began, looking towards her colleague and then back at him. 'We couldn't find a Lauren at the address you gave us. We've had people search inside the property and they couldn't find any signs of her. We've also put out a trace on her name and come up with no record of her being a resident either. We're waiting on hospital records, but if she gave birth in the past few weeks as you say, we should find her, shouldn't we?'

He didn't like the tone the detective was taking now. 'Of course. It's not like I've dreamed the whole thing.'

The detective glanced at her colleague again. 'We're not saying anything right now, Tim. We just can't find any trace of anyone who remembers anything about your movements in the past couple of days.'

'Speak to the neighbours back in the other house. They'll definitely remember.'

'We have, Tim. They're saying they thought you lived alone.'

He made a noise halfway between a laugh and a shout of alarm. 'That's not possible . . .'

Saturday 5 September

Day five of Molly being missing and the media interest had disappeared almost entirely. What at first had been front-page news was now relegated to a small *Information Wanted* section on a local Facebook group. As soon as the police had decided that the most likely thing to have happened was that Molly's mother had taken her child back, the media had moved on. Just another domestic. Another father left to pick up the pieces.

He thought about the likelihood of him ending up in a superhero costume on top of Buckingham Palace, but decided his current luck would see him locked up with a terrorist in some cell.

The detective – DC Hashem – continued to visit him, but seemed to eye him with more and more suspicion by the day. He was surprised she was still coming, but the questions were more confusing by the day.

He was tired of it all. Sleep was a distant memory. He would drop off for an hour or two then jolt awake with his heart beating, stumbling off the couch to pull back the curtains once again. Every noise outside made his heart stop for a beat. He could smell his own mustiness emanating off him.

There was no end for him. Not a happy one, anyway. He felt that with every fibre.

A persistent banging came from the hallway. He jumped off the sofa, moving so fast he knocked over a side table, barely aware of it crashing to the floor as he flung open the front door.

'Oh, come in,' he said, making his way back to living room. He noticed the table upended on the floor and bent to pick it up. 'Sorry, must have knocked it over.'

'It's fine if you got a little angry, Tim,' the female detective said, looking around the room as if it were her first time there. 'It's a trying time, I understand that.'

'Angry? No . . . I just bumped into it,' Tim said, righting the table and then standing to face the detective.

'Do you get angry often, Tim?'

Tim was stuck for a moment, staring open-mouthed at the detective. 'What? Why are you asking me that?'

'I think it's a perfectly reasonable question. Do you throw things around, maybe punch a hole in a wall, or rip a door off its hinges?'

'No, I do not. I can get cross sometimes, but I'm not violent . . .'

'Ah, but that's not strictly true, is it?' the detective said, moving past him and perching on the edge of a chair. 'We know, for example, that you received a police caution for being involved in . . .'

'That was nothing,' Tim interrupted, but then he stopped himself. He breathed in and out and fixed the detective with a stare. 'What has this got to do with anything? Can you tell me what you're doing to find Molly?'

'Can we go over things again? I want to make sure we have all the information on Molly as best as we possibly can.'

Tim wanted to walk out, get away from the woman and from the house. To be back in that moment, in the park, pushing Molly along. Free and happy. Instead, he was forced to stand there and listen.

'Why haven't you been in touch with your parents?'

'We're not close,' he said after a few seconds, trying to remain calm. 'There's no reason to have them involved.'

'We've spoken to them,' the detective said, looking at him with those inquisitive eyes of hers. 'I don't think they were all that happy to find out from the TV that they were grandparents. Bit of a shock, I think you can imagine. Did you not think to get in touch and let them know what was happening?'

'No, I didn't. As I said, we're not close.'

'Falling out? Temper get the better of you?'

This time he made a movement towards the door, but the male detective standing in the doorway stopped him in his tracks. 'Why are you asking me these questions?' Tim said, turning back to the female detective. 'They have nothing to do with Molly being missing. Have you found Lauren yet? That's what you should be doing. Finding her and seeing if she has taken my daughter.'

'Calm down, Tim. Come and sit down.'

He looked back at the male detective who was still staring at him and decided to sit on the sofa. Settled on the edge. 'Please, just tell me what you want to hear. I just want you to find her.'

'We understand that. There are still a lot of unanswered questions, though, which is making our job just that little bit more difficult. So, how about we clear those up and then we will be in a better position to find your daughter. Sound fair?'

Tim nodded, wrapping his arms around himself and leaning forwards.

'You said you'd been with Lauren for just under a year,' the female detective said, confusing him by changing tack. 'Did she ever meet any of your family?'

He was beginning to see how his answers were unlikely to help him. 'No, she didn't. There was no reason for her to meet any of them. I wasn't close to them, so why would I introduce her to them?'

'Did she meet any of your friends?'

'I don't really have any friends. I left all that behind a long time ago.'

The detective made some sort of noise under her breath. 'So, she wasn't introduced to your family, or friends, yet you were living together and she became pregnant. Were you working at the time?'

'Yes, I worked from home. Tech support for various websites. I have my own business.'

'You don't speak to your family, you have no friends, you work from home and your neighbours don't know you exist. That seems a little like isolation to me. Is that intentional?'

He didn't know how to respond, so he shrugged his shoulders instead.

'We've tried to locate Lauren from the information you've provided us with, Tim, but we've been unsuccessful.'

'I don't understand . . .' Tim began, before being interrupted.

'I'm saying, we've checked into every local and national database. We've also checked again at your previous address, with your old neighbours and anyone we could find. No one recalls a woman being there. No one recalls a child being there either. We can find no trace of anyone named Lauren Moran, born on the date you gave us, in the area – or nearby, in fact.'

'That can't be right.'

The detective leaned forwards, placing her notepad to one side. She stared at him.

'Did they exist, Tim? Either of them? What is the truth here?'

Monday 21 September

Three weeks she had been gone.

That's how long it took for him to give in and call for help. He hadn't spoken to the group in years, but it was finally time.

He waited until the train came above ground, leaving the tunnel which ran underneath the River Mersey, and then pulled out his new mobile phone.

'It's me . . . Tim . . . I need help . . . I need the club to help me . . . Yes, I know, again, but that's what it's for, right?'

He could hear the exasperation from the voice on the other end of the line, but managed to set up a meeting for the next day.

Tim was desperate. There was no evidence his daughter had ever existed as far as the police were concerned. Just his word, which wasn't enough.

He'd spent his time wandering around, hoping to catch sight of her. He was certain he would recognise her. There was a small mole, or birthmark, on her right earlobe. He could close his eyes and remember the touch of it on his finger, as he rocked her to sleep, stroking the side of her face and touching her ear. He was the only one who knew that was what would work.

It was obvious to him what had happened. Lauren had found out where he'd gone, attacked him in that park and taken Molly somewhere. The problem was proving that he was right.

The problem was proving their existence at all.

How could Molly be unreal when every fibre of him ached? He felt incomplete and malformed without her.

How could he have made her up?

He blinked and had an image of Lauren cowering from him, as he stood over her. Another second and the image was gone. Replaced by the wheel spinning once more.

He left the train at Moreton station and walked the ten-minute journey from there through a dodgy estate to his altogether nicer one. He pulled his coat tighter around him as the wind picked up and swirled fallen leaves on the ground ahead of him.

He entered the street where the house he'd spent almost a year with Lauren was situated. He'd decide to move back – convinced Lauren would return there if she was going to come back anywhere.

Flashing lights stopped him in his tracks. A police car was parked up outside his house. Another van was there, the words *Scientific Support* emblazoned on the side. He broke into a jog, which turned into a sprint as he covered the remaining few yards at speed. He stopped at the end of the driveway, almost barrelling into a uniformed policeman who was standing guard.

'What's going on?' Tim said, already out of breath, but not caring. 'Why are you here? Have you found her?'

'You need to stay here for a second.'

Tim tried to move past the police officer, but a burly arm blocked his path. He looked towards the house, squinting into the darkness, before a light was switched on in the hallway and two figures emerged.

'Mr Johnson,' a voice called out from the direction of the front door.

'Have you . . . have you found her?' Tim said, his words faltering as he lifted a hand to his mouth. 'Is she OK? What's going on?'

'I need you to come with me,' DC Hashem said, taking her hands out of the pockets of her coat. Tim saw the man standing behind her was the same one that had accompanied her to the other house.

'Tell me now,' Tim replied, words falling from his mouth without him being aware of them. 'Just tell me, is she OK? Please tell me Molly is OK. Where's my daughter?'

'I just need you to come with us now. We'll explain everything down at the station.'

He didn't think he could make the short walk to the car, but he was opening the door and getting in before he realised he'd started moving. Other people headed towards the house, wearing white overalls and carrying shovels. The male detective sat in the back next to him. The car pulled away, Tim looked back at the darkened house and he began to shake uncontrollably. He could feel the man's eyes on him.

He whispered to himself for almost the entire journey back to Liverpool.

'Please let her be OK. Please let her be OK. Please let her be . . .'

PRESENT DAY

PART ONE

An eye for an eye
will only make the whole world blind.
Mahatma Gandhi

I'm a fighter. I believe in the eye-for-an-eye business.
I'm no cheek turner. I got no respect for a man
who won't hit back. You kill my dog,
you better hide your cat.
Muhammad Ali

While seeking revenge,
dig two graves – one for yourself.
Douglas Horton

You

You're consumed with hate.

You think of nothing but desolation and the absolute need to devastate. To destroy. To satiate yourself in vengeance.

You have lived your life in moments of desperation. Each day passing in a blur of perceived normality. Now is your chance to be something more.

You plan. You want it to be perfect. There isn't anything you haven't foreseen and countered for. You cannot be stopped. Nothing will stand in your way.

They must pay for what they have done.

You want the violence. You feel it in every fibre of your body. The desire, the craving. You need to make things right. You need to redress the balance.

You don't see them as victims. You know others will, but that does not matter. You know the truth. You know the public will care little, instead waiting for the next instalment. A reality show to end them all. A true fight to the death, beamed into every living room. No one cares about the so-called victims. They just want the next part to begin.

They're just like you. They love to watch and vicariously experience the thrill of violence and suffering. You know it to be true.

You want the world to die a slow, painful death.

You want to be there to watch it die.

There are faces you see every night, lying in the dark waiting for sleep to consume you. Appearing in your mind without invitation. Making your skin crawl, your stomach churn and hands shake. You feel anger, you feel afraid. You want those faces to disappear.

You want silence. You want to switch off that part of your brain which keeps bringing them back.

Instead of living in a constant state of terror, you decide to do something about it. To switch off those voices and make those faces evaporate. You have plans, you are in control. You know what to do. You have right on your side, you have the tools and the desire to do what is necessary.

You want retribution for what happened.

You want revenge.

One

There was a time when the issue of getting older hadn't bothered him so much. He remembered that time with a fading clarity. Now it needled him, occupying his thoughts without reason. Another year about to come to an end – the onward march towards the magical age of forty.

Aging was becoming wearisome.

Detective Inspector David Murphy looked out across the River Mersey, leaning forwards against the promenade railings. He glanced down at his hands gripping the metal, his knuckles white and scarred, then stared back out across the water. He could see the ferry making its approach towards home in an early afternoon gloom. Darkened clouds were moving above him, moody and plentiful, casting the water below him with a grey shadow. The view across the river was a direct contrast to the one he would experience from the other side of the water: fewer iconic buildings, less industry and none of the bustle of modern life.

Murphy turned and gazed up at the Port of Liverpool building directly in front of him. Its more famous sibling – the Royal Liver building – sitting next to it, the mythical Liver Birds perched atop, looking out over the same view as him. He craned his neck upwards to glimpse a sight of them. Took in the faded stone of the structure and felt a sense of calm wash over him. Some things stayed the same in an ever-changing world. They signified a past which was now being increasingly encroached upon by futurism – the new museums and office buildings growing ever closer to them. One of the newer museums lay to his right – fans of the Beatles given their own altar to worship at within. Further back, a black, glass coffin of a building lying between the waterfront and the city centre. The Albert Dock was visible further down the river, now filled with trendy bars and shops selling to tourists and excited youngsters.

Yet, there were buildings that would always be part of the Liverpool city skyline.

'I decided against it. Looks like it's about to rain any second and there's nothing sadder than eating ice cream under an umbrella.'

Murphy turned to his wife, watching her climbing the few steps up to the promenade to join him, and smiled towards her. 'Could be worse,' he said, wrapping his arm around her as she reached him. 'Could have forgotten the umbrella.'

Sarah lay her head against his chest. 'This is nice,' she said, turning with Murphy as he looked out across the river once more. 'Been a while since we've been down here.'

'Everything's changing.'

'That's modern life for you. Blink and they build something where you were looking last.'

Murphy made a noise at the back of his throat and continued to watch the ferry cross the Mersey.

'I love the fact I'm going back to university,' Sarah said, lifting her head slightly to look around the waterfront. 'But I really wish the holidays lasted a little longer. Could get used to meeting you on your lunch break and taking in the scenery around here.'

'Don't you think you get enough time off as it is? It's like three months off in the bloody summer. More, in fact, than when you were teaching. I'm lucky to get three days off in a row.'

'Should have become a teacher instead then. I'd love to see you try and control a classroom full of six year olds.'

Murphy shuddered at the thought. 'You're OK. I'd rather deal with criminals any day of the week.'

There was still a period of adjustment going on between them, now Sarah had left work as a teacher. She had decided to go back to university, following the trauma they had experienced fifteen months earlier. A violent attack in their home, which had almost resulted in both their lives being ended.

Sarah had wanted to understand what could drive someone to do what had been done to them, so she had decided to return to university and study psychology and criminology. Murphy just wanted to forget.

'You thought about where we're going to eat later?'

Murphy pulled away and looked downwards at Sarah. Sometimes the height difference bothered him, sometimes it didn't register. There was almost a foot between them, he was well over six foot tall, she was not much over five. It led to some odd looks sometimes, especially as she had kept her pre-thirties looks. Whereas he was becoming more weathered by the hour. 'I thought you'd decide for once.'

Sarah began to shake her head before Murphy cut in again.

'I've chosen where we've eaten at least the last six hundred times.'

'You've kept count, have you?'

Murphy couldn't help but smile. 'Smart arse.'

'I'll think of something. Probably in town. I'm not going to be done in Liverpool One until late.'

'Well, don't spend too much money . . .'

Murphy stopped as he received an elbow in the ribs from Sarah. 'I'm spending what I like, knobhead. I've not done any shopping in bloody ages and I need to fit in with the other students. They're all going to be at least fifteen years younger than me in that university. And I'm using my own money anyway.'

'First, ow,' Murphy replied, making a show of rubbing his side, 'bony elbows. Second, I wasn't exactly being serious. I just like seeing you react to my sexism.'

'You're just a wind-up merchant, you are. Anyway, aren't you best getting back?'

Murphy rolled up the sleeve on his suit jacket and checked the time. Looked up at the Liver Building and saw the same time peering down at him. 'You're right. I'll speak to you later, once you've bought half of the stuff in the shops, and bought me something two sizes too small because that's the size you *wish* I was . . .'

'I never–'

'Course you don't,' Murphy replied, smiling down at Sarah and then planting a kiss on her forehead. 'You all right getting back from here? I'm going to flag a cab down if you want dropping off?'

'No, it's all right,' Sarah said, giving Murphy a squeeze and then stepping away. 'I don't mind walking up.'

Murphy made his way towards the Coffin-Building, turning to wave back at her, the smile on his face fading as he moved away. There was something to be said for taking off during work hours and having a blast of normality. Mostly, it just made it more difficult to go back to work.

Within a few minutes, he was in the back of a black cab, winding through the traffic on the outskirts of the city centre, passing the never-ending roadworks on Leeds Street, sweeping round Liverpool John Moores University and eventually turning into St Anne Street.

The too-familiar brown-brick building came into view, Murphy stopped the cab a few yards past and over-tipped the driver.

Five minutes later, he walked into the main office of the Major Crime Unit. He took a deep breath and made his way to his desk, passing the various detectives under his auspicious command.

'Nice lunch?'

Murphy mocked a salute towards DS Laura Rossi and sat down. 'Very. One of those where you don't want to come back to this place.'

'It's why I try and eat in the building as often as possible. Not from the canteen, of course.'

Murphy pulled his chair closer to the desk and moved the mouse, causing his computer monitor to come to life. 'What was on the menu from Mama Rossi today?'

Rossi ran a hand through her long, almost black hair, sweeping it away from her face. 'Just some mortadella, olives and mozzarella on ciabatta. Nothing special.'

Murphy rolled his eyes at her. 'Of course not. Bet it was bloody delicious.'

'You always think that, but that's only because you're used to the shite they pass off as sandwiches in here.'

'Got that right,' Murphy replied, signing into his computer and checking his emails. 'Missed anything?'

Rossi shook her head. 'Still waiting on uniforms to pick up that lad who tried to hold up a post office this morning. Shouldn't take them too long, given he had to take off the crash helmet to be understood. DC Kirkham is taking a witness statement from that assault from last night–'

'The domestic?'

'Yeah. Going to try and do the bloke for attempted murder. CPS probably won't go for it.'

Murphy grunted, reading through the subject lines of a few emails for anything of interest. 'Is she still talking?'

'For now,' Rossi replied, shifting paperwork off her desk and into a drawer. 'Wants him done for everything. *Bastardo* tried to strangle her, so that's sparked something in her.'

'Anything else?'

'Nothing at the moment. Although the boss has been on the phone for the last five minutes. Doing the pacing up and down thing as well. Got a feeling something is going on . . .'

He made to reply when the door to DCI Stephens's internal office banged open. Murphy rolled his eyes at Rossi and turned to look towards the boss.

'David, Laura, when you're ready.'

Murphy glanced at Rossi and shook his head. 'Just when we thought we were going to have an easy afternoon.'

Murphy and Rossi shuffled into DCI Stephens's office and closed the door behind them. The office was as neat and ordered as usual. A single filing cabinet, large desk and leather chair took up most of the space. The only personal touch – a photograph of the boss's family – faced outwards, so those coming into the office couldn't help but notice it.

'Sit.'

Murphy and Rossi followed orders and sat on the chairs placed to one side of the organised desk, waiting for DCI Stephens to amble back to her chair and drop into it with a sigh and a shake of her head.

'This is . . . well, it's not the usual thing I would call you in for.'

Murphy glanced at Rossi, ready to raise an eyebrow, but she was focussed on the boss.

'I have a missing persons report. Normally, it would be dealt with by uniform, as you know, but this is different.'

Rossi glanced at Murphy and his raised eyebrow.

'This is a bit more delicate,' DCI Stephens continued. 'It's a . . . well, it concerns someone we all know.'

'Celebrity?' Murphy said, having flashbacks to a case the previous year which had turned to awfulness within a few hours.

'Not as such,' DCI Stephens said, looking away and moving the notepad on her desk slightly. 'An important person, shall we say. Someone who will be missed.'

'Are we allowed to know his name?' Murphy said.

'It's Sam Byrne.'

Rossi said something in Italian under her breath before Murphy had chance to answer. DCI Stephens spoke for him anyway.

'Yes . . . *that* Sam Byrne.'

Two

There was an uncomfortable silence for a few seconds as they waited for DCI Stephens to speak. Eventually, Murphy grew tired of the performance. 'That young bloke who's up for MP?' he said, sitting back in his seat a little. 'Surprised it hasn't been in the *Echo* already. How long's he been missing?'

DCI Stephens turned her gaze back to them and almost rolled her eyes. 'It's being kept quiet for now. We don't want to have it come out if he's just taking a break or something. He's been gone for a few days at least. Last seen Thursday evening, leaving his campaign office.'

Murphy glanced at Rossi who was keeping her counsel. 'This is the fourth day then. How do we come into it?'

'I . . . sorry, we need someone to look into his disappearance. I've been asked by the higher-ups to put our best on it. Which means his parents have been *exerting* their influence. They want to see if we can find him before it becomes a story.'

Murphy couldn't help but preen a little. It had been a while since he'd been categorised as the best at something. 'What are the details? Who called?'

DCI Stephens brought the notepad on her desk closer. 'Someone in his office. Assistant or something. Got into his car and vanished. No one has seen him, or the car, since. I imagine Byrne's parents had already been onto their friends here, though, once she'd been in touch with them over the weekend. He didn't turn up to the office on Friday, didn't answer his phone that day or any other.'

'He doesn't have any significant other concerned?' Rossi said, speaking aloud for the first time. 'A girlfriend or boyfriend?'

'He's single, which makes things a little more difficult.'

'So we don't know if he has a girlfriend, or a partner we don't know about, et cetera et cetera,' Murphy said, finishing the sentence.

'Exactly. I tried that one with DSI Butler, but he wasn't having any of it.'

Murphy ran a hand over his beard – closely shorn, but dark enough to be noticeable. For now, anyway. He was finding more grey hairs by the day. 'Comes from him then.'

DCI Stephens ignored his hard tone. 'I just need you to look into it, see if there's a simple explanation and then move on. That's all. Nothing major, no big task force or anything like that for now. We want this kept in house.'

'OK, we can do that,' Murphy said, glancing at Rossi for support. She turned away from him slowly, eyebrows raising and dropping back to normal in the time it took to face the boss again.

'Probably a partner we don't know about. A weekend

away has turned into something longer than intended? Have uniforms been to his address, his phone checked, that kind of thing?'

DCI Stephens gave Murphy a dismissive wave. 'You can find all that out yourself. I'm sure they've at least knocked on his door. Just get over to his house and confirm he's not bloody dead or something, then we can knock all this on the head and be done with it. Although I'm sure his mum and dad have already been inside.'

Murphy lifted himself out of the chair and gave a mock salute to DCI Stephens. 'You got it, boss.'

'Don't be that guy, David.'

Murphy waited for Rossi as they exited the office, making their way back to their desks together in silence. A few heads turned expectantly, but Murphy ignored them. He sat down at his desk and waited for his computer to load up again.

'Seems like scut work to me,' Rossi said from opposite him. 'Thought we'd left that behind when we reorganised.'

'Friends in high places,' Murphy replied, opening the short file on Sam Byrne's disappearance that DCI Stephens had already emailed across. He printed it off. 'We need to get some of those.'

'Hardly a major crime, is it? Which is what we're supposed to deal with.'

'Were you prepared to put your foot down and say no?'

Murphy stood and waited to see if Rossi was going to reply. He collected the file pages from the printer when it became clear she wasn't going to answer.

'Nothing much here,' Murphy said as Rossi made her

way around to his side of the desks. 'Uniforms visited his address but got no answer. Nothing out of place. No signs of forced entry or anything to indicate foul play.'

'Means nothing . . .'

'Of course not,' Murphy said, continuing to read through the few paragraphs of information. 'There's bugger all here. We're at square one with this thing.'

'We're best getting started then.'

'Call those uniforms, get them to meet us at the house.'

Fifteen minutes later they were pulling out of the station car park and onto St Anne Street. Murphy shifted the pool car into gear and drove steadily away from the city centre, the area changing as he did so.

'There's a distinct lack of effort around here,' Rossi said, fiddling with the satnav on the dashboard before giving up with it and pulling out her phone. 'I know I say it every time, but they could be doing so much with this place. They can throw up a building in the city centre in a few months but everything else takes bloody ages to do around here.'

Murphy hummed a response. It was difficult to disagree with Rossi's sentiments.

'All those new buildings and regeneration projects going on down at the waterfront and they can't find a bit of money to throw at Scottie Road.'

Scotland Road was the name for an A road which ran from the city centre towards the north of Liverpool and the towns there. What had once been a tight-knit community of people, was now a place of closed-down pubs, old churches, run-down shops, and more speed cameras than Murphy could remember seeing on any other road in the city. There were signs of change, but they were few and far between. 'Everything just seems like it's waiting to be knocked down and forgotten about. Where's this place again?'

Rossi moved a leaf of paper to the top of the folder she was holding on her lap.

'Blundellsands. House is on Warren Road. Won't be a bad place around there. Can't imagine he paid for it himself. He's what, twenty-six, twenty-seven?'

'Always nice to have rich parents. A world away from this type of place,' Murphy said, leaving behind the rundown area of Scotland Road and turning onto Derby Road.

The drive was only twenty minutes, but the monotony of the dual carriageway with its endless stream of traffic travelling to and from the north of the city made it feel much longer. The sun above them kept threatening to make an appearance through large clouds of white, but Murphy's sunglasses stayed in the inside pocket of his suit jacket.

Soon the built-up areas of the city centre and neigh-bouring towns of Bootle and Waterloo were a memory as they entered the leafy streets of Blundellsands.

'Any ideas whereabouts this place is?' Murphy said, slowing down as they turned onto Warren Road. He attempted to peer through the trees that obscured the houses beyond.

'Yeah,' Rossi replied, mirroring Murphy and squinting through the foliage. 'That was number twelve so only a few more up.'

Ten minutes and three wrong houses later, they found the correct address and parked up. The house was set back from the road and looked quite diminutive at first glance, but Murphy realised its appearance was deceptive, as the side came into view. A larger structure was attached to the front facade, almost as if it had once been a small cottage house or bungalow, before being extended into a larger dwelling.

It had been built of white stone, with traditional diamond-patterned leaded lights giving it a much older appearance. The house looked well-maintained and hanging flower baskets adorned either side of the front door.

A marked police car was parked near the entrance, looking almost abandoned, a lone officer sitting in the passenger seat. The driver appeared in the doorway as they approached.

'We got the keys from the parents,' the uniform said as Murphy and Rossi reached him. 'There's nothing different from the other day. No signs of struggle or forced entry.'

'Anything look disturbed at all?' Rossi said, shielding her eyes from the sun as it finally made an appearance.

'No. Just a normal house really. Bit bare, if you ask me. Think he's the only one living here and there's a fair bit of house to fill.'

Murphy took a step closer, ducking underneath a hanging basket. 'Have you been wearing gloves?'

The uniform hesitated before speaking. 'I didn't think—'

'No, you didn't,' Murphy cut in, shaking his head. 'Go and sit in the car with your mate until I ask you to move.'

'No need to be like that. We weren't told—'

'I'm not interested,' Murphy said, taking gloves out of his pocket and snapping them on. 'Just be a good boy and do as you're told.'

The uniform walked away, muttering under his breath. Murphy took his place in the doorway and waited for Rossi to finish putting on her own pair of gloves.

'Any need?' Rossi said, rolling her eyes at him. 'Bloke obviously doesn't think there's anything going on here that requires us to be forensically aware.'

'I'll apologise to him at some point. If I remember. Always good to make friends.'

Murphy took the lead, entering the hallway of the house, the brightness of the outside not permeating within. He almost had to squint to see his way forwards, the lack of light giving a dingy tinge to the place.

'You take the rooms down here, Laura,' Murphy said, pointing towards the various doors, both open and closed, that ran off the hallway. 'I'll be upstairs.'

Rossi nodded and walked through into what Murphy assumed was the living room, he turned and ascended the stairs. A couple of framed prints were displayed on the wall: a vase of badly painted flowers and a country view, the trees of varying sizes and types. He made his way onto the landing and chose a door at random, finding an almost empty room which gave up nothing of interest. The next one was no better – a couple of bookshelves, sparsely filled. There were two more doors. Ignoring the bathroom, Murphy decided on the last bedroom.

A king-sized bed took up space on one side of the room, built-in wardrobes on the other. The curtains were open across the large window, the weak sunshine revealing only dancing dust motes. The room felt abandoned, as though it hadn't been used for a while. It was as sparsely decorated as the other rooms, with only a few more pieces

of furniture. He checked the drawers in the bedside cabinets, coming away with nothing much of interest. There
were some framed photographs of Byrne as a teenager
with various people. One photo pictured him with an
older couple, who Murphy recognised as his parents – the
well-known ex-MP and wife. A small selection of books
of different genres lined a shelf. He checked the wardrobes and found a few suits on hangers, various items of
clothing. There was nothing hiding in a shoebox, or
anything as easy as that.

He took another look around the room, seeing if there
was anything he had missed, and shook his head. He left
the room and met Rossi in the kitchen.

'Anything?' Murphy said. 'Shite all upstairs.'

'Nothing down here either. Few bills, an empty diary
and some films. An iPod dock, but no iPod. Outside is
nice, though. Big, empty garden. Grass has been cut
recently. Probably got a gardener for that.'

Murphy took a look around the kitchen, opening a few
cupboards and a couple of drawers, before standing back.
He looked across at Rossi and folded his arms.

'Does this feel weird to you?'

Rossi smirked a little. 'What? Walking into people's
houses and going through their stuff? Not really . . .'

Murphy smiled back. 'Not that. It's just . . . there's
something not right here. You would expect it to be like a
bachelor pad. You know, messy and unkempt. It's almost
like–'

'No one lives here.'

'That's it,' Murphy said, uncrossing his arms and leaving the kitchen. 'Just look at the place. It's like no one has
been here for months, never mind days. It feels empty.'

Rossi had followed him into the dining room and now followed him into the living room. 'What are you thinking?'

'I don't know.'

Which worried him.

Three

Murphy made his way outside, snapping off his gloves in the process and stuffing them back in his pockets. The marked car was still parked up outside, the uniform who he had encountered on their arrival now leaning against the door on the driver's side with his back to them. Smoke was drifting from beside him, circling the officer's head and then dissipating as it reached higher. The uniform turned his head as Murphy's size thirteen shoes smacked against the concrete path as he made his way towards the car.

'Anything?'

Rossi spoke before Murphy had chance. 'Do you know if he had any other residences than this one?'

The uniform came around the car, the smoke not following as he flicked the cigarette away. 'Robertson has been checking into all that while we've been here,' he said, nodding towards the passenger seat. 'She can tell you.'

Murphy gritted his teeth and made a beckoning motion to the other side of the car, a face within turning towards the sound of her name. He waited for her to exit and stopped gritting as he saw her roll her eyes at Uniform Dickhead. 'What do you need?'

'Brief history. Family, friends, other residences, that sort of thing.'

'Don't have everything yet, but can get it to you. We know about the parents, but no girlfriend or partner we can find. He seems to have this politics thing going on, but nothing else work wise. His campaign office is in Waterloo. Don't have any info on other residences at the moment, but I've been in there. He must have somewhere else.'

Murphy nodded, glancing at Rossi for a second and then back to the female PC. 'Good work. There's a DC Harris back at Major Crime. Can you get in contact with him and tell him what you know. He'll help you with everything else.'

He heard a mutter from the other side of the car, but bit his lip. 'What's your name?'

'Robertson, sir,' she replied. 'Andrea Robertson.'

Murphy nodded again and then turned for his car. Rossi spoke to the uniforms for a little longer, and caught up with him at the car.

'She's cool,' Rossi said, putting her seat belt on and tucking hair behind an ear. 'I like her already. Think she's been around a few scenes now. Him on the other hand . . .'

'A dickhead. Hope we see much less of him.'

'Where to then?'

Murphy shifted the car into gear and pulled back out onto the main road. The sun had disappeared once more, the greyness back outside. 'His office? Can't think of anywhere else we can go. It's starting to feel like a moonlight flit.'

'Same here,' Rossi replied, fiddling with the passenger seat as they made their way out of Blundellsands and back towards the A road. 'That house was weird. Why have a nice place and then live like that? It was a box. Nothing personal at all. No evidence of parties or anything. I know if I was in my twenties with a house like that, it would be full every weekend.'

Murphy indicated and waited for a car to pass before turning. 'Only thing I can think is that it's something like an investment. Waiting to rent it out or something as boring as that. Otherwise, it's just a bit sad.'

'Seems a bit pointless. Can't be cheap to buy up here. Unless his parents own it and they're just letting him stay there. Makes him feel like he's obligated not to mess it up.'

Murphy murmured an acknowledgement and continued driving. The green and red-brick look of suburbia, soon turned back to the grey and brown of industrialisation.

'What if this is the start?' Rossi said, disturbing Murphy's boredom. 'You know . . . what if there's something more going on?'

'It always starts with a body,' Murphy replied, waiting for traffic to pass across a roundabout before driving on. 'You know that.'

'Not always.'

Murphy didn't reply, checking the satnav on the dashboard to make sure he was close.

'I'm sure there's a simple explanation,' Rossi said, leaning back in the passenger seat a little more.

'Who are you trying to convince, me or yourself?'

Rossi made a noise in the back of her throat.

A few minutes of finding somewhere to park, a reverse parking job which only took three tries and a strong word with a passing cyclist later, they were standing outside Sam Byrne's office. The converted shop, thick blinds covering the windows, didn't seem befitting of the man Murphy had glimpsed in local papers and on TV – all tailored suits and trendy haircut

'Looks closed.'

'They always do, these places. Not usually the political party of choice for people in this city,' said Murphy, noticing the blue and white flyers stuck to the window.

'Have to go a bit further north of the city to find those supporting this lot.'

'He must have been popular round here, though,' Murphy said, trying the door handle and knocking on the glass when it didn't open. 'He's going to win, if the opinion polls are to be believed. The *Echo* reckon he's going to piss it.'

'Probably got the young vote. Good-looking fella with a local vibe.'

The blinds were pulled back a little, revealing not much inside, before a lock turned within and the door was opened. A young woman, barely into her twenties, peered out at them.

'Can I help you?'

Murphy could hardly detect any Liverpudlian in her accent – in fact, almost no trace of any accent at all. He introduced himself and Rossi and they were shepherded swiftly inside.

'Sorry about that. We can't have just anyone swanning in from off the street, can we?'

Murphy smirked but didn't respond, instead looking around at the office. An older woman was working at one of the two desks which stood in the centre of the room while several filing cabinets lined the far wall. Every surface was covered in piles of paperwork. Numerous framed newspaper articles and photographs hung on the walls. An enlarged picture of an instantly recognisable Sam Byrne, beaming proudly next to an even more well-known figure, took pride of place.

'Friends in high places,' Murphy said, gesturing towards the photograph. 'Never met the PM myself. I've heard he wishes us well though. Just before another cut arrives.'

Redness spread across the woman's face, pockmarked cheeks losing their initial porcelain quality. 'This is Emma Palmer, she runs accounts.'

Murphy nodded towards the older woman who barely looked up from the computer screen in front of her.

'I'm Charlotte. I'm Sam's assistant.'

Of course she's a Charlotte, Murphy thought. 'Mr Byrne's disappearance has been passed onto us,' he said. 'So is there somewhere Mr Byrne usually works from, on his own, I mean?'

'Just through here,' Charlotte replied, walking away. 'Spends most of his time in his office in the back. We haven't really been in since he . . . since he didn't come in on Friday. He left here on Thursday, but no one has seen him after . . . after I saw him last.'

Rossi stopped Charlotte from stepping into the office, the door was ajar and a little light entered from a window inside. 'Wait here,' she said, mirroring Murphy's actions and snapping a pair of gloves over her hands. 'Just a precaution.'

'You think something's happened in his office?' Charlotte said, the tone of her voice changing for the first time. 'We would have known, surely?'

Murphy pushed open the office door a fraction more, surveying the room before entering. 'As DS Rossi said, it's just a precaution.'

'It can't be something that happened in our offices,' Charlotte said, her voice lower now, almost as if she was speaking to herself. 'We would have known.'

Murphy turned and looked towards her, seeing only the crown of her head as she stared at the floor.

'Laura, do you want to ask Charlotte some questions while I get on in here?'

Rossi gave him a nod and guided Charlotte out. Murphy turned back to the office and crossed the room to the window. He lifted the blinds, the room instantly becoming lighter as a result.

Murphy looked across at the desk, noting the seemingly teetering pile of paperwork, the masses of Post-it notes and the bulging folders on the floor.

Tried to work out where the hell he should start.

Four

Rossi had that feeling once again. A sense of something coming towards her, an impending awfulness. The emptiness lying at the pit of her stomach. Talking to the missing councillor's assistant wasn't helping. The confusion and helplessness emanating from the woman beginning to annoy rather than aid.

'I just don't understand,' Charlotte said, her hands palm up in front of her, before being tucked away again as she folded her arms. 'He's never done anything like this before.'

'What's his normal day like,' Rossi said, opening her notebook and waiting. 'How busy is he usually? What does he do?'

Charlotte leaned back against the counter. 'Should I put the kettle on?'

Rossi shook her head but didn't speak. She waited for Charlotte to start.

'He's very busy at the moment,' Charlotte finally said with a sigh. 'He has a lot of meetings, for a start, then there's all the door-to-doors he's doing. There's hustings with the other candidates. He has a lot going on.'

'I'm sure he does. Do people come here or does he hold meetings elsewhere?'

'All the planning happens here and at the party HQ in town, but he has the occasional meet and greet in these offices. He has to speak to local businesses often and they come here to speak with him. Everyone is concerned about the downturn in the local economy and that sort of thing. We have a lot of people here usually. Campaigns involve a huge number of volunteers. It's just me and Emma that are here full-time. He's keen to begin work on bringing this town back to its former glory.'

Rossi listened as Charlotte outlined more parts of their normal working day, becoming less and less interested as the young girl spoke. She resolved never to take a job in politics.

'How about frequent visitors, does Sam have people who come to see him often? Maybe unconnected to what you would consider to be work purposes?'

Charlotte paused, then looked away. Rossi's eyes narrowed a little as she waited for a response.

'No one I can think of right now.'

Rossi was silent for a few seconds, then made a note on her pad.

Come back to visitors

'How well liked is he in the area? With local businesses, that kind of thing?'

Charlotte perked up a little. 'Oh, very popular. We're doing exceedingly well with local business owners. He's keen to push for better parking regulations, so people can drive here and not worry about being ticketed. That helps out the shops a lot, gets people in the area again. He's very good with people, listens to their concerns and will act on them when he becomes a Member of Parliament.'

There was a pause, then a shake of her head.

'He's a good man. We are all part of his team. We're here to make a difference, you know? To get Britain working again, the way it should. He was all about that. He's been that way all his life.'

Rossi nodded, noting down Charlotte's words, feeling like she was listening to a party political broadcast. 'He's young, though. Anyone have an issue with someone of his age coming in and making changes?'

Charlotte hesitated again before answering. 'That's just politics. You have the old guard, those who want to keep things the same as it's always been. Then you have someone like Sam, who gets how young people think and understands the problems facing those struggling with their own businesses, and he really listens to them. Some people don't like that. It can get heated sometimes, but all politics is like that.'

'Yeah, I've watched Prime Minister's Questions a few times,' Rossi said, attempting a smile. 'They sound like children when they're making those noises from the benches.'

Charlotte did smile back, a flash of perfect white teeth, before pursing her lips once more. 'As I said, it's how it's always been. Sam wants to change all that. You know, really listen to people.'

'Sounds like a Tory version of Jeremy Corbyn.'

'Well, maybe he is. Or will be. That's if he's OK, of course.' Charlotte's bottom lip quivered a touch, before she turned away from Rossi and faced the kitchen counter. 'I think I'll have a cup of tea. Are you sure you won't have one?'

It was Rossi's turn to hesitate. 'Have you got coffee?'

*   *   *

Murphy moved yet another pile of paperwork, wondering if this was going to be the highlight of his day. Tidying up some posh get's office. A posh get playing at being a politician while getting a nice cheque from his parents every month at that, he assumed. He sifted through some of the sheets of paper on top of the pile, but quickly grew bored of reading the minutes of some meeting or other.

DC Hale can go through everything in here, he thought. Just to piss him off a little. Then decided against the idea, imagining the answer to lie somewhere in the mess, completely missed by the young detective constable. Probably whilst he was styling his hair for the twentieth time of the day.

'You won't find anything in there,' a voice from the doorway said, interrupting his thoughts. 'He never keeps it in any kind of good order. I'm always telling him he should file things away, but he prefers to just dump it all on the floor.'

Murphy turned to see the woman who had been sat in the outside office when they'd arrived. 'Emma, is it?'

The woman nodded, but made no move to enter the office.

'I'm guessing you mean this is all just rubbish then,' Murphy said, gesturing to the other piles of paperwork. 'Nothing of interest at all?'

'He keeps anything important in his briefcase. Everything else is by email these days. His desktop is on, but he preferred to use his laptop.'

Murphy looked around, trying to remember if he'd seen a laptop on his cursory glances around the room. 'Let me guess,' he said, turning back to Emma. 'That's usually in his briefcase as well?'

'No,' Emma replied, the unmistakeable lines on her upperlip creasing. A smoker, Murphy thought. 'He has a nice little bag for that.'

Murphy suppressed a huff. 'We've been to his house up in Blundellsands. Didn't see a laptop or a briefcase there. Is he the type of person who would leave that sort of thing lying around, forgetful, maybe leave it on a train? I've seen politicians do that sort of thing.'

Emma almost smiled. 'No. He was very protective of that sort of item. He knew the importance of keeping confidential information safe.'

Murphy scratched at his beard, wondering what was being left unsaid. 'I can't imagine he gets paid all that much for the work he does here. Does he have another job or something?'

Emma shook her head. 'Devotes all his time to the campaign. His house was left to him. A family member, I seem to recall. An aunt, or grandparent. So he doesn't need to worry about paying the mortgage.'

Murphy figured as much. Money goes to money. 'So, help me out here. We've been to the house, which didn't look lived in all that much. And we've been here, where there's nothing of note according to you.'

Emma faltered for a second, then seemed to compose herself. 'I'm not sure what Mr Byrne does in his spare time. I just run through the accounts, the expenses, that type of work here. We work on speeches, how he presents himself publicly, all of those things. I don't run his personal life. I suppose if you want to read through those files you would need some sort of order or something?'

'I imagine so,' Murphy replied, finally understanding what she was driving at. 'Unless we suspect a danger to life, in which case we can go ahead and take them with us. What do you think, Emma? Do you believe Sam's life may be in danger?'

'I wouldn't presume anything, detective,' Emma said, fixing Murphy with a stare. 'Of course, that's not my job. All I can say is that this behaviour is very out of the ordinary for him. I can't imagine what would keep him away for this length of time without being in touch and letting us know if all is OK, or not, as the case may be.'

Murphy nodded and stood up fully. His knees and back clicked as he did so, whilst he swallowed back a noise. 'Thank you. You've been a great help.'

He waited for her to leave before pulling out his phone. 'Kirkham, I want you to come up to Waterloo.' Murphy rattled off the address to the DC. 'Bring some evidence boxes. There's a lot to take away.'

*   *   *

'So, what are you thinking?' Rossi said, once they were both back in the car. They had parked around the corner to make it a little easier for Kirkham and a uniform to lug the boxes of files to their own vehicle. 'Something isn't right, I know that much, but what?'

'That older woman, Emma, she was trying to tell me something. Without actually telling me, more's the pity.'

'Well, let's bring her in. See if we can get her to talk. Isn't that what we usually do?'

Murphy swigged back some water from the bottle he'd taken from the office. It was lukewarm with a bit of an aftertaste, but it was enough to quench his thirst. 'I don't think she's the type to cave under questioning. I think she's sworn to keep her mouth shut about all kinds of secret things. I suppose every politician needs someone like her. Someone willing to say nothing, even when someone like us comes calling.'

'Sounds almost like you admire her for it?'

'You don't?'

Murphy waited for Rossi as she picked up his bottle of water, gave it a look and then placed it back down in the holder. 'Doesn't make our job much easier, that's all. The guy has gone missing, seemingly without trace, and she stonewalls us. Surely she should be helping us out as much as possible?'

'Yeah, but there's still some kind of code or something. I guess she's not sure that he hasn't gone missing of his own accord. It's only been a few days, remember. Which tells me that she knows something about the way he lives outside of this world.'

Rossi raised an eyebrow. 'Something we need to know then. A young politician, good looking enough to get what he wants. We're always hearing gossip about politicians. Those *bastardos* don't seem to have any limit. We could be looking at literally anything here.'

'True, which makes things more difficult,' Murphy replied, taking out his phone and scrolling down his contacts list. 'Doesn't mean we won't find out, though. Someone will be willing to talk. There's always at least one.'

Rossi hummed under her breath as Murphy put the phone to his ear and waited for an answer. 'Graham, it's Murphy,' he said once DC Harris answered. 'Listen, I need as much background info on Sam Byrne as you can find . . . Yeah, including stuff we shouldn't know about . . . No, as quietly as possible . . . Boss doesn't want this getting out too far . . . Cheers, mate.'

Rossi waited for him to end the call on the phone before speaking. 'What's your gut telling you?'

'Not sure,' Murphy replied, wondering if the sight of a uniformed copper outside Byrnes's office was too much. He was supposed to be keeping things under the radar and a uniform going in and out of the guy's office removing stuff was probably not the best idea. 'Something feels dodgy about the whole thing. I think there's something we're not aware of right now.'

'I agree, for what it's worth. I think something's happened to the guy. Someone in the public eye like this, they don't just bugger off for a long weekend or more and not tell even an assistant. That house wasn't right and there's something off about those two women in his office.'

Murphy didn't reply, staring out of the car windscreen towards a bookshop on the opposite side of the road. 'Seems well liked in the community from what I can gather. The shops around here are dying a death and he's promised them all kinds. If he can do even a little bit to help them, I can't imagine he's disliked, even if he is a Tory. Seems like he was heading for the top as well.'

'Another career politician,' Rossi said, tutting to herself. 'At least this one didn't go to that Eton.'

Murphy smirked then started the car up. 'Silver linings,' he said, taking the handbrake off and pulling out onto the road. 'That's why I like you, Laura. You always see the positive.'

'It's the only way to get through the day.'

'Agreed. Now let's go and see his parents. Finally.'

Five

Murphy checked the address on the sheet once more before handing it back to Rossi. He tried fiddling with the satnav again, but gave up when he spotted Rossi pulling out her phone.

'It needs updating or something,' Murphy said, turning the thing off and resisting the urge to throw it out of the window. 'Have you found it?'

'Yeah,' Rossi replied, squinting at her phone. 'Go to the end of Sefton Lane and I'll direct you from there.'

'Ever been to Aughton? Can't remember if we've ever had a job that far out together.'

'Probably at some point. Maghull isn't far from it and I've definitely been there. Can't remember offhand.'

'It's barely Liverpool anyway,' Murphy said, accelerating along the A road and passing a slow-moving car. 'Near enough Ormskirk. Edge Hill Uni is just round the corner, but that's about it. There's not much going on from what I remember. Not quite Formby, but near enough.'

They reached the edge of the city, the suburban area revealing itself once again. More tree-lined roads and large houses. Murphy sometimes forgot that the house he now lived in could probably match up to any here. His days on a council estate in south Liverpool now long behind him.

'Have you got the names of the parents there?' Murphy said, waiting for traffic to pass by before turning left onto Green Lane. 'I know his name, obviously, but I don't know the wife.'

'Arthur and Mary. She's the second wife, I imagine, as he must be getting near eighty now. Sam Byrne is only twenty-six, so even allowing for a late pregnancy, she can't be more than sixty odd. Seem to recall something about it, but I don't tend to keep up with ex-MPs' family lives.'

Murphy nodded and turned right towards Maghull and then onto Liverpool Lane North, away from the more familiar town and further north. 'I suppose it wouldn't be right if the whole city looked like this. For a start, I think we'd lose our status as part of that northern powerhouse that's always talked about but never appears.'

'It would be difficult to make certain parts of the city look like this,' Rossi replied, checking her phone screen again and pointing to the right. 'You'd have to move the locals about as well while you were at it. Can't imagine that would go too well.'

'This looks right,' Murphy said, pulling into a side road of more recently built houses. 'Not bad at all here. MPs must get nice pensions.'

'Alongside all the money they make in business on the side.'

Murphy didn't bother replying. The last thing he wanted at that moment was to get into a discussion about politics with Laura Rossi. Even he wasn't that stupid.

'How are we approaching this?' Rossi said, turning to Murphy as he stopped the car outside the house. 'Are we going to go with the premise that he's missing and presumed in danger, or missing of his own accord ... or just buggered off for a long weekend and neglected to mention it to anyone?'

Murphy shook off his seat belt and took out the car key. 'Let's see what they have to say first. They're the ones who want to keep things quiet, more than his actual work colleagues, or whatever we call them. They must have a reason for that, which means there's something not right. Usually if someone in the public eye is a victim of crime or whatever, their face would be plastered over every newspaper and TV news channel within hours.'

'I guarantee someone will speak out soon enough. Then it'll be everywhere.'

Murphy opened the car door and waited for Rossi to exit the other side. 'We'll cross that bridge when we come to it and then try not to jump off the damn thing as well.'

They walked up the driveway, not for the first time admiring a house from the outside. 'It always fills me with some kind of weird feeling when we see houses like this in Liverpool,' Murphy said, enjoying the sight of the house. I guess even though I live in the city I still expect everywhere to look like it's about to fall down, like it does on the telly.'

'With some of the places we've seen, are you really that surprised?'

Murphy lifted his hand to knock on the door but didn't get the chance to. It was opened inwards, almost knocking back the person inside with its swiftness.

'Hello, detectives,' the man filling the doorway said. 'I was told you'd be arriving at some point today. Detective

Inspector David Murphy and Detective Sergeant Laura Rossi, I guess?'

'Pretty good guess,' Murphy replied, giving a sharp glance at Rossi. 'Do you need us to come inside, or do you know how the rest of the day is going to go as well?'

'Sorry, my preparedness can be off-putting sometimes. It's something my wife complains about also. Please, come in.'

Murphy stepped inside, Rossi following behind him. They waited for the former MP to show them which way to turn. The hallway was suitably grandiose, matching the house's facade. The aforementioned former Member of Parliament wasn't keeping himself in as good a condition as his dwelling, however. Murphy remembered some of the more cutting depictions of the man back in the eighties. A rotund man, with wrinkled skin and a comb over, he was the Eric Pickles of his time. He was even larger now with jowls that flapped when he spoke, although from a quick glance Murphy thought some attempt had been made to live a healthier life.

'Just through here,' Arthur Byrne said, extending an arm to his left as he faced them. 'Mary will be joining us presently. Can I offer you some refreshments?'

Murphy shook his head. 'That's OK, Mr Byrne,' he said, walking into the room that had been indicated and taking stock. 'Sit anywhere?'

Arthur came in behind Rossi and nodded his head, the folds of skin under his chin wobbling around as he did so. Murphy thought of that Churchill dog from the adverts and suppressed a laugh. Rossi stopped short, then continued to walk into the room, looking around the room with widened eyes. Murphy tried to ignore the various ornate pieces and headed for a seat.

'As I said, Mary will be with us shortly,' Arthur said, standing as he waited for Murphy and Rossi to take up opposite ends of an uncomfortable sofa. He stood before them with his hands clasped together in front of him. 'I'm sorry to meet with you in these circumstances. I have followed your careers with much interest. You have done much for the city and its community. I do hope you know how that is appreciated.'

Murphy looked towards Rossi who was still staring at the furniture in the room. He followed her gaze to a particularly well-carved, deep-brown bookcase, the pattern at its top edges remarkable in its design.

'Doesn't need saying,' Murphy said, tearing his eyes away and back to Arthur Byrne. 'Just doing our job. Nothing more than that.'

'On the contrary,' Arthur said. Murphy half expected him to add *my dear chap* to the end of the statement. 'I believe you two and your team go above and beyond the call of duty on many an occasion. That's why I asked if you were available.'

'Really, that's interesting,' Murphy replied, shifting his bulk on the sofa and gaining Rossi's attention. 'I guess you believe Sam hasn't just neglected to mention a short trip?'

'No, Detective Inspector Murphy,' Arthur replied, looking towards the hardwood floor beneath his feet. 'I believe he's at a critical point in his life and would not leave at this time. I am extremely worried about his safety, given the amount of time he has been out of touch. When we were informed at the weekend that he hadn't arrived into the office on Friday, we didn't think much of it. When we couldn't get a hold of him over the weekend well . . . let's just say it's inexplicable behaviour from Sam. I contacted DSI Butler personally this morning, asking for your assistance. Four days is just a little too long.'

'Tell us a little more about him,' Rossi said, finally finished with admiring her surroundings and joining Murphy in conversation. 'He's young for an MP, or should I say prospective MP, isn't he?'

Arthur looked up, then made his way to a chair opposite them and carefully settled his bulky frame upon it. 'Sometimes we find our calling early. Look at that young Scottish woman. I can never pronounce her name, but she was still in university when she was elected. Never mind that it's representing that party from north of the border who would see the union split, she is still representative of a shift in politics. She could do with a bit more life experience, of course, but that's the generation we're left with now. Sam is older than her, but I think he could have got elected at any point. He has something about him, which I imagine he inherited from me. He knows how to work a room, how to make people believe in him.'

'He's winning at the moment,' Rossi said, opening her notebook as Murphy sat back a little in the sofa and allowed her to continue. 'By some margin, as well. Not very easy in our city, coming from your particular political affiliation. I don't think you ever stood within Liverpool, did you?'

'No, I don't think I would have been an MP for as long as I was if I'd stood in Liverpool, Ms Rossi,' Arthur replied, a chuckle escaping from his lips.

Murphy tensed as Rossi bristled beside him. He was DI Murphy, she was Ms Rossi. Sometimes you can boil the prejudices of a generation down to a simple act.

'Has he always been interested in politics,' Murphy said, speaking before Rossi could make a remark back. 'Or was that something he followed you in doing? The family business, if you will?'

'He needed some guidance, especially as his exam results failed to live up to expectations. He was sent to the best private school we could afford, but whilst we wanted him to move onto Oxford or Cambridge, he couldn't quite live up to that. We were happy he made it into the City of Liverpool University. He hasn't looked back since.'

Murphy inwardly shuddered at the mention of the university. A place he would rather not think about too much. Another case, another time.

'Of course,' Arthur continued, resting his hands on his substantial stomach, 'we had hoped he would be amongst a different crowd, but Sam has a way of standing out. He excelled in debates, worked very hard and achieved what was needed.'

'He wasn't always working hard,' a voice said from the open doorway. Murphy turned to see Mrs Byrne appear in the room. 'Spent many a night getting up to all kinds in those clubs in town. I blame those friends of his. They led him astray far too often.'

'Mary—' Arthur began to say, before his wife cut him off.

'No, they need to know everything. If you ask me, detectives, he will have got himself into some kind of trouble. Always easily led. You want to find Sam, look at who he was spending time with and they'll give you the answer. It's not like he is unfamiliar with the *unsavoury* aspects of life.'

Six

Murphy refused a drink once again, as Mary waited in the doorway having asked if they'd like tea or coffee. Murphy, worried that accepting would break the flow of conversation, was pleased Rossi also turned down the offer of refreshments.

'My wife, Mary, detectives,' Arthur said, standing up and waiting for Mary to join them. Murphy felt compelled to do the same, leaving Rossi still sitting on the sofa. 'As she says, Sam did enjoy his time in university, as youngsters are wont to do. He still graduated with a first class degree, however.'

'In politics, though, dear,' Mary said, lowering her eyes at her husband before turning back to Murphy and Rossi. 'Couldn't even talk him into doing a combined degree. Something in economics, perhaps, or even history. I suppose it doesn't matter much now.'

Murphy sat back down, letting his eyes rest on Mary for a second before moving away. She was much as he'd expected. Immaculately turned out, her make-up freshly applied, she looked to be around mid- to late-forties, but Murphy guessed she was almost a decade older. Compared with her husband, she was aging well.

'Yes, detective, I don't look my age, thank you for noticing so vividly.'

Murphy felt the blush rise to his cheeks, but shook his head and carried on. 'Nice to meet you, Mrs Byrne. I'm sure your husband has informed you already who we are.'

'Of course,' Mary replied with a wave of her hand. 'Always an odd boy is Sam. I'm sure this is another one of his games. I hope it is, anyway, or I will be very cross.'

'Games?'

'Not important,' Arthur cut in, giving his wife a look of admonishment she took with a roll of her eyes. 'What is important is that we make sure my son is safe, isn't that right?'

'Of course,' Murphy replied, trying to hide his enjoyment of the pairing. Something bugged him, though: the difference in the reactions of the two to their son's disappearance. He filed it away for later scrutiny. 'Which means we need to know as much as possible about Sam's life now, in order to discover what's happened.'

'I know the way these things work. I listened to a whole one of those podcast things recently about missing people. Some crime writer or something hosted it. Was very interesting. Anyway, that means I know how it's usually nothing bad that has happened and that the missing person turns up within a few days or so. Still, Sam is not your normal everyday type of person. He's . . . important.'

'Quite,' Rossi said, scribbling something Murphy couldn't see on her notepad. 'Sam left university and went straight into politics then?'

Arthur cleared his throat. 'Yes, something like that. I had to place some calls to get him some experience, of

course, but he moved upwards quickly. Became a councillor and then began this journey into being a fully fledged
Member of Parliament. Quite the rise, you would say.'

'I wouldn't say anything, Mr Byrne,' Rossi replied,
giving him a flash of a sneer and looking down again
before Murphy could give her his own look of admonishment. 'Has he always been a good boy, or has he been into
any kind of trouble growing up?'

Murphy looked back at Arthur, expecting him to be
annoyed with Rossi, but he seemed to have brushed it off.
He was slightly disappointed. It would have been fun to
watch Rossi make him squirm.

'He got himself into some scrapes as a teenager, but who
doesn't at that age?' Arthur said, speaking before his wife
had a chance. 'He's been concentrating on his future since
then. He knows it wouldn't do for him to be getting into
any kind of trouble if he wants to fulfil his ambitions.'

Murphy glanced over at Mary who still had her mouth
open as if to speak. She caught his eye and looked away
quickly. He watched her absent-mindedly brush away a
little dust on the side table next to her chair.

'How about now?' Murphy said, moving his gaze back
to Arthur. 'Any kind of threats or unwanted attention?'

'You know how things are these days, detective. All
that internet nonsense and so forth. I'm sure he receives
all kinds of abuse on there every day. However, the internet has also been hugely important for the campaign. He
is young and privileged, but not a Jacob Rees-Mogg type.
He's not taking his "nanny" out with him when he
canvasses. He's just like them. Only not like all those lefty
types the universities seem to be breeding these days.'

Murphy sensed Rossi tense up again.

'*Cazzo*,' Rossi said under her breath. Murphy knew what the word meant and hoped Arthur and Mary Byrne didn't.

'Anything specific you can think of?' Murphy said, when it didn't seem as if the pair had taken any Italian language lessons in their retirement. 'Something out of the ordinary he may have mentioned?'

'Not that I can recall . . . Mary?'

Mary was still looking away from the group, quiet since her initial outburst. 'No, nothing like that. I'm sure he would have told us if there was.'

'How about friends? Do you know the names of them at all? We don't have many contacts for him at the moment.'

'Oh, yes, he has many friends,' Arthur said, sitting back, hands now clasped on the arms of the chair. 'There was a whole group at university he was very close to. Can't imagine they haven't stayed in touch.'

'That's lovely,' Rossi said, tapping her pen against the notepad on her knee. 'Any names at all?'

Arthur glanced at Mary again, pursing his lips and grimacing. 'Erm . . . Mary, what was the name of that one chap, with the hair?'

'Simon. Simon Jackson. I think he's from Manchester originally. We don't have any phone numbers. I'm sorry. Not the done thing these days, I suppose.'

'That's fine,' Murphy said. 'Any other names you can provide to us would be great.'

'I know a few first names, but that's about it. We weren't especially involved in that part of his life.'

Murphy waited as Rossi wrote down an array of names, each more middle-class sounding than the previous one.

'Sorry we can't help you more on that,' Arthur said, clasping his hands together. 'He was far too busy lately with the campaign, so I'm sure he didn't have much of a social life anyway. Just the way of things. I'm sure you'll be able to work some of that computer magic and find the people from the information Mary has given you. I can't imagine there being a need to bother any of them, however. I'm sure his disappearance will be connected to what is happening in his life now.'

Rossi raised an eyebrow at Murphy and gave a slight shake of her head.

'OK,' Murphy said, shifting forwards on the sofa so he was perched on the edge. 'Well, at the moment we're investigating various avenues of interest. We've been to his house, but we didn't exactly get much of a sense of him from there.'

'That doesn't surprise me,' Mary said, smoothing down her skirt as she spoke. 'We don't go there much, but we're always telling him to make it more homely. Find someone to start courting and have a family. That always played well for Arthur. Everyone knew he was a family man, which helped immeasurably in getting him re-elected so often.'

'He still has it,' Arthur said, his voice booming across to Murphy and Rossi. 'Only a month until the by-election and he is considerably ahead of the Labour candidate. Not a surprise, really, given the mess that party is in right now.'

Murphy held up a hand to stop Arthur going further into the politics. 'Is there anything at all you can think of, any reason why he might have left now, or may be in danger?'

Arthur and Mary exchanged glances and waited a few seconds to reply.

'Nothing would make him suddenly take off in the middle of a campaign such as this,' Arthur said as Mary sat open-mouthed again. 'He has been brought up correctly and understands his obligations perfectly well. Something must have happened to him for him to disappear in this manner. I would very much like for you both to find out what that is and bring him back to us, Detective Inspector Murphy.'

'We'll do our best, sir,' Murphy replied, standing up and at once towering over the pair. 'If you do think of anything,' he continued, trying to catch Mary's eye, 'please don't hesitate to get in touch. I'm sure you know how to do that, but here's a card with our relevant information on it anyway.'

Murphy produced a card from his back pocket and laid it on the coffee table in front of Mary. She leant forwards and made it disappear before Arthur had chance to move.

'Thank you very much, detectives,' Arthur said, getting to his feet slowly and with some effort. 'You have our every trust that you can get to the bottom of this.'

They were shown to the door without further preamble. Murphy glanced back to see Mary still sitting on the chair. She seemed lost in herself now, without the pretence of a show to put on.

Once outside, Rossi finally let rip.

'*Mannagia alla miseria*. Politicians,' she said, spittle flying from her mouth. 'And Tories at that. Nothing but a bunch of *carogna*. Did you see the way he spoke only to you, never me. Sexist bastard.'

Murphy continued to walk, hoping to get further away from the house before Rossi really started to shout.

'Honestly, these types of people run the country and we wonder why it's in such a mess.'

'We don't have to like them to help them.'

'That should be the official police slogan,' Rossi replied, reaching the car door and huffing when she realised Murphy hadn't keyed the automatic locking yet. 'We didn't get a single helpful thing in there. Pointless conversation. We're nowhere with this thing.'

'She knows something,' Murphy said, unlocking the car and climbing inside. 'The way she was on the verge of saying something every few minutes. She has something to say. I'm hoping that a few more days of Sam being missing will make her talk. They didn't seem all that upset, which was weird.'

'All a front. Stiff upper lip and all that shite.'

'Suppose so. For now, no, we don't have much, but hopefully they've found something back at his office. There's a bit of secrecy going on around this thing.'

'To be expected, I suppose,' Rossi said, clicking her seat belt on just as Murphy pulled out into the road. 'I bet if we really knew what went on with MPs behind closed doors, we'd never vote any of them in.'

'You say that like it would be a bad thing.'

Rossi laughed, filling the car with its distinctive sound. That's when Murphy knew he'd made Rossi laugh properly . . . when his ears were still ringing a few minutes later.

'I'll give you that one,' Rossi said, pulling her notepad out and studying the notes she'd made. 'A bunch of first names and a Simon Jackson. I really hope we don't have much trouble accessing Byrne's social media accounts. Otherwise, this could be a very long and boring process.'

'I'll leave that to you and Graham to sort out,' Murphy said, grinding his teeth at the mere mention of social media. 'Wouldn't know what I was doing anyway.'

'You still refuse to get with the programme? Everyone is online now. Stop resisting it. You're missing out on trolls, political arguments, echo chambers and pictures of cats. What more could you want?'

'I'll live,' Murphy replied, bringing the car to a halt at a set of traffic lights. 'I can think of a hundred and one other things I'd rather torture myself with before joining those sites.'

'I give it another six months, then you'll cave.'

'Keep dreaming. I'm more likely to visit Goodison Park than open a Facebook account.'

Rossi laughed, but the noise of it didn't fill the car this time. 'We'll ask the university as well, but can't imagine we'll get far with that one. What did you make of them anyway? Have to say, when Mary walked in with the tanned tights and sensible shoes, I thought I'd end up disliking her more. Turned out she was OK.'

'She's definitely hiding something about her son. I doubt we'll ever know if the dad has his way, though.'

'Oh yeah, it's all about the correct image with him. All about the *campaign* and how that's going. That's why we're having to keep everything in the dark. If it gets out that a prospective MP has gone missing and then he turns up looking sheepish with a few love bites and a three-day hangover, he would probably lose a fair few votes. Not very professional. What about that house, though ... amazing furniture in there.'

'You could do a whole hour of the *Antiques Roadshow* in just the living room, or whatever they want to call it.'

'Probably a *morning room* or something,' Rossi said, taking her phone out and keying the screen. 'I'll put Graham on the list of names, but I don't think we're going to get very far with just this. We need something a bit more concrete.'

Murphy slowed the car as traffic built up in front of them. Thought through the meeting with the missing man's parents once again in his head.

Something wasn't right. And he wasn't sure he wanted to find out exactly what that something was.

Sam
Four Days Earlier

He enjoyed pain. Particularly carried out on others. Women especially. He liked seeing the hurt in their eyes. The awareness of their helplessness reflected back at him, knowing he could end it at any point. Under his control, his power. There was something about that kind of thing which really got him going.

Problem was, not all women liked his particular brand of play. In the past, he'd had too many whiny bitches who became worried about their safety as soon as he started playing. Idiots. As if he would put himself in danger for some whore who didn't like it when he went a bit far.

That's all they were, really, he thought. Playthings, objects for him to derive pleasure from.

It wasn't his fault he had been driven to this mindset. They had done that. All that talk of equal rights and safe spaces. It was his world. He was the one in power. If they wanted to take some of that, they would have to deal with the consequences.

That was how he had dealt with the changes in the world around him. His father had instilled in him the importance of power. How he had to take it, make it his and never let it go.

Once he had made it through the next few weeks of the campaign, he would have everything he needed.

He would have his pick.

For now, the urges had become too strong. He needed a release and she was a willing and cheap solution.

'Put these on,' he said, handing the clothes to the woman. He turned away as she swiped a hand across her nose and began undressing. He didn't want to see her until she was properly attired.

'If you want any of that weird shit, that costs extra,' the woman said, a rasp to her voice which set his teeth on edge. 'You hear me? You have to give me more if I have to do anything like that.'

'You're getting paid well enough,' Sam said, pinching the bridge of his nose and trying to maintain control. 'I'll give you three hundred quid just to shut the fuck up.'

'My lips are sealed,' the woman said, unable to keep the glee from her tone. 'Well, until you need them to be open.'

'Are you dressed?'

The woman murmured a yes. He turned round to see her properly. She was a little older than he would have liked, but he would see past that. The short plaid skirt, the white blouse, the tie loose around her neck. It would work.

'Walk this way and keep quiet.'

He led her to the bedroom in the back of the flat, the lights off so she couldn't see what was inside. He felt a slight touch of hesitation when they reached the doorway, but a gentle nudge kept her walking.

'Lie down on the bed.'

She complied, as they always did. Their stupidity driven by the desire for money. To feed an addiction. It sickened him.

'Close your eyes,' he said, crossing the room and opening the bottom drawer of the bedside table. 'Now.'

She did as she was instructed, lying down fully on the bed now. He moved quickly, placing the blindfold over her eyes. 'Turn over,' he said, not wanting to touch her yet. She did as she was told, lifting herself and turning over. She raised her lower half in the air, but he pushed it down with an elbow and leaned over her. He snapped a manacle hanging from the bedpost around her wrist.

'Hey, what are you doing?' she said, lifting her head up off the bed and turning towards him.

'Shut up, or you won't get your money. You'll do as you're told and be out of here within an hour. Keep talking and you'll get nothing.'

The threat was enough, just as it always was. He was surprised it worked, but then he didn't understand the way these people lived.

He snapped another manacle on her free wrist, then tied her ankles to the bedposts at the end of the bed.

The gag was last.

He stood over her, the straps in place and secure. He could feel the shift instantly; the fear exuding from her feeding his desire.

'You're being paid to be here,' he said, taking off his shirt one button at a time. 'Stop your whining.'

She shook her head, tears springing from her eyes as she turned her head towards him. He was enjoying this already.

'You have one job. To satisfy me. That's all you have to do. If you don't, then we don't leave here until I am. Simple. There is no getting away from here, not until I say so.'

He waited for her to nod her agreement, then looked her over. It would do.

He opened another drawer and removed what he needed. He moved back to the bed and smiled as she winced at him lifting her skirt up.

She wasn't expecting the first whip of the cane across her. She began to struggle, but couldn't move more than an inch or two. He brought the cane down again, more forcefully this time. He closed his eyes as the sound of her screaming into the gag filled the silence.

He kept going, one hand bringing the cane down over and over, the other hand giving himself pleasure.

She passed out at some point, her blood now spilled out on the bed and beyond. He took a plastic bag and straddled her back. Jumped up and down a little to bring her back to consciousness.

When he was done, she was nothing to him. For ninety minutes, she had consumed him, but now, she was just a problem to deal with. He wasn't sure if she'd recognised him, but he felt certain that she wasn't about to talk. He let her off the bed, barely watching as she limped gingerly away from the bedroom.

'Remove the clothes and get dressed. Five hundred. And you don't talk to anyone or I'll find you.'

She sniffed, tears still cascading down her dirty face. She reached with shaking hands for the money he was holding towards her.

'I mean it,' he said, not letting go of the money. 'I'll

come looking for you and no one will hear from you again, got it?'

She nodded, her whole body trembling now. He released the money and watched her leave, a thin smile on his face. He heard the door close and began chuckling softly to himself. He grabbed the clothes off the floor where she'd left them, placing them in a plastic bag and taking them back to the bedroom. Stopped for a second to take in the bloodstains and results of his work.

'Well done, Sam,' he said softly to himself. 'That was a great performance.'

He heard a knock at the door and frowned. 'What the fuck does she want now,' he said, moving towards the door and checking the peephole, but seeing no one there. He opened the door slowly, then flew backwards as the door was slammed into him. He landed on the floor, instant pain in the bottom of his back. A figure stood over him, a black balaclava covering their head.

'What the fuc—'

A bolt of electricity entered his body before he could finish his sentence.

'You're going to follow me out of here. You'll do as you're told, or I'll keep firing this thing at you until you can't breathe any more. What do you think?'

Sam didn't answer. Couldn't. He was still trying to stop shaking as he lay on the floor. The figure above him wiggled the taser in their hand, soft laughter coming from the darkness.

*   *   *

There was something he hadn't known about being on the receiving end of brutality.

You start to wish for an end. Of any kind. Death was beginning to look like a preferable option than what was being done to him. Endless pain, in waves of torture and spilled blood. Mental and physical. Both as bad as the other.

He was beginning to rethink his position on the use of these methods against enemies of war. Something he wouldn't have ever thought possible before then.

He just wanted it to end.

Sam believed in God. Worshipped Him in his own particular way. Enough to appeal to a certain section of society but not too much to put off younger people who put less stock in those ideas. He was a modern Christian. Belief without responsibility.

Now, he wondered if there was anything out there when this was ended. Wasn't too sure he cared enough at that moment. He welcomed the idea of darkness. Of emptiness. Of anything but the bright light shining in his eyes.

'Please . . . please, no more.'

The words escaped his lips, cracked and swollen, rasping breaths following them. The cackle of laughter surrounded him, high-pitched and echoing.

'When I say it's done, it's done.'

Always the same answer.

'I can't take anything else,' he said, his voice sounding alien to him now. 'Just tell me what you want. I can get you anything. Just, please, tell me.'

Silence was the only response. His leg muscles burned underneath him, thighs on fire from being made to kneel for hours on end.

'I'm an important man,' he said, his throat protesting against the cruelty of speaking. 'Just tell me what you want from me. Money? I can get you as much as you need. Please, name a price. I want to make you happy. I want to make you stop this madness.'

'I don't want anything. I have what I need. I have you.'

The voice bounced around him, turning from a whisper to a shout in a second. The smell of smoke made its way through the hood, he heard the noise of something being cut or sawn into pieces. Sometimes the smells and noises meant something to him, other times not. He was never sure if pain was about to arrive, or if they were playing with him.

He wasn't sure about anything any more.

He'd always been the one in charge. The master. Now that control had been snatched from him.

'What should I do with you now? Maybe I should cut off parts of your body one by one. That would be fun, wouldn't it? That would be justice for someone like you.'

He shook his head, which was the only part of his body he could still move. He felt the now familiar pressure on the back of his head, as something was wrapped around his mouth area, cutting off his voice once more.

Sam was screaming into nothingness.

'There's something you should know, Sam. You made this happen. This is no one else's fault but your own. That's not to say I'm not enjoying this. This has been such fun. All fun has to end at some point, though. I know this. You know this.'

Sam realised he didn't want the end to come. He still wanted to live. As much as he wanted the pain to stop, he didn't want this to be the end. He could feel tears fall from his eyes and run down his cheeks, his shoulders hitching as his muffled cries escaped.

He didn't want to die.

'First, I'm going to list your crimes. Then we'll sentence you for them. And we're talking proper sentences. The punishment must fit the crime, isn't that right? That's fair, right?'

He wasn't expected to answer. Sam knew that. The decision had already been made. Before he had been brought to this place, wherever it was. He'd been sentenced long ago.

On some level, he knew he deserved it. For all he had done in his life.

Now, he was helpless and had to wait.

He didn't have to wait long.

Seven

There was a sense of boredom creeping in, which Murphy knew wasn't a good sign. A missing person could sometimes be an interesting case but, more often than not, it was a whole bunch of work for little to no reward. There were just too many cases, too many people missing, for it to be any other way.

He'd thought he'd left that sort of thing behind him. Now, any missing persons case which came into the division was usually shifted elsewhere, unless there was an extreme likelihood of violence or similar.

Turned out, all you needed was for the missing person to be vaguely in the public eye, and the case was forced upon him to deal with.

It was all about who you know. As with everything in life.

'They've found his email password,' Rossi said from her desk opposite him. 'Just got access now. *Pazzo* left it on a Post-it note on his desk. Should mean that we will be able to get control of his social media accounts. If you think that's right, of course?'

Murphy leaned back in his chair and thought for a second. 'Do it, but only because of the circumstances. I'm sure his parents would be happy with us for doing so and not give one about privacy issues. As far as we're aware, he's missing, presumed in danger, so we use anything we can.'

'We've already been through his sock drawer, the very definition of invading privacy,' Rossi said, a ghost of a smile on her face. 'Probably boring anyway. He's a prospective MP, desperate not to get into any scandal until he's been in the actual job for more than five minutes. I imagine he'll have scrubbed the thing clean.'

Murphy gave her a look.

'OK, odds are there's something,' Rossi said, the ghost smile becoming real now. 'Still, he looks far too clean-cut and a bit geeky for anything too weird. We'll get access and let you know.' Rossi beckoned to DS Graham Harris, who wheeled himself over to her side of the desk. They began to speak in low tones.

Murphy went back to recent John Doe cases, of which there were an alarming number. Most would be identified quickly, but some would be left to drift: the homeless, the missing, the immigrant, the loner. All lying in a morgue in the centre of Liverpool with no one to claim them as their own.

Most were too old to be Sam, but a couple caught his eye. He prepared a message and sent it to the coroner, thankful that he didn't have to do so in person. Dr Houghton wasn't exactly the first man he would choose to spend time with. The antagonism between them had been one-sided for a long time, but Murphy's dislike of Houghton had grown and now the feeling was more than mutual.

'Couple of deads in the morgue to look into,' Murphy said, waiting for Rossi's head to pop up from behind the monitor. 'Nothing that promising, though. Same age bracket, but one is almost pointless checking out. How are you getting on over there?'

'Facebook is open, just waiting for Twitter. Only messages to do with work, from a cursory glance. Will take us time to go back any further.'

'If he is in danger, there's a possibility they'll have been deleted anyway.'

Rossi clicked her pen against her teeth for a few seconds. 'Any word on his phone?'

Murphy checked his notes. 'Last switched on four days ago, which is the same day he went missing. Bounced off a mast in the city centre, but nothing since then. Must have been out in town.'

'What time was that?'

Murphy looked again. 'Some time just before midnight.'

'Could be on CCTV, we could track him from that.'

'Already on it,' Murphy replied, dropping his notes onto a stack of others which he would get around to shifting off his desk at some point. 'Not exactly a small area to check though. There's also the issue of how long this'll stay out of the media for. The more we check into things, the more likely it is someone will talk.'

Rossi shrugged and looked back at her computer. 'Not sure why we're keeping it quiet anyway. If he turns up, all's well. If he doesn't, then we're going to need all the help we can get.'

'Can't disagree with you there,' Murphy replied, turning away and looking over towards DCI Stephens's office. 'I think that'll change soon enough. Just the way of things. There's no way this'll be kept quiet for much longer.'

Murphy lifted himself off his chair and made his way towards DCI Stephens's office. He knocked once, waited for a response, then knocked again when there was no answer.

'Come in.'

Murphy made his way inside, nodding when DCI Stephens held up a hand at him as she finished on the phone. The office was about the only thing that Murphy envied about the DCI position. However, everything else that went with the job outweighed the joy of being able to collect his thoughts in private. He had enough on his plate as it was without the pressure that came with being in that sort of authority.

'OK . . . OK . . . Look, we'll talk later.'

He tried looking elsewhere and stared at a box file on a filing cabinet, wondering why she'd allowed him inside whilst still on the phone.

'I know . . . I can't talk now . . . Bye.'

Murphy tried not to jump when DCI Stephens slammed the phone down on the desk. Definitely a bad time.

'Yes, David,' DCI Stephens said, a trace of impatience already apparent in her voice. 'What can I do you for?'

'Erm . . . I just wanted to give you an update,' Murphy said, giving her a quick glance before looking down at her desk. 'About the Sam Byrne case.'

'Yes, of course.'

Murphy updated her on the afternoon's events. It didn't take long, which he hoped was an indication of where they were. 'We're just waiting on a few things to come back now,' he added when he'd finished. 'We haven't really got much to go on and if you want things kept quiet, I'm not sure if there's anything else we can do.'

'I think we both know that's a situation that isn't going to be possible for very long. I've told DSI Butler, who seems to be the main point of contact with the parents, but you know what it's like with these types of people. Everything swept under the rug, a large piece of furniture then placed over that rug ... we're just going to do our best and see what happens in that regard.'

'Good to know,' Murphy said, breathing a little easier. 'I'm not sure if there's anything else that we can do. You know what it's like with these things.'

'All too well,' DCI Stephens replied, straightening up the papers on one side of her desk. 'If anything else major comes in, then we can talk. But for now, let's see if we can get this dealt with quickly and out of our hair before the end of the week. Sound fair?'

Murphy made as if to salute then thought better of it. 'Yes, boss.'

He left her office and made his way back to his desk. Checked the clock on the wall and sighed when he saw the time. Another hour or two and it would be evening. He had left Sarah on the waterfront at one p.m. Five hours later and everything was so different. He'd texted her a few hours earlier to say he wouldn't be able to meet her as planned, but imagined she'd be home by now. He picked up his phone to call her, then noticed a note on his desk. He placed the phone back down and picked up the note instead. Read it once and then threw it towards the bin.

'Only one unidentified in the morgue now. And it's the least likely one.'

Rossi gave him a quick look before going back to her computer. 'That's good, I suppose. We've found some things on here, but not sure how they relate.'

Murphy stood up and walked round to her side of the desk. 'What have we got then?'

'Tons of messages from female admirers. Apparently there are still women out there who'll sleep with Tories . . . who knew?'

'Good start,' Murphy said, ignoring Rossi's remark. 'Anything that looks like something that's gone further.'

'Most are just standard responses. Thank yous and hope you vote for me and or my party, et cetera, et cetera. He's talked a bit more with some of them, but nothing too explicit. There are three women who sent pictures after he asked them to, but they've gone to phone after that.'

'What do you mean?'

'Exactly what I say,' Rossi said, flicking between tabs on the computer screen. 'He's asked for their number and that's the end of the conversation. We're getting in contact with them now, but we're talking months between these things. Last message was three months ago. Worth checking, but don't hold your breath.'

'Anything else on the other one . . . Twitter?'

Rossi huffed and switched tabs again. 'Nothing in direct messaging. He doesn't seem to respond to anyone on there at all. He posts quite regularly on Twitter – much more regularly than on Facebook – but just standard campaigning things at the moment. There are automated tweets going out most days, so even though it looks like he's been posting he hasn't been in reality.'

Murphy didn't bother asking what she meant. It was unlikely he'd understand afterwards anyway. 'Where's Graham?'

Rossi murmured a 'dunno' and went back to clicking on her computer. Murphy spotted DCs Hale and

Kirkham sitting at another desk and decided to speak to them first.

'Anything from the office stuff?' Murphy said when he reached them. He leant one hand on the desk, towering over them. 'You've had a couple of hours now.'

'Nothing yet, sir,' Kirkham replied, whilst Hale busied himself again. 'We're going through stuff, but there's a lot of unimportant info. Graham has taken a bunch of stuff away to work on properly.'

'Keep at it,' Murphy said, standing up and brushing down his shirt. 'I'm sure there's something in that lot we should know about.'

'Will do, sir.'

Murphy turned, giving a quick glance at the almost empty board at the head of the room and making his way back to his desk. There was a commotion from behind him and a loud shout.

'Shite, who left this here?'

Murphy paused and turned to see DC Graham Harris berating another DC at the other end of the room.

'I'm in a bloody wheelchair and you leave things lying on the floor? Just bloody move it.'

Murphy waited for DC Harris to wheel over towards them, Rossi now up out of her seat to see what was going on.

'Honestly, health and safety around here is shocking,' DC Harris said as he made his way to their bank of desks. 'I'm sure some of them have a bet on to see who can flip me over.'

'You can rest assured, Graham, that if that happened, someone would be flipped over themselves for the trouble.'

'Good to know,' Harris replied, wiping a hand across his glistening brow, taking away some of the shine. 'Anyway, I think I've found what that woman at Sam Byrne's office was intimating might be of interest.'

Murphy grinned, happy to be right for a change. 'What is it? Secret hideaway abroad? Stash of money?'

'Almost right. He has another property. An apartment just outside of town, near the student accommodation on Mount Pleasant. He rents it, under a business name. Found it going through the books. Must be a tax thing.'

Rossi came round from her side of the desks. 'I bet he's holed up there. Shall we pay him a visit and close this thing before we manage another hour's overtime?'

'Why not?' Murphy said, grabbing his coat and following Rossi out the door.

Eight

The light was beginning to fade as they entered the apartment building and made their way up the stairs. Posters adorned the walls, all of a political nature, all displaying various proclamations along the same theme. The free-form thoughts of left-wing idealists, Murphy noticed.

'You would think with these places being so bloody right-on, there'd be a lift or something,' Rossi said from behind him, already sounding out of breath.

'Told you to pack in the smoking,' Murphy said, waiting at the top of the stairs for Rossi to make her way up. 'Only on nights out, my arse.'

'Nothing to do with that,' Rossi replied, joining Murphy at the top. 'I just hate stairs. It's all right for you with legs the length of the Mersey.'

'What number is it again?' Murphy said, turning and facing the two rows of doors ahead of them. 'Twenty-eight?'

'Close. Eight. Last one on the right. This place brings back memories.'

'You stayed in student digs? Your ma and auld fella are just down the road. Could have saved a fortune.'

Rossi shook her head. 'I was nineteen and wanted out of the place. Five brothers, and me a student. Three of them were still at home, and between them and my mum and dad, the questioning after a night out got too much. Shared a flat up the road with a couple of others. It's mostly students around here, always has been.'

The converted block was situated on Mount Pleasant, a road which led up towards Abercromby Square. A Tesco Express with student accommodation above it was only a couple of doors down. The building they were in provided housing for private tenants and students with a little more money behind them. It hadn't stopped the fly-posting, though, Murphy thought.

'That door doesn't look right,' Rossi said as they reached number eight. Murphy stood to the side of her as he waited for her to knock. 'The handle has been screwed with.'

Rossi knocked once, then again when there wasn't an answer. Murphy extended a finger and pushed on the door. It opened slowly in front of them.

'Told you it wasn't right,' Rossi said, her voice louder now. 'Police, we're looking for Sam Byrne.'

Silence came from inside the flat. Rossi announced their presence again, only this time with more force. Murphy poked his head forwards into the darkened hallway, listening for any movement.

'Are we going in?' Rossi said, a whisper in his ear.

'Of course,' Murphy said, stepping into the flat. 'I don't think there's anyone here.'

'Famous last words . . .' Rossi said from behind him, following him inside. Murphy allowed his eyes to adjust to the darkness. Now he was a few steps into the flat, he could hear a low noise coming from a room down the hall. He took the telescopic baton he'd been carrying in his belt and extended it to his side. 'We're inside. Door was unlocked and we're concerned for the safety of Sam Byrne. Anyone in here should make themselves known to us now.'

Murphy waited a few seconds for any movement, then pressed ahead when he heard none. His heart began beating a little faster, his eyes were wide, watching for any sudden movement ahead of him. Now his vision had adjusted, he could see five doors, all leading off the single hallway. They were all closed. Murphy opened each one in turn, Rossi by his side as he did so.

He opened the living room door first, which turned out to have a kitchen attached. The curtains had been drawn, but it was still light enough to see it was unoccupied. The next door revealed a small closet, followed by a bathroom. Both similarly empty. There were two doors at the end of the corridor, one with light creeping out from underneath the door, one without.

Murphy went to the darkened door first and knocked, the sound muffled by his leather gloved hand. He opened the door when there was no answer. He waited for his eyes to adjust to the darkness within, but he knew there was no one inside. A musty smell assailed him.

'One more,' Murphy said to Rossi, his voice matching her previous whisper as he moved to the other door and knocked on it. The sound echoed around the small hallway. 'We're coming in, if you want to make yourself known to us, now's the time,' he said, his voice bouncing back off the door. A glow emanated from beneath the door, light spilling into the gloom of the hallway. He could hear low music, a distant bass drum and melody coming from within the room. He tried to place the music, but couldn't quite catch it.

'I'm opening it,' Murphy said, taking hold of the handle. 'Standard pro.'

Rossi tensed beside him and he opened the door.

He swept the room in a second, the inside much smaller than he'd been expecting. Rossi was behind him and opening a wardrobe door in the time it took for him to realise they were alone in there. The glow was coming from a red light fixed to the wall. The light buzzed, making the low sound Murphy had registered when they'd entered the flat. Music was playing softly, coming from a speaker with an iPod dock on top of it. The window was covered in thick, black material, tacked to the wall so it couldn't be removed.

Most of the space was taken up with what looked like a king-sized bed, a raised pole on each corner. The bed was clear of a duvet or blanket – just a sheet tinged red by the light was covering the mattress. The overhead light blinked on and Murphy turned to see Rossi standing next to the light switch.

'*Dio Mio . . .*'

Murphy turned back to the bed to see the red light hadn't been the only thing giving the bed a flash of colour. The white sheet was stained in places. Red and brown marks, sometimes in large circular spots, others just small smears. There were restraints built into the bed; chains and manacles hanging down from the bedposts. There were stains on the wood of the bedstead and marks etched into the grain.

'What the hell is this?' Murphy said, dropping his baton to his side. He removed his gloves and reached into his pocket, taking out a packet of latex gloves. He snapped open the packet, placed the gloves on and moved closer to the bed. 'Most of these don't look recent.'

'There's a box here,' Rossi said from the other side of the room. 'Seems to be full of sex toys.'

'Usually we have to go hunting for those.'

'Most of these don't look like the normal ones we'd find anyway.' Rossi stepped to the side and, after putting on her own gloves, lifted something in the air. 'Ball gag.'

'I've only ever seen one of those in that film ... what was it called? The guy with the wig, what's his name?'

'John Travolta. You're thinking of *Pulp Fiction*. I wish it was the first time I'd seen one of these ...'

'The less I know about your private life the better,' Murphy said, thinking the levity of his tone sounded odd in that room.

'Not a chance. I've had some terrible cases over the years,' Rossi said, placing the gag back in the box where she'd found it. 'We need forensics in here.'

'You reckon?' Murphy said, looking at the bedside table. There was a glass ashtray, which was empty but stained black on the bottom. He opened a drawer to find boxes of condoms and another large sex toy. 'I think you were right about MPs,' he said, closing the drawer and steeling himself to open another one. 'They are all a bit weird.'

'Told you so.'

Murphy opened the middle drawer and found a box of red candles, some with melted wax hardened on the sides. The bottom drawer held a small black book, which Murphy took out and placed to one side.

'We're both ignoring the obvious thing in the room,' Rossi said, standing at the foot of the bed. 'What do you make of it?'

Murphy looked towards where she was pointing. On the wall above the head of the bed were printed slogans displayed in picture frames, all surrounding one phrase which had daubed directly onto the wall.

SLUTS - WELCOME TO PAIN

Murphy moved closer and winced. The rest of the words on the wall were similarly offensive.

'This guy is off the charts,' Rossi said, wrinkling her face as she approached the wall from the other side of the bed. 'Do we have to find him?'

'Yes,' Murphy replied, turning away and snapping off a glove. He reached into his pocket and pulled out his mobile phone. 'I'd really like to get an explanation for a start. I want to know if everything that happened in this room was consensual.'

'You think something might have happened to him here? Seems like bloodstains on the bed. Maybe he got too strong with someone and they didn't like it.'

'I think we have to consider it may have been the other way around . . . Hello, it's Murphy. We need a forensics team here . . . No, no body, but a shit ton of other stuff we need to look at now.'

Murphy continued talking as Rossi made her way out of the room and turned on lights throughout the rest of the flat. By the time he'd ended the call, she'd made her way back to the bedroom.

'It's definitely his place,' Rossi said, handing him a few envelopes. 'All have his name on them. Gas and leccy bills in his name. Couldn't find one for water. There's more stains in the bathroom, but apart from a chair and TV in the living room, there's nothing else here. This wasn't somewhere he spent much time.'

'Given his house up in Blundellsands, I don't think he spent much time being normal anywhere.'

Rossi murmured an agreement, then went back to looking at things in the room. 'Got a tablet here,' she said after a minute of looking. Murphy poked his head up from underneath the bed. 'Battery's dead, but I don't even want to know what's on it.'

'Can those things take photos and videos?'

'Can you please move into 2016 at some point? It's like being partnered with Inspector bloody Morse. Yes, they can take photos and videos. Just like that thing in your hand does.'

Murphy narrowed his eyes at her. 'All right, smart arse. I don't own one of them, so wasn't sure, that's all. Put it down and let them bag and check it. We've got enough other stuff to deal with anyway.'

'Neighbours?'

Murphy nodded. 'Getting late, though. Unless we find a murder weapon in the next half hour, it can wait until tomorrow morning.'

'Good, but we'll do prelims with them first. We should make sure he's not been back here recently, and ask when they saw him last.'

'Exactly,' Murphy replied, checking the time on his phone and rolling his eyes at it. 'We'll get uniforms to knock on some doors. I also want to know who lives in this block, who are students, who aren't. If this is something that goes on here.'

'What, a building for BDSM?'

Murphy thought for a second, but wasn't sure of the answer. 'That's what we have to find out,' he said eventually. 'I'm starting to think he's gone missing for a reason now. And that we need to find him soon, because if he's the one dishing out the pain, revenge will be on someone's mind.'

You

You look down at your hands. Blood drips to the floor from your fingertips. You are covered in it. His life slides away as you watch, the droplets pooling around your feet.

You have done it. You are a murderer. A killer. This is it now. This will be how you will forever be. There won't be a chance for repentance. You'll live with what you have done for the rest of whatever life you have left.

You tortured the man. You have no regrets.

This won't keep you awake at night. You already have enough to do that. It won't be his face staring up at you in the moment of his death, that won't be it. He'll be there, but it will be from another time. Another place.

Another face.

No one has a soul. You don't believe in nonsense like that. You know you are just a set of synapses firing, nerves and impulses. That is all. There is no heaven to be barred from. No hell to be damned to for all time. You're just an evolved animal, now with real power.

The man, lying broken on the ground next to you, deserved to die.

It wasn't just for what he'd done in the past. It was for the things he was doing now. His actions caused this to pass. He hadn't learned his lesson. Hadn't tried to change. He had to be stopped.

That is your truth. Your verdict. You weighed up the good and bad and made the call.

You don't grieve for him or anyone else. You don't feel guilt.

They deserved their fate.

You already know the answer.

You just don't want to face it.

There is only one ending you can envisage for yourself. You don't see yourself lying on a beach in a foreign country, free and clear from the nightmares. No one will understand. You will be castigated. Burnt at the stake. Judged by the crowd and deemed a monster.

That will be your legacy.

The people you are destroying now are the most deserving. You know that. You know everything they did and didn't do. You know all their dirty little secrets.

You enjoy seeing them in pain. This is justice. The ultimate penalty for the worst crimes.

You know they thought so little of people beneath them that they would never understand any other way.

This is what they deserve. All of them.

You are just carrying out what needs to be done.

You are right.

You are true.

You are not stopping until it's over. Until your list is complete.

Nine

It was almost nine p.m. by the time they could leave the building, leaving the preliminary discussions with the immediate neighbours in the hands of the uniforms who had arrived. Murphy had received word that one of the occupants had used Sam Byrne's name almost instantly, which meant it wouldn't be long before the drums started and social media would be abuzz.

Sam Byrne's name was about to be discussed online by a large number of people. It had taken seven hours, but he'd managed to keep it a secret longer than he'd first imagined.

If anything, it would mean he would have a little more help now. Given what they'd found at the flat, the blood-stains and evidence of violence, it was unlikely things were going to turn out OK.

He tried to put it to the back of his mind as he drove home, turning up the car stereo as he put a barrier between work and home life. The music helped, giving him a sense of finality to the day. It helped, too, that the familiar songs were old classics which he'd listened to endlessly.

It didn't take much time to drive home, but the journey was still longer than he wished. They had recently moved house, which had made the journey more interesting for a week, but now it had become as commonplace as the previous commute had been. He pulled into the driveway of the new place, still unsure of the way it looked from the outside, but he supposed it didn't matter. He didn't spend much time staring at the outside of his own house.

Murphy waited for the song to finish before leaving the black Citroen. He locked the car, double checking it before letting himself into the house.

'Tell me there's some tea going,' he shouted, slipping off his shoes in the hallway and then taking off his coat and jacket. 'Bloody starving.'

'It's in the dog, you dirty stop-out,' came the reply from the living room.

Murphy smirked, moving through to the living room where he found Sarah sitting in front of the TV. She was in her usual spot on the couch, legs tucked underneath her, phone in hand. He spied the screen as he moved across and gave her a kiss. 'That would make more sense if we actually owned a dog. Still playing those damn games?'

'Got to fill my time waiting for the man of the house to return, haven't I? And I'm enjoying the calm before the storm of coursework and essays and all of that stuff. Would you rather I was polishing the silverware, wearing an apron or something?'

'We have silverware?'

Sarah pushed him away with her foot and sat up a little more on the couch. 'You just missed Jess. We got a takeaway in, seeing as you cancelled on me.'

'Sorry about that. Work, you know . . .'

'Of course I do,' Sarah replied, finally taking her eyes away from the mobile phone screen. 'Tea's in the oven. Ordered your usual for you.'

'And kept it warm for me. Aren't you the best wife a man could ask for,' Murphy said, leaving the room and making his way into the kitchen.

'Don't be a smart arse, it doesn't suit you,' she shouted at him from the other room. He chuckled softly under his breath, before burning his hand on the uncovered plate in the oven.

'Remember to use oven gloves.'

'Yeah, I know, I'm not an idiot,' Murphy said, waving his fingers in the air before running them under the cold tap. 'Where's the tray?'

'On the side, where it always is.'

Murphy looked around at the fifteen possible sides in the kitchen and was about to ask again when he spotted it.

A few minutes later, he was sitting in his chair watching TV and eating what would have been a nice chicken korma two hours earlier. It barely touched the sides as he shovelled it in, hardly caring that it tasted like reheated rubber.

'That telly is still not in the right position,' Murphy said between mouthfuls. 'Half the screen is blocked by the mantelpiece.'

'I've checked and it's definitely not half. If I move it any further over it may as well be next door. Just move your chair over a bit.'

Murphy huffed a little, but didn't say any more. He was the reason they'd had to move in the first place, given what had happened in their previous home. Someone coming in and disturbing the feeling of safety there. It didn't matter that the intruder was currently in prison, awaiting sentence for multiple murders, it would never have felt right staying there. Murphy was happy to move and make a fresh start.

Still, the damn TV was in the wrong position, so he could moan every now and again.

'What's going on at work then?' Sarah said, placing her phone down on the side table next to her and lifting a cup of tea to her mouth. 'Haven't seen anything online about a major incident.'

Murphy shoved another forkful of korma and pilau rice into his mouth, giving himself a few seconds to think of an answer. It wasn't long enough. 'It's nothing.'

'Now that's interesting,' Sarah said, putting her cup down and drawing herself up so she was almost kneeling on the couch. 'Something top secret, David? Can't even tell your wife what you're working on?'

'Something like that,' Murphy said, realising there was no naan bread left and that was the reason why he'd almost cleaned the plate. Usually there would be food left if he'd eaten an entire naan by himself. 'I doubt it'll be secret much longer, though.'

'Oh, this is getting juicier by the second. Someone famous then?'

'I'm not saying. Let's just say politics around here is about to get a lot more interesting.'

Sarah shook her head and sat back into the sofa, uncurling her legs from underneath her and finishing off the cup of tea. 'I doubt even your job could make politics interesting.'

Murphy didn't reply, instead he concentrated on finishing off his food, placing the empty plate on the arm of the chair.

'Jess was telling me about a case she's just lost. Bloke being done for murder. Another domestic. She seemed quite pleased not to have won, to be honest. First time I've seen that.'

'It happens every now and again. Even defence lawyers have a conscience. Sometimes.'

They fell into an easy silence, Murphy feeling his eyes droop as the television – or the half he could see anyway – blared away in the corner.

* * *

There was a moment, then it came. That feeling of familiarity mixed with comfort. It didn't matter what had happened in the time she had spent away, as soon as she walked in and felt that, it was all OK. Everything was right, the way it was supposed to be, the way she wanted it. Her house, her place.

Darren was on his feet and in the hallway before she'd even closed the door behind her. He was less familiar. It didn't matter that he'd moved in six months earlier, it still meant there was a smudge in the life she had created in her own home.

Not that she would have it any other way. For now.

'You're home late. Is everything OK?'

Rossi stayed silent as she removed her coat and pulled her shoes off her aching feet. She made her way into the living room, leaving Darren leaning on the stair banister behind her. She began moving things closer to where she usually sat on the couch. The coffee table was pulled nearer, joined by a smaller table.

'Where are my slippers?'

'I tidied them away, under the stairs,' Darren said, hovering in the doorway. 'Tried to keep things neat around here.'

'Well, don't do that,' Rossi said, moving past him into the hallway and opening the door to the cupboard under the stairs. She spied her slippers and dragged them out. 'I mean, do do that, with the tidying. Just don't move my stuff about. I leave things in certain places for certain reasons.'

'OK, OK,' Darren replied, holding his hands up, still standing in the living-room doorway. 'If I'd known your slippers had a special place where they lived, I would never have moved them.'

Rossi finally got her right slipper on her foot after three tries, then stood up. 'I'm sorry, it's just been a long day. Thank you, but don't do it again.' She tried to smile at the end, but it still came out a little harsher than she'd intended.

'Have you eaten?' Darren said, walking up the hallway past her and into the kitchen. 'Only I don't think there's much here and I got something earlier on. Need to do a shop . . .'

Rossi's chin dropped to her chest and she sighed inwardly. 'It's OK,' she said, following him. 'I've got some of me ma's polpetti in the fridge.'

'Oh, OK. I didn't realise. Do you want me to do anything?'

'No, it's fine, go and sit down, I'll be in soon. Won't take me long.'

The kettle was filled and switched on by the time she heard sound from the television in the front room. She pulled out her phone and propped it up on the kitchen counter and was watching the news on it within a few more seconds. She found an unopened packet of pasta then took the meatballs out from the fridge and emptied them into a pan.

She was half-watching the news, stirring the polpetti on the stove, when Darren appeared at the kitchen door again. Rossi had her back to him, but sensed him standing there watching her.

'What?' Rossi said without turning round.

'Nothing,' Darren replied, his voice closer to her. 'I was just making sure you were OK. You seem a little tense.'

Rossi felt his hands on her shoulders and closed her eyes for a moment. 'Just a long day at work, that's all. Sorry if I'm being a little short with you.'

'That's OK,' Darren said, leaning down and planting a kiss on the top of her head. 'I'm used to it now. Hasn't exactly been an easy day for me either, so I understand.'

'Busy or difficult?'

She felt his hands leave her shoulders. 'Just someone not making it who should have. That's all. I know I'm only an anaesthetist, and we don't usually have much to do with patients, but sometimes you can't help it. Only a kid . . .'

'That's horrible,' Rossi said, breaking spaghetti in half and placing it in a pan of boiling water. 'Poor parents.'

'It's made me think about things,' Darren said, leaning against the worktop. Rossi leaned past him to pick up the salt cellar and added some to the pan.

'What's that?'

'How I don't want to wait around for my life to start. I want to do things quicker, have things quicker.'

Rossi turned her back to him and stirred the meatballs in sauce. Waited for the hammer to fall.

'I want to start a family, I want to move into a proper home, with you. I want . . .'

Rossi allowed the words to drift away and instead concentrated on moving the spoon around the pan, occasionally breaking up the dried spaghetti in the other pan to make sure it didn't stick to the bottom. She was no longer allowing Darren's words to penetrate her mind, the sound becoming a droning noise in the background.

'What do you think about that?'

His last question got through. Rossi didn't answer, instead moving away and taking a plate from the cupboard and busying herself trying to find some Parmigiano for her meal.

She didn't want to think of an answer. She just wanted to relax, eat and not worry. She didn't want to answer and ruin everything.

Terrified of what that answer might mean for the future.

Ten

There's a truth to some of the things shown in crime dramas on TV. There's also much fiction. Murphy didn't enjoy watching them, preferring something mindless instead. He enjoyed reading true crime books every now and again, but it wasn't often.

Crime just wasn't something he wanted to see dramatised.

What they don't show you in those programmes is the hours of boredom, the endless monotony of writing reports and filling out forms. The wasted moments, hanging around, doing nothing but wait for others to work and finish their responsibilities before you can get started.

Sitting in his car outside the flat which had been Sam Byrne's secret hideaway was one of those times. As bleary-eyed students made their way up the hill of Mount Pleasant towards the university, he was stuck in an increasingly uncomfortable car seat.

'Freshers' week starts earlier each year,' Rossi said, mobile phone in her hand. 'There's a statement coming from his parents soon. We knew it wasn't going to be kept quiet for long. Nothing we could do about that.'

Murphy grunted a response, shaking his head and grinding his teeth. 'Still, a day? I know the boss'll be understanding, but that prick Butler will be a nightmare to deal with from now on. We couldn't keep the thing under wraps for twenty-four hours.'

Rossi sighed and ran her free hand through her hair, pushing it back from her face. 'Do we know who blabbed yet?'

'It'll be one of the people who live here. Mixed with a "source" inside the department. That's how it works these days.'

Rossi sniffed and went back to scrolling through her phone. 'So far, it's not really anywhere but online. The *Echo* have got it, obviously, but not much on *Sky News* or the BBC. Could be that we'd feed it by commenting.'

Murphy rubbed the bridge of his nose and wondered when things had changed so much. When he suddenly had to consider things like this?

The news of Sam Byrne's disappearance had broken overnight and only increased from there. Now, his name was trending on Twitter and an endless stream of people having a field day with the story on social media. That was the world he lived in now, Murphy thought. When normal, everyday people believed they had a right to comment on everything, even if they knew nothing.

'I don't know,' Murphy said eventually, more to fill the silence than anything else. 'If he's just buggered off some-where, maybe this'll make him check in and we can get on with actual police work. If not, then maybe we'll find him sooner because of it. Or we'll never find him because someone panics, or we find him *because* someone panics.'

'That's a lot of possibilities in one sentence. It was

always going to happen. There's no way someone in the public eye, especially a politician, is going to disappear and no one find out.'

'Suppose you're right,' Murphy said, lifting his radio and speaking into it for a few seconds. 'Let's go.'

They both exited the car, Murphy stretching a little as he did so, glad to be out of the confines of the vehicle.

'Will anyone be up at this time?' Murphy said, giving a nod to the uniform waiting outside. He waved over to DC Kirkham who was standing on the other side of the road, turning away as he bounded across. 'You know, students and that. They're not usually early birds.'

'Do you believe every stereotype you hear?' Rossi replied, taking the lead and opening the door which lead into the communal hallway. 'They'll be up. It's whether they'll be in that'll be the issue.'

'Uniforms say no one has left since last night. They knew we were going to be interviewing them this morning. They probably told them why as well, which is why they're still here and discussing it on bloody Twitter.'

Murphy held the door open for DC Kirkham, who muttered a thanks as he joined them in the hallway.

'OK, let's split this up. A floor each?' Murphy said, looking at the two younger detectives.

'Sounds good to me,' DC Kirkham said, a touch of eagerness to his tone.

'Laura, you take the ground floor, I'll take the second. Jack, you take the first. Remember, no names mentioned. Just allow them to talk.'

Murphy waited for DC Kirkham to start ascending the stairs before speaking to Rossi in a low voice. 'If they push, let them know a little bit, but we need to find out

exactly what's been going on in that flat. Finish up quickly
and join Jack. I don't want him screwing anything up.'

Rossi gave a nod and then turned away, knocking on
the first door, the sound reverberating around the hallway. If they weren't already awake, the whole place would
be by now, Murphy thought. A minute later, he was on
the top floor, walking swiftly over to the door opposite
the flat Sam Byrne had rented. The door was opened
while he still had a fist in the air, knuckles unused on the
wood.

'Hello, are you them?' a voice said from within. Murphy
looked down, and then down a bit further to locate the
voice. A small, mousy-looking woman peered over glasses
up at him. 'We were told you might be knocking.'

Murphy introduced himself, looking past her into the
flat for anyone else lurking there. 'Mind if I come in and
have a chat?'

'You're not allowed to question me and enter my home
if I don't want you to, or without a caution being read.'

The girl, because that's what she was really, he thought,
was trying to maintain eye contact with him, but was failing. Her hands shook a little as she held the door. Murphy
tried to make himself half a foot shorter, but settled for
tilting his head and smiling thinly.

'Nothing to worry about,' Murphy said, attempting his
'soft' voice. 'Just a few questions about the flat opposite
yours, that's all. Can I come in and explain?'

The woman hesitated, then she opened the door a little
further and allowed him to enter. He waited for her to
close the door and followed her into the living area. The
flat was the same layout as Byrne's flat opposite, just in
reverse. He looked around, widening his eyes in surprise

as the expected chaos of student digs failed to materialise.

'Nice place,' Murphy said, still trying to allay the woman's fears. 'You keep a tidy home.'

'Flatmate's room is more what you'd think a student flat would be like,' she replied, pushing her glasses up her nose. 'I'd offer you a drink, but I don't really want to.'

Fair enough, Murphy thought. 'Not a problem. What's your name? You still haven't told me.'

'Claire,' she replied, folding her arms across her chest. 'Just Claire for now.'

'OK, Claire. As I said, just a few questions and then I'll let you get on. Mind if we sit?'

Claire hesitated again, biting her bottom lip, before moving over to a sofa and sitting on the far end of it. She motioned to a chair tucked under a small kitchen table on the other side of the room. Murphy moved across and pulled it out. The room wasn't exactly spacious, but it had been nicely put together: one sofa, a flat-screen television opposite it in the corner of the room. The kitchen area was behind him and seemed clean enough. There was a faint smell of lavender in the room and a healthy-looking potted plant stood on the windowsill. There were a few prints on the walls, but no photographs. He imagined they would be in her own room, the flatmate doing the same. This would be a communal area, purposely kept clear of anything personal.

'I don't know anything,' Claire said, fixing Murphy with a stare. 'So I don't know why you need to speak to me.'

'Let's not be too hasty, Claire. You don't know what I'm going to ask yet.'

'It's about the flat over the way. As I said, I don't know anything.'

'Let's start at the beginning,' Murphy said, pulling out a usually unused notepad. 'How long have you lived here?'

'A year. Just about to start second term at uni.'

'Which one?'

Claire's shoulders relaxed a little. 'City, up the road.'

'What are you studying there?'

'Physics,' Claire replied, arms now by her side. 'Very difficult and not for the faint-hearted. I have some studying to do actually, so if we could hurry up . . .'

Murphy held up a hand of acceptance. 'Where are you from originally?'

'Preston. Would you like to know what my parents do for a living, or how they met? Maybe you would like to know my grandmother's shoe size? I don't see what any of this has to do with why you might be here.'

'I'm sorry,' Murphy said, unhappy with how the apology tasted in his mouth. 'You've lived here for a year. Do you know many people in the building?'

'A few, not many. We tend to keep to ourselves here. Thankfully, the price of the rent keeps away the ones who are at university primarily to test the parameters of their liver functions. We're a little more studious here. Of course, there's a few people who aren't even students.'

'Was the person who lived in the flat opposite one of them?'

Claire didn't respond for a few seconds. 'I didn't really know him.'

'But you saw him?'

Another few seconds went by in an uncomfortable silence. 'I may have done. I didn't know at the time who he was.'

'Who do you think he is?'

It was Claire's turn to tilt her head at Murphy. 'I think we both know that's a ridiculous question, Mr Murphy.'

It had been a while since anyone had called him 'Mr', thought Murphy, trying not to show his annoyance at the fact she couldn't even manage to call him detective. 'How about, just for my sake, you tell me. Just to make sure.'

'Sam Byrne,' Claire said, looking away from Murphy and towards the switched-off television. 'The man standing for MP in the by-election coming up. They say he might win.'

'I don't know about that, but we are talking about the same person at least. When was the last time you saw him?'

'I'm not sure. I hear him out in the hall now and then. A week or so, maybe. I suppose he's been busy recently. I don't think he lived here, to be honest. We would only see him every now and again. His post would pile up downstairs in the pigeonhole.'

'Did you ever speak with him?' Murphy said, crossing one long leg over the other. 'Ever borrow a cup of sugar or something?'

'No, not really,' Claire replied, ignoring the attempt to lighten the mood. 'Just a quiet nod if we passed each other out in the hallway. It's a bit difficult to ignore someone who lives only a few feet away.'

'So, you've never heard anything out of the ordinary there? TV too loud or anything like that?'

Claire thought for a moment, began to speak, then stopped herself.

'What is it, Claire?' Murphy said, uncrossing his legs and leaning forwards.

'Well . . . it's probably nothing, that's all. I don't want to create a problem, or exacerbate an existing situation.'

Exacerbate, Murphy thought. That was a new one. 'We're trying to help Sam, that's all,' he said, keeping his calm. 'Any information will be treated with the utmost respect.'

Claire breathed in and pulled on a few strands of her hair. 'I've heard a few things coming from the flat, but I just thought it was a television on too loud, that's all. Sometimes . . . well, they sounded too real.'

'What did you hear?'

'Screams.'

Murphy nodded, but didn't say anything. He waited for Claire to keep talking.

'I thought it was just a horror movie, that's all. There was something else, though. Happened a while ago, so probably has nothing to do with anything.'

'Go on, Claire,' Murphy said, trying to keep the eagerness out of his tone. 'You never know what might be helpful.'

'Well, this is a few months back now. I came home late from working at the library in uni. The hallway was quiet and I was about to let myself into the flat when his door opened. A girl came out crying, really quietly but it was loud enough for me to hear her. He came out and shepherded her back inside and just gave me a look, as if he was apologising. I just put it down to an argument or something.'

'You don't seem certain about that.'

Claire shook her head and seemed less sure about what she was saying. 'I don't know. There was something about the whole situation I didn't like.'

'What was it?'

'It was like . . . It was as if she didn't want to be there and he was making sure she wouldn't leave. He didn't drag her back in or anything like that. It was just a feeling. I wanted to say something, but didn't think it was my place, especially if I was wrong.'

Murphy finished writing and considered Claire's words again. Looked up at the young woman and tried to make sense of what she'd told him.

Eleven

A few minutes after Claire had told him about hearing screams and a crying girl in the hallway, Murphy was saying goodbye and leaving his card. There was patently nothing else she was willing to say, which made things a little more difficult. Just another piece in what was becoming an ever more complicated jigsaw.

Murphy made his way to the other neighbouring flat, knocked a few times, then slid a contact notice under the door when there was no answer. The flat was on the same side as Claire's had been, so he wasn't expecting much more from the occupant. It was another item which needed ticking off the list, however.

'How are you getting on?' Murphy said, joining DC Kirkham on the floor below as the younger man exited the last flat. 'Anything useful?'

'Not really,' DC Kirkham said, flipping open his notepad. 'Bloke in number five works nights and was just pissed off I woke him up. Wasn't much help at all really. Couple in number four were on their way out the door to a lecture. Both studying history, both originally from Manchester, both had no contact with the person who lives in that flat upstairs. No answer from number six.'

'Did you get all their names?'

'Of course,' Kirkham replied, eager rather than annoyed. 'Although number five refused to give me a surname. Didn't matter, as I spotted it on an envelope on the way out. He didn't know anything really, but does remember seeing Byrne last week sometime. Couldn't be sure of the date.'

'The couple hadn't seen him either?'

'George – that's the tall one according to my notes – remembers seeing someone he didn't recognise one day going up the stairs ahead of him. He wasn't sure if it was someone who was visiting at first, but then he saw him picking up post from the pigeonhole downstairs another time. Didn't get a good look at him, so wasn't sure who he was. James – the short one, obviously – he has never seen him at all, but now knows all about it, of course. Has hundreds of followers on Twitter and Instagram apparently. Not sure why he felt the need to tell me that . . .'

'Right, good,' Murphy said, making his way down to the bottom level. 'Not about it being all over social media, of course, but at least we have a general framework to work with. I want you to go back to the station and start writing that up and we'll meet you back there. Get Graham to look at CCTV in the area and pull everything for the past seven days. Tell him to be prepared to go back further. We're working on a theory that he went missing Thursday night, as that's the last time anyone saw him, but we need a complete picture of his movements around here in the days leading up to it and after.'

'Yes, sir,' DC Kirkham said, putting away his notepad and standing up straight. 'Anything else?'

Murphy shook his head and watched him leave. In the time he'd spent talking to Claire, the young detective constable had visited three places. He wasn't sure if that was a good or a bad thing. He dithered for a second, unable to decide between waiting for Rossi in the car or in the lobby of the building. He settled for the latter.

'I miss uni,' Rossi said, closing the door of flat number three behind her. 'The hours, damn I miss those hours.'

Murphy checked his watch. Only seven minutes waiting. Not bad. His patience was getting better. 'Anything?'

'Not much,' Rossi said, following Murphy out of the building and onto the street. She waited for him to open the car and climbed inside before continuing. 'Flat one was out. Flat two wouldn't put his phone down long enough to speak to me, even after I asked nicely. So I asked not so nicely and he told me he knew who Sam Byrne was and that he had seen him in the building on a few occasions. Thought he was just visiting someone, though. An old friend or something, he thought. I think he's the one who has been talking non-stop online about our activities here. A uniform has tipped him the wink. The residents were milling about last night in the hallways, while forensics were doing their job, so one of them must have known Sam stayed in the flat.'

'That'll be flat seven – Claire. Lives opposite Sam's place. I spoke to her.'

'Right,' Rossi said, waiting a few seconds to see if Murphy was going to continue, but he kept quiet for now. 'Flat three didn't know a thing, but I don't think they'd notice anything happening from any distance further than the end of their noses. No idea what they're doing at university. Can't see that ending well for them. Thick as bloody pig . . .'

Murphy waited for Rossi to finish ranting, which took a while as she went from speaking English to Italian half-way through a sentence.

'There's not enough to go on,' Rossi said, once she'd finished. 'Byrne's missing under suspicious circumstances, but I don't see a threat to life here. Unless you got any more on your floor?'

Murphy told Rossi what he'd learned from Claire, throwing in DC Kirkham's results as he did so. Once he'd finished, they both sat in the car watching the forensic officers exit the building, packing up their white van.

'Think they'll have the answer?' Rossi said, turning towards Murphy.

He thought for a second and then shrugged his shoulders. 'No idea. I'm still not sure what's going on here. Everything points to something happening to him, but we don't have a single concrete idea what that could be.'

'We were told about this less than twenty-four hours ago, so maybe we're just not seeing it yet.'

Murphy murmured an agreement, lifting the radio out of its cradle as it crackled to life. DCI Stephens's voice filled the car, making Rossi reach across and turn down the volume a little.

'David, is Laura with you?'

'I am,' Rossi said, her brow creasing as she frowned at the mention of her name. 'Everything OK?'

'Yeah, just wanted to make sure. I want to let you both know that DSI Butler will be making a public statement regarding Sam Byrne in the next thirty minutes. Couple of the broadsheets have taken an interest in his disappearance, so a discussion has been had with the parents. They'll be releasing their own statement at the same time. I guess we can't keep things quiet very long in the current climate.'

'I hope you know it was none of us that released this info,' Murphy said, hoping the edge to his voice was coming across on the radio. 'We kept it as quiet as possible.'

'I know that, David. It was never going to be a secret once we got involved. That's the nature of things, no matter what some people think.'

Murphy mouthed the word 'Butler' towards Rossi who rolled her eyes in response.

'How are you getting on at this flat he rented?'

Murphy updated her on the morning's activity. 'Here's Jack now,' DCI Stephens interrupted as Murphy summarised DC Kirkham's interview highlights. 'He has his determined look on,' she said.

'I gave him a couple of tasks to sort out,' Murphy said, glancing at Rossi who was already staring out the side window at nothing in particular. 'Listen, is there anything we're not aware of here? We've found certain things at this flat, which don't exactly match up with what we know about Byrne so far. Anything that'll surprise us down the line that we could be told about now?'

There wasn't an immediate answer, just radio silence, which made Rossi turn her head a little. Finally, DCI Stephens spoke.

'Let's talk more later. Nothing to worry about at the moment. Just keep on with what you're doing for now.'

She finished the call, leaving Murphy with a quizzical look on his face.

'A flat he tries to hide,' Murphy said, extending a hand and ticking off items with a finger. 'Which doesn't look lived in, with a bedroom that looks like a torture chamber, complete with blood and whatever else stains. A neighbour who has heard screams and seen crying women in the hallway. Yet, he's the one that's reported missing. It's four days before we're brought into it. He's in the public eye, possibly about to become a Member of Parliament. His car disappears but nothing else. Except maybe his laptop. What the hell is going on here?'

Rossi shaped as if to answer, then stopped herself. Murphy waited, one hand now on the steering wheel.

'My best guess?'

'Go on,' Murphy said, wondering if hers matched his at all. 'I'm all ears.'

'This was a place he didn't want anyone finding out about. He was doing something here. This wasn't a one-off thing, he's had this flat a while. He's in the public eye now, so he's kept it hidden, but something drove him back here. I'm thinking someone found out about it and what he does.'

'And that'll be what is key here,' Murphy said, finishing the thought. 'Finding out what he does here and why. Then we'll be getting somewhere.'

Thirty minutes later, they were back at the station, gathering the few officers and detectives who had found themselves attached to the case. Murphy watched the television on the wall as DSI Butler gave his statement live on the news channel.

'*All our efforts are being directed towards finding Sam Byrne safe and unharmed . . .*'

'Talk about an overestimation on numbers,' Murphy said, his voice almost a whisper as he talked to himself. 'We barely have half a dozen people on this.'

'It's hardly a big case, though,' DC Hale said, sidling closer to Murphy. 'Some bloke who has gone missing, that's all.'

'Which is why we have our DSI giving statements from his ivory tower and a MCU working the case?'

DC Hale started to reply, then kept his mouth shut. Murphy looked him over and waited for another remark, but it didn't come. He didn't bother giving him any more time to change his mind and instead turned to the others who had been watching silently behind him.

'I know missing cases are usually a ball ache and best avoided, but you've all heard by now who it is and who is giving statements on our behalf.'

There were a few turned heads and whispered words.

'That means we're going to be on the clock. It also means that within hours we're going to be under scrutiny from the outside again. Sam Byrne was a prospective MP, ahead in local polls and well liked within the community he wanted to represent. He was a Tory . . .'

There were a couple of heckles at that, but Murphy carried on as if he hadn't heard them.

'. . . which means he must be doing something right if he was about to be elected in this city, of all places. I want you out there, finding out what the real feeling was about him, whether he had anyone stridently against him, things like that. We have one full name for a friend, and a whole bunch of first names. I want a couple of you combing through his social media accounts to find out who these people are.'

There was a noise towards the back of the incident room, the sound of a phone slamming down. Murphy looked past a few heads to see DC Kirkham waving at him.

'What's going on, Jack?' Murphy said, making his way towards the DC.

'They've just found Sam Byrne's car by the Rocket.'

'Not exactly gone far then . . .'

'Not just that,' DC Kirkham said with a smirk, then looking past Murphy at the rest of the incident room. All eyes were on him. 'It's parked up just off the dual carriageway, near the bypass. Someone has just called it in.'

'Right, well, now we have his vehicle at least–'

'I haven't finished,' DC Kirkham interrupted, still not showing any impatience. 'There's someone inside it. A body.'

Murphy felt his stomach drop a few floors.

NINE YEARS EARLIER

City of Liverpool University

It wasn't the university they were supposed to attend, but it wouldn't matter much. Some of them had careers already mapped out in front of them. Sam Byrne would be an MP like his father. Simon would join a legal firm. James would work with his father in the City, moving back down to London. Tim was more single-minded about being his own boss and wanted to create his own company – helped by family money, of course.

They would all be successful. That much was certain.

Sam was the catalyst. The creator. They didn't even need to be from the same background really, simply the same mindset as him.

Ambitious, greedy, selfish and committed.

He had contacts before arriving, secured by his father, so he knew two fellow politics students would be in his group. He would target economics and business students next.

They had some local flavour, provided by a mature student, a few years older and wiser. He wasn't pure-bred British, but he was in there at the beginning. A history student who was trying to make something better of his life.

They were an exclusive band of eight by the end of the first semester, but Sam had further plans to recruit more. They would be the 'grandmasters'. Others who joined, they would be less important. The local pub provided the backdrop to what would become the official moment the Abercromby Boys Club began.

'There are points of order we must adhere to if we are to ensure our survival. Firstly, no one discusses the group with outsiders.'

'The first rule of Abercromby Boys Club is we don't talk about Abercromby Boys Club . . .'

'Very funny, Tim. Let's be serious here. There won't be many people outside of this room who will understand what we're doing here. There will be people who castigate us and try to shut us down. We must not break the code.'

'Are we sure about the name? Only it's the same as that clothing brand in America.'

'It took hours to agree on that one. Let's not go through that again. The university is situated on Abercromby Square. It makes sense.'

'Fine, fine, what's the second rule?'

'We must exert our influence over the many. We may only be eight strong at the moment, but we must act as if we have the influence and power of eight thousand. We are the forebears of what will become a long-lasting group. We will pass on our wisdom to others. Next year we will become the welcoming party for a new batch of intakes. This is the beginning, gentlemen.'

'Bullingdon Club for the north. I'm sure that'll go down well in the south.'

'We're going to be better than them. For one, we won't have any of the bizarre initiations they have down there.'

'*I heard you have to do something with a dead pig.*'

'*That's just rumours. My dad would never have fucked an animal.*'

'*Well, that won't be happening here . . .*'

'*That's a shame. That's the only reason I turned up.*'

'*Tim, enough with the jokes. We will have rituals, but they will be proper ones. They will be essential for new members.*'

'*We need to write these down.*'

'*I've already done that. Your overall responsibility is to the other members of this group. One succeeds, we all succeed.*'

'*What do we get out of this?*'

'*We all help each other. We all use whatever contacts we have to make things happen for one another. We look after each other, if someone screws up. That's how these things work.*'

'*And this will help get us women?*'

'*Of course it will.*'

'*Good, that's what I want. Sluts. Bring them on!*'

'*Keep your voice down, Neil. There's a simple rule to getting any woman you want.*'

'*What is that then?*'

'*I'll tell you, Paul. Three easy letters to remember. I-I-P.*'

'*And that means what exactly?*'

'*I'll tell you if you let me finish a sentence. I-I-P. Isolate. Inebriate. Penetrate.*'

'*I'll drink to that!*'

They had been successful and become more powerful than they could have ever expected. On their campus they became legendary. They were young and clever, able to make the university turn a blind eye to anything disreputable using their family's influence.

Sam had thought it would be a way to make connections, to solidify his position in life, but it became more than just a way to meet people who could help him get to where he wanted to be. Their club quickly became notorious for its alcohol-fuelled incidents and its members' desperation to fuck anything that moved.

They knew they were better than everyone else there. They were wealthy, smart, good looking, and knew how to get on in life. They were bred for this. They would all be successful, they would all get whatever they wanted.

Sam knew that if people perceived them to be powerful, to be worthy of admiration, then they were. It was as easy as that. People were easily controlled in that way.

A dress code was implemented. Suits were worn on a daily basis, and none of that store-bought rubbish. Tailored suits had to be worn at all times. There was a difference in the standard, of course, but even the least expensively dressed amongst them looked better than what anyone else on campus. Sam had the best, which was expected. A Savile Row special for most days. Immaculately pressed and worn.

That was how they got respect. That was how a reputation was earned. If each member looked as if they were a *somebody*, half the job was done.

Membership numbers grew. More rules were implemented. Keeping fit was one of them. They would go the gym on an almost daily basis, to keep up the look properly. They had to look the part, that was vital.

'It's easy. It's seventy per cent what you look like, twenty per cent how you say something, ten per cent what you actually say.'

'And who said that?'

'I don't know, do I? Someone important, let's leave it at that.'

'So, you're saying if George Clooney came out and said something racist or the like, some people would forgive him based purely on what he looked like?'

'Pretty much. If Mel Gibson had said what he said earlier in his life, people would still watch his movies.'

'I think they still do . . .'

'Yeah, because those religious ones he makes now are being watched by normal people.'

Another rule governed the way they interacted with people outside of the group. Male non-members were tolerated – especially if they were useful in some way – but they were still considered inferior.

Women . . . they were a different story.

'So, what's an alpha?'

'It's what we have to learn to be. Right now, you're all pretty much gammas.'

'I have no idea what the fuck you're on about.'

'Think about it. Men do things because they think they'll impress girls. Men demean themselves to be noticed. Men place women on pedestals and think they're everything that is needed for a good life.'

'Too right . . .'

'Don't interrupt. Put that in the rules as well. We're proper men. We're different from the rest of the brutes out there, so let's have some decorum.'

'Sorry, carry on.'

'Gammas are bitter, unattractive, unusual. They simultaneously despise and worship women.'

'What's an alpha then? And how do we become one?'

'Most can't. An alpha male is the tall, attractive man.'

'That rules out short arse over here then . . .'

'Fuck you . . .'

'Stop. Remember, men, decorum. You're forgetting about perception again. Just because he's four foot nothing . . .'

'Five nine, thank you.'

'If you're five nine, I'm eight foot one . . .'

'Last warning, don't interrupt again. As I was saying, just because he's short doesn't mean he can't be perceived to be anything he wants to be. He just has to live that life. An alpha is the life and soul of any party. It's who everyone looks up to. He's the smart, successful man with a beautiful wife. He's the captain of the rugby team, with no scars or marks destroying his looks. He's athletic, he's fit. Men want to be him, women want to be with him.'

'How do women play into this?'

'An alpha sees women for what they are. That they exist only for our needs to be met. Physically and socially. That is all. Alphas don't care about women any more than that. Betas, they like women a little more. It's totally fine whichever you feel you fit in. Any lower than an alpha and you're not fit for this thing of ours. However, I would much prefer you were all sigmas, but that probably won't be possible. I will not be in a group with a bunch of gammas though.'

'What's a sigma?'

'They're almost the pinnacle of male dominance. They get the most women, the most respect. They're hated by alphas, as they don't understand how they work the game. They don't respect an alpha's dominance, as they understand that they are better than they are.'

'This is more confusing than the socio-economic history of the Middle East.'

'It'll all become clear, don't worry.'

'So, we dress better, look after ourselves, create the perception that we're people that need to be noticed, and women will come running?'

'Don't believe me?'

'No, it's not that. I just want to make sure I'm understanding.'

'You watch. You think anyone else around here has planned like we have? No. Of course they haven't. They'll be out there now, those men who think all they need to do to take a girl home is flash a smile and buy a drink, but think about it. They won't have the necessary tools to make those sluts disappear once they're done with them. We will. We'll use and abuse.'

'I-I-P?'

'I-I-P, indeed.'

*   *   *

They had to stand out. They had to be more than they were.

They didn't realise that this was the beginning of their end.

That soon, they would all be something else. Something they had never intended to be.

*   *   *

By the final year of studies, things had changed immeasurably. They had the respect and attention they had always deserved. The original eight had become seven for a short period, before the mature student who had departed was replaced. A student who had better connections, better prospects.

Sam was the creator, but the others had done more than their fair share.

They were kings. The grandmasters. The club was now numerous in members, but they were the originals.

Everyone wanted to be them.

In the meantime, they were still third year university students, wanting to go out and have a good time every week. Which they did, easily and with abandon. Their parties had become legendary – taking place in various private establishments in the city, paid for by pooling their money together and using their influence to get what they wanted.

That was where she presented herself. The girl who would change everything. Who would sully everything they had worked so hard to create.

The bitch who tried to ruin all that they had created.

The party had been planned well in advance by the committee of the Abercromby Boys Club. It was to be the party to end all others. Only the right kind of people were invited: the rich, the good looking, the ones who might be useful to them. That was their modus operandi, which had worked well in the past.

They had booked the VIP area of one of the top clubs in Liverpool, one usually reserved for whichever footballer or celebrity was in the city that weekend. The committee had taken over the entire floor. Guest list only.

Sam noticed her first. That was always the way. He would zero in on one girl, making her his sole goal for the night.

'*She doesn't look right.*'

'*She looks fucking amazing, what are you talking about?*'

'*Look at her. She's too young. She shouldn't be here. Who brought her?*'

'*Why do I care? I want her. I can have her. That's the way things work around here.*'

'*Be careful. She looks about fourteen, for fuck's sake. Don't fuck this up.*'

'*She looks ripe for picking. I just hope there's not much grass on the pitch, if you know what I mean . . .*'

'*That's disgusting, Sam, you dirty bastard.*'

'*Why are you laughing then?*'

That was the way Sam was, always looking for the freshest face, the easiest fruit to pick. A low-hanging branch he could bend to his will.

Eventually, Sam had grown bored of her, catching the eye of an even younger-looking girl. Tim was still interested, though. James and Paul had watched him move towards the girl and lean in so she could hear him over the loud, pumping music. He placed a hand on her shoulder and smiled, moving her across the room to the bar and ordering her a drink.

They watched as he waited for her to turn away so he could slip something into her glass.

'*I don't know why he doesn't just use Rohypnol. Would be much easier.*'

'*He prefers them to be alert. He's not some dirty rapist or anything. Ecstasy works better.*'

'*Still, seems like a whole load of hassle that could be done better.*'

'*Maybe you want to show him how it's done instead?*'

The women who came to their parties were nothing but things to be conquered.

They watched in a kind of admiration as the girl's behaviour began to change as the drug started to take effect. She pawed at him, dancing up against him as he stood rigid, looking down at her. A little open-mouthed.

He looked like a wolf. She was little Red Riding Hood and he wanted to devour her.

They loved to watch it happen.

They had watched it unfold this way many times before. Even done it themselves.

The wolf had his prey and wanted to share it with them. They all wanted a taste of that fresh meat. Blonde hair cascading down her back, flawless features, the glimpse of curve beneath a short, tight skirt which could have doubled as a belt.

They wanted to be a part of it.

They wanted to be as one.

With that, they all took their piece. They all took what they believed they deserved. They had their fun and set themselves on a course which would irrevocably alter the future of their lives.

She was nothing to them. A slut who was asking for it. That's all she was.

They were wrong.

PART TWO

PART TWO

PRESENT DAY

You

Murder takes planning. That's if you want to get away with it for long enough. You could snap and kill someone at any point, if you really wanted to. You would be caught straight away, but you could still do it.

You think about that as you're standing on the platform. The rumble as a train gets closer. You shut your eyes and imagine pushing the man standing too close to the edge into its path. Feel that man's blood and brain matter splatter your face as he is wiped away. All it would take is one quick shove in the back and it's done.

That's all that is separating all of us.

To get away with it, though, you need to plan for hours on end. Researching techniques and thinking about what could possibly be discovered from what was left behind.

You can't be caught yet.

There had been a moment when you thought it would matter more. That doing what needed to be done would resonate and mean the beginning of the end. In reality, it was an end of the beginning. Things would never be the same.

Psychopathy was something that had only existed as words on a page for you. Now, it means more. You have a recognition of it, a realisation that the elements have always been there under the surface but not fully existent. Now, they're out in the open. There for anyone to see. Everything and nothing has changed. It was a true dichotomy of mind.

You have it now. That sort of split personality. A compartmentalisation of thought and action. Regret and guilt forgotten, cast aside like elements of a bad equation.

You have a list. Eight names, to be crossed off one by one.

It all requires strength. Mental and physical. Some of those on the list were larger in size than you, which had proved an issue to overcome and would do in the future. It matters little. Your desire to right the wrongs committed, to bring balance and stability back, motivates you to be stronger than they are.

You are doing good via evil. Shades of grey, no right or wrong.

It is life. Decisions made, action taken, the aim of equilibrium never quite attained.

Now you have started, you can't stop even if you want to. The only way is to keep going, moving forwards and doing what needs to be done. That's the goal now.

That's why your list is growing smaller, because regret and guilt have been discarded, abandoned as if it mattered little. It is just a feeling. A concept.

You have no guilt.

Just the yearning, craving desire to do it all again. To feel that power as life left the room and became nothingness. When breath ended and one less life was in that place. When an empty shell was all that was left behind.

Justice. To feel that control over what existed and what didn't.

To feel it over and over again.

A reason to keep going.

To end it all. To bring them all to their knees.

To snuff out their lives from existence.

Until only one is left.

Twelve

If someone went missing and was then found dead, it would be at that point that Murphy would usually become involved. That was just the way of things. It didn't happen often, but that was normality for him.

It wasn't this way. Not normally.

Murphy moved round the car, careful not to get in anyone's way as he did so. Everything would be examined, nothing left to chance. Everything they did here could prove important down the line. Everyone on the scene knew that now.

'This is a big one,' Murphy said, his voice only just above a whisper. 'We're going to be up against it from the start.'

'Could be worse,' Rossi replied, matching Murphy's tone. 'Could have been a kid. Then we'd be seriously under scrutiny.'

Murphy looked down at Rossi and tried to think of an argument. Decided against it and instead kept moving. The main activity was taking place at the back of the car.

'What do you reckon, circular saw or do you think they put a bit more effort in?'

'I don't really want to think about it,' Rossi said, brushing her hair out of her face with one hand. 'I'm just glad the tent is up already. Don't really want to chance pictures of this one getting out.'

'Can you believe the guy took one when he found it?' Murphy said, unable to hide the disgust in his voice. 'What kind of person does that?'

'Just the way things are these days. I'm betting he regrets it now.'

They had arrived an hour earlier to a scene of confusion. Murphy had started directing things before he'd even placed a foot out of the car. A couple of uniforms were standing over a middle-aged man who was on his knees looking up at them, shaking hands raised above his head. A mobile phone had been lying on the ground in front of him.

'Honestly, I didn't do nothing, I was just taking it, just in case. I haven't got anything to do with this. Honest. Please, just let me delete it.'

Murphy had shouted towards another uniform who was directing traffic away from the scene and told him to call transport police, if he hadn't already done it. He waited for the forensics van to pull in further up the road, then had made his way to the car which was sitting at the side of the dual carriageway.

The boot was open, a small length of rope hanging off the top.

'I thought I was helping. I put myself in danger. It could have been anything in there.'

Murphy had approached the back of the car, Rossi only a couple of paces behind him. Once the body had come into view, he'd winced.

'*I would never have opened it if I'd known what was in there.*'

'*That's why we turned up and you're taking pictures? Fucking disgusting.*'

Murphy had left Rossi at the car and walked over to the uniforms. Told them it was time to put the guy in the back of a car and remove him from the scene.

That's where he was now. Still in the back of a marked police car, peering out the rear window every few minutes. Murphy snapped off his gloves and made his way over there.

'What's his name?' Murphy said to the uniform standing outside of the car. 'We're going to have a word.'

'Only gave us his first name. Harry. Refused to do any checks as he wants to speak to a solicitor. Think he thinks we're going to do him for something. Not sure what like.'

'I could probably think of a few things,' Rossi said, joining them at the rear of the vehicle. 'Are the photos still on the phone or did he delete them before you took it off him?'

'Still there. He dropped it before he had a chance to do anything.'

'Good,' Murphy replied, walking round the car to the driver's side. He opened the door and waited for the uniform to get out. 'Won't be too long, just want a word.'

Murphy squeezed himself into the driver's seat, moving the seat back as far as it would go and removing his knees from around his ears. 'Sorry about that,' he said to Harry who yelped when the seat shot back. 'Long legs.'

Rossi opened the passenger-side door and got in with ease. 'Phone is here,' she said to Murphy, handing him an evidence bag. 'Harry's battery is low, but you can see the photos if you want.'

Murphy shook his head and turned slightly in his seat. He adjusted the rear-view mirror and stared at Harry sitting in the back seat. He looked to be about mid-forties, his face lined with life, greying hair rising from his temples. A podgy stomach protruded over too-tight jeans. He was slumped to his side, eyes screwed shut, shoulders heaving every few seconds. 'You're sniffing like a coke head, mate,' Murphy said, staring in the mirror. 'Anything else you want to tell us? Laura, write down that Mr Harry here needs a full body cavity search as well, once we're at the station.'

'I don't do drugs,' Harry said, his voice somehow small enough to get lost in the car.

'What was that?' Murphy said, cupping a hand to his ear. 'Didn't quite catch it, what did you say?'

'I don't do drugs,' Harry replied, louder now.

'Good to know. Although if you did, maybe it would explain what you were doing this morning, wouldn't it?'

'I didn't do anything.'

Murphy exhaled through his nose. 'Is that really going to be your defence? We find you at the boot of a car, taking pictures of a mutilated body, and you're going to just tell us you didn't do anything?'

'I didn't know . . .'

'What? That someone had been brutalised and killed, so probably didn't need their dignity destroying any further?'

Murphy continued to stare at Harry in the mirror, but the man remained slumped over.

'Sit up. Now.'

Harry slowly pulled himself up as Murphy's voice stopped echoing around the car.

'Let me tell you what's going to happen,' Murphy said, lowering his voice. 'You're going to tell us everything you saw, heard, smelled and touched. Then you're going to go down the station with the fine police officers outside, and they'll explain to you how to go about purchasing a new phone. Understand?'

'I want to speak to a solicitor . . .'

Murphy chuckled to himself, nodded towards Rossi.

'At the moment,' Rossi said, turning round and looking directly at the man in the back seat, 'we can charge you with destroying evidence, compromising a crime scene, accessory after the fact, obstructing justice, causing a public nuisance . . . Should I go on?'

Murphy held up a hand and looked in the mirror again. Harry was looking back, filmy eyes betraying him. He was scared. Hopefully enough to talk.

'Now, we can avoid all that if you just speak to us,' Murphy said, tapping the steering wheel with one hand. 'If you're just a witness to something, then we can treat you very differently. So why don't you just start answering our questions? What were you doing here?'

There was silence for a few seconds, another sniff, then Harry started talking. 'I was just having a walk, that's all. Noticed the car and thought something wasn't right.'

'What time was this?'

'About eleven thirty, midday. I went over and opened the boot and found what was in there.'

'Why did you open the boot, Harry?' Rossi said, notepad in hand as usual. 'Seems a strange thing to do, just opening the boot of a parked car.'

'I saw someone,' Harry said quietly. 'Walking away from the car. I noticed him fiddling with the boot and leaving it open.'

Murphy exchanged a look with Rossi. '*On the rob*,' he mouthed. Then, 'Tell me exactly what you saw.'

'Some guy, that's all. He was bundled up, which I thought was odd, you know, because it's still quite warm. Had a big black jacket on, a hoodie underneath covering his face. Looked shifty, like. I stopped and watched him and he went to the back of the car and was messing with it.'

'What was he doing?' Murphy said.

'They was tying a rope and spring around the boot, so it was a bit open, but not fully. Meant you could just unhook it and open it up like.'

'Then what happened?'

'Well, I waited a little bit, just to see what he was going to do next. He just walked off, down the road. Quick like, didn't seem to want to hang around. I went over and thought I could see something inside. So I opened the boot up.'

'Do you often go around opening other people's cars?'

Harry didn't answer, just shifted in the back seat. Murphy waited, but moved on when it became obvious the man wasn't going to answer. 'What about this guy you saw. What can you tell us about him?'

Harry shrugged his shoulders. 'I don't know. I told you, he was all bundled up. Couldn't see him properly.'

'How tall was he? Was he white, black, Asian, what?'

'Not that tall,' Harry said, looking out the side window. 'Small really. About five six, five seven. Bulky, but that might have been all the clothes he had on. Seemed to be normal really. Think he was normal colour . . .'

'What's normal, Harry?' Rossi said, her pen pointing at Harry.

'You know, white. Not one of them coloureds or muzzies or whatever.'

Murphy gave a slight shake of his head. Casual racism alive and well in 2016.

'He had gloves on as well, so it'll be my fingerprints on the boot,' Harry said, suddenly sitting up and leaning forwards. 'I had nothing to do with it, though. Don't try and pin it on me. There's no way I'd have anything to do with anything like this.'

'No, you just like taking pictures of it,' Murphy said, annoyed now. 'Which way did he walk?'

'Down towards Statton Road, that way. Went in a hurry like, but not, if that makes sense?'

'Not really,' Rossi said, putting her notepad away. 'We're going to have more questions for you. You can go with the officers out there to the station. Someone will speak to you there.'

'You're joking, aren't you?' Harry replied, the shaking now beginning to disappear. 'I've got to sign on later and I've got stuff to do.'

'Probably should have kept your phone in your pocket then,' Murphy said, opening the car door and getting out. He waited for Rossi to exit, then walked back towards the tent. He ignored the shouts from the back of the marked car as he did so, waiting for Rossi to join him.

'What are you thinking?'

Murphy looked around, spotting a couple of cameras as he did so. 'CCTV will probably corroborate his story. Just wondering how far we can track whoever did this.

They've gone some way to disguise themselves, but in broad daylight like this? Seems ballsy to me.'

'Obviously our guy in there didn't have anything to do with it?'

'Well, we've been wrong before, but I doubt it,' Murphy replied, taking a soft mint from a packet in his pocket and sticking it in his mouth. 'Doesn't mean he doesn't know more. He's not going anywhere for now.'

Murphy stuck his hands in his pockets and watched the forensics team as they moved back and forth from within the tent. The road remained closed off and traffic was already building up in a lengthy tailback, a few scattered horns sounding in the distance.

Thirteen

It was a couple more hours before Murphy and Rossi were able to leave. With no joy from the nearby houses, they had been forced to widen the search perimeter to look for possible witnesses. They'd marked out on a map possible routes that a person walking away from the car might have taken. Uniforms would take over now, going door to door. Which left little for them to do at the scene, especially as the body was about to be removed.

'The guy isn't exactly the most trustworthy witness we've ever had,' Rossi said, clicking on her seat belt. 'He said towards the estate, but it could easily have been the exact opposite direction. It's a lot of doors to knock on without knowing if it's going to lead to anything.'

'Still got to do it,' Murphy replied, taking off the hand-brake and moving away. 'Car looked clean inside, but hopefully there's a receipt tucked away somewhere. A nice close-up picture of the suspect getting a McDonalds drive-thru would be nice.'

'Those things are always shockingly shit anyway. You would think CCTV would be in HD by now.'

'You know why it's not,' Murphy said, passing drivers still stuck in traffic on the opposite side of the A road. He saw a few shaking their heads at him as he drove past, probably oblivious to what was happening. He hoped. 'No storage for that kind of thing. We just have to make do for now.'

'I know. Just annoying that's all. Settled in the new house yet?'

Murphy took one hand off the steering wheel and scratched the side of his beard. 'Getting there. Still a few boxes need unpacking and putting somewhere. I swear this house is smaller. Seems like we're tripping over things constantly. Should be a much bigger place, given it's not as nice an area as where we used to be.'

'It's still bloody nice round there,' Rossi said, laughing to herself. 'You'd think you'd moved to Kenny or Norris Green. It's Crosby for Christ's sake. You're a few years away from going full posh and moving to Formby.'

'On a DI wage? You must be joking.'

'And Sarah going back to uni. Once she's graduated, you're definitely going. Bet you a fiver now. It'll be there or Gateacre.'

'Not a chance of Formby,' Murphy said, indicating and turning into Edge Lane Retail Park. 'They'd throw me out of there in five seconds with this accent.'

He drove through the McDonalds, ordering two coffees and a large fries to share.

'My mam would kill me if she knew I was eating this,' Rossi said, grabbing a handful of fries as Murphy drove away. 'This is not the food an Italian should be eating.'

Murphy took a swig of his coffee, realising he should have read the warning on the outside of the cup first. 'How's it going with you and Darren anyway?' he said, trying to cool his burning mouth, to no avail. 'Still in the honeymoon period?'

'He's there, like, all the time,' Rossi said, blowing into the coffee cup. 'Never get any peace.'

'That's the point in living with someone, Laura. It means you have to share space with them and actually want to as well.'

'I know, I know,' Rossi replied, still blowing into her coffee. 'I just didn't think it through properly. Thought I'd be used to it by now. I quite liked going home to an empty house, deciding what I want to watch on TV, what to eat, all that sort of thing. Now we have to discuss everything and neither one of us is very good at making decisions on small things. He's even started talking about having a family and buying a bigger house. It's ridiculous.'

'You'll get used to it,' Murphy said, risking another sip of coffee and then swearing under his breath at making the same mistake again. 'Looks like we've got something here to keep you out the house for a bit anyway.'

'Not wrong there,' Rossi said, taking another fistful of fries. 'Why do you think they cut him up? Usually means they're going to dispose of the body in a different way. They've cut him up and stuck him in the boot of a car and left him to be found on purpose.'

'Ever tried lifting a dead weight? My guess is this is someone working alone, couldn't lift him and needed to get him out to the car. Easier in a few parts.'

'I do so love my job,' Rossi replied, staring out the window as the houses flashed by. 'Where else could you have a conversation like this?'

'I can't think of anything worse to do to someone after they're dead. Cutting them up and that.'

'Never heard of necrophilia?'

Murphy raised his eyebrows at Rossi and waited for the lights to change. 'OK, you win. That's much worse. For that, you can finish off the fries. Lost my appetite all of sudden.'

'Don't mind if I do,' Rossi said, grabbing the box and chomping down the rest. Murphy shook his head and continued driving.

They were back at the station within fifteen minutes, despite having to negotiate the ever-increasing traffic near the city centre. Murphy sat in the car a few seconds after Rossi had got out, closing his eyes and breathing a little.

Steeling himself.

Walking into the incident room, he was glad of the quiet moment he'd taken. DCI Stephens was standing at her office door, arms folded and waiting.

'David, please,' she said as he made his way in. Murphy beckoned towards Rossi who was further into the room than he was, but DCI Stephens put up her hand. 'Just you for now.'

Rossi made as if to say something, then turned away, keeping quiet. Murphy was still a little further behind, so it took him longer to work out what she'd seen.

'Just back from the scene?' DCI Stephens said as he approached. 'Not spoken to anyone else yet?'

'Was just going to check in with you first, before we go see the parents,' Murphy said, making it to the door finally. He saw what had made Rossi turn away and quietly accept the non-invitation.

'Sir,' Murphy said, stopping at the door and waiting for DCI Stephens to make her way behind her desk. 'Wasn't expecting you here.'

Detective Superintendent Gareth Butler didn't stand up, settling for smoothing out a crease on his immaculate black trousers instead. He was aging well, a hint of silver at his temples, which only served to make him look more distinguished. 'David. Good to see you,' DSI Butler said, almost sounding sincere. His accent showed no trace of Liverpudlian, which had set Murphy on edge from the first meeting they'd had years earlier. 'How is the family?'

Murphy ignored the comment, knowing DSI Butler cared little for an answer. 'It's him,' Murphy said, making sure they knew from the start. 'Or, if it's not, someone has gone to far too much trouble to make us believe it is.'

'Do we know any specifics yet?'

'Just that he's been found, someone was witnessed leaving the scene, and that we hope he was dead before being cut up.'

'Quite . . .' DSI Butler said, swallowing and pursing his lips. 'That bit was true then. I was hoping that wasn't a confirmed situation. Ghastly.'

'He's being removed from the scene as we speak,' Murphy continued, still facing DCI Stephens. 'Post-mortem will be carried out later today. I've made sure of that.'

'Good, good,' DSI Butler said, Murphy turning to him finally. 'This will be a very delicate case, David. I think we need to treat it as such. His family are well respected within the community, so any salacious details will need to be cleared through me before being released.'

'I have a feeling there may be one or two of those already. We have already discovered certain things about his personal life we didn't know before.'

'I trust you have been working with the utmost care and respect for his privacy,' DSI Butler said, fixing Murphy with an unblinking stare. 'We don't want this getting out of hand with the media and the whole thing turning into a circus.'

Murphy returned the stare. 'My team will work as they always do. We'll find whoever has done this and stop them. That's our job.'

The two men looked at each other, DSI Butler breaking first and looking over to DCI Stephens.

'I assure you, you'll have all the resources you require,' DSI Butler said, leaning forwards in his chair. 'The MCU has our full support in this matter.'

'Thank you, sir,' DCI Stephens replied, propping her elbows up on her desk and steepling her fingers together. 'I can assure you that we'll do all we can for the Byrne family.'

'I have already informed them of developments,' DSI Butler said, leaning back and looking out towards the window. 'I imagine you'll want to speak to them yourself, David, which is fine and correct. I would just impress upon you the importance of remembering that this will be a difficult time for them. Please treat them with the respect they deserve.'

Murphy bit down on his lower lip. 'Of course, sir,' he said after a few seconds. 'Wouldn't work any other way.'

DSI Butler continued looking out of the window, nodding his head slowly. Eventually, he turned and faced the room again, standing up from his chair. 'Excellent. I'm sure we'll be speaking again soon.'

Murphy stood and shook DSI Butler's hand, he waited for DCI Stephens to show the senior officer out then sat back down, gripping the sides of his chair tightly before realising he was squeezing a bit too hard and crossing his arms instead.

'Politics,' DCI Stephens said, once she'd closed the door and moved back to her side of her desk. 'Always the bane of my life.'

'Never been interested, boss,' Murphy replied, stretching his legs out and crossing one ankle over the other. 'There's something iffy about the whole thing, though. I hope we're not going to be hampered. This is going to be a difficult enough case as it is, without being messed about with.'

'Let me deal with that, if or when it happens. Just get on with your work and let me know if you have any difficulties.'

'Will do,' Murphy said, straightening up and resting his hands on his knees. 'Anything else before I brief them lot out there?'

DCI Stephens shook her head, lifting her phone before Murphy had even left the room.

Murphy crossed the incident room, reaching his desk in a few long strides. Rossi looked up, raising her eyebrows at him.

'Well, what's the damage?' Rossi said when Murphy didn't speak.

'Nothing too bad. Just top brass bullshit. We're just going to have to brace ourselves for a shit-storm if we don't clear this up quickly and with little fanfare.'

'Not sure that's going to be possible given that flat he kept quiet. I've made sure the two scenes are now linked. Are we thinking the flat might be the original kill site?'

'Hope so,' Murphy replied, moving an old file from on top of his desk to a drawer. 'Would make things easier.'

'Forensics should be back on that soon enough. Might be overworked now, of course. If it's his blood on the walls and around the room, we at least know where square one was.'

'Can you grab whoever is here and ask them to head for the briefing room. We need to get things moving as quickly as possible.'

Rossi nodded and was up gathering people within a few seconds. Murphy took out his phone and fired off a quick text to Sarah.

New case. Body near the Rocket. Will be late in. xx

He turned back to an emptying incident room. He lifted himself out of his chair and headed to the briefing room.

'Just a quick update,' Murphy said, when the final person was sitting down. A number of faces looked back at him, not as many as there would be the next morning, he thought. 'We've got several officers already out there, so this is for you lot in here. A missing person has now become a probable murder victim. Victim is tentatively identified as Sam Byrne.'

He tapped a pen against his thigh as he waited for the whispered voices to die down. 'He was found at approximately midday, in the boot of a car which was parked near the Rocket, on the corner of Edge Lane and Talbotville Road. Possible witness is downstairs now. Kirkham and Hale can take an official statement from him. He called us, but also opened the car boot up and apparently took pictures of the body inside.'

'Fucking weirdo,' a voice said from the other side of the room.

'It's possible he also saw someone leaving the scene, so make sure you get as good a description as possible, lads,' Murphy said, ignoring the interruption. 'He gave Laura and me a brief description at the scene, but it wasn't enough to go on.'

Murphy waited for Kirkham and Hale to acknowledge his request then he turned to DC Harris. 'Graham, I need all CCTV pulling from the area. I want the whole route tracked. We need to know where he travelled from before parking the car, what time he arrived at the scene, where he went afterwards, the usual.'

DC Harris wrote down the info and nodded to himself. 'Think we're well covered around that area. Shouldn't be too difficult.'

Murphy turned to Rossi, who stepped forwards and spoke. 'We've got uniforms in the area now, doing the door to doors and that. There's another crime scene being investigated at the moment, as most of you will be aware. We're waiting for forensic results on that and more info will be given as soon as.'

Murphy wrapped up the meeting and waited for the room to empty, leaving Rossi and him alone in the briefing room.

'We need more angles on this and fast,' Murphy said, perching himself on the desk at the front of the room. 'Have to be ahead of things this time.'

'You mean we're not doing the usual "question everyone and hope one of them confesses"?'

Murphy returned the smile and silently hoped it wouldn't come to that.

Fourteen

Murphy had decided long ago there was no dignity in death. No '*she went peacefully in her sleep*' or '*he wouldn't have felt a thing*' changed the reality of things. It didn't matter how you went, there was still no dignity once you were gone.

In the job he did, he had experienced each facet of death, all of them coming down to single factor. Once your body had become just an empty vessel, once life had disappeared, it didn't matter what was done to it. Dignity wasn't a high priority. Finding out what had happened was more important.

Still, looking at the dismembered corpse of Sam Byrne as it lay on a post-mortem gurney, Murphy was rocked a little. He'd seen shocking things in the past, but dismemberment was something which always seemed the worst imaginable. There was no dignity here.

'Clean enough cuts.' Dr Houghton's voice boomed through the silence. 'Almost definitely a mechanical implement.'

'I had money on a circular saw.'

'You'll probably win that bet,' Houghton replied. 'Although I do detest the idea of betting on this sort of thing, David.'

'You don't like betting on anything to do with death? We won't include you in the death pool any more then, if you like?'

'You're joking, aren't you? I have good money on one of those boyband members being an early casualty.'

Murphy chuckled softly, ignoring Rossi rolling her eyes beside him. 'Any idea how he died?'

'Well, given his head is separated from the rest of his body, I'm not ruling out that having something to do with it.'

'Fair enough,' Murphy replied, taking his turn to roll his eyes. 'Post-mortem dismemberment?'

'Yes, I believe so,' Houghton replied, moving around the body parts with a speed that belied a man of his size. 'If you want to take a closer look I can explain better.'

'That's OK,' Rossi said, not looking up from her note-pad. 'I'll take your word for it.'

Murphy shook his head, trying not to be too vigorous about it. 'Looks like he was beaten as well.'

'Tortured, more like,' Houghton said, measuring yet another mark on the torso. 'Burn marks, whip marks, bruises, open wounds . . . he will have been in a great deal of pain.'

'Given that flat we found, are we sure it wasn't welcomed?'

Murphy turned to Rossi and nodded slightly. 'Might have a point.'

'He was stabbed a number of times, in the upper chest and legs. No ligature marks around the neck. We'll have to do further tests, but cause of death is looking likely to be related to the blood loss he will have suffered.'

Murphy looked at Rossi and motioned towards the door with his head. He turned back to Dr Houghton. 'Full report by the morning?'

'Ever known me to take my time when it comes to these things?'

Murphy stared at the doctor with what he hoped was disdain. 'You want me to answer that honestly?'

He left before the doctor had chance to reply, pushing through the doors and out into the hospital corridor. The basement always seemed colder to Murphy. Not just in temperature. It was as if the air had been sucked out of the place. The life of the bustling corridors above them invisible.

'What do you reckon then?'

Murphy turned to the waiting Rossi and tugged on his bottom lip with his teeth. 'We need forensics back on that flat. It's looking more likely that's our kill site. The marks on his body would fit with what we found in there.'

'Still doesn't get us much closer to finding out who did it.'

'I think we're a long way off that yet,' Murphy replied, offering a piece of chewing gum to Rossi and taking one for himself. 'We don't know enough yet.'

'Are we going to see the parents again?' Rossi said, taking the gum and placing it in her mouth. 'I know Butler has taken over in that regard, but we should probably still speak to them.'

'Of course we are,' Murphy said, beginning to walk away. 'There's still a few unanswered questions there.'

'Just a few?'

Murphy checked his watch as they walked back to the car park. 'Already getting late. Bloody starving. Wonder if they've ordered food back at the station.'

'I hope so. I could eat a dead horse.'

'Probably will be if they've ordered from that place on London Road again.'

Rossi sniggered. 'Don't even joke about that. Although the thought of an entire command coming down with dysentery during a murder case is funny.'

'Funny?'

'OK, maybe not ha ha funny. What would happen though?'

Murphy made it to the outer door, holding it open for Rossi who waited for him to walk through first instead. 'We'd be replaced faster than you can say "coming out of both ends".'

'Lovely image.'

'I have a way of painting a picture with words,' Murphy replied, opening the car. 'Back to the station, hope to eat, then over to the parents. Plan?'

'Plan.'

They drove the short journey from the hospital to the station in near silence, contemplating what they had just witnessed. The brown brick building appeared in front of them, the drabness of it sucking the life out of them more than the post-mortem had.

Murphy didn't wait for Rossi, who he left swearing in Italian at a vending machine. He climbed the four flights of stairs and pushed his way into the incident room. He ignored the increasing paper mountain on his desk and made his way over to the murder boards at the back of the room.

An attempt had been made at creating a new board for Sam Byrne, but whoever had done it hadn't had their heart in it. Murphy wiped some of the unrelated notes away and picked up a marker and began writing.

'Pictures of Sam Byrne here,' Rossi said, coming up behind Murphy. He was concentrating too hard to be startled, but gave a little motion of his head. She began sticking them to the board with Blu-Tack as he wrote.

'What was the name of the friend Sam's mum mentioned the other day?'

Rossi stuck the last picture on the board and then took out her notepad. 'Simon Jackson. We also had a few first names that Graham was looking into, but I'm not sure what's happening with them now. He'll have been on CCTV all afternoon.'

'Make sure someone is on that,' Murphy began to say, but realised it was futile as Rossi had already gone. He waited for her to finish talking to the closest DC, informing them of their new job. 'Thank you,' he said once she'd returned to his side. 'Simon Jackson shouldn't be too difficult to find. The others, maybe not so easy. Make sure follow-ups are done on the flat as well, catch up with the people not home earlier on.'

'It's all moving along very quickly,' Rossi said, snapping open an energy drink and slugging some back. 'We've gone from a missing case to a murder case in a day. Can't be a coincidence.'

'What do you mean?'

'As soon as we get involved, he turns up dead in the boot of his own car. I think someone got spooked.'

'Depends on when he was killed, I suppose. We were at the flat the same day we were put on the case—'

'Odd that one of his own staff would lead us there,' Rossi said, interrupting Murphy. 'Somewhere supposedly secret and she may as well have written the address down for us.'

'True,' Murphy replied, placing the lid back on the marker and putting it back. 'We need to speak to Emma Palmer again. We'll need to interview all of those people helping out on the campaign.'

'That's a lot of people.'

Murphy stretched his arms above his head and yawned. 'I know, but you never can tell who has the right info.'

'That Charlotte will be devastated,' Rossi said, also yawning. 'Got me started now.'

'Come on,' Murphy said, walking away. 'Let's go see the parents and see what they have to say.'

*   *   *

Murphy looked at the biscuits on the plate longingly, his stomach making a few noises. He decided against reaching for one, however, thinking it was probably not the best impression to make. Getting crumbs all over the floor of grieving parents was probably best avoided.

Not that they were showing much grief. Not outwardly, anyway.

'Thank you so much for coming,' Arthur Byrne said, removing his glasses and cleaning them with the edge of his jumper. 'Such a ghastly business. We will help in any way we can.'

Murphy glanced over at Mary Byrne, who was sitting rigid on the same chair she'd sat in on the previous day. Her hands were seemingly glued to her knees, white around the knuckles.

'We've notified the correct people,' Arthur continued, placing his glasses back on. 'We want to make sure the media treat this with the respect it requires.'

'I assure you we're going to do all we can to find out what happened to Sam,' Murphy said, repeating the same thing he always said to those left behind. 'Is there anything you can think of which might help us in that endeavour?'

First time he'd used the word 'endeavour', though, he thought. That was new.

'I'm afraid we can't give you anything more than we did yesterday. There's simply nothing else we can think of which could lead to this.'

'What kind of relationship did you have with Sam,' Rossi said, leaning forwards which gave Murphy his cue to sit back.

'A good, healthy one,' Arthur replied, still stoic and resolute. 'He was our son and we were proud of him.'

Murphy waited for a falter which didn't come. The British stiff upper lip was in fine form.

'Did you speak regularly?'

'I spoke to him on a number of occasions recently, just to keep him focussed on the by-election. I wanted to make sure he didn't let the opportunity slip. However, he was doing so well without my help.'

'How about you, Mary?' Rossi said, turning to Sam's mother. 'Did you speak to him more than your husband?'

'Once a week,' Mary replied, staring past the two detectives at the wall behind them. 'He was very busy, so it was just quick phone chats. I haven't seen him in a while.'

'I know this is a difficult time for you both, but I really need you to think about any possible reasons Sam may have been in danger. If he was mixed up in something potentially dangerous, however small.'

Mary looked at her husband who didn't return her gaze. 'No. He was not involved in anything that could lead to something like this happening. He was a good man. Was trying to do right by his community and his country.'

Murphy watched Mary whilst Arthur spoke, frowning as she gripped her knees more.

'Mary, look at me,' Murphy said, his voice deliberately soft. 'If you think you know something, and really want justice for your son, then you need to tell us.'

She shook her head in response, but he could see hesitation.

'I imagine it was one of those bloody people being let into the country. Have you checked it wasn't a terrorist incident? I hope you have. Open borders and damn liberal minds cause things like this to occur to good people . . .'

'Arthur, do please stop,' Mary said, her hands now shaking. 'We both know what's going on here . . .'

'That's enough. We don't need to talk about any of that.'

Murphy looked over at Rossi who was staring at Mary.

'We can't keep this quiet. It's impossible. They should know everything.'

Arthur stood up, Murphy shifted forwards on the sofa waiting for him to make a move.

'There are things that people outside of this house do not need to know,' Arthur said, looming over his wife who sank back in her chair a little. 'Unimportant information that will only besmirch our son's reputation. Do you want to do that to him? Really, now?'

'You think his image matters more than getting justice for our son? You're not worried about him at all. You're worried about yourself. That's how it's always been.

You're scared that he will damage your credibility. Your reputation.'

Murphy and Rossi watched the exchange in stony silence, looking between the couple as if they were watching a tennis match. In this case, a tennis match fuelled by thirty years of pent-up anger.

Arthur stood over his wife for a few seconds longer, then crossed the room to a large wooden bureau. His hand was poised over the handle. Murphy guessed it was where he kept his alcohol, but that he wasn't prepared to start drinking in front of them.

'Might I suggest something,' Rossi said, lifting herself off the sofa. 'How about Mary and I go and make some tea and have a chat.'

Mary looked up and gave a slight nod. Arthur still hadn't turned round, but his hand dropped to his side.

Rossi waited for Mary to walk out of the room before turning to Murphy and mouthing, '*Talk to him.*'

Murphy watched her leave, then looked at the great bulk of Arthur. He had to stop himself from sighing.

Fifteen

The kitchen, a cottage-style set-up with exposed brick and wooden beams overhead, was much as Rossi had expected given the type of house Arthur and Mary Byrne lived in. There was a large Aga, which took up most of the space along one wall, and a farmhouse sink beneath the window. Mary crossed to the kettle situated on the thick wooden worktop and switched it on.

'I'm sorry about my husband,' Mary said, her back to Rossi. 'He is so ingrained with his former life that he doesn't understand that sometimes we have to think a little more emotionally about things.'

'That's OK,' Rossi replied, pulling a white chair away from the small table. 'It's a difficult time for you both. We understand that.'

'I just don't want us to keep something quiet that could be important. Especially when it's because someone is concerned about the way it makes them look. Like anyone would care any more. Arthur hasn't been an MP for over ten years now. He's been forgotten about, but he doesn't want to accept it.'

'What is it, Mary? What do you want to tell me?'

Mary waited for the kettle to finish boiling. The other two people in the house had been forgotten, Rossi thought. She waited for Mary to make the tea and bring over the drinks to the table. Mary produced a small jug of milk, which Rossi added to the mug in front of her, but no sugar was offered, which was annoying.

There was a hesitation as Mary looked towards the kitchen door, as if suddenly remembering the two men in the house. Then she sat down opposite Rossi, cradling the mug in her hands as if to feed on the warmth resonating from it.

'Sam was always a precocious child,' Mary said, staring down at the table surface. 'Always wanting to do something, or talk about things on his mind. He was reading very early, talking in full sentences sooner than any child I'd known before. Very intelligent. The problem was he would become bored easily. Nothing was ever enough for him. There was always something else he thought he should be doing. That's why he failed to get into the universities in the south. He could never focus when he was younger.'

'You didn't have any other children?'

'Couldn't,' Mary replied, shutting down that avenue of questioning quickly.

'He still managed to achieve a lot,' Rossi said, blowing on her mug a little. 'It takes effort to get to the position he did.'

'He was intelligent, as I said. Once he calmed down a little, knuckled down at university, he was always going to do something important. There were other things, though, which influenced him.'

'What things?'

'Power,' Mary said, tracing a circle with one finger on the table. 'He had the same lust as his father. He wanted to be respected by the many, not just the few. Politics has that effect on people. It seduces you into thinking you're in a position which is exalted. That you have an effect on people's lives. He enjoyed that belief.'

'What was he like outside of that life?'

Mary gave a tight-lipped smile. 'He was always very polite, staid and proper. With the right people.'

'There was another side to him?' Rossi asked, glancing around the kitchen and frowning as she tried to work out what was missing in the house. 'One that he didn't show to just anyone.'

'We tried our best with him, we really did. I wanted him to know that there was nothing that would make us think any less of him. He was our son. We wouldn't turn our backs on him.'

Rossi studied Mary, the older woman was still looking down at the table. 'What are you trying to say, Mary?'

'Well . . . I assumed wrong. That's all.'

'Assumed what wrong?'

'I thought perhaps he was *different*. That he was single because of another reason.'

Rossi had to stop herself from sighing audibly. The usual dancing around the topic, which she saw so often from the older generation when it came to anything to do with sexuality. 'You thought he was gay, that's it?'

'I wouldn't put it so bluntly.'

'And you were wrong about that? Was he worried about his sexuality?'

Mary shook her head. 'No, I was wrong. He wasn't that way. There was something else, though. Something he didn't want us to know.'

'Did you know about the flat he kept in town?'

There was another hesitation from the woman. Rossi waited patiently for an answer.

'I don't know much about his private life.'

'That's not an answer.'

'I don't want to go into many specifics. There have been a few issues over the years we have had to deal with, that's all. He didn't have a normal life in that regard.'

'What kind of things?'

Mary didn't answer, seemingly noticing the tea in front of her for the first time. She took a long sip, then set it down and looked at Rossi. 'Whilst he was in university, he was part of a group of friends who got up to some high jinks. Arthur had to smooth over some difficult moments, but there was nothing serious.'

Rossi felt there was more, but didn't want to push too hard. 'What kind of moments?'

'As I said, nothing too serious. They would drink, as students do these days, and sometimes that led to over exuberance. A few local businesses weren't too happy. That was all easily sorted out, however.'

'There are other things, though, aren't there?'

'Girls. More than one. I never knew specifics, but eventually we had a girl turn up here,' Mary said, looking away and screwing her eyes shut. 'About a year or two ago. Just came up and knocked on the door.'

'What girl?'

'She never told us her name. She could barely speak, poor thing. Began to ramble on about our son, about what he'd done to her. About what he and his friends had done.'

'What did she say?'

'She was so upset. Crying and wailing. I brought her in the house, because I didn't know what else to do. She . . . she said he had done things to her. Unspeakable things. Against her will. She was unstable. Crying one minute, angry the next. She wanted justice, she said, but no one would believe her.'

Rossi swallowed and tried to remain calm. 'What did you do about this?'

There was a pause as Mary considered her words. 'I couldn't believe a word of it and she was so out of control emotionally. I had Arthur send her away. We didn't know what else to do. We didn't believe we could have raised a son who would do such things. Arthur said she was quite plainly lying – that she just wanted money or something.'

'You told Sam about her visit?'

Mary nodded, her eyes becoming teary for the first time since Rossi had arrived at the house with Murphy. 'It was the first time I had seen real, aggressive anger in him. He was in a rage. Even Arthur couldn't calm him down. He was so filled with fury. I'd never seen him like that before.'

'What happened next?'

'He said he would sort it out and we never heard about it again. I asked Arthur about it a while later and he said it was all taken care of. I was . . . I didn't want to ask any more.'

'Did you ever learn anything about the girl who came here? A name, or something like that?'

Mary shook her head. 'I didn't want to know. It wasn't something I had any interest in getting involved with. Sam seemed to be OK the next time I saw him after that and he sent me some flowers to apologise. That was enough. Now . . . now I'm worried he may have got himself into trouble and couldn't control it.'

Rossi sat back in her chair and took in the information. Formed a picture in her mind of a different Sam Byrne than the one she'd first imagined.

Realised what was missing in the house.

Photographs. There were barely any family pictures in the house. She recalled seeing one or two in the living room, but they weren't exactly displayed prominently. It was a show home. It was a facade.

'The only thing was . . . when I first spoke to Sam about the girl, he didn't ask about her name. All he said was "which one".'

'Which one?'

'It was like he'd been expecting it to happen. That someone was going to turn up and say these things, but he couldn't be sure who it would be.'

*   *   *

Murphy settled back into the sofa as Arthur Byrne paced the floor. He moved quickly for a man of his years and weight. Every few turns he would remove his glasses then place them back on again, shaping as if to speak, before changing his mind.

'What do you think they're talking about in there?' Arthur said, stopping in front of Murphy.

'I have no idea,' Murphy replied, looking up slightly at the older man. 'Why don't you sit down and talk to me while they're away.'

'I don't understand the point of all this,' Arthur said, turning around and facing his chair. 'What does it matter what Sam did in the past. It has nothing to do with what's happened to him now. That's guaranteed.'

'What did he do?'

'It's not important,' Arthur said, his voice getting quieter. The older man dropped into his chair. 'He's dead. What does it matter?'

'Because if you want me to find who did this,' Murphy said, moving forwards and perching on the edge of the sofa, 'you're going to have to tell me everything. We need to know.'

Murphy clenched his teeth to stop them grinding together as Arthur removed his glasses once again.

'He was just a boy really. All of them in university are. We coddle them too much these days, so that when we send them off to the big wide world, they're not real men. Not like when I was younger. Now, every Tom, Dick and Harry from a council estate gets the chance to go to university. Time was, you were there on merit. It was your family that got you there. It's all changed now, of course. Now, you can walk off the damn street and get a degree.'

'You're avoiding the subject here, Arthur.'

'I know, I know. He was a boy. Eighteen, never been away from his family. His mother would still press his shirts for him, for Pete's sake. Give young boys like that an opportunity on a plate, what did they expect?'

Murphy felt his stomach tumble over a few rotations. 'Boys?'

'Yes,' Arthur replied, his glasses now discarded on the arm of the chair. 'It seems Sam had organised some kind of club whilst at university. They would convene at a pub on campus but they also met at all the best restaurants and bars. It was a group of like-minded souls, who all swore to help each other. A secret society of sorts. I was a member of something similar at Oxford, years ago. Liverpool had never seen anything like it before.'

'A kind of Bullingdon Club, is that what you're talking about?'

'I don't really know if the comparison fits, but it's close enough.'

Murphy stood up, walked over to the bureau and picked up one of only three photographs in the room. 'This is them, isn't it?'

'Yes,' Arthur replied, without looking up at him. 'Eight of them. They got into a little trouble during their final year.'

'Tell me about that.'

'They were just exuberant young boys. They chose the wrong girl to party with. She woke up the next morning making accusations. It was all sorted out.'

'What sort of accusations?'

'I think we can both read between the lines, can't we?'

Murphy bit his lip. 'Were the girl's accusations made official?'

'No, I managed to stop it before it got that far. It wasn't the only time their parties got a little out of hand. She was the only one who turned up again a few years later though. Look, this will have nothing to do with what's happened to Sam now. Mary . . . she won't let this lie, that's all. She believes in all that karma rubbish. She thinks Sam may have done something bad when he was younger. She was always worried that it would come back to haunt him later on, but it was just boys being boys. These girls . . . they were just looking for a payout, that's all. As soon as that one found out who a couple of the boys' fathers were, she invented a whole story.'

'Who are the other men in this picture, Arthur?'

Arthur shook his head in response. 'I don't want to give out that information. You can't make me.'

Sixteen

Murphy waited at the car for Rossi to finish speaking to Mary Byrne. Through the living-room window he could spy Arthur, still sitting in the chair were he'd left him. Murphy leaned against the car, blowing some warmth into his hands as the surrounding air became cooler by the second.

'New best friend?' Murphy said as Rossi made her way down the path towards him shaking her head. 'I just hope you got something more than I did.'

'She told me a story.'

'I bet she did,' Murphy replied, opening the door and getting inside the car. He whacked on the heating as soon as he'd started the engine, shaking his head as Rossi got in and removed her jacket. 'Do you not feel the cold?'

'I do, but it's still warm out. It's you getting older and feeling an invisible draught everywhere we go.'

'Less of the old. Come on, what did she say? We need to compare notes.'

Rossi explained what Mary had told him, Murphy cutting in every now and again to confirm the similarities and differences between the two stories they had been told.

'What do you reckon then? Think it has anything to do with his death?'

Murphy paused for a few seconds, trying to make sense of the information they had so far. 'Everything is jumbled up at the moment. It's like we're getting parts of a complete story, but it's all out of order. We need to go back to the beginning and work out where it all starts.'

'Because the start would be somewhere else?'

'You talk back a lot more these days.'

'You can blame that on *me* getting older,' Rossi replied, smirking and running a hand through her hair. 'I think you're right. Nothing has made sense yet. It's quite obvious that he and his friends at university have possibly raped a young woman – maybe women – and it's been hushed up by his father and his powerful friends. Is that enough for someone to take revenge on him in this way years later?'

'I think we've both seen revenge taken for much less.'

'True, I suppose,' Rossi said, giving Murphy the go-ahead to pull out after checking the road on her side was clear. 'I still think we're missing something.'

'I'm hoping CCTV and forensics from the flat will clear up his last movements. That'll answer a few questions.'

'He was cut up. That's not something you do unless you have something against the person. Surely? This is either another ever-so-delightful serial killer on our shores, or it's personal.'

'Could be both,' Murphy replied, hoping he was wrong. 'Weirder things have happened around here lately.'

'Ever think we're getting more violent?'

'Not us personally, I hope?' Murphy said, flashing Rossi a grin. 'Unless you want to confess to something?'

'No, I mean as a species. Seems like everything is getting worse the last couple of years. Murder in the news, on the streets . . . enough to drive you to drink or religion.'

'It's never as bad as that.'

Rossi tapped her fingers against the dashboard as she leaned forwards. 'Think about it. I've heard coppers themselves say they don't want to go to Liverpool One or the Trafford Centre because they're worried about being killed in a terrorist attack. We have domestics every damn day, which seem to be becoming more violent every time. People are starting to treat life like it's a bloody video game.'

'It's never as bad as you think,' Murphy said, grin now disappeared. It was a conversation he'd had with Sarah on occasion. Especially now. What kind of world were they living in? 'There's always bad in the world. That's just the way of things. Before these bad guys, we had other bad guys. We just know about every move this lot make, because they want us to know. We know every damn thing these days. I'm not even forty and I remember a time when I didn't know everything a shitty group halfway round the world was doing. It keeps them going, knowing we're afraid.'

'We shouldn't fear?'

'Of course we should,' Murphy said, trying to look past Rossi as they pulled up to a junction. 'But we can't let it control us. We're scared of the wrong things, that's all. We should be scared about how we're going to fill the time we have on this planet. Not what could end it.'

'Suppose so,' Rossi replied, moving back against her seat finally and allowing Murphy to see out of the passenger-side window. 'It's still frightening.'

'I don't think we're in the best position to judge how violent society is anyway. We see too much of the bad to be non-biased. It's like some coppers – uniforms usually – who think everything they see on shift is the truth about society. They think there's a bunch of scroungers and benefit cheats out there, because that's all they deal with day to day. They think all the residents from certain estates are lost causes, and that Katie Hopkins is the voice of bleeding reason.'

'Not all of them,' Rossi said, but even Murphy could tell she wasn't in total opposition to what he was saying. 'And it's not like CID is much better.'

'True. We're all human. Some of us can't think much for ourselves, that's all. We're all led by our own prejudices.'

'Confirmation bias.'

Murphy turned to look at Rossi, a question mark on his face. 'What's that mean?'

'It's a psychology thing. You need to learn this stuff now Sarah is studying it. Basically, we all look for things that confirm our own preconceptions. So, you have someone who has grown up believing a certain group is a certain thing, usually by being taught that information from a parent or similar. They become a copper, spend every night breaking up fights and taking down burglary reports. That all feeds into that bias. Like people who think all students are lazy, or all Muslims are terrorists. Doesn't matter if you come along and show them it's a small minority doing those things, it's already in their head that a certain group of people who are all the same.'

'How the hell did we get here?'

Rossi peered through the windscreen. 'It's the right way, what are you talking about?'

'I don't mean on this road,' Murphy said with a laugh. 'I meant onto this subject. It's a bit heavy after the day we've had.'

'I have no idea. Nice to know you have a soapbox though. Big improvement from the dour one-note guy you were when we first started working together.'

'Careful, Laura,' Murphy said, giving Rossi the side-eye. 'I'm still the boss round here.'

Rossi mimed pulling a zip across her mouth and throwing away a key.

'I'm just tired, that's all,' Murphy continued, one hand on the steering wheel, the other resting against his forehead. 'I have no idea what the hell has happened the last couple of days. We weren't even supposed to be given a case like this in the first place. Now we have a dismembered body, a possible historical sexual assault and a Z-list probable MP with a secret flat filled with blood-stained walls and bed, and a bunch of sex toys I don't even want to think about.'

'That's about the size of it,' Rossi said, digging around in the glove compartment. She pulled out her phone. 'I'm going to find the seven other people in that photograph. Even if it bloody kills me. Simon Jackson is the first on my list. Put me down for a late one tonight.'

Murphy grunted in response. He stopped in the car park behind the station before pulling out his own phone.

'I'll follow you up,' Murphy said. Rossi raised a hand in response, still staring at her phone as she walked away from the car. Murphy checked a few emails, deleted some updates. He brought up his contacts and scrolled to W. For wife.

'Hey, it's me,' Murphy said when Sarah answered. 'Going to be late home, so don't wait up if you're tired or anything.'

'No worries,' Sarah replied, the sound of the TV being muted suddenly in the background. 'Might still be up anyway. First lecture tomorrow.'

'Nervous?'

'A little bit, yeah. Also want to get ahead of the others. Do a bit of studying, you know?'

'There's a bottle of white in the fridge, but keep the red on the side for me, will you? I will drink it at some point.'

'That's what you always say. I think Jess had that the other day.'

Murphy shook his head, adding 'ring Jess' to his internal list of things to do. 'Of course she did. I've got to go.'

'Have you eaten? Only I know what you're like . . .'

'I will get something here now.'

'Make sure you do. And be careful. I'm not paying off this mortgage on my own if anything happens to you.'

'I'll be at the office, so unless there's a terrible stationery injury, I think I'll be OK.'

Murphy heard a muffled laugh over the line, quickly shut down. 'Watch those staplers. Speak to you later.'

Murphy said goodbye and ended the call. The car park was quieter now, the light fading around him. He could hear the traffic from the nearby road, still busy for a Tuesday night, as it always seemed to be.

The incident room was bustling with activity when Murphy entered it a few minutes later. The detective constables still on duty were huddled in front of screens, going through CCTV from various sites in the city, a few sergeants were being updated by Rossi in another part of the room. DCI Stephens's office was empty and dark, which was unsurprising. The perks of being higher up in the food chain, Murphy thought.

'Graham,' Murphy said as he reached his desk. 'How are you getting on with the CCTV?'

'It's much as the guy at the scene said,' DC Harris replied. 'Here we are, I'm just piecing the whole thing together now.'

Murphy waited for DC Harris to cue up the footage, then watched the screen from over Harris's shoulder.

'There's the car being driven down Queens Drive, approaching the roundabout. He goes onto Edge Lane, then takes a right into Warnerville Road. Reappears at the bottom of Talbotville. You obviously can't drive back onto Edge Lane from Talbotville, so it looks like the site was chosen specifically for the fact that it was on a busy road, but not easily accessible.'

'Maybe,' Murphy replied, studying the footage, wishing not for the first time the technology was better. 'Seems to be being driven carefully. Nothing erratic or irregular there.'

'If I could get closer, I bet he'd have his hands at the ten and two position.'

'So, where did he come from before Queens Drive?'

DC Harris sighed and opened another file of footage. 'I've got him joining from Mill Lane, near the Premier Inn in West Derby. Before that, we're trying our best. Looks like they've come from the Croxteth area, but it's difficult to pick him up at that time of day. We'll get there.'

'OK, I understand. What about after the car is dropped off, have we got him leaving?'

'Yes,' DC Harris replied, moving to another file now. 'Here we go.'

The car appeared on screen again, parked up near the bollards at the end of the street. A figure in black got out of the car and moved to the boot of the car, his back to the camera. 'He's working very quickly,' DC Harris said, leaning back in his wheelchair. 'Confident like.'

'There's our friend there,' Murphy said, pointing to another figure nearby. 'Look at the way he's just hanging around waiting. On the rob or what?'

'Look,' DC Harris said, slowing down the footage. 'It's almost like he glances towards the camera here, but his face is covered.'

'Zoom in as much as possible,' Murphy said, looking around for a chair but settling for leaning against the desk when he couldn't see one. 'That's it, is that the best we could get?'

'Yeah, pretty much. Sorry, but I think we're dealing with someone who didn't want to be seen.'

'Where did they go after that?'

'Back down Talbotville Road and into the estate there. Lost him, sorry.'

Murphy stood up, shaking his head. 'At least we know our friend from the scene was telling the truth. Keep looking. See if he reappears anywhere nearby in the hours afterwards.'

'Returning to the scene, you mean?'

'Yeah,' Murphy replied, looking over towards where Rossi was crouched behind another desk. 'Sometimes they do that.'

'No problem. I think Jack has something from the flat for you.'

Murphy nodded and looked around for DC Kirkham, but couldn't see him. The television at the end of the room caught his eye. He grimaced when he saw who was on screen.

DSI Butler, in all his livery, stood holding court in front of the media. He had a grave look upon his face as the ticker along the bottom of the screen informed the country of the breaking news.

PROSPECTIVE CONSERVATIVE MP FOUND DEAD IN LIVERPOOL

You

You watch the television, perched on the edge of a sofa which cost more than a small car. They are discussing your handiwork. Your act of murder.

The thrill of it threatens to overwhelm you. You sneak a look at the door, expecting it to crash open at any second.

You wait. Your heart hammers in your chest, so fast you wonder if you could have a heart attack right there and then.

They are talking about what you've done, in serious tones, beamed into living rooms around the country.

You are infamous.

Infamy. You wonder if your name will soon be spoken in the same breath as some other notorious killers. You wonder how you stand up next to a Jeffrey Dahmer or Richard Ramirez. A Levi Bellfield or Ted Bundy.

Aileen Wuornos. Fred and Rose West.

There's always a clamour to find out why someone has ended the life of another. People need to know why and how. That's just the way things are. Why did someone have to kill another person? Why did they deserve to die? Questions, questions, questions.

Murder isn't as bad as it's made out to be. It's even lauded in some circumstances. It's something people don't mind, as long as certain rules and boundaries are adhered to. No one thinks too much about the loss of life of an enemy, or people deemed to be in opposition to them. In war, all bets are off.

This is a type of war. You are certain of that. People may not understand, but these eight men have to be stopped. They can't be allowed to continue, infecting humanity with their presence and lust for more and more influence. There has to be an end point for them.

They must pay for what they have done.

Cause and effect. They have done wrong and now they will face the consequences.

Guilt can make people do things they never thought possible. That is something else that has become clear. Living with one of the strongest emotions known to humankind is almost impossible. Unless you have moved on from such things as conscience. Unless you know how to counteract the guilt and live through it.

That knot in your stomach can disappear. So can that feeling of unending dread, the fear of a knock at your door ending your mission before it has come to its natural end. There's a way of making your way through life without those feelings.

You sit back and watch the drama you have created unfold. Planning your next move.

Seventeen

Murphy yawned for what felt the thousandth time and shrugged when Rossi looked up from her desk at him. The incident room had thinned out a little as the evening drew on, but there were still a few people dotted about. Each with their own little task to be getting on with. Hoping to be noticed for doing their jobs.

'Knock it on the head if you want,' Rossi said, looking at her computer screen again. She had a laptop open to the other side of her, switching between the two screens as she saw fit. 'You'll only end up missing something.'

'I'll give it a bit longer,' Murphy replied, rewinding CCTV images back again and rewatching what he'd missed during his stretch and yawn. 'You can bet they'll be wanting a better answer than *we don't know a thing* tomorrow morning. We need a timeline.'

'What have you got so far?' Rossi asked, moving away from her desk and coming around to his side. 'He was reported missing when, Sunday or Monday?'

'Over the weekend, but I think he was gone by Friday. He left the office on Thursday, so we're working back to that point.'

'Someone at the apartment block said they saw him Thursday evening?'

'Heard him,' Murphy said, sketching out the timeline for the umpteenth time on a blank piece of paper. 'Could have been someone else, I suppose. They weren't exactly sure of the time.'

'CCTV covers the entrance?'

'We haven't got that yet, so I'm working from the nearest one we can get. Outside the Tesco, just a few doors away. It's busy, though, so it's slow work.'

'Thursday evening, I'm not surprised. Start with a narrower timeline and work from there?'

'Tried that,' Murphy said, dragging the images back to the beginning again. 'I think this is him, but I'm not sure. Could be anyone.'

Rossi leaned forward and studied the freeze-frame, seeing only a blurred image which was of no use to anyone. 'Did the resident say what time they thought he left?'

Murphy shook his head. 'I'm going to have to go through it completely. Or wait for the CCTV from the apartment block.' He left the images running and turned to Rossi. 'How are you getting on?'

'Think I've found Simon Jackson,' Rossi said, placing a hand on the back of her neck and rubbing some life into it. 'Graduated from university the same year as Sam Byrne, now lives just outside of Manchester. Works in the legal sector or something. I'll contact him tomorrow morning, when it's a more suitable hour.'

'Good work. Could do with the other names on that list, though.'

'I've been thinking about that,' Rossi said, looking past Murphy at the images on the screen playing behind him, then back to Murphy. 'The names that Mary Byrne gave us the other day are probably right, no matter what they both say now. I've looked through all of Sam's social media accounts and got a few possible positive matches from that. I think I've found one – Matthew. His Facebook profile states that he attended the same university as Byrne, and he shared a few messages with Sam a while ago. Nothing of interest within the messages, but there's a connection of sorts. He's a strange one as there doesn't seem to have been any activity on his social media accounts for a few months now.'

'What's his full name?'

'Matthew Williams,' Rossi replied, checking the notepad in her hand. 'I'm trying to work out where he lives now.'

'OK, cool. Making some sort of progress . . . What?'

Murphy turned to see what Rossi was frowning at. The screen behind him was still playing through the CCTV, now a few hours on from the beginning.

'Take that back a bit,' Rossi said, leaning forwards and taking control of it herself before Murphy had chance to. 'I'm sure I've just seen something.'

Murphy slid back on his chair, allowing Rossi to take over. 'What time is this at?'

'I don't know . . . wait . . . there, do you see it?'

Murphy peered at the image on the screen, trying to see what Rossi had noticed. 'Give us a clue, what am I looking for?'

'There, look, that woman,' Rossi said, pointing at a figure moving away from the camera. 'Here, let me show you again.'

Rossi took the footage back a little, a woman appearing, looking around, then moving away. She was brushing past people as if they weren't there, bumping into a couple as she moved between them. Then, she was gone.

'She was getting away quick, but I'm not sure what . . .'

'You don't recognise her?' Rossi said, rewinding the footage once again. 'No, you won't, you didn't meet her. Remember that case I was telling you about, the old man and the prostitute?'

'You told me about it last week,' Murphy said, motioning for her to continue. 'My memory isn't that bad yet.'

'Yeah, well, she was the sex worker.'

'Right. You can tell that from this picture?'

Rossi nodded, taking the footage back further, trying to work out the exact moment when the woman entered the scene. 'Definitely. You can tell from the hair, look,' Rossi said, pointing at the screen. 'See that there, that's the beads in her hair. The ones that got stuck.'

'Right, well, that's all well and good, but I'm not sure what that means . . .'

'Well, this isn't her usual place of work for a start,' Rossi said, watching the scene unfold once more. 'She's definitely trying to get away from somewhere. Is it just a coincidence?'

'There are no coincidences,' Murphy replied, staring at the woman leaving the frame. 'Someone once told me that.'

'Think about it. Sam Byrne has a secret flat that's used for God knows what. The state of that bedroom, what if he uses it to bring women back there and something went wrong.'

'He went too far?'

'Exactly,' Rossi said, standing up fully. 'Piece that together with what we've been told by other residents, about women crying in the hallway. We need to speak to her.'

'What we need is the CCTV from the apartment. Make sure she's been there.'

'Hopefully have that tomorrow,' Rossi replied, moving away from Murphy's desk. 'That will give us a better timeline. And maybe a suspect.'

'Possibly. I'm not counting any chickens yet, though. Which reminds me, any of that pizza left?'

'The gannets over there took the last pieces,' Rossi replied, pointing towards a huddle of DCs on the other side of the room. 'That was what time, ten forty, ten forty-five?'

Murphy looked at the timestamp on the CCTV footage. 'Yeah, around then.'

'This would fit. Especially if she comes back with someone, to clean up and that. I don't think she could get him downstairs on her own.'

'I think we're making a big leap here,' Murphy said, forwarding the footage and looking for the woman to reappear. 'But I take the point. It's about the best we've got so far.'

'Better than nothing.'

Murphy checked his watch, then the clock on the wall. 'Think it might be time to knock this on the head. Hopefully we'll have a more complete picture tomorrow.'

'Won't hold my breath,' Rossi said, stretching her arms above her head. 'Something tells me this case isn't going to be a cut-and-dried one.'

'Optimism, that's why I love working with you,' Murphy replied, giving Rossi a smirk. He pulled out his phone, swiped to the right and typed out a message.

You still up and about?

'At least I'll get some time to myself when I get in,' Rossi said, shutting down her computer and putting the laptop into a bag. 'He's on earlies the next few days, so goes to bed at ridiculous o'clock.'

'Well, don't be up too late on that thing,' Murphy replied, pointing towards the laptop bag she was holding. 'Need you bright and alert first thing.'

'Yes, Dad,' Rossi replied, driving the knife right into the gut of Murphy's self-esteem. 'More likely I'll fall asleep on the couch watching something I've Sky-plussed from a decade ago.'

'That reminds me,' Murphy said, grabbing his coat and pushing his chair in. 'I keep hearing this phrase "Netflix and chill", what does it mean?'

Rossi stared at him for a few seconds, then shook her head. 'There's no way I'm discussing that kind of thing with you. Especially after just calling you Dad.'

Rossi left Murphy standing by his desk. She shouted a goodbye over her shoulder as she headed for the door. His phone buzzed in his pocket and he took it out with a smile.

'She always falls for it . . .' Murphy said to himself, opening his phone.

Always fuckin' up. Coming round?

Murphy typed a reply and shouted a farewell to the officers working the nightshift in the incident room. He left the station and entered the car park, pulling his coat tighter to him as the unseasonably wintery air hit him. September may have only just begun, but summer was forgotten. He keyed the fob in his hand and heard the familiar sound of the car unlocking only a few feet away.

In a few minutes, he was on the road, turning up the volume on the music in the car. The Scottish band, Deacon Blue, blared from the speakers, talking about a Real Gone Kid. He had added it to his playlist recently, after seeing a local boxer use it for their ring entrance, the song transporting him back to the eighties in an instant.

Scousers always have the best taste in music, he thought. Even the boxers know good music and they get punched in the head for a living.

It was a fifteen-minute trip from the station to Jess's house, which took Murphy less than ten now the traffic had dwindled. The once busy roads had quietened and, late at night, it became clear what Liverpool was – a group of towns bordering a city centre which didn't sleep all that much.

Deacon Blue gave way to another eighties staple in The Waterboys, Murphy's playlist sounding like it hadn't been updated in thirty years. He was still trying to work out how many contemporary songs were actually on it, when he pulled up outside Jess's house and turned off the engine.

He made his way up the short path, trying to forget a time when he would visit for another reason. A time when a blond, tousled-haired kid would try to barrel him over with glee. Before he could stop himself, Murphy remembered the last time he'd seen the boy. Seventeen years old, a shotgun being held against his head by a man Murphy was supposed to have stopped. He shook the memory away and knocked on the door, then rang the doorbell when there was no answer.

'It's usually the other way round,' Jess said, opening the door and letting Murphy pass by her. 'Not used to getting you here.'

'Yeah, well, I thought it was my turn to clutter up your living room.'

'I never clutter up your house,' Jess replied, closing the door behind them and following Murphy into the living room. 'I give it character.'

'Are you calling me and Sarah boring?'

'Of course not,' Jess said, crossing over to her spot on the couch and dropping into it. She closed the lid on the laptop next to her and turned a little to face him. 'I'm just saying I make it more interesting.'

'And we thank you for it,' Murphy replied, sitting down on the opposite couch. He ignored the picture on the wall above him, the kid he'd remembered outside now forever a teenager. 'Still not sleeping much?'

'The house is too quiet. I should move really. Maybe get a nice apartment somewhere nearer town.'

'You'd only be awake worrying about the mortgage on one of those places. Remember that celeb couple from last year, ChloJoe? Quarter of a million pound apartment, that was.'

'Bet it was nice,' Jess said, moving across the couch and finding the television remote under a cushion. 'Wouldn't mind having a doorman and all that. With what I'd make on selling this place, I'd clear most of that.'

'You've been here for years,' Murphy replied, looking at the TV as it came to life. 'Can't just up and leave.'

'Why not? What's keeping me here?'

Murphy felt the ground beneath him get a little shaky. Whilst they didn't talk about Jess's son and what had happened to him all that much, it was always the giant elephant in the room. Sometimes it was wearing a tuxedo, dancing the 'Macarena', and singing the national anthem out of tune. 'It's your home, Jess. Lot of memories here.'

'Maybe that's the problem, Bear.'

The old nickname she'd had for him had returned to use recently. After her son, Peter, had died, she had blamed Murphy for his death. Punishing him for not doing more to save the boy. Years had passed before their more than twenty-year friendship had slowly been repaired to the point where she felt comfortable enough to use that damn nickname he wished had stayed lost.

'What do you think?' Murphy said, pointing towards the television. *Sky News* was showing a report about Sam Byrne's demise along with shots of Liverpool and interviews with locals. 'We're not exactly making much headway.'

'Maybe someone finally realised we were about to elect a Tory in Liverpool and decided to sort it out?'

'I'm starting to think politics has very little to do with any of it.'

'Never discount it,' Jess said, flicking around the channels before landing on a live poker show. Cards flashed up on screen as various men and a sole woman stared at each other. 'Politics makes people do really stupid things.'

'I'd say more, but you know how it is.'

'You're worried I'd be defending whoever gets charged? You know that could never happen. We're too close. I'd drop that case faster than you can say antidisestablishmentarianism. Or however you say that word.'

'You're asking the wrong person there,' Murphy said with a chuckle. 'I failed English. Could barely string a sentence together at school.'

'You got better at it,' Jess said, laughing. 'Had to in your line of work. I've read some of the reports you've put together. They're not bad. Some are even readable.'

'I was so nervous during that first entrance exam. You were with me, remember?'

'Of course,' Jess said, leaning forwards on the couch. 'You wanted a shot of brandy and I only had Hooch in that poxy little student flat I was in.'

'Hooch,' Murphy said, his voice echoing off the walls, joined by a clap as he slammed his hands together at the memory. 'God, that stuff tasted like boiled shite.'

'You got through the exam.'

'I know, I know . . . it just always feels like there's something closing in on me when we get cases like this. That they move too quick to catch mistakes or clues or whatever.'

'You'll get there, you always do. No matter what, you're there at the end.'

Murphy nodded, relaxing a little as Jess spoke. There had been a growing uneasiness within him all day, which he couldn't put his finger on. Speaking to Jess had eased that somewhat.

Made him feel almost normal.

* * *

Rossi waited for Murphy to leave, then made her way back up to the incident room and back over to her desk. She switched on her computer, hoping she had the same access as Murphy. She waited patiently for it to boot up, then sat down sharply in her chair as it came to life. She let the laptop bag drop to the floor with a soft thunk, then her other bag went on the desk, clattering against pens.

She ignored the looks from the few detectives still left in
the incident room and concentrated.

She pulled up the CCTV footage Murphy had been
going through, hands shaking a little as she watched the
images appear and speed past. She cued up the time she
wanted and watched. She rewound and watched again.

There was a moment when she thought she'd been
mistaken. That it was someone else. On the fifth watch,
she accepted the truth.

A man appeared on the edge of the frame, looking
around as if he was waiting for someone. He walked a
little further, then checked his watch. He came into full
view as people passed him by on either side. He looked
up towards the camera and Rossi paused the image.

She knew the man.

It was her brother.

Eighteen

Anxiety and tension. Those were the two features of the incident room that morning. Murphy could feel them, both battling for superiority over each other. He tried to ignore it and read the forensics report from Sam Byrne's apartment with a detached view. But he could sense it still, the drawn faces of the various detectives in the area surrounding him beginning to grate.

Rossi was late, which didn't help. He was too used to having her around now. Years earlier, he had worked more or less alone. A variety of ever-changing sergeants working alongside him, there for the shared glory rather than an actual partnership. He'd forgotten for the most part what that was like. He'd grown accustomed to having her by his side.

'Graham,' Murphy shouted over to DC Harris, waiting for him to turn his wheelchair round to face him. 'Is this the full report?'

'As much as we got,' DC Harris replied, wheeling himself over to Murphy's desk. 'Nothing good on there?'

'Just confusing, that's all.'

Murphy turned as the main door into the incident room banged open and Rossi rushed in. She had a glow of sweat across her brow, her hair cascading over her face, thick and dark. She had only one arm in her jacket, half of it swinging by her side, her laptop bag banging against her other side. She was holding a bottle of Lucozade in her mouth.

'Sorry . . . excuse me . . . sorry,' she mumbled.

Murphy waited for her to make it over to her own desk, he raised his eyebrows questioningly.

Rossi placed the bag down on her desk, then removed the bottle from her mouth. 'I know, I know. Just had a bad night, that's all. Had to go and see someone before work.'

'Not Darren trouble again, I hope,' Murphy said, letting his eyebrows drop and turning back to the forensics report. 'I like this one.'

'Haven't seen him to have any trouble. This was something else. Personal.'

'Really? I've never known you to have anything secret around here.'

'Well, there's a first time for everything, isn't there?' Rossi said, snatching her jacket off and throwing it underneath her desk. 'What have I missed?'

Murphy waited a second or two, then thought better of pushing it. 'Forensics report is back. On the apartment.'

'Right, so is it the kill site?'

'I'd say no,' Murphy said, throwing Rossi over a copy. 'Five different blood donors from the bedroom, none match Sam Byrne. We have other . . . fluids, from him, but no blood. Three blood donors have all come back as DNA matches to people in the system.'

'*Cazzo, bastardo,*' Rossi said under her breath. 'Serial?'

Murphy hesitated for a second, then shrugged his shoulders. 'Better question is why they're in the system already.'

'Why is that then?'

'All three are women. All three on prostitution charges. Haven't got the other two donors, obviously, but I'm pretty sure the three we do have are alive. One of them was last picked up on Saturday night. After Sam went missing. We're going to see another one now.'

'OK, take me back a step, because I think I've missed something.'

Murphy leafed through the report again. 'I'm saying the blood found in Sam's bedroom is from a variety of sex workers. And now I have to find out why it's there and what the hell was going on in that apartment.'

'What else is in there?'

'Lot of matches to Sam, but no blood. Semen and other bodily fluids, but the blood is all other people.'

'You know where the sex worker is then?'

'Yeah, flat in Anfield. Works a patch regularly down that way. She's well known to local uniform.'

'Give me a second,' Rossi said, bending down to find her coat. 'Who is it that we're going to see?'

'*We're* not going anywhere. I'm taking Hashem with me. Be good to get her out in the field for a change.'

'Are you going to do this to me every time I'm late,' Rossi replied, sitting up and leaning forwards on her desk. 'Leave me out of things, punish me?'

Murphy gave her a smirk, then stopped when he saw Rossi's nostrils flare. 'No, that's not why. I need you to go and see Simon Jackson. You and Kirkham. We got in touch with him this morning. He's willing to speak to us.

Although, we haven't told him what it's regarding. So you'll have to tell him that we believe it is Sam who we found.'

Rossi's shoulders relaxed a little, nostrils going back to normal. Murphy gave a sigh of relief. The last thing he wanted to do was annoy Rossi any more than she already was that morning.

'OK, cool,' Rossi said, looking away towards the ceiling for a brief moment. 'I agree, Abs should be going out there more. About time.'

'Glad you back my judgement,' Murphy replied, trying the smirk again and waiting for a nod from Rossi. 'We'll talk later, yeah?'

Rossi grunted a response at him.

Murphy made a *let's go* motion towards DC Hashem and waited for her to spring up out of her chair. She bounded across the room towards him, her headscarf bobbing up and down with her. She slowed down and readjusted it as she reached Murphy. He looked down at her, wondering if the constables were getting smaller each year, or if he was getting taller.

'Ready?' Murphy said, handing the address over to Hashem. 'I'll drive.'

'Yeah, definitely,' Hashem replied, almost beaming. Murphy was always a little shocked when the broad Scouse accent sprung from the new DC's lips, but he knew that was just his own problem. He already had an Italian Scouser on his team, it was hardly groundbreaking to have a Muslim one as well. 'Anfield? Was hoping it was that one who has loads of followers on Twitter.'

'Who's that then?' Murphy replied, letting DC Hashem move past him and out in to the corridor.

'Some blonde-haired, big-breasted woman. Has hundreds of thousands of followers on there. She calls herself an escort, you know, the way some of them do these days.'

'Never heard of her.'

'Yeah, well, she's like a mini-celebrity. Wouldn't mind meeting her. She posts pictures of her rabbits . . . not that kind of rabbit . . . real ones.'

Murphy raised an eyebrow at the young DC, wondering at what point he'd lost control of the conversation.

'Anyway, looks like she's got a nice place, that's what I mean to say. Must make a lot of money.'

'Abs, I know we don't do this a lot, but just for future reference, I'm not really into learning about local celebrities. Not even when they're escorts and post pictures of their rabbits online.'

'Got it, sir,' DC Hashem replied, a thin smirk on her face.

Murphy relaxed his shoulders. 'So, do we know anything about the woman we are going to see?' he asked.

'Only what was in the system. Thirty-two, three kids, but they all live with their grandmother. Charged on numerous occasions, but never done any time inside. Found with class A once, but managed to get away with it, by the looks of it. And her blood was found at Sam Byrne's flat. So weird that, like. You would think them two would be polar opposites.'

'We're all the same deep down.'

Murphy earned a solemn nod from DC Hashem and felt good for about at least a second. They made it downstairs and into the car park without another word, but it didn't last much longer.

'You know, I was pleased when the North and South Divisions were merged. I've heard nothing but good about working in this office and they were right.'

'That's nice to hear,' Murphy said, almost regretting his decision to leave Rossi with Kirkham. 'It'll probably end up feeling about the same, you know.'

'You're joking, aren't you? Everyone here is too scared to say anything about me. Wasn't like that in the South Division.'

'What do you mean?' Murphy replied, frowning a little as he unlocked the car and got in. 'Scared to say what?'

'You're messing me round, right? I'm not only a woman, but a Muslim one as well. If I was a lesbian I'd have the trifecta. Since we've been here, I haven't heard one "bomb in your headscarf" joke whatsoever. They're all shit scared you'll pitch them through the window or something.'

'Well, it's good to know that, I guess. Although I would have hoped it being 2016 would have made a bigger difference to people's views.'

'You'd be surprised how much people don't like change.'

Murphy shook his head and started the car, driving out of the car park and onto the main road. It was a ten-minute drive to Anfield on a good day, but it was fifteen minutes later when they turned off Walton Breck Road and onto Feltwell Road. A mass of terraced houses, most of which looked as scruffy as the residents within, greeted them. A few kids played in the road, booting a football which had probably been brand new a decade earlier. They sauntered onto the pavement as Murphy drove slowly towards them. A bare-chested man sat outside one of the houses, smoking and watching the kids, whilst two women wearing bright pink vest tops stretched to maximum capacity chatted outside another.

'What number is it?' Murphy said, turning to DC Hashem and then back to the road in case another couple of kids came out.

DC Hashem told him and continued peering out of her side window. 'Here it is,' she said, already snapping out of her seat belt.

Murphy slowed and pulled into an empty space. There hadn't been many cars parked along the road, but there seemed to be more the further down they had gone. The houses on one side had also begun to change, seemingly nicer in appearance than further up, with dark-wood double glazing and well-kept front yards.

Murphy turned off the engine and pulled the key from the ignition.

'Anything I need to know before we knock?' DC Hashem said, one hand on the door handle. 'Only, I don't much like surprises.'

'Just follow my lead, don't interrupt but don't be afraid to ask any questions. Take as many notes as you can.'

'Right, cool,' DC Hashem replied, getting out of the car. Murphy followed, joining her on the doorstep as she pressed the doorbell outside. Within, they could hear the tinny response to the push of the button, then a dog barking.

'I don't like dogs,' DC Hashem said, glancing up at Murphy then back at the door. 'They don't seem to like me all that much either.'

'Sounds like one of those tiny ones.'

'They're the worst,' DC Hashem said, a nervous laugh spilling from her lips.

'It'll be sound, don't worry.'

The door was unlocked and a voice from behind the door began shooing away what Murphy assumed was the dog they'd heard. The door opened slowly and a face appeared.

'Yeah?'

'Vicky Whitlaw?' Murphy said, trying to keep his voice as light as possible.

'Who wants to know?'

That would be a yes then, Murphy thought. 'Detective Inspector David Murphy and Detective Constable Abs Hashem from the Major Crime Unit, can we have a chat please?'

The door opened a little more, the face peering at them both. 'ID?'

Murphy already had his in his hand and showed it to the woman. DC Hashem fished around in her pocket and finally produced hers.

'What can I do you for?'

Murphy tried his most trustworthy look and tilted his head a little. 'You think we could do this inside?'

'Have you got a warrant?'

'Do we need one?' DC Hashem said, tilting her own head now. 'It's not like we're here mob-handed. We just want to have a little talk with you, that's all.'

There was a moment when Murphy thought the door was going to be slammed in their faces. Instead, Vicky Whitlaw stepped to one side and let them in.

'Thanks, Vicky,' DC Hashem said, stepping forwards into the room immediately in front of them. She rubbed her hands together and looked around as Murphy followed her in. 'Hey, it's nice in here.'

'What were you expecting?' Vicky said, standing at the doorway with her arms folded. 'Some dosshouse, just because of what I do?'

'No, just surprised because my place is a bloody pigsty. I can never be bothered doing anything. Do you live on your own? Only I do, so that's my excuse. If I'm the only one to see it, who cares?'

Murphy watched as Vicky's shoulders relaxed a little, giving a casual shrug. 'I just like a nice house, that's all. Although the whole place ain't mine, like. Got Polish neighbours upstairs.'

'How is that?'

'They're not bad for foreigners, like,' Vicky replied, unfolding her arms and coming into the room. She stood in front of the window and leaned on the ledge, hands behind her. 'Had to have a word when they were hanging their washing out the upstairs window. But, yeah, not noisy or anything. Was worried when they moved in, with them being not English like. No offence.'

'Why would I be offended?' DC Hashem said, accent thicker than ever. 'I was born in the Women's, love. Grew up in Bootle. Don't come more Liverpool than me.'

Murphy enjoyed DC Hashem's ability to make even a barbed response sound like a jokey retort.

'Oh, I don't mean it like that . . . what are you here for anyway?' Vicky said, as if she was suddenly remembering that strangers were in the house. 'I haven't done anything.'

'Not saying you have,' Murphy said, looking around to find somewhere to sit, then leaning on the mantelpiece instead. 'Actually, we were more interested in whether you had a complaint to make?'

Vicky's brow furrowed. Murphy could see her mentally rewinding through her last few clients. 'Not sure what you mean?'

'Well, we're investigating the death of Sam Byrne . . .'

'Oh, for fuck's sake . . .'

'And we found something interesting at one of his residences.'

'I know what you're talking about,' Vicky said, standing up straight and folding her arms again. 'And I'm telling you now, that little prick got what was coming to him. Had nothing to do with me though.'

Murphy nodded, thinking out what he was going to say next, but DC Hashem spoke instead.

'We found your blood at his apartment in town. How did it get there, Vicky?'

Vicky dipped her head into her chest and when she spoke her voice was quieter than it had been. 'Not by choice.'

'What does that mean?'

'It means, I'm glad he's dead.'

Murphy lifted his hand from the mantelpiece and rubbed it along his chin. 'What did he do to you?'

Vicky raised her head and looked at Murphy. 'Would you believe me if I told you?'

'Why do you think we're here?'

'Well, you're here now,' Vicky said, looking away from Murphy and towards DC Hashem. 'I didn't think I'd be telling anyone this. Once I knew who he was, I didn't think anyone would care.'

'How did your blood end up on his walls?'

'He's a monster. Well, he was anyway. You ask me, it's better for everyone that he's ended up dead. Before he killed someone himself.'

Nineteen

There was something about driving out of Liverpool and towards Manchester which set Rossi's teeth on edge. It didn't feel right, no matter how many times she did it. It was as if she were entering a foreign country, one in which she both didn't belong and wasn't wanted.

It was the accent that did it.

The two cities' rivalry had grown with the football clubs, and their battles on the pitch, back when she was in uniform especially, had become something tangible and violent. Football hooligans may have been a thing of the past in most places, but on match days between the two biggest clubs in the north west, violence suddenly became a family pastime.

Rossi and Kirkham got out of the car, walking in step as they headed towards the exit. The building which housed Simon Jackson's offices was high above them, the ornate entrance from the car park only the first thing to impress Rossi. The second was the lobby of the building. All silver and white, the polished marbled floors gleaming beneath them. People zipped back and forth, all wearing well-cut suits and expensive aftershaves and perfumes. There was an air of privilege seeping out of every pore of the place. Rossi turned to check out a particularly well-groomed bloke as he walked past, before deciding there wasn't enough to grab hold of there.

'JC Enterprises,' Kirkham said, reading from the list on a board next to the reception desk. 'Eighth floor. Which is good. Was worried it was going to be higher than that.'

'Not a fan of heights?'

'Not particularly,' DC Kirkham replied, looking around and spotting the lifts at the end of the vast space. 'Have you ever been up the Radio City Tower in town?'

Rossi shook her head, thinking of the tall building which stood out on the Liverpool skyline. It had been dwarfed only by the Liver Building in the past, but since all the new investment had been ploughed into the city centre, taller office buildings had overtaken it. She remembered hearing a comedian a few years earlier describing the tower as looking like an upside-down lampshade and finding it difficult to disagree with him.

'I have,' DC Kirkham said, pushing the button for the lift and stepping back. 'It's windows all around you up there. Floor to ceiling. Great view, but I couldn't really appreciate it as I was edging around the place, scared to get anywhere near the glass to look out.' DC Kirkham turned to her and grinned, the image of a little imp springing to Rossi's mind.

'Used to be a revolving restaurant,' Rossi said, letting DC Kirkham enter the lift ahead of her before following him inside. 'Imagine the same thing, but only moving around as well.'

DC Kirkham shivered for effect, the same grin plastered on his face. Rossi looked down at the notepad she'd taken out of her pocket as soon as she'd entered the lift.

She read the notes she'd made before leaving the office an hour earlier, annoyed with how brief they were.

'What does this guy do again?' DC Kirkham said, stepping out after Rossi when the lift came to stop. He lowered his voice. 'Something swanky by the looks of this place.'

'Some kind of legal firm, apparently. Not sure what his role is.'

The lift had opened up to a small corridor, decorated in the same silver and white as the downstairs lobby. In front of them were large glass doors with the words JC Enterprises etched in curling script.

Rossi pushed her way through the doors, putting her other hand in her pocket and removing her ID, keeping it palmed.

'Can I help you?' the impossibly tanned woman behind the reception desk said, giving Rossi and Kirkham the once-over.

'We're here to see Simon Jackson,' Rossi replied, keeping an even tone. She tried and failed to hide her accent, which earned a raised eyebrow from Tan Woman.

'Is he expecting you?'

Rossi raised an eyebrow of her own. 'Should be.'

'Right,' Tan Woman said with a nod. She may as well have said No, he's bloody not and never will be, in Rossi's opinion. 'And your names are?'

This was the bit Rossi had been looking forward to. 'Detective Sergeant Laura Rossi and Detective Constable Jack Kirkham. From the Major Crimes Unit in Liverpool. Think that'll be enough?'

Tan Woman moved quickly, picking up the phone and turning in her swivel chair. She spoke into the receiver in a hushed tone. She was done in seconds, turning back to them with a toothy smile. There was a smudge of red lipstick on one dazzling white tooth.

'He'll be with you in a few seconds.'

Amazing what a title can do, Rossi thought. 'That's excellent to hear,' she said instead, stepping back from the desk. 'We'll wait here nice and quiet.'

Tan Woman had lost a little bit of confidence now and simply nodded meekly in response. Rossi almost felt guilty for a millisecond, then forgot Tan Woman existed as Simon Jackson entered the lobby.

'Is this them?' Jackson said to Tan Woman, eyes darting between her and Kirkham. Rossi was given a slight once-over, but his attention was on Kirkham.

This will be fun, Rossi thought.

'Simon Jackson?' Rossi said, interrupting Tan Woman before she had chance to speak. 'Have you got somewhere private we can have a chat?'

'Yes, please, follow me.'

Rossi glanced towards Kirkham and then followed Jackson. She could see rows of desks to one side, behind glass-panelled doors, but was led away from them. She was glad of it, the banks of people all wearing headsets had set off something nasty inside of her.

'Just here,' Jackson said, holding an office door open. 'Can I get you anything, tea, coffee . . . my solicitor?'

It was said as a joke, but Rossi didn't smile in return. She was pleased to see DC Kirkham didn't either. 'No, thank you. Hopefully we'll be out of your hair quite quickly.'

Rossi walked over and plonked herself down on one of the chairs facing the only desk in the room. She waited for DC Kirkham to do the same, then had a gander at her surroundings. It was much as she'd expected the office of someone like Simon Jackson to be – neat, orderly, sparse. Very white, to match the outside decor, with a few certificates on the wall behind where Jackson now finally sat down. There were a couple of photographs underneath the degree certificates and another one in a frame on his desk, next to the Apple Mac taking up most of the room. Rossi leaned forwards to look at it. 'Family?'

'Yes, wife, Sophie, daughter, Emily.'

'Very nice,' Rossi said, sitting back in the chair and looking out of the large window to the side of where they were sitting. 'Nice view as well.'

'Thank you, although I didn't have much to do with it,' Jackson replied, running a hand through his hair. It was longer than Rossi had expected, and had a Hugh Grant foppish look to it, a single curl flopping down onto his forehead after he'd finished with it. Jackson wasn't particularly tall, but only if you were looking for it. He was slim, but well built with it. There was a nice figure underneath the suit he was wearing, she guessed, but the whole look wasn't exactly impressing her.

'What's this about then?' Jackson said, affecting an air of relaxation. Rossi wasn't buying it, but took it anyway. 'Not often I get a visit from Her Majesty's finest.'

'You know where we're from?'

'The accent does really give it away. Liverpool, I assume?'

'You're right. Somewhere you know well?'

'Of course,' Jackson replied, leaning back in his chair and crossing his fingers over his midriff. 'I studied at university there a fair few years ago.'

'You've done well, getting your own office before you've even turned thirty.'

'Yes, well, hard work, that's all.'

'I'm afraid we're not here with the best of news,' Rossi continued, ignoring the remark. 'It's my duty to inform you of the passing of someone you knew quite well when you were a student.'

'Really . . . who?'

Rossi shot a look at DC Kirkham, who was silently studying Jackson.

'Sam Byrne. He was found dead yesterday morning.'

'Oh, that's terrible. What happened to him?'

Rossi was trying hard, but she was unable to quieten the annoyance Jackson's performance was provoking. 'I was sure you would know already, what with it being on the national news. You don't keep up to date with what's happening around the country?'

Jackson hesitated, caught in a lie, Rossi presumed. 'I went home yesterday and went straight to bed. Didn't catch up on things, sorry. It's a total shock to me.'

'Really? Then it's a shame you had to hear it from us.' Rossi decided to move past what was obviously an untruth. 'Did you keep in touch with Sam once you'd graduated?'

'Well, I'm not sure what you've been told, but we weren't all that close really. We had some time together at university, but we weren't good friends. Certainly not lately, anyway. I haven't spoken to him in a long time.'

Rossi nodded, removing her notepad from her jacket pocket. 'When was the last time you spoke to him?'

'Oh, it will have been years ago. Maybe three, four years ago. I'm not sure. I've been so busy–'

'Do you keep in touch with many people from university?' DC Kirkham said, cutting in. 'Any relationships that have lasted since then?'

Jackson shifted in his seat, removing his hands from where they'd been resting on the desk and placing them on the arms of his chair. 'No, not really. I don't keep in touch with anyone. I'm too busy working and they have their own lives to lead. It was all such a long time ago now. Years, in fact. I'm sure you understand.'

'Help me understand this then,' DC Kirkham said, lifting a finger and pointing to the wall behind Jackson. 'Why would you keep a picture of yourself with Sam Byrne and six other gentlemen, if you weren't all that close?'

Rossi almost grinned, watching as Jackson opened his mouth, becoming more pale by the second.

Twenty

There was a noticeable change in the atmosphere now, Murphy feeling like a spare ornament as Vicky sat down and wrapped her arms around herself. The room had grown colder somehow, as if they had let an evil spirit inside, allowing it to fester and become bitter.

'He was wrong,' Vicky said, the bravado she had shown when they had first arrived now a distant memory. 'Gone in the head. I've had some shit in my work before, I know the worst of the worst. Men who treat us like scum, just there to satisfy whatever they need. This was different though. He wasn't normal.'

'Tell us what happened,' DC Hashem said, sitting on the threadbare sofa opposite the one Vicky was slowly drawing back in to.

'He picked me up on a Tuesday night, about a month ago, I think. No, I know it was. It's not like I would forget really.'

Vicky smiled, but there was no warmth to it. Murphy shifted across and perched himself on the arm of the sofa DC Hashem was sitting on.

'Must have been about ten, ten thirty at night,' Vicky continued, seeming not to notice Murphy. 'Maybe a little later. He wasn't someone I'd seen before, not on our patch anyway.'

'Where was this?'

'Do I have to say?' Vicky replied, eyeing DC Hashem with suspicion. 'Only I don't want to have a load of us lose a good patch.'

'It would help a lot,' DC Hashem said, scribbling notes in her pad.

'Can you promise not to stop us working down there?'

DC Hashem turned and looked at Murphy, who decided to give her a small nod.

'Fine, it's down near Regent Road, near the old ware-houses. Bankfield Street. We keep moving about, but that's more or less where we feel best. Usually all we get is lonely auld fellas, desperate for a bit of attention. Can do five or six of them before midnight.'

'This guy was different, though,' Murphy said, steady-ing himself as he moved a little and the sofa made a loud creaking sound. 'Sam. He didn't just want a handjob in the front seat of his car?'

'No, not at all,' Vicky replied. She had become almost emotionless, her words coming out in a stiff, staccato manner. 'He pulled up alongside us – there was only three of us standing there at the time, but we weren't stood next to each other, of course. He checked us all out, then came to a stop beside me.'

Murphy looked her over, wondering if there was some-thing about her appearance which marked her out. She looked younger than the age he knew her to be. Small, diminutive. She could easily pass for a teenager on a dark night. He logged it for further thought.

'He rolls down the window and I speak to him. He's not bad looking at all, which meant I didn't worry at first. He seemed normal. Young, fit. Looked like he'd had a shower, which if you've been doing what I've been doing, you suddenly start appreciating a lot more.'

DC Hashem gave her a tight grin which didn't travel to the rest of her face. 'What did he say to you?'

'He said he needed someone for a few hours,' Vicky continued, shaking her head as if she was trying to free the memory of what had happened that night. 'Offered me a ridiculous amount of money.'

'How much?'

'Five ton.'

Murphy's eyes widened. From what little he knew about the business, five hundred quid was more than women working on the street would usually make in an entire week.

'I couldn't really turn that money down,' Vicky said, looking away from them now. 'He was in a really nice car, wearing a suit which looked really good, and I just trusted him. He had one of those faces. Of course, when I found out who he was, I wasn't surprised that he was doing so well. He could sell a lie like no one I've ever met before.'

'What kind of car was it?' DC Hashem said, not looking up from her notepad.

'Silver Audi,' Vicky replied without missing a beat. She then reeled off the first part of his number plate without pause as well. 'I knew he had the money, but I still wasn't sure, like. Then he said he'd pay me half up front, the rest when we got to where he wanted to take me. I didn't really think twice, to be honest. Just gave the nod to the other girls, just in case, then got in the car.'

'What happened next?'

'He drove into the city centre, which made me feel a bit safer, then past Lime Street and up that road that goes towards the uni there. Parked up in a car park behind the building and we went up to his apartment. It was all normal until we got inside.'

Murphy made a mental note to check the car park behind the apartment block, to see if there were any records kept by on-site staff. If there were any staff, of course.

'The lights were all off and he only put on a couple of lamps. Couldn't really see much, the lights were all red, but it didn't look like what I'd been expecting. It wasn't lived in, you know what I mean? He made me take my clothes off and change into something else.'

'What did he make you wear?'

'It was like a schoolgirl outfit, which isn't really out of the norm. Had to do that before. It was when he took me into the bedroom that things got worse. I didn't want to be tied up, I never normally let that happen, but he wasn't even listening to me by that point. He was stronger than I'd thought he would be, so I just let him get on with it. All I could think of was the money. It was more than I'd earned in a long time and it wasn't like he was hurting me then.'

Murphy could sense where things were leading and held a hand up to stop Vicky. 'Are you comfortable with me being here, Vicky? I can step out if you want.'

'No, it's fine,' Vicky replied, fixing him with a stare. 'It's not like you're anything like that. I can tell.'

Murphy wasn't sure whether to be flattered or not. He decided he would be.

'He had me in different positions, but it was never any effort to move me. He was just throwing me around, wherever he wanted me to go. He took pictures, I know that. There was a tablet or something on one side and he kept picking it up. There was no noise from it, but I know what he was doing. At first, he was just using things on me, without lube which hurt like a motherfucker, but I just got on with it. I was talking to him at first, like I thought he'd want, but he made me stop. Took my knickers and stuck them in my mouth.'

It was DC Hashem's turn to squirm uncomfortably now, but thankfully Vicky was still oblivious to the two of them.

'It turned bad pretty quick. He had me on my front, arse in the air, which I thought was just going to be the sex thing and we'd be done. Then he moved away and I could feel something being stroked against my back. Something thin. I knew what it was when it came down on me.'

'Cane?'

'Yeah, I think so. You tell me,' Vicky said, standing up and turning around. She lifted her top and revealed her lower back. The marks were faded, but still noticeable. Criss-cross lines of red and silver. Murphy tried to count them from where he was perched, but gave up after a couple of dozen.

'Christ,' DC Hashem said under her breath. 'How long did he do this to you?'

'I didn't keep track of the time, to be honest. Bit hard to, you know, when you're trying to stay alive through the most pain you've ever been through. And I've given birth three times, so I know pain.'

'Did he stop at that?' Murphy said, half-expecting the answer to be negative.

'No, he wasn't done by a long shot. Once he'd whipped me raw, he . . . he had sex with me from behind, but he had his hands around my neck as he did. At first, it was just pressure on the back of my neck, but then he moved his hands to the front, so he was proper choking me.'

'*Ya lahwy*,' DC Hashem said under her breath, earning a sharp look from Murphy. It was bad enough when Rossi had an outburst in Italian, now he had someone exclaiming in Arabic.

'I started seeing spots,' Vicky said, continuing as if she hadn't heard DC Hashem say anything. 'Thankfully, he was finished before I proper went under. I thought he was going to kill me. I thought I was done, finished. I thought I was going to die in that room, after everything he'd done to me.'

'After he was, erm, finished, what happened?' DC Hashem said, more pale than Murphy had ever seen her before.

'There was like a switch that went on. Not that he went back to being nice or anything. He just threw my clothes at me, untied me and wanted rid of me as soon as possible. I bolted out the door, half-dressed, but he brought me back inside to give me a bit of a speech. Told me he'd track me down, kill me, my family, all that sort of thing. If I talked about what happened there, of course. I was so scared, I just did as I was told and agreed to everything he had to say. He gave me the rest of the money, said he'd find me if I told anyone, then got me out of the door. Bastard didn't even give me a lift back.'

Murphy closed his eyes for a second, swallowing down the bile of information they'd just been given and trying to make sense of it.

'Why didn't you tell anyone what happened to you, Vicky?' DC Hashem said, notepad forgotten now as she leaned forwards with her elbows on her knees. Murphy could see she wanted to reach out and touch the young woman, but there was no chance of that happening.

'Apart from the fact he threatened me? Who would have believed me? I went to the hospital, but didn't really tell them anything and they weren't interested in knowing. I found out who he was a day or two later, when I was still in two minds about what to do. I knew I wouldn't have stood a chance. I went to his apartment by choice, took his money, and that was it. I would have been laughed out of your place. Even if I was a normal girl he would have still won. His type always do.'

Murphy wanted to argue with her, but found it difficult to disagree. No matter his personal feelings on the matter – he would have a very different form of justice for any man who did what Sam Byrne obviously enjoyed doing – the fact remained that it became an argument between two sides. When you factored in that only six per cent of rape cases reported actually resulted in a conviction, it was clear which side was winning.

He gripped the side of the sofa a little harder and wondered if it would be better to let Sam Byrne rot, rather than waste his time finding his murderer.

*   *   *

Rossi waited for Simon Jackson to formulate a response to DC Kirkham's question, trying to keep a sly smile from passing her lips. The young man was floundering, beginning to speak, before stopping himself and trying again.

'It's a very simple question, Mr Jackson,' Rossi said, standing up and walking past him and over to the wall. 'Why would you keep a photograph of yourself with our murder victim hanging up on your wall if he was just an acquaintance you had little to do with?'

'I . . . I don't know.'

'Oh, come on, you can do better than that. You don't get to the position you're in here, with a lovely wife and young child to boot, if you can't answer easy questions.'

'I like to keep things. For sentimental reasons.'

'You think of Sam Byrne in a sentimental way? That's a little surprising given what you've said so far.' Rossi was closer to him now and could see the beads of sweat start to form on his forehead. She lifted the photograph off its hook on the wall and looked at it more closely. Sam Byrne was centre stage, dressed in black tailcoats and wearing a large bow tie. The rest of the group were similarly attired, all wearing the same uniform.

'That's you there, isn't it?' Rossi said, moving to Jackson's side and holding the photograph at his eye level. She could see his breathing become shorter and heavier. 'Right next to Sam Byrne. Nice outfit.'

'Do I need to have someone here?' Jackson said, noticeably paler now. 'I'm not being accused of having anything to do with what happened to Sam, am I?'

'Of course not,' Rossi said, moving away from him and taking her seat, still holding onto the photograph. 'As long as you tell us the truth from now on, I won't take your lies as evidence that you are trying to hide your involvement in my investigation. Sound fair?'

Jackson swallowed and wiped a sleeve across his brow.
'OK, that's fine.'

'Let's start with the rest of the people in this photograph. Can you tell me their names?'

'Starting from the left,' Jackson said, leaning forwards
as Rossi placed a finger underneath each face. 'That's Paul
Wright, James Morley, Timothy Johnson, myself, Neil
Letherby, Sam, Matthew Williams, and Christopher
Roberts. Eight of us. We were the original members. More
joined later.'

'And what is this? Some kind of club?'

'Of a sort, yes,' Jackson replied, some colour returning
to his cheeks now. 'We met in the first months of university. We had something in common, all of us, in that we
were supposed to be elsewhere. Our families had all had
high expectations for us, Oxford or Cambridge, that sort
of thing. We'd all been privately educated, but not applied
ourselves enough to join the elite. So, we created an elite
ourselves.'

'And what did you do in this club?'

'Nothing out of the ordinary. We held parties, helped
each other out in our respective studies, that sort of thing.'

'Why would you pretend not to be close to someone
you were patently very involved with?' DC Kirkham said,
looking up with his pen in hand. 'That doesn't make much
sense to me.'

'I . . . I panicked. That's all. I have a highly pressured
job here. I can't have anything like this going on around
me. I don't want to be involved in things of this sort. It
was all such a long time ago.'

'We're talking a few years here,' Rossi said, growing
impatient with Jackson's explanations. 'It's hardly like

you haven't seen each other in decades. You're not old men reflecting on a youth gone wrong. This is recent enough that you need to be upfront with us.'

'I understand.'

'When was the last time you saw Sam?'

Jackson hesitated, the colour draining from his face as quickly as it had returned. 'Years ago. Probably about the time when we graduated . . .'

'I hope you don't play poker,' Rossi said, giving Jackson a stare. 'You have a terrible tell when you're lying.'

Jackson didn't say anything at first. Rossi remained mute, waiting for him to speak first.

'I've seen him a couple of times since then, but not for anything more than a brief catch up. The group of us would check in from time to time, but honestly, I have no idea how this has happened to him. I have nothing to do with that, no involvement whatsoever.'

Rossi somewhat believed the latter part, but there was something about the beginning of the sentence which didn't ring true.

'Just a catch up? Nothing more than that?'

'Nothing,' Jackson replied, his voice quieter. 'We all went our separate ways after graduation. I couldn't tell you anything about his life now, other than what I have read in the papers. A Tory MP in Liverpool . . . that would have been something.'

'It would have been something all right,' Rossi said, sniffing at the thought. 'How about any of the others?'

'The same. An occasional email or text. Christmas cards, that sort of thing.'

'There's nothing else you think we should know?' DC Kirkham said, pen poised in the air, pointing directly at

Jackson. 'Anything that will help us in this enquiry? I don't really want to have to come back here.'

Jackson shook his head slowly, but Rossi wasn't convinced by the performance.

'Here's my card,' Rossi said, placing her details on his desk in front of him. 'If you remember anything else, if there's something you want to tell us later, get in touch.'

'I will, of course,' Jackson said, reaching across and picking up the card. 'Huh, that's funny.'

'What is?'

'I knew a Rossi, or something similar sounding anyway. Back in first year, he came to a couple of the meetings. Could have been Roserto or Roberto. Rossini? Something like that, I think. Can't imagine there are many Italians in Liverpool.'

'More than you think,' Rossi said, her pulse quickening. She glanced at DC Kirkham, who was busy packing up his stuff. 'Used to be a little Italy near Lime Street, you know.'

'Hmmm,' Jackson said, his brow furrowing as his face creased up in concentration. 'His name was Vincent or Victor. One of the two.'

'Can't help you,' Rossi said, heart hammering against her chest. 'Well, I think we have enough here, don't you, Jack?'

Kirkham looked at Rossi then at Jackson, frowning a little. 'Yeah, I guess so.'

'If we need anything else, we'll be in touch,' Rossi said, standing up and turning to face Jackson. She shook his proffered his hand. 'You have been very helpful.'

'I'll send something to the family. It seems right to.'

Rossi was already halfway out the door and didn't respond. She was too busy wondering what her brother had become involved in. Her heart rate didn't decrease as they made their way to the car, or on the drive back into Liverpool. Just the single thought running over and over in her mind.

Don't be involved in this, Vincenzo. Don't be involved in this.

Twenty-one

It was mid-afternoon by the time they had all reconvened back at the station. Murphy was chewing on the last bit of his sandwich, putting off the inevitable march over to DCI Stephens's office and presenting the mess of the case they had so far.

'At least we have names to go through now,' Rossi said across the desk to him. Murphy was still a little annoyed by her lateness that morning, but was more concerned by what he was sensing from her now. There was something going on behind the DS's eyes, but he couldn't work out what it was.

'That's definitely an avenue to explore,' Murphy said, putting his suspicion to one side. There was more to worry about right now. 'Along with the fifteen million other things that seem to be going on.'

'No suspect, though,' Rossi replied, swiping her hair away from her face. 'That's an issue.'

'You're telling me. All we seem to have at the moment is a bunch of blokes looking like dickheads in bow ties, a girl turning up at the parents of the victim saying she's been raped, and a sex worker explaining in great, horrible detail how her blood turned up at his apartment. I wouldn't exactly be surprised if this whole thing started to get worse before it got better.'

'One thing at a time? The usual?'

'The usual, yeah,' Murphy replied, gathering his notes up and accepting the inevitable. 'I'll speak to the boss and then we'll have a gathering.'

'A gathering? I like that. Makes it sound like we're going to have an office party or something.'

'You supply the vol-au-vents, I'll bring the cheese and pineapple on the sticks.'

Rossi laughed, but it was only on the surface. There was definitely something going on, Murphy thought, but he put it down to relationship issues again. He stood up and made his way over to DCI Stephens's office, taking in a deep breath before knocking and entering.

'David, what's the latest?'

No preamble, straight into it. Murphy usually preferred that, but at that moment he was hoping for at least a few more seconds to try and make sense of what he was about to say. No such luck.

'It's all a bit of a mess,' Murphy said, deciding honesty was the best course of action. 'I know more about this guy, but none of it's pretty.'

'Let me have it,' DCI Stephens said, leaning forwards on her desk, fingers intertwined in front of her.

Murphy gave her the whole lot, every detail they had discovered so far. He paused every now and again to answer a question or three from DCI Stephens. When he had finished, she looked as confused as he felt.

'So, he was a bastard.'

It was a statement rather than a question, but Murphy still replied. 'Seems to be that way. I'm guessing he was picking up prostitutes and treating them in the same manner as the one we spoke to earlier. Must have been his *thing*.'

'Everyone has something.'

'Yeah, well this is a bit different. Regards how it plays into his murder . . . I can't say yet.'

'Working theory?'

Murphy pursed his lips and sucked on his teeth. 'Could be that he got involved with the wrong sex worker. Someone took exception to the way in which he used them for what he wanted. This is strong violence being used against them, after all. Laura knows a woman caught on camera nearby on the night we think he went missing. We're trying to track her down as we speak. Uniforms knocked at last known address, but there was no answer. There's also the question about the girl who turned up at Sam Byrne's parents' house.'

'Said she was raped,' DCI Stephens said, leaning back in her chair and folding her arms. 'Possible that it could be a revenge for that?'

'If we have learned anything recently, we should be open to any possibility.'

'True enough,' DCI Stephens said, looking past Murphy at the wall behind him. 'You know Butler isn't going to like any of this, right?'

'With all due respect, boss, I'm not really bothered what he thinks about what we uncover.'

'Yeah, well, I think we both know he'll want to keep as much of this out of the press as possible.'

'Not my call,' Murphy replied, shifting in his seat and glancing towards the door. 'It won't come from me, unless we need it to.'

'What do you mean?'

'Well, for example, if we decide it is something to do with what was happening at that apartment, we'll need to speak to anyone who may have experienced what the others have. In that case, we'll have to put out a call for more witnesses.'

'Yes, we can cross that bridge when we come to it. Do we have any kind of timeline yet? Maybe that'll narrow things down a bit more.'

'We have a working model of one,' Murphy said, thinking of the dates and times marked up on the murder board, hardly any of which had been confirmed. 'To be honest, we're in the dark regarding most of his movements since Friday last week. ANPR didn't pick up his car until yesterday morning, which could mean he was either driving around out of sight, or his car didn't move for four days.'

'Last seen leaving the office on Thursday, not seen at his house in the meantime?'

'Uniforms visited his neighbours up there, but they hadn't noticed anything out of the ordinary. To be fair, the houses are so set apart that it doesn't surprise me. It's not likely that you would notice your neighbours coming and going at all.'

'We do have a mess here, don't we?'

Murphy went to reply, then thought better of it. 'Best we can do is wait for forensics to come back on the body. Post mortem wasn't much help, but we haven't had anything back from them yet. Let's hope there's something there that gives us a new lead.'

'I think we have more than enough here to start shaping the investigation. Tell me more about this university thing.'

'Well, this is more Laura's wheelhouse,' Murphy said, glancing towards the door once more, wondering if he should pull her in. 'There was some sort of club that he was a part of, which apparently gained a bit of a reputation. Laura seems to think there's more to it, but I'm not sure how it will relate to this case now.'

'What kind of club was this?'

'From what we can gather, some kind of private club which had only a few members at first, but they became quite influential. Sort of like one of those things they have down south, you know, MPs and prime ministers getting into positions of power because of who they know, et cetera. Not sure how successful it was, being in Liverpool and about as far from those places as it's possible to get, but it sounds like its members had a bit of a reputation. Connections from outside who could help them secure well-paid jobs, influential families smoothing any *exuberance*, from what we can tell. Besides Sam, the other member that we know about works in the legal department of some sort of investment bank or whatever it is. We're tracking down the others now.'

'For what reason?'

It was a good question, one which Murphy didn't really have an answer for. 'Covering every angle,' he said eventually, going for something safe as a response. 'If there's something in his past which has caught up to him, seems right that we find out more about this university stuff. We're also looking into the constituency where he was standing for MP. See if there were any issues with locals, that sort of thing.'

'Some headcase who didn't like him?'

Murphy shrugged, holding his hands up in mid-air. 'As I said, covering every angle. I agree, for what it's worth. I don't think it'll be something as simple as that. Seems much more personal.'

'There's also the matter of where he was during the weekend.'

Can't argue with that, Murphy thought. 'We're working on it. That's all I can tell you.'

'It's enough, I suppose,' DCI Stephens replied, smoothing down her hair with one hand. 'I'll let Butler know, so he can update the press with whatever info he deems appropriate.'

'Happy not to have to deal with that at the moment. Just another headache.'

Murphy left soon afterwards, crossing back to his desk and slumping into his chair. Rossi gave him a look, but he just shook his head.

'Got some good news if that helps?' Rossi said, standing up and bringing a few leaves of paper around to his side of the desk. 'We've tracked down a couple of the guys from the club Simon Jackson told us about. Hopefully we'll have the rest shortly.'

'What do we know so far?'

'Not a lot,' Rossi replied, leaning against his desk and dropping the papers in front of him. 'Just last known address, occupation, the surface stuff.'

'This name rings a bell,' Murphy said, pointing at a name in the middle of the list of eight. 'Timothy Johnson?'

'He went by Tim, apparently,' Rossi replied, taking her phone out of her pocket. 'Haven't got to him yet. What are you thinking?'

'Tim Johnson . . . not exactly an unusual name. Probably someone else.'

'Google's not exactly helping me out,' Rossi said, giving him a quick glimpse of her phone and the results of a search. 'I'm sure we'll find out soon enough.'

'Paul Wright and James Morley,' Murphy brought up their respective entries on his computer screen. 'Both have minor records.'

'That'll be why we found them so fast. Both had cautions for public indecency, which gives you a bit more of an idea of what this club was really into.'

'I can already tell I'm not going to be impressed,' Murphy said, gritting his teeth together.

'Let's just say the two of them were close enough to invite someone else to get in between them and they were caught in public doing so.'

Murphy grimaced, reading between the lines was more than enough for him. 'Right, great, and this was when?'

'Seven years ago, whilst they were still at university. Which leads me onto another question . . . do we approach the uni about this? See if they can tell us any more?'

'Send Hale and Kirkham up there. I'm not sure we need to revisit that place any time soon. It's not like we're their favourite people to deal with.'

Rossi sniggered and sucked in a breath. 'It's been what, three or four years? I'm sure they've forgiven us for being the reason they were two psychology lecturers down after we'd finished with them.'

'Wasn't exactly the best publicity for them,' Murphy said, remembering the events which had occurred a few years earlier. 'Plus, they were harbouring murderers. If you ask me, it was their own fault. Probably should have done a more thorough check.'

'What, make sure they hadn't ticked the box which said "Have you knowingly killed, or planned to kill, a fellow human being?" I'm not sure even the CRB ask that.'

Murphy joined Rossi in laughing. Sometimes, that's all they could do to get through days such as these. 'I suppose not. Anyway, I think we need to concentrate on the events taking place now. I'm not sure what we're going to achieve by bringing Sam Byrne's uni days into this investigation. Unless something else comes up, of course.'

'No problem,' Rossi replied, standing up from the desk. 'I'll hand this stuff to someone else and get back to tracking down the woman from the CCTV. Have we got anything from the apartment block yet?'

'I don't know, Graham was sorting that out.' Murphy turned his chair and looked for DC Harris, spotting him talking to DC Hashem on the other side of the office. 'Graham, got a minute?'

DC Harris looked over and held up a finger. Murphy waited for a few seconds as DC Harris finished speaking to Hashem then wheeled over to his desk. Rossi had returned to her desk now, fiddling with her chair before she sat down.

'Where are we with the CCTV from the apartment block?' Murphy said, turning his chair to face DC Harris. 'Thought we'd have that by now.'

'We have a slight problem with it,' DC Harris said, moving his wheelchair back and forth. 'Turns out it was non-operational from Thursday into Saturday.'

'Really?' Rossi said from across the desks. 'Coincidence or had it been tampered with?'

'Well, they thought it was just a technical issue, but obviously it might be something else now.'

'When did this come up?' Murphy said, gripping the sides of his chair a little harder.

'This morning while you were out,' DC Harris said, his wheelchair coming to a stop as he recognised the change in Murphy's tone. 'Don't worry, I've sent someone out to check up on it. See if we can get anything from it forensically.'

'Good to know that now, but maybe I could be told about things sooner next time?'

DC Harris nodded, looking away from Murphy. 'I was going to,' he said in a low voice. 'Just hadn't had chance.'

'That's fine, but let's try and keep everyone up to date with everything from now on. We've got a tough one here and things like CCTV being tampered with could be important. I need to know about stuff like that straight away.'

'Noted.'

Murphy nodded to himself then glanced over at Rossi. She was pretending not to be listening in to the conversation, but he knew she was taking in every word. Usually she wasn't shy about hiding her nosiness, but here she was pretending not to hear a thing.

It was another weird Rossi-moment to add to the list.

Sometimes, Murphy thought, the idea that there was something such as gut instinct was ridiculous. Other times, it didn't seem so out of the ordinary.

Right then, his gut was telling him something about Rossi. He just wasn't sure what it was.

Twenty-two

There was a growing ball of dread in Rossi's stomach. A knowledge that the path of her life was about to twist and turn, events spiralling out of her control. The clouds turned grey above her, as if they were aware of what was about to happen.

The first droplets of rain began to fall as the familiar bright blue Peugeot pulled to a stop just in front of her. She waited for the driver to shut off the engine, then walked the few yards towards the car. Rossi smiled tightly as the driver's door opened and her brother appeared.

'Didn't think you were coming?'

'Well, I didn't think you were going to wait any longer for me,' Vincenzo Rossi replied, shutting the door behind him and coming round the front of the car. 'Seemed pretty urgent.'

'Well, we'll soon find out if it is,' Rossi replied, sneaking a glance at her brother's face, studying it for any sign of tension. 'You OK if we go to the pub?'

'Depends,' Vincenzo said, loosening his tie a little. 'Is this an elaborate sting, where a bunch of your mates are going to pull me over in a couple of hours and do me for drink-driving?'

'I think you're safe, Cenzo.' Rossi took the lead, moving with pace towards the pub a little way down the street. 'It'd be a massive waste of police time and, besides, I couldn't exactly do that now, could I? Ma would kill me.'

'True. She'd have you on slicing onion duty at the next get together. How is she anyway? Haven't seen her or Paps for a while.'

'Maybe you should go and see them then?' Rossi said, pushing open the door to the pub and making her way inside. She reached the bar and spied a woman serving an old bloke further down. Vincenzo stood at her side, digging around in his pockets for money she knew wouldn't appear. 'They're serious about this restaurant thing, you know? Papa thinks it'll be good for them to have something to do in retirement. Keep telling them they're in their sixties and could probably do without the stress, but you know what they're like.'

'I haven't eaten properly in a while, so I'm probably due a visit.'

Rossi finally got the barmaid's attention and ordered for the two of them before Vincenzo had chance to say anything. A fiver didn't cover the cost of the two pints, so she had to scrabble around for some change in her jacket. Vincenzo took the drinks over to a table in the corner.

There was still a hint of the heartbreaker about Vincenzo, Rossi could see. The lines on his face were more prominent than she remembered, and there were more and more flecks of silver at his temples, but that smile had been the cause of many a tearful girl appearing at the front door of their home when they were growing up. She had lost friends because of her brothers – good friends at that – but that was just the way of things. Vincenzo wasn't the worst of her five brothers – that had been Antonio – but he had a well-earned reputation in the area they had lived. He had that twinkle in his eye still, but sitting across from him now, she also saw something else. The dark rings under his eyes, the wince as he lifted the pint glass to his lips, the stare he kept giving the exit.

'You all right?' Rossi said, slipping her jacket off and placing it on the empty seat between them. 'Seem a bit off today?'

'Yeah, I'm fine,' Vincenzo said, attempting a smile which did little to convince Rossi. 'Tired, that's all. Work has been ridiculous lately. It's all good though. What's up with you? Not often you want to speak to me. Usually if you need one of the boys you go to Gino.'

'It's not me that needs anything,' Rossi replied, taking a long swig from the pint in front of her. The lager was flat, only a whisper of head at the top of the glass, but she barely noticed. 'I wanted to talk to you about something.'

'Sounds serious . . .'

'Could well be. I'm not sure yet. Depends how this goes.'

Rossi watched Vincenzo closely as he drank from his own pint. There was no tremble to his hand, no shaking or nervousness she could pick up. He seemed bemused by her presence, but unwilling to voice it.

'You're going to have to give me something more to go on here,' Vincenzo said, fixing her with his blue-eyed stare. 'Beginning to get a little worried.'

'You were what, thirty-three, thirty-four when you went back to uni?'

'Thirty-four. I wouldn't use the word "back", though. It wasn't like I was ever there when I was younger. If you remember, I wasn't the most likely Rossi to ever do well academically. Took me a while to get into that mindset.'

'You did well when you eventually got there,' Rossi said, looking away from her brother. She played with a beer mat, rolling it around the table. 'Keep in touch with anyone from when you were there?'

'Not really,' Vincenzo replied, mumbling his way through the two words. 'Long time ago, isn't it? And I wasn't exactly the same age as most of the people there.'

'I need you to be sure of this. Is there really no one you keep in contact with from back then? This is important.'

'What's this about, Laura?' Vincenzo said, looking at her again. She held his gaze as she waited for him to speak. 'I don't know what you're talking about.'

'Have you been following the news at all?'

There was the slightest bit of hesitation. 'Yeah, course. You're working on the case, I assume?'

'Depends which one you're talking about.'

'Why don't we drop the *stronzate*. What do you want to ask me? Because this is all starting to seem like a trap.'

'Did you know Sam Byrne?'

'No. There, you happy? I was at university at the same time as him, but that's it. Nothing else.'

Rossi felt she knew when someone wasn't telling her the truth and this was one of those times.

Her brother was lying to her.

'Are you sure about that? Only I get the feeling you might have known him. What about Simon Jackson? Do you remember him?'

'What is this?' Vincenzo replied, sitting back and causing his seat to scrape against the floor. 'I'm not going to sit here and be questioned like a criminal. I'm your brother. You should show me a little respect.'

'How about you show me a bit of respect and answer my questions. Truthfully.'

'I'm not listening to this,' Vincenzo said, standing up, his chair scraping back even further. 'Tell Mama I was asking after her and that I'll be over to see her soon. Maybe you can get hold of me and apologise when you feel like it.'

Rossi watched her brother leave. Her hand shook as she lifted the half-empty glass in front of her, necking it in one go. She risked a look around her, making sure no eyes were on the corner of the room where she was sitting.

There was a sense of losing control. That she was opening a box full of things she didn't wanted to see. A box that couldn't be closed.

Her brother was involved. She knew that now. Could read it in every line on his face, every dark swathe underneath his eyes.

She just didn't know to what extent.

*   *   *

Murphy placed the phone back on his desk and turned to face Rossi's empty chair without thinking. He opened his mouth to speak, but then thought better of it. The last thing he needed right then was for the rest of the team to have any evidence he was losing his mind a little.

Which he was, when he went to study the murder board at the back of the office and tried to work out what the hell was going on.

At that moment, all he was sure of was that Sam Byrne was definitely dead, and that was only because he'd seen his dismembered body for himself. Without those pieces, he would have still been checking for a pulse.

'Nothing about this makes any sense,' Murphy said, looking down at DC Harris. Graham had joined him there, waiting patiently for him to speak before saying anything. 'Was there really nothing else CCTV-wise?'

'The Tesco one is the best we have,' DC Harris replied, leaning on one arm of his wheelchair. 'We have some from further away, but with the vic's car likely being in the car park behind the apartment block, it seemed a little redundant. We have the car being driven out of the back street that runs along the building . . .'

'Benson Street . . .' Murphy said, picking up a pen and beginning to write on the murder board.

'Right, Benson Street – which is a one-way street, by the way, something I didn't know – and then onto Renshaw Street. We lose the car pretty soon after that. Whoever was behind the wheel was driving out of the city centre, but I'm not sure what help that is.'

'This is Thursday night, right?'

'Yeah,' DC Harris said, picking up his pen as Murphy stood poised with his own in the air. 'Late Thursday, into Friday morning possibly.'

'Right, so we have three full days, before he's killed some time on the Sunday night.'

'Dead at least seventy-two hours, according to the post-mortem report, so that's correct.'

'Three full days, so where was he? No outside contact, his phone is off, so no pings off any towers.'

'Not just off, battery and sim card removed.'

'Good point, so wherever he goes from the apartment, it's highly likely it wasn't too much time before he met with his killer. No pings from what time that evening?'

DC Harris didn't even look up. 'Eleven twenty-three p.m.'

'I'd kill for a memory like yours, Graham.'

'Bit inappropriate, given what we're talking about here. Can't be too careful in this PC world.'

'I always preferred Dixons myself. Anyway, it's pretty likely, given what happened to the CCTV at the apartment block, that he was taken from there. We don't know where, or by who, but at least we know that for certain. I can't see it being by choice either.'

'What time did you see the prostitute Rossi recognised on the CCTV?'

'About ten, I think. Maybe ten thirty. Not sure, but that sounds about right.' Murphy really did wish his memory was better. DC Hashem joined them at the board, leaving DCs Hale and Kirkham talking amongst themselves.

Murphy opened the file he'd been holding and leafed through the information inside. 'Eight names, all in a close-knit group at university, what do they have to do with this?'

'My guess,' DC Harris said, taking the CCTV logs from Murphy's proffered hand, 'is probably nothing. We're being sidetracked by extraneous info. I think we need to concentrate on the prostitute. If she was there at that apartment – and given Sam Byrne's previous, it's likely she was – then she'll be the last person to have seen him alive.'

'Rossi is working on finding her now,' Murphy replied, staring at the names of the seven men Sam Byrne had been friends with while at university. 'Quite a few people we've spoken to has mentioned this group he set up at university. There must be some reason for that.'

'Throw the names up there anyway,' DC Hashem said, cutting in to the conversation. 'Can't hurt.'

'Suppose not,' Murphy replied, smiling at his new favourite DC. Sometimes you just take a shine to people. 'We need to track them down anyway. See if they've been in touch with him.'

Murphy wrote the names quickly, stepping back and clicking the lid on the pen when he was finished. 'The most important thing is tracking down that woman. Graham is– Where are you going?'

DC Hashem had made some sort of noise and scurried off. Murphy saw her rush over to her desk and almost send her chair flying as she tried to sit down on it.

'Something has got into her the last couple of days,' DC Harris said, turning to face Murphy. 'I'm telling you, they're getting younger and more clumsy by the day.'

Murphy wasn't listening, instead watching as DC Hashem began clicking furiously on her laptop. He walked over to her, still holding the marker pen and file in his hand.

'How old was Sam?' DC Hashem said as Murphy reached her side. She wasn't looking at him, eyes fixed on the screen in front of her.

'Twenty-seven,' Murphy replied, one hand on the back of her chair as he leaned in to see what she was looking at. 'Who's that?'

There was a photograph of a man on the screen who looked vaguely familiar. He was in his mid-twenties with scruffy hair. His face was thin, drawn, as if he hadn't slept in a good week or so.

'Meet Tim Johnson.'

Murphy turned and checked the list of names he'd just scrawled on the board. 'That was quick.'

'We did him last year. I'm surprised you don't remember the case . . .'

'There's a fair few in the city. I can't keep up to date with all of them.'

DC Hashem turned towards Murphy, causing his arm to slip off the back of the chair.

'We did him last year . . .'

'You've said that . . . what for?'

'Murder.'

*   *   *

Vincenzo Rossi pulled over his car as soon as he felt he was far enough away from the pub. He pulled out his mobile phone before leaning back and closing his eyes, breathing hard.

'It's OK,' he whispered to himself. 'Everything will be OK.'

He put the phone to his ear once he'd found the right number and pressed dial.

'It's me . . . No, it's OK . . . She knows, which means they all do . . . About the club, about me being involved, I don't know what else . . . Well, I didn't think to ask, did I? Jesus . . . Where are you now? . . . Go to the other place . . . I think it's best . . . OK, see you soon.'

Vincenzo ended the call, pinching the bridge of his nose and closing his eyes again.

Shook his head and wondered how the hell he'd got himself into this mess.

Tim Johnson

It had been a year since she'd been taken, but still that final image rolled around his mind. The pram wheel spinning, the darkness which had engulfed him. The weeks which had followed, the feeling of desperation growing as no one came to his aid. The months on remand for a murder he was certain had not occurred, and had nothing to do with him.

The trial had been a sham. He couldn't believe he could be convicted without a body.

He was a murderer without a victim.

Every day, he wondered if this was the moment they would realise their mistake. Whether today would be the day he would be let free, so he could finally do what he was supposed to.

Find his daughter.

Find Molly.

There was no one on the outside helping him. His family – what was left of it – had turned their backs on him. They believed the lies which had been told, the veil of unreality that had been created around him. The club he had given so much of himself to at university had similarly left him to rot.

A story had been told before he'd had a chance to give a different point of view. He was waiting for the twist in the third act, but they thought his imprisonment was the final scene.

'*This isn't real. How can this happen? I loved her.*'

His solicitor hadn't believed his side of the story. He could tell that just by looking in her eyes. There was a veneer of sarcasm to everything she'd said, an attempt to try and make him come out and say what he'd done, just to make her job easier.

'*We need to find her. Then everything will be OK. She has Molly. It's obvious.*'

Back on that cold night, a year earlier, he hadn't known that he wouldn't be able to walk free again. That it would be the last time he would have the choice to do as he pleased. Taking away someone's freedom, for something they hadn't done . . . there was little he could think of that was worse.

'*I'm not lying. I'm not mentally ill. I don't have any issues. She exists. They're lying.*'

He had been put in the back of that car, watched the lights fade around him, and had almost accepted his fate. When they had begun to question him, he had simply told the truth. He had told the detectives all about his and Lauren's relationship – the truth this time. He had thought that would help, but it only made their eyes grow darker as they looked at him.

'*I haven't done anything wrong. I shouldn't be here. You have to help me. I don't care if I'm in prison for the rest of my life . . . please, you have to find Molly.*'

He had started to realise what was happening during the second interview. The room wasn't what he had been expecting – the cold, bare walls designed to feel constricting, the metal chairs, the detectives stood over him screaming at him for the truth . . . those hadn't existed. It was almost like a small office, albeit one without windows. A large table stood between him and the two people who would be the only people he would speak to for days. They looked like normal people, just two random strangers that you'd pass on the street. They didn't look like hardened investigators. They hesitated, stammered, mixed up their words, just like regular people.

They would take his life away.

'It's ridiculous. How can they say what they've been saying? There isn't even a body. None of this makes any sense.'

On and on, for hours and hours, asking the same questions again and again. It was relentless. Tell the story, tell it again, tell us a different story. Hell was repeating yourself over and over, with no reward for what you had to say. It hadn't taken him long to realise what they were thinking.

'Molly is real. Lauren is not dead. She has taken my daughter and framed me for this. I don't know why. She hates me for no reason. I don't understand any of it.'

Questions would start with Molly. What was she like? How had she looked the last time he'd seen her?

That single image would return constantly. The pram wheel spinning and turning and circling, making him dizzy and sick as it moved around his mind.

Within a few hours of that first day in that police station in South Liverpool, he had begun to see what was going to happen to him. They'd shown him pictures of bloodstains on the ground. They'd shown him ripped pieces of fabric, clumps of discarded hair. They'd asked him about those things as if he knew what the answers were.

He'd tried to be honest. To be unaware of what they were implying. It had been too late, though, they had formed the story in their own minds and were only wanting it confirmed by him.

'*This can't be real. It can't be happening. You have to stop this. I don't care if my DNA is there. I don't care if you've found a weapon, I didn't do it.*'

He would come back to Molly and ask his own questions. They would bat them back as if they didn't mean anything.

They had waited until the second day before they dropped the bomb.

Molly didn't exist. She was a figment of his imagination. A story he had invented to help him get away with the murder of a woman whose name wasn't really Lauren. The woman was named Irenka Dubicki, and she was missing. Some Polish immigrant. According to them, she had worked close to where he'd lived and he had become obsessed with her, creating a life which didn't exist. He was another lowlife, another statistic. Another man who had killed a woman he supposedly loved.

Maybe there had been a relationship, they'd said, but it was nothing like what he'd told them it had been. There were no witnesses to attest to the fact that they'd been together that long.

They had told him that they met men like him every day. Someone who had gone too far. One argument too many. He had invented a story about a woman called Lauren and a daughter called Molly, only because he had been scared of being discovered. Maybe because the guilt over what he had done to Irena Dubicki was too much to take. That was all.

'*Why would I make up a story about having a daughter? It makes no sense. None of it. The story doesn't look right at all. Surely you can see that?*'

It didn't matter. They had evidence. They had no body, but that didn't matter. They had motive, they had opportunity, they had Irena Dubicki's DNA and blood on a knife. The body of Lauren, or Irenka, as they were now calling her, had disappeared.

Tim had just wanted the story to stop.

There was no Molly. There was only the sick mind of a killer.

That was their story.

How could he argue against it? He didn't use social media, he didn't keep in close contact with anyone outside of his house. He didn't have friends, he had acquaintances. He had turned his back on the close-knit group he had been a central part of at university and he'd tried to start again. No one knew he had met Lauren and become a father.

He'd thought Lauren was his way of escaping his past. He had been wrong.

He couldn't escape his past.

It was karma. He was paying for mistakes he had made. He could feel that on one level.

On another, it was just another example of the people he had come to hate. A gender which had caused nothing but hurt and agony for him in his life.

'*You're just like the rest of them. Like that fucking Muslim bitch who arrested me in the first place. You're not going to help me. I'm going to rot here and you'll be happy about that. This trial is a sham. I'm going to be sentenced to life and you'll move on and not care what happens to me afterwards. I'm going to die here, you know that, I know that. And no one cares. They bought the lies and deceit and that's me done for.'*

He had no hope. He was just another statistic. Another innocent man jailed for something he hadn't done.

How many more of him were out there? How could any man believe anything they were told if this was where they ended up?

He wasn't a father any more. He wasn't a loving partner.

He was a killer.

That's all people would see when they looked at him. His future was behind prison walls, with no freedom.

No way out. No way back.

Gone.

IN THE BEGINNING

Formless and Empty

The pain wasn't supposed to be real. It wasn't supposed to exist. There had been moments when she believed that. That the pain she felt wasn't authentic. That it was just a figment of her imagination.

She hadn't expected it to hurt, deep inside her. A lingering, dull ache. Not something that would live with her for years after. A burned memory she would carry with her across years of brokenness and disappointment.

Pain was something other than hurt. She knew that now. There was a whole other level of agony she could experience, which made the rest of her experiences in life fade to nothingness in comparison.

She couldn't look at herself in a mirror for very long any more. She struggled to look people in the eye, afraid of what they would see staring back at them. She didn't like the same things she had before that night: TV programmes, films, music. There was a black hole within her now that she didn't think would ever be filled.

It hadn't started like that.

University was supposed to have been her chance to become something more. A way out of her boring life. An opportunity to find out who she really was as a person, to cultivate a personality which would last into adulthood.

It was also supposed to have been fun. It was, for the first few months – the lectures becoming of secondary importance as she made friends and had nights out in Liverpool. A group of them had formed – all from different parts of the UK, coming together in a strange city, helping each other become accustomed to the strangeness of being away from home. They'd been living in the same student accommodation, all hiding in their own rooms for the first week, before tentatively coming together in the communal area during the first semester.

Learning to make friends all over again, like the first week of secondary school.

She had been studying politics and international business, deciding early on that she had probably made a mistake. The other students on the course all seemed to be much more knowledgeable than her – with the added caveat that the lecturer seemed to want to skew things to a left-wing perspective unfortunately – but there were some enjoyable parts of the course. She just had to look for them a little harder. She wasn't about to give up, she was there for a reason, even if some days she forgot what that reason was. Her father had instilled in her the importance of university education and she was always willing to accept what he had to say.

The girls she lived with had made a pact early on not to discuss personal politics. They would rail against injustices and perhaps touch on ways of dealing with them, but it never went further than that. They all had the privilege of making that choice, of course. They knew that.

She had become aware of the Abercromby Boys Club during her first week of university. The group was well established by then, its members refusing to wear what other students wore. Instead, they were always decked out in posh suits with never a hair out of place. Over the weeks of her first term, she'd noticed them here and there, on campus and in town. They were almost insidious, blending into the background one minute, taking over the next. She would be working in the library, only to look up and see them take over an entire bank of desks. They had a certain look to them, which marked them out from the people around them. They were hated by so many, but it was only jealousy. Everyone wanted to be connected to them in some way.

'*I don't get it. They look like absolute idiots. Why would anyone speak to them, let alone spend nights out with them?*'

'*I don't know, I think they look all right. It's nice to see them make an effort.*'

'*You like the suits? Even the ones with bow ties they wear?*'

'*Makes them look sophisticated.*'

'*Remember, underneath that suit, they're still teenage boys. Only one thing on their minds.*'

They were a curiosity she'd wanted to learn more about. She'd noticed a few of the lads on her course had joined the club – their dress sense changing overnight, the way in which they spoke to people becoming more arrogant and less friendly.

She'd gravitated towards them, wanting to know more about what they did in those clandestine meetings she knew went on. There was a part of her which had been drawn to them, she'd wanted to know their secret.

It was months before she'd been invited to one of their infamous parties.

She'd begun to earn jealous looks from some of the girls she lived with, while others actively discouraged her from getting closer to the Abercromby Boys Club. They don't understand, she had thought.

She'd wanted to tread her own path, but she'd also understood the importance of being in the correct social circle. She could see those men belonged to something more, were doing something more, and she'd wanted to be a part of it.

She couldn't have foreseen the danger. She didn't make a mistake. It was supposed to be harmless fun.

It shouldn't have been her fault.

The first party had been nothing special. A bunch of students drinking and making fools of themselves – only wearing more expensive clothes and accessories than the other students out that night. What it had taught her was that there was a hierarchy within the Abercromby Club. The upper level of management, or "grandmasters" she had heard them referred to as. It hadn't been difficult to spot them – eight men holding court in their own sectioned-off area of the large party.

There had been something exciting about the whole set-up. These eight men had created something, using money and power to get whatever they desired.

She'd wanted some of that power. That was her goal.

She hadn't made a mistake. Somewhere, deep down, she knew that to be true. Despite what she would hear people say, there wasn't anything she should have to feel guilty. She shouldn't have been blamed for what happened. Saying it was a mistake inferred she bore some responsibility for the pain.

That couldn't be true. She was the victim.

Still, it didn't stop the experience following that night. The pain of it. The haze of her memory wasn't where it was found. There was no pain there. Only flashes of uncertainty, the occasional glimpse of what had happened to her.

Memory is a stranger sometimes. It's something untrustworthy. The experiences she believed she had gone through couldn't be depended upon.

The pain came from what had happened later.

That was what she wanted to rectify. That's what she wanted justice for, not what happened on that night. She didn't know enough, couldn't rely on the firmness of her recollections.

She only had one clear memory. One certainty rising above the fog of doubt.

That had to be enough.

Darkness

There was a time before and a time after. Two separate parts of her life, in which everything was compartmentalised. The memories of the before part were now tainted by what came afterwards. There was no solace to be found in earlier recollections, knowing what followed.

She'd become a different person after that night. It had shaped the woman she became. The experience had altered the fabric of her being, forever noticeable and known.

People say you shouldn't let the awful things that happen to you affect the person you are. That things are best left behind, that you should get over them, move forwards and put it all behind you.

Those people are delusional. It's impossible to forget something which takes away everything you ever believed about yourself.

There had been others who felt she was somehow partly responsible. That she had to accept her behaviour was somehow a factor in what happened.

She had believed those voices for a long time.

These were the facts, as best she could remember them.

Yes, she'd gone to that party willingly. Yes, she'd wanted to become involved with certain people there, in order to be in with the right people. Yes, she may have had too much to drink that night. Yes, she'd dressed to impress, provocatively and without worry. Yes, she may have flirted with some of the men and enjoyed the attention she received.

What she hadn't done was say yes to any of the things that had happened after her memory had faded and became fuzzy and distorted.

She wasn't under the impression that consent was something intangible. That it was something which couldn't be understood by seemingly bright and intelligent men. The absence of a forceful no, isn't an embodiment of a yes.

It mattered little. She'd known the whisper campaign had started.

'*You heard about her. Cried rape after she fucked a bunch of them at the same time.*'

'*Fucking slut.*'

'*Makes it harder for proper victims, that does. Just because she woke up and regretted what she did, doesn't make them rapists all of a sudden.*'

'*Yeah, should be ashamed of herself.*'

Everybody knew what had happened that night, even if she didn't. That's how she felt. They were all talking about her and what she had done. She knew what their thoughts were, as well. Had read enough about them online to know the reality of her situation. She was a liar, a slag who was just looking for attention.

She'd had no choice. She'd had to leave. There was no way back for her at that place. All the studying she had done, all the hard work, undone by one night.

Not that it mattered by that point. She was already gone.

She'd left university, unable to take the constant stares and the talking behind her back. It had felt as if she was the centre of an attention she didn't want or need.

She'd felt alone.

Just the one image in her head. One face. She'd filled in the gaps from blurred fragments of memory and what they'd said to her the next day.

'*You were shit, love. Lay there like an ironing board.*'

'*Thought you'd be well up for it.*'

'*Yeah, happy enough at the beginning, weren't you?*'

'*Here's your taxi fare. Do us a favour and don't come back to one of our parties.*'

Confusion and bewilderment. Those were the two points of reference for the morning after. There was no reason for her to be in that situation. No facts she could point to. Just a fractured reality of what had occurred.

Her life had been ruined by one night. The years following had only increased the hurt.

Until now.

She'd never thought of herself as a vindictive person. Someone who had violence within them. That had changed in the days after that night. She'd wanted revenge for everything that had been done to her. For the way they had treated her – like a piece of meat to be fought over by the pride. She'd wanted to inflict pain to make them pay for what they had forced upon her. They deserved payback for what had happened to her.

She hadn't been able to go back home. Her father couldn't hide his disappointment with her. She'd stayed in Merseyside, moving over to the Wirral.

It was there that she'd first seen one of them. Years later. She'd still been rebuilding her life, trying to make sense of what had happened to her. Then, bang, there he was.

Tim Johnson.

Him.

She wanted revenge.

And she was going to get it.

Hovering Over The Waters

There was someone she'd watched a documentary about. A serial killer in America, Aileen Wuornos, who had killed a series of men over the course of a couple of years. There were arguments over why she'd done it, but her opinion was that something had broken inside Wuornos. That she couldn't take what was happening to her on a regular basis any more and she'd decided to fight back. It didn't matter which men were victims of her anger and rage, they were all the same to her.

She had felt that same rage. That same anger. The need to burn it all down. To bring an end to every life, so hers was never in danger again. She wanted to save another woman from going through what she had, but that was only a insignificant part of her thinking. It was more selfish than that.

There was a need to strike back. To punish and get justice for what had happened to her.

She had tried to do it the right way. To go through the correct channels and report everything that had happened to her in the right fashion. Never again. It was a joke, a way of making you feel as if you were doing it the proper way without actually achieving anything.

When it's one word against another, those without power always lose.

The idea of actual justice became foreign to her. She had thought that she was destined to live her life with nothing but hurt and pain to show for what had occurred that night. As her memories returned, the pain grew stronger, turning into agony and suffering.

The dreams were the worst. Beginning with indistinct shapes, blurred and formless, rapidly turning into nightmares. She would wake up, covered in sweat and breathing hard, thinking there was someone in the room with her. Someone in her bed. Someone in her mind.

There was no escape. Not from the thoughts in her own head. Over and over, the same thing again and again.

No escaping the need for something else.

Justice. Payback.

Revenge.

PART THREE

PRESENT DAY

You

You're sure they're closing in. You know they'll eventually work it all out and try to stop you before you've finished.

That means things have to happen sooner. You decide to take action before that net closes over you.

Starting with Matthew Williams.

He's still the snivelling, dribbling wreck he has been for the previous few hours. Oblivious to what is going to happen to him, how these are the last moments of his life. The misery and sin he has inflicted on people will be no more. He will be gone, no longer able to harm anyone else.

Matthew Williams will be missed only by those who don't really know what is beneath the surface of his persona. They don't know about his black core, the darkness which hides there, the evil which lies within the man. Williams himself won't even acknowledge these truths. He would pretend to be a good man for the rest of his days, given the chance. Not that you're going to give him that opportunity.

You're going to kill him. Just like the others.

You know there's no way Matthew Williams will feel

guilt for what he has done. He doesn't believe he has done anything wrong at all.

That's what these men are like.

Matthew Williams's pleas of mercy echo around the abandoned warehouse, driving you crazy with their repetitiveness. The setting is apt; the desolation and despair seeping out of every wall gives the scene even more menace and threat. No one will find you here. You and he are alone.

The ball-peen hammer is heavy, which gives it a sense of finality. It will take more than a single swing, you know that, but it will begin and finish the job.

The only sounds you hear are the sniffing and hitching breaths of Matthew Williams and the crinkle of the white paper suit which covers you. You hold the hammer aloft, the weight of it burning your upper arm.

The hammer makes a dull thud into Matthew Williams's face as you swing it down. Again and again, turning his face into a bloodied mess of bone and blood and brain matter.

You start giggling, then laughing loudly, as you become the only breathing thing left in the building.

Afterwards, you stand over the body, trying to work out where the facial features used to be. The hammer is a dead weight in your hand now – a simple tool waiting to become a weapon again. You feel it drop out of your hand and it clatters to the floor.

You're in the moment, as you've heard people say. Everything is happening now, in the present. It has meaning.

You don't know what to feel. The violence you have inflicted on someone stares back at you and you have nothing left to give.

You wonder if everyone is the same as you. If, when pushed, everyone could do what you've done.

You blink, once, twice, your breathing still heavy and long. You swallow, waiting for the inevitable.

There are no sirens racing towards you. No angry shouts, no one telling you to get down on the floor. You hear nothing but the sound of your own breath. You can imagine there are rats scurrying about in hidden crevices, but you don't hear them.

You look down at your hands, noticing the shaking for the first time. They are different than they had been before. They look misshapen, gnarled, inhuman. There is something animalistic about them, bloody and scarred. You blink and they appear normal again, slightly blood-stained, but otherwise normal.

The wreck of life still lies at your feet, unmoving and broken. You stare at it for a while, waiting for any signs of breathing to return. You know it isn't possible, but still you linger.

You know it won't be too long before the emptiness within you returns.

You begin to pack up, leaving the body for last. You know that will be the most difficult thing to deal with. You don't have to worry about cutting up this body. You planned this one out better. Not as much distance to travel.

You make your way outside, fresh air hitting you with a blast, taking your breath away. You can smell the River Mersey close by, the salty murkiness of it, as it bleeds into and from the Irish Sea. You wonder what it would be like to strip down and feel the cold water on your bare skin. You clean your hands in the moonlight, making sure there's nothing there that would be noticeable from a glance.

You don't feel anything and begin to worry about the lack of emotion. You were supposed to feel something – fear, guilt, horror, responsibility – but nothing was there. You feel numb.

You know it's not enough. Not yet.

There is a list. Eight men, all written down, waiting for their turn.

You have to keep moving forwards. Making a new plan, working out your next step.

You wonder what to do next. You know the answer, but suddenly the weight of the situation begins to bear down on you. You want to sleep, close your eyes and not open them again. You know that can't happen. You know that you have to keep going.

You shove those feelings to one side, leave the note on the top of the empty shell of Matthew Williams and walk away.

Back to what is supposedly normality.

Twenty-Three

'What if it is just a coincidence?' DC Hale said, leaning back in his swivel chair, legs spread wide. 'Two guys who knew each other in university, one gets done for murder, the other ends up dead. Two very different situations, two separate cases. I think we might be putting too much emphasis on this.'

'It's still weird enough to note down, though,' Rossi said, catching up on the previous hours' events on her return. 'I don't like it.'

'There's no pattern,' Murphy said, standing up and moving over to the murder board. 'Yet. Two out of eight is nothing. If we suddenly start finding out the rest of them are in prison or dead, then we can talk.'

'Well, maybe we need to find the others then. Make sure there isn't anything going on? It would have an effect on the investigation if it has anything to do with a club the victim created years ago.'

'True, Jack,' Murphy said to DC Kirkham who was standing next to DC Hale, chalk and cheese if ever there was a comparison to make, he thought. 'You and Hale can get onto that.'

'All six?' DC Hashem said from her own desk. 'Me and

Graham could take some on as well, maybe? Means things go quicker.'

'You're right, Abs,' Murphy replied, shooting DC Hale a look as he exhaled too loudly. 'Only it's five, as we know where Simon Jackson is. You and Graham chase up Paul Wright and James Morley. Graham, just help where you can, because I still want you to look at CCTV images from where Sam's body and car were found. Jack, Mike, you can knuckle down in finding Matthew Williams, Neil Letherby and Christopher Roberts. Find out where they are by this evening, please.'

'What are we doing?' Rossi said, once Murphy had joined her back at their interconnected desks. 'You delegate all this stuff out and leave us with nothing.'

'Oh, we have something,' Murphy replied, giving her a smirk. 'We're going to see the woman you recognised.'

*   *   *

Two prostitutes in one day, Murphy thought. His standing was really going up in the world. They drove towards Liverpool 8, the Toxteth area of Liverpool, the roads around them becoming quieter as they left the city centre, Murphy tried to put what they had learned in previous hours out of his mind.

'All that matters is her story now,' Murphy said, almost to himself. 'Nothing else.'

'She was potentially the last person to see him alive. That's if I'm right, and she saw him at all, of course.'

'Sounded like she did when I spoke to her on the phone,' Murphy said, slowing down for a set of traffic lights on the A561 – which Murphy couldn't help but call the Speke Road, even if he was miles away from the town where he'd grown up. The road, which lay parallel to Riverside Drive on the banks of the Mersey, ran from the city centre dissecting the city and various smaller towns as it did so. Murphy looked out the window at his surroundings. There was a large Tesco store on his left, as there always seemed to be these days, and a bloke walking an aggressive-looking Staffie. The man's trackie/black shoe combination wasn't really working for him but the dog was probably enough to stop anyone from telling him that.

Murphy drove through the lights and turned left onto Melville Street, pulling into Peel Street a couple of minutes later. A sea of purple bins lined the street, waiting to be either picked up or moved from the roadside by the residents.

'Not bad houses, these,' Rossi said, waiting for Murphy to turn off the engine as he parked up. 'Wish they'd do something about the whole area.'

'Don't hold your breath on that one,' Murphy replied, straightening the car and parking up. 'It's a flat anyway. All of these houses are probably the same now. Divided up and let out. It's the new retirement plan. Wish I'd bought a load myself a few years back.'

'Do they still sing that Robbie Fowler song on the kop?'

Murphy remembered the old song which he'd sung himself at Anfield – the home of Liverpool Football Club – to the tune of 'Yellow Submarine'.

We all live in a Robbie Fowler house, a Robbie Fowler house, a Robbie Fowler house.

'Not that I've heard in the past few years. And his name is God, thank you very much.'

There were a few new-build houses on the street, but for the most part, it was a glorious mix of pre- and post-war architecture, revealing the dichotomy of a city still clinging on to the past whilst trying to move forward into the future.

Murphy waited for a group of three women to pass him, all of them giving him the eye as they walked by. Not the nice kind either. It was the *we-know-what-you-are*-type stare, which spoke of the area's long-held grievance against the police.

'This one?' Rossi said, joining Murphy and looking briefly towards the women, who had begun to speak in low voices now they were further away. 'Looks a bit nice for her.'

'Have you not been here before?' Murphy replied.

'No, I only dealt with her at the station.'

'Well, then, yeah, this one.'

They climbed the steps and looked for Tania Waites's name by the entrance buzzer. Murphy pressed the button for flat C, waiting for an answer before pressing it again.

Above them, a sash window opened up and a face appeared and disappeared in short measure. 'Yeah?' A tinny voice crackled through the speaker.

'It's DI Murphy . . . David, we spoke on the phone.'

There was a long pause, which went on for so long, Murphy almost pressed the buzzer again.

'Come up,' the voice crackled again.

A buzzing sound came from the door and Rossi pushed it open ahead of Murphy. There was a small hallway in front of them with a staircase directly ahead of them. They made their way upstairs, the creak of every step screeching through Murphy like nails on a chalkboard.

'Might come back here with some nails for those floor-boards,' Murphy said, joining Rossi on the second landing. 'Can't stand that noise.'

'Tania?' Rossi said. The front door leading into the flat had been left open, but no one was there to greet them. 'You in here?'

'Come through,' a voice said from within. Murphy followed Rossi inside, closing the door behind him. There wasn't a hallway as such, just a door leading into the living room.

Rossi pushed that door open as well, making her way inside, Murphy close behind her. The living area was bright, a couple of large sash windows taking up almost the entire length of one wall. Wooden laminate covered all the floors, and a nice modern kitchen adjoined the living room. When it was empty, Murphy imagined it would look fantastic in photographs on Rightmove or the like.

It wasn't empty.

The furniture was sparse, but what there was of it looked like it had been modern back in the seventies. There was a small flat-screen TV perched on a bedside cabinet in the corner of the room. The walls were bare, save for a clock on one wall, which would have showed the correct time around four hours earlier.

Tania was standing by the window with her back to them. Smoke drifted from the cigarette in her hand and out through the open window. The smell of tobacco hit them as they moved further into the room.

'Did you close the door after you?' Tania said, her back still to them. Her accent wasn't Scouse, but there were some traces of Liverpudlian in her pronunciation. 'I don't want anyone else thinking they can just waltz in.'

'You remember me, Tan?' Rossi said, moving across the room to stand near her. 'We met a few months ago.'

Tania lifted her head slowly and glanced at Rossi and nodded. 'Back for another crack?'

'Nothing like that,' Rossi said, staring at the cigarette in Tania's hand. Murphy had given her props for keeping off the habit, but it was difficult when it was in your face. 'I think you know why we're here.'

'Your man back there knows as much,' Tania replied, taking another drag from the cigarette, then letting it fall out of the window to the ground below. Murphy took a step forwards and saw the marks on the back of her neck for the first time. Yellowed bruising, darkened circles around them. Tania covered them with her hand as if she knew he was looking at them.

'Do you want to sit down?' Murphy said. 'We just want to talk to you for a bit.'

'Why not?' Tania said, giving Rossi a tight smile and moving over to the rickety cane sofa. It was the only place to sit in the small space which left Murphy hovering opposite her. As much as a six foot four inch lump could hover, anyway.

'I'm guessing you know why we're here,' Rossi said, perching on the windowsill, which Murphy had decided wouldn't support his weight. She had no such issues, though. 'It's about last Thursday night . . .'

'Of course it is,' Tania said, leaning back in the sofa and crossing one leg over the other. She was wearing tight jeans, but her feet were bare. A low-cut top was covered by a black cardigan, but it slipped to reveal more marks around her throat. 'I was thinking of coming in, but you know how it is.'

'What happened?' Murphy said, thinking getting to the point was probably right for the situation.

'I think you can guess,' Tania replied, removing the cardigan and revealing more skin. Her arms seemed untouched, apart from a few slight marks, but the chest area was worse than Murphy had guessed. 'A punter got too much. Will pay the next two months' rent, though, so there's that.'

'Can you take us through what happened.'

'Got picked up – or should I say, I was taken on a "date", just to cover myself – and he seemed nice at first. Then it went wrong very fucking quickly. What do you want me to say?'

Murphy could see the veneer of guardedness was close to cracking.

'Let's go a little slower,' Rossi said, removing her notebook from her pocket. 'You were picked up from where?'

'Not telling you that. I'm not stupid.'

'Fine, we'll come back to that. Who picked you up?'

'Well, it's good you asked me now, as his face has been everywhere since yesterday, otherwise I wouldn't know. It was that guy that got killed. The MP guy.'

'Right, so he picked you up and took you where?'

'An apartment on Mount Pleasant in town. I thought I was made, you know, because it was a nice bit of cash like. Seemed all cool and that, but I should have been on my game. It was a bit too good to be true, but I just got blinded by the fucking Audi and nice suit. I should know better.'

'You went back to the apartment. What changed?'

Tania was silent for a few seconds, her voice a little quieter when she spoke again. 'He did. He was so nice in the car, when he picked me up and that. Then, as soon as we got in that apartment, he totally changed. He was just barely speaking, you know. He asked me to wear something, then took me into this bedroom at the back.'

Murphy knew the story that was coming next and he really didn't want to stand there and listen to it again. It would be the same as the one Vicky had told him that morning. Another tale of sickening violence.

Not for the first time that day, he questioned whether he really wanted justice for Sam Byrne, or if he was just going through the motions.

Twenty-four

Murphy waited for Rossi to finish up at the counter, tutting quietly to himself as she unfurled the plastic covering of the cigarettes and removed one. He took the rubbish from her and placed it in the bin outside as she fiddled with the brand-new lighter.

'You've been doing so well,' Murphy said, walking back to the car as Rossi tried to get the cigarette lit. 'Seems a shame to start back up now.'

'You think I can listen to *merda* like that and not smoke? You must be out of your mind.'

Rossi inhaled another long drag and blew smoke towards the clouds above them. 'What a bastard.'

'Seems to be the prevailing opinion of the guy.'

'I just want to say screw it, let him rot. Whoever snuffed him, good luck to them, all the best. Did us all a bloody favour.'

'We can't do that . . .'

'Would be damn nice to, though,' Rossi said, interrupting between drags of her cigarette. 'He was going to be an MP. *Dio Mio*. Doesn't bear thinking about.'

'I think he would have fitted in quite nicely with that crowd. They're hardly running a monastery down there in that London.'

That earned a grin from Rossi, but it wasn't enough. He could see she was steaming, and he was working out how he could calm her down before returning to the station. Wondered if it was pointless or even needed. 'We can't have people killing someone in our city and then cutting up their body. Doesn't seem the best way of dealing with these issues.'

'No, you're right,' Rossi replied, rubbing her eyes with her free hand and steadying herself against the car. 'Castration would have been enough.'

Murphy winced at the mere mention of it, but didn't argue with her. It wasn't as if he was about to disagree with the idea. It would save a lot of time.

'What now then?' Rossi said, stubbing out the cigarette and immediately removing another one from the pack. 'She doesn't know anything about what happened after she left the apartment and I believed her when she said she hadn't told anyone about what went on. All we have to do is check with the hospital anyway. She said she was there all night. I think this might be a dead end.'

Murphy thought for a second, sticking his hands in the pockets of his long coat. 'It goes on the list of things we need to keep in mind. She didn't really seem the type to just let something like that go, but I don't think she had anything to do with what happened to Sam Byrne.'

Yet another thing.

'It's a pattern, isn't it?' Rossi said, rubbing her eyes again. 'Maybe someone did something about it. A nice vigilante for a change. Would make our job easier.'

'I can't see our big boss being too happy about that story, somehow.'

'Butler can do one if he thinks we're going to sugar coat this for anyone. People need to know what he was like. Might stop those bastards ever trying to get elected in this city again.'

'Not sure that has anything to do with what's going on here ...'

'No, you're right,' Rossi said, bending down to stub out her cigarette on the ground and then tossing it towards the bin. 'They're all the bloody same. Doesn't matter what colour they're representing.'

Murphy waited to see if she was going to light another one, then unlocked the car door when she stood silently by the passenger-side door.

It was only a short drive back to the station, but it felt much longer in the oncoming rush-hour traffic. The radio was playing quietly in the car. Murphy and Rossi listened as the chirpy radio presenter introduced the evening news bulletin. The main story was of no surprise to them.

'Police are still investigating the death of prospective Conservative MP Sam Byrne who was found on Tuesday afternoon. His parents have described Mr Byrne as being someone who was always looking after other people's interest ...'

'That's why he wanted to work for the community, to give something back. He was always thinking of others. The city of Liverpool has lost something with his passing. We have lost our son, but the city has lost someone who would have fought for every hard-working man and woman out there.'

Murphy listened in silence as Arthur Byrne's voice filled the car. Gone was the faltering tone of the previous day, in its place, the Arthur of old. The ex-MP, always ready with a quip or slick sound bite, had returned. Murphy wondered if he was enjoying the spotlight again, or if he would rather be back at home, sitting in his chair and sliding into comfortable retirement.

'*Cazzo,*' Rossi murmured under her breath as Arthur Byrne's voice gave way to DSI Butler's.

'*Anyone with any information, please do not hesitate to get in touch with my officers. This is a sickening and despicable crime and an innocent man has been brutally murdered. We won't stop until we have the perpetrator off the streets of this great city of ours.*'

'Have you heard anything from his campaign people?' Rossi asked, turning off the radio.

Murphy had a sudden jolt, as if something was revealed to him then snatched away. It was the mention of Sam Byrne's office, but something else was nagging at him, a thought he couldn't quite catch. It was beginning to annoy him. 'No, which is very strange. What's the likelihood they're still there now?'

Rossi checked the time on the car dashboard, then pulled out her phone. 'It only just turned five . . .'

'Not sure that matters,' Murphy said, interrupting Rossi as she scrolled through her contacts list. 'It's not like they've got any work on at the moment.'

'You're joking, aren't you?' Rossi replied, lifting the phone to her ear. 'They'll already be working on the next guy they're going to put forward.'

Murphy grunted in response, hoping people would allow bodies to cool at some point before moving on. He remembered whose body it was and decided to get over it.

'Hello, it's DS Rossi here, is that Charlotte? . . . Good, you're still in the office? . . . No, we're just going to pop in, if that's OK? . . . Now . . . OK, great, see you soon.'

Murphy waited for her to end the call. 'Still there then?'

'Yeah, which sounds about right. She's staying there until we arrive.'

It was another half an hour before they arrived back in Waterloo, the day dimming around them. The street outside the shop-cum-office was still packed with traffic. Rush hour was in full swing, but there were still cars jammed bumper to bumper in the parking areas outside the shops on either side of the road.

Murphy managed to squeeze the pool car into a space a little way down from the office, meaning they only had to walk a hundred yards or so back up the road. It was enough time for him to do a little window shopping in the various places still open.

'Has this road ever been that great?'

'Probably at some point,' Rossi replied, moving between two parked cars and waiting to see if the traffic was stationary before stepping out into the road. 'It's hardly like it's going to be anything other than this these days.'

'This' was a collection of charity shops, bookies, convenience stores and a single bookshop – which Murphy actually quite liked the look of, despite not being an avid reader. He was still only halfway through Steven Gerrard's autobiography, with no end in sight.

'It must be popular with some people,' Murphy said, joining Rossi on the other side of the road. 'It's mad busy down here with cars.'

'There must be quite a few commuters. Train station is close by.'

Murphy looked back towards Waterloo train station entrance and shrugged. He let Rossi lead the way towards

Sam Byrne's campaign office and stood behind her as she knocked.

They were let in by Charlotte, the young woman still as fresh-faced as ever, her youthfulness making them both feel tired and jaded in comparison.

'I can't stay long,' Charlotte said, closing the door behind them. 'We've got yet another meeting on this evening.'

'Trying to pick up the campaign again?'

'Something like that,' Charlotte replied, looking at Rossi for a moment before turning away. They followed the young woman into the main office, Murphy looking for and finding Emma at her desk. 'Anyway, what can we help you with? We've said as much as we can already. Didn't think we'd be needed again so quickly.'

'Just a follow up, really,' Rossi said, removing her notebook from inside her jacket. 'We'll talk to you separately to save you some time.'

They had worked that out in the car, the two detectives pairing with the women they had spoken to a couple of days previously. Murphy nodded and waited for Charlotte and Rossi to leave, then walked over to where Emma was sitting.

'How are you getting on?'

Emma eyed Murphy, then turned her chair to the side and picked up a bundle of paperwork. 'Well, it's not been a great week, if you must ask. You know, given my boss has been murdered and cut up. HQ aren't helping much either. They're just worried about losing momentum.'

The woman's bluntness didn't shock him. Everyone experienced grief differently. 'Still think you can win the by-election without Sam?'

'You must be joking,' Emma replied with a tinny laugh. 'He was the only reason we got this far. We're done now. Too much bad press over this whole thing. Whoever comes in won't have the rapport with the locals that Sam had. We may as well pack up now.'

'You won't, will you?' Murphy said, leaning against a filing cabinet near Emma's desk. It shifted slightly as he put his weight on it, making a scraping sound against the floor. He straightened up a little, just in case it was about to collapse. 'They're not going to give up just like that.'

'Of course not, but we all know what's going to happen now.'

Murphy could sense something, a similar feeling of anticipation to the one he had picked up the other day. 'What are you expecting?'

'I think we both know what is going to come out about Sam.'

'Humour me.'

Emma gave him a withering stare, then shifted the paperwork she had set down on the desk to one side. 'He was a bastard. A smarmy one at that, which is the worst kind to be.'

'You were aware of what he was doing in his spare time.'

It wasn't a question. Murphy knew now why she had been so amenable when he'd spoken to her before. She had suspected what Sam Byrne was doing in his private life and didn't want it to continue.

'I knew something was going on. Something he didn't want getting out,' Emma said, unable to look Murphy in the eye. 'What was I supposed to do, though? He was the boss. It wasn't just him I would have to contend with either. It would be the people around him too. I bet you'll never even know they exist, but they're there. Making sure everything runs smoothly, that nothing can come out that might embarrass the party. That's the way these things are run.'

'Why are you here then?'

'Because I believe in the greater good,' Emma replied, still looking away. There was an uncertainty to her answer, which Murphy took to mean she wasn't quite as sure about this belief as she had been a few weeks earlier. 'We needed a candidate like him around here. Someone who could start to have some effect in the area. I know what you're thinking, but for a Tory, his politics were OK. I've supported Labour for the past twenty years, ever since I was sixteen and started being interested in politics. The party isn't the same any more, so I moved to the Conservative Party. I hoped he would stop his extracurricular activities once he was elected.'

Murphy shook his head, not for the first time wondering about the ability of people to leave their morals at the door in pursuit of selfish aims. It was life in the twenty-first century.

'You need to be straight with me,' Murphy said, moving closer so he was now in Emma's eyeline. She still averted her gaze from his, but shrank back a little. 'If there's a chance that what happened to Sam may have something to do with what he was doing either here, or related to here, then you need to tell us.'

'What do you think it could be?'

'I don't know. Maybe someone found out about what he was doing and decided to try and use it to their advantage? Bribe him or something. I need to know if anything out of the ordinary has happened here recently.'

Emma glanced up at him. 'There is something, but he said he was going to take care of it and it meant nothing.'

'What is it?'

'A man came here. Late one evening. I think he thought Sam would be alone, because he'd waited until Charlotte and a few others had left first. He banged on the door and I made Sam open it. This guy came in and started shouting at Sam.'

'What about?'

'How he hadn't changed and that the past was about to come back and haunt him. That he couldn't get away with it any more.'

Twenty-five

Rossi stood in the kitchen, waiting for Charlotte to recover from yet another crying fit. It was becoming a little annoying, but she could understand the young woman's reaction to the situation she had found herself in. Charlotte was still a teenage girl in so many ways, Rossi thought. Real life hadn't really been a problem until now.

'I just don't understand any of this,' Charlotte said between hitching breaths, dabbing at her eyes with a bit of kitchen roll. 'I just came here to help, you know? And now all of this is going on.'

'Is there anything you want to tell me, Charlotte?' Rossi said. She was trying to keep the conversation on track with varying degrees of success. 'About Sam.'

'I don't know what you mean.'

Rossi was becoming a little more impatient by the second. She had sensed that Charlotte was holding something back in their first meeting, and the feeling was stronger now. 'I think there's something you want to tell me.'

Charlotte shook her head, but there was no force to it.

'Are you worried about what will happen if you tell us something? If people within the party find out? What is it?'

'There's nothing . . .'

'You know, Charlotte, I do this every day. This is my job, talking to people in these situations. No one ever wants to talk. We're all the same. We all want the quiet life. We all want to ignore tough issues and act like everything is normal. Well, look around you. This isn't normal. Nothing that's happened in the past week is. I suggest you start talking to me. If you don't . . . well, I can't promise that the outcome will be a happy one.'

Charlotte listened to her speak, eyes wide and puffy from the crying. Her hands were shaking in front of her and she rested them by leaning on the kitchen counter. Rossi waited for her to speak, prepared for another battle.

'He wasn't a nice man,' Charlotte said finally, her voice quiet and almost childlike. 'I'm sorry.'

'Don't apologise,' Rossi said, moving to Charlotte's side. 'I just want to hear the truth. That's what we all want, so we can make sure something like this doesn't happen again.'

'He wanted things from me. Things I didn't want to do. It was endless, the comments, the suggestions.'

'What kind of things?'

'He used to say that he liked the fact that I looked so young. That I was nice and unused. He would ask me if I was still a virgin, but it would be more crude than that. It was constant. He would ask me about my private life in the most disgusting way, but I never said anything about it.'

Rossi tried to keep her cool, but it was becoming more difficult with each passing sentence. 'Did he ever do anything physically?'

Charlotte didn't reply at first, the silence answering the question for Rossi.

'I don't want to say anything more about it,' Charlotte said, not answering the question. 'It was a difficult time for him, there was a lot going on . . .'

'I'm not interested in the excuses he would give, Charlotte. I just want to hear the truth of the man, that's all. He made life difficult for you. His behaviour had nothing to do with what was happening to him.'

'It was just . . . banter.'

Rossi shuddered at the use of her most disliked word in the English language. 'It's amazing the sort of behaviour people try to explain away with the word *banter*,' Rossi said, spitting out the final word with all the venom she could muster. 'He was responsible for his own actions. The only thing I need to know is if it had any relation to what happened to him. Is this behaviour indicative of the man?'

'It was just the way he was with me,' Charlotte said, tears being held back at that moment. 'I don't think he was like that around other people. He had this side to him, which just came out sometimes. He was a good man, underneath it all. Honestly, he was.'

Rossi tried to work out what line of thinking would lead anyone to call Sam Byrne a good man, but failed. The more that was revealed about the guy, the more she really wished she'd never heard the name.

The fact that her brother was involved with him in some way was what really burned, however. She still had no idea how, but the thought that someone she had grown up revering – as she had all her brothers – was somehow linked to Sam Byrne hurt in a way that she didn't think would be easy to recover from.

She needed to know how Vincenzo Rossi was caught up in this mess. Without anyone finding out.

*   *   *

There was a stony silence between Murphy and Rossi as they made their way back to the car. He was too lost in his own thoughts to notice it much, but he was aware of it on the periphery. It was something which was bothering him, but it seemed irrelevant.

'What did Charlotte have to say?' he said, once they were in the car and on the road back to the station. 'She seemed to be upset when she showed us out.'

'It was just more examples of Sam Byrne being the last person who probably deserves any kind of justice,' Rossi said, going on to relate the conversation she'd had with Charlotte. Murphy listened with a growing sense of displeasure, gripping the steering wheel in front of him in lieu of an actual live Sam Byrne to grab around the throat.

'What does it all mean?' Murphy said, once Rossi had finished speaking, glad that the silence had lifted. 'What does it have to do with his death?'

'He was a deeply unpleasant man, probably someone who craved power, just so he could keep raping women.'

'And that got him killed?'

'I think so,' Rossi replied, pushing the button on the side of her door and letting the window down a little. 'We've heard the same thing now from a number of women. Not only did he have no problem in saying the most disgusting things, but they were all framed around one type of fantasy.'

'The young thing?'

Rossi gave him a sharp look, which Murphy accepted. 'Sorry, I know, not the best way of putting it.'

'Damn right,' Rossi said, looking away from him again. 'He liked the sex workers he took back to his apartment to look like young girls. He liked Charlotte because she looked young. I don't know if that has anything to do with his murder, but it's worth thinking about. What if someone got wind of it? Wouldn't be the first time we've had a vigilante in the city.'

'True,' Murphy replied, thinking back only a few years to one particular case. One that had affected his life in a major way. 'I don't feel like that's what is going on here, though. This feels more, I don't know . . .'

'Weird?'

'Well, yeah, but there's something we're missing.'

Rossi didn't answer him, allowing the cogs of his mind to grind into action.

'What about this guy who just shows up one evening? I don't even know how to go about tracking him down.'

'Did she even know when it was?' Rossi said, pausing between gulps from an energy drink.

'Not really. Narrowed it down to a month or so ago. I showed her the picture of Sam and the other members of that club at university. Said she didn't recognise any of them as being the guy.'

'Could just be an angry constituent, I suppose.'

'Maybe we should talk to the guy in prison? Probably has nothing to do with it, but can't hurt, can it? Maybe there's something linking the fact he's in prison and Sam's death. Seems a bit of a coincidence, two out of the eight being indisposed.'

He turned to Rossi, waiting for a response, but she was staring glassy-eyed out of the window to her side. 'What do you think?'

'About what?' Rossi replied, slowly turning her head back to him. 'Didn't hear you.'

'Right, nothing, doesn't matter.'

Back at the station, the mood hadn't lifted much. DC Hashem was still working on finding one of the men on the list, whilst Hale and Kirkham were on the phone to Neil Letherby's partner and someone who might know Chris Roberts respectively. Murphy dumped his keys on his desk, looked over at the boss's office and put his hands on his hips when he saw it was empty.

'Where's she gone?' he said to DC Harris. 'Only just coming up to seven.'

'No idea,' DC Harris replied, rubbing his left eye with the palm of his hand. 'I've been glued to this screen for the past couple of hours. Everything is starting to get a little blurry.'

Murphy walked around to DC Harris's desk, CCTV images on his screen coming into view. 'Anything?'

'Nothing. Sorry. I have gone over and over it, but there's just no clear sighting of anyone. It looks planned to me. Very careful job. They knew where the cameras were, so have managed to either avoid them, or cover themselves sufficiently to make sure they couldn't be recognised.'

'What's the best we've got?'

DC Harris paused the video he'd been studying, clicking open another tab. 'This is it,' he said, moving out of the way of the screen. 'All we can make out is a hunched-up figure over a steering wheel, wearing some kind of black jacket with a hood, or a hoodie, sunglasses and something else covering ninety-five per cent of their face. It's not enough.'

'Keep working on it. Send it over to the forensics team as well. They have the numbers to go through it frame by frame if needs be.'

'No problem.'

Murphy turned to face the office, scanning for anyone who could possibly alleviate the feelings of helplessness which were threatening to overwhelm not just him, but everyone else in the damn room.

He saw DC Kirkham put the phone down and lean back in his chair, covering his face with both hands.

'Jack, what is it?'

DC Kirkham turned in surprise as Murphy made his way towards him.

'Anything?'

'Well, I'm not sure,' DC Kirkham said, standing up as Murphy reached him. 'Could be nothing, but, well, I'm not sure.'

'Doesn't matter, just tell me.'

'I've been trying to track down Chris Roberts – which hasn't been easy, as you can imagine with a name like that – and I think I have. All the details seem to match up.'

'What did he have to say?'

'That's the thing. I couldn't speak to him. He killed himself ten months ago.'

Murphy rocked back on his heels a little. 'OK, that is weird. That's three of the eight names with either prison or death in their lives.'

'That's not the end of it,' DC Kirkham said, breathing a little harder now. 'I spoke to his business partner. The inquest determined suicide, but no one who knew him believed the verdict. There's been some kind of campaign to overthrow the verdict.'

'Right, this is getting a little more interesting. Tell me the details.'

DC Kirkham pulled his notepad off the desk and began reading from it. 'He was found at the bottom of a cliff down south, with marks on his hands and arms. Post-mortem categorised them as looking like defensive wounds at first, but then they found a video on his phone. It was taken as a suicide note.'

'We don't even write those things down any more? Bloody hell . . .'

'It was him, on video, saying he couldn't live any longer, a few more things as well, but ostensibly that the guilt was just too much.'

'Guilt over what?'

'Didn't say and his business partner told me none of his family or other friends could tell anyone what it could be. Local police looked into things, but there was nothing. The family think he was coerced into saying it, but there was no other evidence that could suggest murder, so everything pointed to a suicide.'

Murphy leaned on the back of DC Kirkham's empty chair, steadying himself as it almost tipped over. 'Another coincidence?'

'They're piling up now, to be frank, sir.'

'You're right, they are,' Murphy said, scratching the back of his head. 'Three out of eight . . . I don't like those odds.'

By the next morning, the tally was four, which moved the odds even further out of Murphy's comfort zone.

Twenty-six

It was a month since he'd seen Sam. Now, he was dead.

Vincenzo Rossi felt nothing.

He shouldn't have gone there but things had spiralled out of control and into a situation he'd had no intention of being involved with. He'd stupidly thought Sam would be willing to do something about it all.

All Sam had been interested in was how things would look for him and his campaign to become MP.

Vincenzo had gathered as much information as he could about what had happened to the group since leaving university. Visited them all one by one.

They had no idea what they had left behind. The lives they had destroyed.

One in particular. Someone who couldn't be saved.

He shouldn't be involved in any of this, he thought now. If he could turn the clock back, he would return to that day two years earlier, when she'd first come to him, and stop himself promising anything.

Now, it was all too late. That first meeting had changed all their lives.

No, if he could, he would go back to an earlier date. Nine years ago. That first meeting they'd had in the pub.

He should have stood up as the voice of reason. He was the older member of the group, the one they might have listened to.

Instead, he'd let them carry on. Stood on the sidelines as they grew in number and power. He could have done more back then.

Now, things had gone too far.

He tried her number again, but voicemail kicked in immediately. He hoped it had come to an end. That he could breathe easier and that he didn't have to worry that his sister and a bunch of her copper mates were about to boot his door in and arrest him.

What did they have on him? What evidence could have been left behind?

He couldn't be sure.

Vincenzo put the cigarette in his mouth, a small tremble in his hands as he flicked the lighter and inhaled the first glorious drag.

He knew everything was going to crumble soon. That his world would change forever. His future would be altered and malformed. All the work he had put in to make his life better would ultimately be for nothing.

He would end up in a cell, he thought. Maybe even next to his old friend Tim Johnson. That would be karma right there.

He should have said no. He should never have helped her.

How could he have let her do it all on her own?

Sam was dead. Others were too. And it was his fault. He was to blame for the whole thing.

There was no way around it. It was his responsibility.

They all deserved it. Every last one of those eight men in that club deserved exactly what was happening to them.

'Why do you feel guilty then?' Vincenzo whispered to himself, the smoke filling the car around him. He slid the window down a touch, allowing it to drift out into the night.

There had to be a better way than this, he thought.

A way out.

Twenty-seven

The scene was almost exactly as it had been two days earlier – an open car boot revealing the bloody contents within. Any other time, it was possible that it would have ruined Murphy's day, but it was almost as if he'd been expecting it.

Now, there was another dead body to deal with. It was becoming sickeningly normal. The sight of the blood, gore and guts; he felt like he could become immune to it all. The horrors of the wider world had already been on his doorstep for the previous few years. Each time, it was supposed to horrify and disgust, but it was now becoming . . . expected.

Secretly, wanted. Needed. The easiest way to stop a killer was for them to make a mistake. Another corpse increased the possibility they may have made one.

'At least he's had the decency to leave us something this time.'

He didn't respond to Rossi, instead reading the note which had been passed to him. It was in a plastic see-through sealed bag. Block capitals, neat and precise.

I AM A DIRTY RAPIST KILLER

Then, in smaller script underneath.

FIVE DOWN – THREE TO GO

'Who's the other one?'

'Other one what?' Rossi said, looking back at him. 'Going to have give me more than that.'

'It says five. If we count the guy in prison, Sam, this guy and the one who committed suicide, that's four. Total. This says five.'

'Got me. One of the ones we haven't tracked down yet, I suppose. We hadn't tracked down James Morley, Paul Wright or Matthew Williams when we left last night, from memory.'

'I wonder if this is one of them,' Murphy said, walking away from the boot to the front of the car. 'Another nice car. Fifteen plate, so can't have been cheap given the make.'

'They all seem to have been doing well for themselves.'

'Until recently.'

'The body hasn't been cut up this time.'

'You're right,' Murphy replied, moving backwards slowly and taking in the entire scene. 'Easier to move.'

'What's that?'

'The car is closer to where the murder took place. Didn't have to move the body very far at all. Sam Byrne was dismembered for ease of transport.'

Rossi was pulled aside by a uniform. The scene around them was becoming more crowded. Tape had been strung up around the area, but it did little to stop people coming up to look, including the local media.

A throwback to its era as one of the main shipping docks in the country, there were warehouses lined up further out of the city centre, often disused and abandoned. Some attempts had been made to make use of some of them, but there were many which were left to ruin. Large, red brick buildings which loomed over the Mersey, dotted along Regent Road. A throwback to another era. Whereas some, like the Stanley Dock tobacco warehouse, had been earmarked for regeneration projects. Destined to become home to yet another apartment block, unaffordable to most in the region probably. Others weren't so lucky.

Murphy stood with his hand against his forehead, shading his eyes from the sun which had decided to make an appearance that morning. He glanced across at the car outside the warehouse again and shook his head. The boot was horrific, but the bloodier scene inside the building said much more.

'We've got an owner for the car.'

Murphy turned to find DC Kirkham standing behind him, one hand in his pocket, the other hanging limply by his side.

'It's Matthew Williams. I'm guessing it's probably not a coincidence.'

'I wouldn't imagine so, no. So that's the connection. We were right to have the suspicion.'

'I guess so. I'm not sure what we do with it, though. It doesn't seem like it's much to go on.'

Murphy sighed, wondering if there was ever going to be a time when people around him would be more imaginative.

'Think about it,' he said, taking DC Kirkham to one side, away from the uniforms milling about. 'We've got a list of eight men, all part of the same group at university. They've been involved in things we're not yet aware of, but we know at least one woman who showed up at Sam Byrne's parents' house saying she had been raped. We already know what this sort of university club can be capable of, don't we?'

'Well, if that pig story was even half correct, with the prime minister–'

'Yeah, exactly,' Murphy said, cutting in before DC Kirkham got any more graphic. 'So, let's say these men have done something which leads to someone wanting revenge. Is it not possible that's what we're seeing here?'

Murphy showed Kirkham the note he was still holding, the words sketched on the paper. 'We need to find the girl who went to Sam Byrne's parents. I can't see any other reason for that message to be here, can you?'

DC Kirkham opened and closed his mouth.

'Good, glad you agree,' Murphy said. 'Take Hale and put everything you can into finding the girl. Go back and check reports, which I guarantee won't mention any of their names. Just look for reports of sexual assault and rape involving university students around that time. Hopefully that information will still be on file. Laura and I will go for a little visit.'

'Who to?'

'Our man in prison. I think it's time we heard what he has to say.'

*   *   *

Whilst Matthew Williams's broken body was being removed from the scene of his discovery, Murphy and

Rossi were on yet another motorway, on the way to meet Tim Johnson.

'Surprised he wasn't in Walton.'

'They seem to ship our murderers out to Manchester these days,' Murphy replied, shifting in the passenger seat as Rossi drove. 'And we get their ones, of course. It's like a shit exchange programme.'

'Didn't have a problem with getting in there. Tim was eager to speak to us, apparently.'

'Good, let's hope that bodes well for what we're going to be asking him.'

Rossi shaped as if to speak, then stopped herself. She paused a few seconds, Murphy waiting for the words to come out.

'What is it we're going to be asking him, exactly? Only, I can't imagine a convicted murderer will cooperate with people like us.'

'Depends if he still wants to say he's innocent,' Murphy replied, trying to read the file containing information on Tim Johnson and his conviction as Rossi speeded up and passed another car on the motorway. 'He might want to be seen as helping us out, to make himself look better or whatever.'

'I don't know. Seems like a long way to go for probably not very much. Feel like we should be back at the scene. The body probably hasn't even got to the morgue yet and we're not even in the same bloody city as it.'

Murphy had stopped listening, reading the notes on Tim Johnson's case instead. 'Convicted without a body, which isn't very usual. Especially as it was apparently only a year ago that the victim went missing . . .'

'Missing kid or something, wasn't there?'

Murphy hummed in response. He was trying to remember the case himself, but it had been dealt with by another division in Liverpool. 'I remember bits of this, but it's not very clear. Guy reports a baby being kidnapped in Sefton Park, claimed it had been snatched with the pram he was pushing. It was big news for about two days, then it just disappeared. Next thing you know, the guy – who I'm presuming is Tim Johnson – was arrested and charged with murder. He had moved over to Liverpool in the week prior, from over the water. Some woman over there was killed or something.'

'So, the murder takes place over on the Wirral?'

'Apparently so.' Murphy continued to read, shaking his head more vigorously with each turn of the page. 'This is crazy, even for here.'

'What's that?' Rossi replied, glancing across at him.

'It's a bizarre story,' Murphy said, trying to work out where to start. 'It gets really weird from the time he was charged with the murder. Turns out the baby didn't exist. He'd made the whole thing up: the kidnap, the fact he had to escape the mother . . . everything. They were working on the theory that guilt over him killing this woman had sent him over the edge.'

'*Mannagia* . . . that is bizarre. I remember him being up in court, but missed that. Surprised it wasn't bigger news.'

'I imagine his family managed to keep most of it out of the papers. According to this, his father worked on Fleet Street for a long time. Some favours being called in there maybe.'

'Still, it's a juicy story. So, no body?'

'No, just a lot of blood, which indicated that there was

a catastrophic event, in which survival would be almost impossible. They could pinpoint movements, place Tim at the scene with DNA, all kinds of stuff. Looks like they're not expecting a body to turn up, though. They reckon it was ditched into the sea.'

'Top end then, rather than the Mersey?'

'Exactly,' Murphy replied, turning over another page of photographs. 'They said he had access to a boat of some sort. Took it out from Moreton shore a couple of miles, weighed down her body and dumped it over the side into the Irish Sea. Unlikely they'll ever find it.'

'These things don't usually stay hidden forever,' Rossi said, her knuckles on the steering wheel turning white. 'I'm surprised he didn't end up in Ashworth, with all that talk about making up a baby.'

'Huh, yeah, you're right. How did he think he was going to get away with that kind of lie?'

'Does it say anything in there? What's in his statement?'

Murphy leafed through the pages, finding the initial statements and reading through them. He opened the window a little as the motion of the car and reading at the same time kicked off his motion sickness. Fresh air blasted into the car, as Rossi speeded up in the fast lane.

'First interviews he spent most of the time asking about "Molly",' Murphy said, swallowing back saliva. 'Then he went to no comment as soon as his solicitor arrived ... Christ ...'

'What?'

'Nothing. Just read who represented him at trial. It was Jess.'

'Small world,' Rossi said, shaking her head. 'Not a conflict, is it?'

'Probably not. Will mention it just to make sure.'

Rossi nodded, going silent as Murphy continued to read. He looked away from the pages every few seconds, wishing he'd read it all before getting in the car. 'Surprised she lost this one, actually. With no body, it's usually a very difficult prosecution. Bet it pissed her off royally.'

'It sounds like it would have been dealt with properly for CPS to get that far. Must have been a load of evidence against him.'

'Does look that way. Thing is, if he hadn't made up the kidnapping thing, it's unlikely he would have been caught for it. He called attention to himself by doing that. Although, I suppose guilt can make you do some crazy things.'

'Who was the victim?'

Murphy went back a few pages and found the page he wanted. 'Irenka Dubicki. A Polish-born woman, came over to the UK about a decade ago. Lived alone, had no family over here. It seems there might have been a relationship with Johnson, but the police were never sure.'

'So, we have one guy dead, who liked to hire prostitutes and abuse them. We have another who killed a woman he may or may not have been in relationship with. It's not exactly a great advert for that club they were all in.'

'What's the chance all of the eight men on that original list have had similar issues in their past?'

'I'd say quite high,' Rossi said, slowing down as a lorry crossed into the middle lane and tried to overtake another lorry going three miles an hour slower in the inside lane.

Murphy sat back in the passenger seat, closing the file on his lap and staring at the back of the lorry in front. He began to feel normal again as they approached Manchester and the prison that held Tim Johnson.

It also contained the man who had killed Murphy's parents, but he tried to put that fact to the back of his mind.

Twenty-eight

There was something broken about the man in front of them. It wasn't apparent if that was because he'd spent a year in jail or if the weight of his guilt had suddenly crashed down upon him. The grey flecks in his stubble and dark rings under his eyes spoke of more going on under the surface. He had gained weight since he had been photographed on his first arrest, his face rounder and his stomach extending over the jogging bottoms he was wearing.

Murphy studied Tim Johnson without speaking, half-listening as Rossi explained why they were there. There was something familiar about the man – not him exactly, but his demeanour. He had seen it before, but couldn't place it. Johnson's eyes flitted between the pair of them, his breaths coming hard and fast.

'Do you understand that, Tim?' Rossi said as Murphy tuned back in. 'We just want your help with an ongoing investigation.'

'Have you found Molly?'

The eagerness with which it was asked unsettled Murphy. The lie was still there, slipping easily out of Johnson's mouth. It didn't bode well.

'We're not here to discuss that,' Rossi said, Murphy watching as Johnson's shoulders dropped. 'We want to know about the club you were a part of at university.'

Johnson began to shift in his chair. 'I don't know what you mean.'

'Of course you do. It was a group you founded, along with seven other students, back in 2007 when you started university in Liverpool.'

'It was nothing . . .'

'Of course it was,' Murphy said, leaning forwards on his elbows, the metal table hard and cold. 'It took up a lot of your time, I imagine. Creating something like that often does.'

'I don't know what you mean.'

'Come on, Tim, let's be honest here. We're not here because we don't know anything. We just want your help. Do you want to do that or not?'

'I . . . I don't know how I can help.'

Johnson had a soft accent, Murphy thought. Southern, but not west counties. Closer to the London boroughs and surrounding areas. Posh, clipped tones, which jarred in the place they were sitting. He glanced at Rossi, giving her the nod.

'Let's start at the beginning,' Rossi said, sliding her file in front of her and opening it. 'You start the club along with seven other young men. Why? What was its purpose?'

'I don't know really,' Johnson replied, his voice quiet in the small room. He had pulled up the sleeve on the grey sweater he was wearing so that it covered his right hand. He leaned on his balled-up fist, occasionally stroking his stubble with the corner of the sleeve. 'The Abercromby

Boys Club. The name doesn't really do it justice. It was supposed to help us all out. It wasn't my idea.'

'Whose idea was it?'

'Sam Byrne's. He seemed to know what he was talking about. He made it sound like we have whatever we wanted by being a part of it. We had to wear certain things, work in certain circles. We'd all be compensated well once we left university and began our careers. Great jobs, making a lot of money. That sort of thing. We could achieve whatever we desired, he reckoned.'

'What was the reality?'

Johnson stared at the metal table, tracing a pattern on the surface with his left hand. 'Pretty much what I'd expected. We were young, didn't really want to do much else other than drink, meet girls, that sort of thing. I wasn't sure what the point of it was.'

'You went along with it, though.'

'Yeah, it was fun. After the first year, we started recruiting more members. It was getting bigger every semester and it was all the right people joining. Those with money and power. Well-known families, that sort of thing. I wasn't expecting anything like it at a university in Liverpool. It felt like we were building something better for the place. Somewhere that was inviting for young people all around the country, those who didn't get into the better universities . . . that they could still be someone.'

'Right, and how did you achieve that?'

Johnson hesitated; unsure of himself, Murphy thought.

'We would just . . . help each other. We were all well connected. We all came from good backgrounds, which meant that we knew many people in business and politics.'

'You've heard the news about Sam,' Murphy said, using the mention of politics to shift the conversation.

'Yes,' Johnson replied, looking at Rossi before shifting quickly away. 'Is that why you're here?'

'Partly. We just want to know more about the background of the man.'

'Do you think him ending up murdered is because of something we did back then?'

Murphy didn't say anything, wondering how much to give away. 'That's a possibility,' he said, deciding it was probably the best answer in the circumstances. 'We're looking into everything.'

He watched as Johnson's breathing became a little harder, then glanced down at the man's sleeve-covered hand as it began to shake.

'I don't know what could have happened that would have anything to do with this. It was just a silly club. We didn't do anything that deserved this.'

'Tell me about the parties,' Rossi said, looking down at the file in front of her. 'What went on at those?'

Johnson swallowed and didn't respond straight away. 'They were just parties. You know, drinking, men, girls, that sort of thing. By the last year, they had become the place to be.'

'And you all took advantage of that,' Rossi said, looking up at Johnson and waiting for him to look at her. 'It must have been something else for you boys. All of a sudden getting all this attention. Tell me, was this the sort of thing that went on at your various private and boarding schools?'

'Not really.'

'So, it must have been a nice situation to be in. You're all used to spending your time with other boys. Now, suddenly, you're surrounded by young girls. And they all want to be with you, don't they?'

Johnson began to say something then stopped himself. He went back to tracing patterns on the metal surface again.

'There's one incident we do want to speak to you about,' Murphy said, bending his head to try and meet Johnson's gaze. 'Involving a student in your last year.'

'I don't know what you mean.'

'I think you do. It's written all over your face. You're worried about something coming up in this conversation. It's that, isn't it?'

Murphy waited for Johnson to reply, but there was only silence. He pushed on regardless. 'I want to have a guess at what happened, then you can correct me if you need to, sound fair?'

Johnson still sat in silence, the finger moving slower across the table.

'As a group, you're all used to women throwing themselves at you. The eight of you have some prestige because of this club. If someone wasn't amenable to your advances, it wouldn't sit well, would it? So, what happens, is that you do it anyway. All of you, or some of you. You take a young girl from one of your parties and something happens behind closed doors. You all think she'll keep quiet, but she doesn't, does she?'

'I don't know what you're talking about . . .'

'You were there,' Rossi said, hands flat on the table. Murphy could see the pulse in her cheeks as her teeth clenched together. 'You know what happened.'

'Depends which time,' Johnson said, his hands no longer shaking. 'There were a lot of parties.'

'If it was all Sam Byrne, that's all we need to know,' Murphy said, cutting in before Rossi had chance to say anything. 'We just need to know the truth.'

'Sam was always the one looking out for that sort of thing. He was a cad, a real ladies' man. They all wanted him, that was for sure. He never did anything wrong.'

'Are you sure about that? Only you don't sound like you are.'

Johnson tugged on his bottom lip with his teeth. 'Explain to me why I should help you?'

Murphy had hoped that question wouldn't come up. 'Why don't you tell me about Sam?'

'No, tell me why I should do anything for you?' Johnson leaned back in his chair, his body shaking now. 'It's because of all of you I'm here in the first place. I should be out there, finding my daughter and living my life. Instead, I'm stuck in prison for something I haven't done, while Molly is out there in danger. Or even ... I don't know.'

Rossi gave Murphy a look as Johnson collapsed onto the table with his head in his hands. They didn't have any leverage here, which pissed off Murphy royally. 'Look, Tim,' he said, as Johnson's shoulders hitched from silent tears. 'I don't know the full story, but I promise once we're done with our investigation, we'll take another look into what happened. Something is going on with regards to your original group members, so I do want to check that you weren't involved in that.'

'Really?' Johnson said, lifting his head a little and exposing his face. Murphy didn't believe in being able to read people to the extent some professed to. Yet, there was something in Johnson's expression which jarred with him. If Johnson had really killed the woman he was in prison for, then it was an Oscar-worthy performance.

'You just need to help us,' Murphy continued, carefully working things through in his head. 'Is there anything you think we should know?'

Johnson sniffed and propped himself up on his elbows. 'I don't know. There were rumours, that's all. There was eight of us, so we weren't in each other's pockets. We would split into smaller groups. Some of us were closer than others. We mostly lost touch after we left university, but I knew if something happened I could call on them.'

'Did you? When this all started?'

Johnson hesitated, looking between Murphy and Rossi then back at the table. 'No.'

It was the first time during the interview that Murphy could definitely say Tim had lied. He decided to leave it alone.

'What happened in your final year? Something did, didn't it? That's why you took yourself away and had little to do with them.'

'There was one girl. It wasn't right,' Johnson said, his voice quiet again. 'I told them that.'

'What wasn't right?'

'What . . . they did to that girl. It didn't need to happen, but they wouldn't listen.'

'You need to tell us everything you know,' Rossi said, keeping her voice strong and even, her knuckles growing whiter as she gripped the table.

'I wasn't there, honest. I found out later, when she was going around telling everyone what happened. Some first year, I don't know her name, just recognised her from the campus. She was always buzzing around us. She wanted to be close to us, as so many did. She looked so young. Sam liked them looking like that.'

'Like what?' Murphy said, trying to keep his feelings under better control than Rossi. She was gritting her teeth again, and experience told him that even though she was usually able to keep check of her emotions, it wasn't working right now.

'Young, like teenager age, I guess. He liked that look. I don't know what happened that night but it wasn't the only time it happened. It was the first time someone made a complaint, though. She ended up leaving university, but I heard she was still sniffing around years later. Sam's parents rang me and asked about it. Thing is, you've got to understand, these girls were up for anything the night before, but then the next day it would be all different.'

'Walk me through what you know to have occurred that night,' Murphy said, trying to work out the man in front of him. He seemed meek, broken, but there was something about the way he spoke, with such emptiness and a lack of empathy, that worried at him. He couldn't shake the feeling that Johnson was lying. Then he remembered they were in a prison, with a convicted murderer, and he shook it off.

'I don't know really,' Johnson said, glassy eyes landing on Murphy and staying there. 'I saw them the next morning, I think. If I'm remembering the right night.'

'Who's them?' Rossi said, pen in hand. 'Names.'

'I don't know. It could have been any of us. We would meet up for coffee the day after these parties and we were always full of it. I remember that night a bit clearer, that's all. Mainly because of what happened afterwards. It was a close call. Sounded like she was right up for it, but we were worried as well, you know?'

'No, I really, really don't,' Murphy said, then stopped himself from saying any more. 'What happened after that?'

'She apparently started talking. Changed her mind and decided they had done something she hadn't wanted them to. I knew those guys and they weren't like that. It wouldn't be their fault if she'd decided the next day that she didn't want to be known for being that type.'

Murphy felt as if the air had been sucked out of the room. They had heard so many similar stories over the years that it wasn't really surprising to hear. It was the complete lack of thought which always jarred with him.

'We're talking multiple men and one first year student . . .'

'It happened all the time. These girls, they'd be throwing themselves at us constantly. Yeah, they'd be drunk, but they weren't saying anything that night. They'd come back with us willingly and it wouldn't be until they started feeling guilty the next day that they'd say anything was wrong. Not our fault. It's not like they were saying no, was it?'

'Probably weren't saying yes, either,' Rossi said, the words coming out in a hiss.

'Why was this girl different?' Murphy said, trying to keep things on track and not jump over the table and teach the young guy a lesson. 'If this sort of thing happened often, why do you remember her?'

'I don't know.'

'I think you do,' Murphy said, not letting it go. 'The memory of this one came back to you so easily. You knew exactly what we were talking about. Why?'

Johnson shrugged, shutting down after being so willing to speak before.

'Want to know what I think,' Rossi said, leaning towards Johnson. 'I think your hatred of women has landed you here. I bet you were there that night, that's why it comes back to you so easily. You know exactly what happened, because you were in that room. When you leave university, and you don't have your pick any more, it festers inside you. That's how you are found guilty of murder, because you couldn't handle it not coming so easily to you any more.'

'You really don't know a thing, do you?' Johnson said, fixing Rossi with a stare. 'Typical. I knew one of your lot back at university.'

'What lot?' Rossi said, Murphy bracing himself to get in between them at any moment.

'You're Italian, aren't you? All the same. Nothing but illogical passion. He was like that. Come to think of it, you share his name.'

'I think we should leave before I do something,' Rossi said, turning to Murphy and beginning to get out of her seat.

'Rosti ... no, that's not right. Rossi, that's what you said. Vinny Rossi ring a bell? A relative from the boat, perhaps? He was a mature student, who wanted to be one of us. We got rid of him, but not before we found out what he was really like.'

Murphy turned back to Johnson as Rossi grabbed the file from the desk and headed for the door. 'What did you say?'

'They all know each other, these Italians. Just like that Polish lot. Ruined my life, them coming over here. You've got to help me. I can't let my daughter become another *slut* like the rest of them.'

Murphy stared at Johnson as he dissolved into tears once more. He looked over at the door where Rossi waited.

Once, a few years earlier when they had been stuck in a car waiting on something or other, he had asked Rossi how she remembered all her brothers' names. It had been a jokey conversation in which Rossi had repeated their names so many times that by the end even Murphy knew them all.

He remembered Vincenzo Rossi. He also remembered that he had returned to university as a mature student.

As he headed after Rossi, he realised that he'd been wrong about what had been bothering her. It wasn't anything to do with her relationship.

It was her brother.

Twenty-nine

DC Kirkham checked the details again, then twice more, just to be sure. The whole case was becoming more convoluted by the day, he thought. It wasn't about to get any easier either. Another body, another death. It was almost like clockwork.

He'd decided early on just to keep his head down and do as he was told, ignoring the voice inside him which only spoke of dark days ahead.

'We're losing control,' he said under his breath as he walked over to the murder board at the back of the incident room. He lifted up the marker and added the details of what he'd discovered in the past few minutes.

'That the girl's name?'

Kirkham turned to see DC Hashem standing behind him, holding a cup of tea out towards him. He smiled, thankful for the interruption.

'Cheers,' Kirkham said, taking the cup off her and blowing on the surface before taking a swig. 'Yeah, that's her name. We're going to have to track her down now. Nothing in the system that's recent.'

'What do you think about this whole thing?'

Kirkham didn't answer, turning back to the board and its various weblike diagrams, moving from name to name, act to act. He wasn't about to try and make sense of the whole thing.

'It doesn't seem likely that this is anything to do with her, does it? I mean, on her own, doesn't make any sense.'

'No, not really. Stranger things have happened, though.'

'I think revenge is key here. Someone is offing all these blokes for a reason.'

Kirkham stepped aside as DC Hashem took the pen from his hand and added a single word next to Paul Wright's name on the board.

'Dead?' Kirkham said, reading DC Hashem's writing. 'Another one?'

DC Hashem turned to him with a smirk. 'Just found him now. Another suicide, apparently. Can't be a coincidence, can it? That's our number five.'

'Doesn't explain why one of them isn't dead, though, does it?'

She shrugged in response, Kirkham moving back to his desk and placing the cup down on the Tranmere Rovers coaster an ex had bought him. It was the only thing he'd kept from the relationship, mainly because he couldn't be bothered replacing it. He lifted up the phone on his desk and tried calling DI Murphy, unsurprised when it went to voicemail after a few rings.

'What's the latest?'

Kirkham looked up to find DC Hale standing near his desk, looking at him while chewing a sandwich. Crumbs fell to the ground in front of the DC, sending chills through the mess-hating Kirkham.

'While you've been busy eating that, we've got a name for the girl who we think was assaulted whilst Sam Byrne was at university. Also, Abs has found out Paul Wright's whereabouts.'

DC Hale looked down at his sandwich and snorted. He devoured the rest of it in one mouthful. 'Good on her,' he said, Kirkham getting a clear view of the half-chewed bread and ham before it was swallowed down.

'Yeah, it's good work.'

DC Hale leaned forwards and covered his now empty mouth. 'Not saying it makes up for ISIS, but she's getting there.'

Kirkham clenched his fist under his desk, but took a few breaths before answering. 'You'd better be careful saying stuff like that. Murphy will bounce you out of here so quick your feet won't touch the floor. You saw what happened with that Tony Brannon guy.'

'Oh, for fuck's sake, it's just a joke. Can't you take a bit of banter?'

Kirkham decided not to keep the conversation going any further, already foreseeing the end of it. As soon as he heard the words 'freedom of speech' he'd have to batter Hale to death with his empty sandwich carton.

Instead, he tried the phone again, waiting patiently for it to ring out before leaving a message this time.

'Hello, sir, it's Jack. Can you give me a ring. It's urgent.'

*   *   *

Murphy looked at his phone, putting it back in his pocket as the number flashed up. It could wait. He looked across at Rossi, who was still refusing to meet his eye, much less talk to him.

'I need to know,' he said, trying again.

'There's nothing to say.'

It had been that way since they'd left the prison, Rossi rushing ahead of him and sitting in the driver's seat, eyes fixed forward and unwilling to acknowledge him when he tried to speak to her.

'This isn't going away,' he said, placing a hand on the dashboard, the car braking suddenly as Rossi almost missed a turn-off. 'You need to explain what's going on.'

'Nothing is going on.'

'Who do you think I am, Laura? You think I'm the type to just let something like this go? He knew your brother. Vincenzo has something to do with this, doesn't he?'

'I'm not saying anything.'

Murphy suddenly had an urge to shake her. This wasn't the way to deal with this situation and he was sure she knew it. Instead, she'd decided to clam up and say nothing. 'You're making this worse. Have you spoken to him at least?'

'I don't think I should say anything to you,' Rossi said, giving him a sideways glance. 'We both know what's going to happen next, don't we?'

'No, we don't, because you won't talk to me.'

'I'll have to declare an interest and I'll be off the case. Simple as that. I should have done it a while ago. For that, I'm sorry.'

'I don't understand what's going on here. Just explain it to me.'

Rossi sighed heavily, such a large breath escaping her that he thought it would fog up the windscreen. 'I don't know if I should.'

'Try me.'

He waited for her to continue, happy that she had at least decided to slow down the car as they joined the motorway heading back to Liverpool. 'His name came up when we went to see Simon Jackson.'

'Yesterday,' Murphy said under his breath. He could almost feel his blood pressure rising.

'It could have been anyone, because he didn't give me a first name. He couldn't remember it. I went to see him.'

'Vinny?'

'Yes,' Rossi said, shoulders slumped now as her hands slipped to the bottom of the wheel. 'I thought I would just check. See if there was anything there. I'd worked out they were at uni at the same time, but I was hoping it was just a coincidence. That there was another Rossi that year or something. No such luck.'

'How involved was he?' Murphy said, trying to keep his voice on an even keel.

'Not at all, from what I can tell. Vinny wouldn't really talk to me about it. Got quite defensive, but I think that's just because I was asking him. It's nothing.'

'I'll decide that, Laura.' He turned to look out the passenger-side window, elbow resting on the edge as Rossi nodded in response. 'Were you going to tell me about this?'

'I didn't think it was important . . .'

'Not important?' Murphy said, his voice echoing around the car. He breathed in and tried again. 'Of course you did, which is why you didn't mention it. What a mess.'

'I don't see what it has to do with anything. Vinny was at university at the same time as they were, that's all.'

'Two of them have mentioned him now. He must have known them quite well for that to happen. Were they studying the same courses or something?'

'I don't know,' Rossi replied, but he could tell already that she knew more. 'I don't think so.'

'What else is there?'

Rossi glanced across at him as he kept his eyes locked on her. She looked away and back at the road. 'Nothing.'

'This isn't good,' Murphy said, turning his head away from Rossi. 'I don't know what to do here . . .'

'Why do you have to do anything? It's not a problem.'

'Are you joking? This is a delicate situation as it is. If this went to CPS, what do you think they'd say about it?'

He waited for an answer, but Rossi had gone quiet. She had withdrawn into herself, as he'd seen her do before.

'What's the full story here? I need to know.'

'There's nothing else,' Rossi said, her voice barely audible over the noise of passing cars. 'That's it. He knew them at uni, hasn't spoke to them in years.'

'I can't believe you didn't tell me about this . . .'

'Oh, can we stop with the holier than thou *merda*. You've got a short memory, you have.'

'What are you talking about?'

'Have you forgotten what happened last year? With that missing girl? You don't think that was a conflict of interest?'

Murphy shook his head, but felt the ground he was on becoming more icy by the second. 'That's a totally different–'

'Bullshit,' Rossi said, banging the steering wheel with one hand as she did so. Murphy wasn't sure what he was surprised about – the fact she had shouted at him, or that she'd used an English swear word.

'It's one rule for you, another for the rest. Just like always.'

'That's not fair,' Murphy replied, trying to calm down the situation, but probably making it worse, now he thought about it. He was suddenly very aware that they on a motorway travelling at over seventy miles per hour and he wished he'd waited until they had arrived back at the station before discussing this. 'You understood what was going on back then.'

'Yeah,' Rossi said through gritted teeth. 'It was your problem so it obviously meant something completely different. A girl went missing, we were assigned to the case, despite you possibly being her father.'

'It didn't matter, did it? We were taken off it, once something bigger came along.'

'And if it hadn't, would you have removed yourself from that case? Would you have told people we were actually looking for someone who you were possibly the father of?'

Murphy hesitated, knowing the answer but unwilling to give it up that easy.

'Of course you wouldn't,' Rossi said, continuing without waiting for an answer. 'Yes, people associated with our case may have heard of my brother, or even been friendly with him, but it has no bearing on this case. I think you've jumped ahead of yourself, thinking that way. It means absolutely nothing. Simple as that.'

Murphy tried to think of a better comeback line, but had to concede the point. There wasn't really anything to it, now he thought about it. 'Are you sure about this? Only, if this becomes a problem further down the line . . .'

'Do you think I'd keep anything quiet now? It's done. I've spoken to him and he says he doesn't have anything to do with what we're looking into. Whether or not he did anything back then, who knows? He's not involved now, though. That much is certain.'

Murphy scratched at his beard and leaned his head back a little. 'Right, OK. Well, let's not make a big deal out of this. Just, let me know if anything else comes up involving one of your brothers. There's enough of them that something like this was likely to happen at some point, I guess.'

Rossi didn't return the smile he gave her as he tried to alleviate the tension which had grown inside the car. It fell from his face as he turned back to the window at his side.

*   *   *

Rossi fixed her gaze straight ahead, the traffic thinning out as they made their way along the motorway. Murphy had stopped talking, which helped a fair amount, but her heartbeat still hadn't slowed. She was glad of the steering wheel; she was able to hide the shake of her hands by gripping hold of it tight.

She had lied. There was no getting out of it now. All it would take would be for someone to go over that CCTV footage from near Sam Byrne's apartment, someone who knew what her brother looked like, and it would be the end.

There was a moment when she had considered telling Murphy everything. That she had seen her brother in the images, confronted him and known he was lying.

Instead, she had lied. Simple as that. Played the whole thing down, as if it hadn't mattered at all. Pretended that the whole thing hadn't kept her awake the night before.

She had to keep up that pretence.

The whole thing was a mess, as Murphy had so delicately put it. There was no way she was going to be removed from this case, though, she thought. She was there until the bitter end. No matter what it meant for her or her family.

Rossi continued to drive, wondering how and to what extent Vincenzo was involved in the investigation. Nothing about the case seemed like something he would be implicated in. Yet, people kept mentioning his name, he had lied to her when she had met up with him and there was the small matter of him being near a murder victim's apartment the night he went missing.

No, he was involved somehow. Being taken off the case would mean she would never find out the truth.

Would mean not being able to protect him.

Thirty

Murphy surveyed the room, now holding many more bodies than the previous few days had, and glanced over at the thin face of DSI Butler. He was in full preening mode. The smell of his expensive aftershave was washing over the room and having an effect on everyone in there. His mere presence meant something to the people in attendance, as if they were being visited by the pope or Kenny Dalglish.

It shouldn't have annoyed Murphy, but as was so often the case, it damn well did.

'Right, settle down,' Murphy said, attempting to remain in charge. 'You know why we're all here, so let's not waste any more time. We now know eight men were part of a club at university and half of them are dead . . .'

'David, if you'll allow me,' DSI Butler said, stepping forwards and giving him a look that would curdle milk. 'We probably shouldn't get too far ahead of ourselves here.'

'I thought you were going to allow us to make these connections?'

'Of course, that's your job, David,' DSI Butler said, giving him a soft smile before turning to the crowded

room. 'I just want to make sure everyone is aware that
there are a number of factors in this investigation that we
have to consider. Of the four men dead who were a part
of this club, two of them committed suicide. Both of those
inquests ruled that there was no suspicious events
surrounding their deaths . . .'

'Which we'll obviously be looking into now,' Murphy
said, knowing he was getting a look from DSI Butler as he
interrupted him. 'There are coincidences, then there's
something we can't ignore.'

'Do we need to have a chat outside?' DSI Butler said,
coming to Murphy's side and whispering with his back
turned to the rest of the room. 'Only I don't think this sort
of thing should be spoken about in front of everyone here.'

'Give us a minute,' Murphy said, then made his way to
the door, DSI Butler stalking after him as he did so. The
officers held their silence until the two senior officers left,
voices breaking out as Murphy closed the door behind
him.

'I thought we had agreed that we weren't going to link
the two facts just yet?'

Murphy shook his head slowly, as DSI Butler hissed the
question at him. 'I never agreed to anything.'

Which was true. He had stood and listened as DSI
Butler had urged him to drop the whole boys club angle
whilst standing in DCI Stephens's office ten minutes
earlier.

'I thought we had an understanding,' DSI Butler continued, trying to fix a steely stare on Murphy. The fact he
was doing it from six inches lower than him was diminishing the impact somewhat. 'This is a very delicate
situation . . .'

'It's really not, sir,' Murphy said, deciding to interrupt his superior for a change. 'We're carrying out a murder investigation. During the course of that investigation, we have learned from numerous witnesses that there is some link to a shitty club the victim founded whilst at university. Further, we found out that one of the original eight members is in prison for murder. Then, it turns out, two others have committed suicide. Add that to the fact we now have two bodies currently rotting in the local morgue, I make that five out of eight. There's a note attached to our latest dead body saying "five down", which makes it sound like there's another three to go, right? And you think we should just ignore all that?'

'No, I'm not saying that,' DSI Butler replied, hands on slender hips and almost pouting. Murphy looked down at him with his arms folded, waiting for more bullshit to be forced out. 'I'm only saying that we should tread carefully. *You* should tread carefully. There are things going on here that you're not privy to.'

Murphy stared down at DSI Butler, breathing heavily through his nose, mouth closed. 'I don't even care enough to find out what the word "privy" means,' he said, his voice barely above a whisper. He didn't wait for a response, pushing his way back into the meeting room. A few heads turned to see him enter, but most kept their stares to the front. Rossi was sitting motionless in her chair, not looking up at him, whilst DCI Stephens was trying to burn a hole in his head judging by the way she was looking at him.

'Right, let's start again,' he said, once he was standing in front of them. He glanced up, seeing DSI Butler standing in the doorway before walking away. He looked back at the sea of faces and tried not to think about what was probably going to happen to him once the meeting had ended.

'Two men found murdered on the streets of our city. Both in horrific circumstances, which have shocked the community – meaning, there's a bunch of people out there who are looking for any excuse to rip us a new one. So I want your full attention on this and this alone. We find the person who did this now. I want him locked up as soon as possible. Sound good to you?'

He didn't wait for an answer. 'Good. This is what's happening.'

Murphy continued to talk, giving out various tasks for the men and women present. The most salient were saved for the DCs in his command, but the uniforms were properly briefed as well. Best to use them for what they were good at; walking around looking important and talking to the locals.

'Anyone who thinks they've seen anything, you speak to me first. We've got calls coming in, but we know how useful that sort of thing is usually. Doesn't mean we don't look at everything though. Find out what you can. Patrols at every scene, et cetera, et cetera. You know the drill. We've been here before.'

Murphy carried on talking, saying the same things he'd been saying year upon year. It wouldn't matter; he would be saying the same thing to them again soon enough, he thought. Another case, another victim.

'I know it's getting late, but I want us out there. The media are all over us right now and you know from experience that that never ends well.'

A few short laughs followed on from that comment. He knew the next one wouldn't get as many. 'We need to find the other three men on that list out there and offer them police protection until we've got someone for this.'

Heads turned to look at each other and eyebrows were raised. They had quite plainly heard the conversation he'd had with DSI Butler outside. He was sticking his neck on the line and they knew it.

'It doesn't matter if they're connected or not. I just don't want anyone else turning up dead who doesn't need to.'

Murphy continued to talk, bringing those who had questions up to speed patiently. It was another thirty minutes before he was outside in the incident room, surrounded by the DCs he trusted.

'Right, fill me in. What's been happening while we've been gone.'

'Matthew Williams hadn't even visited Liverpool in the past two years,' DC Hashem said, her eager face looking up at Murphy. 'I spoke to his partner, who's in total shock. She's absolutely distraught. Doesn't understand how he's ended up here.'

'Is she coming down now?'

'Of course,' DC Hashem said, her voice lifting at the end of the two word sentence. 'Bit of a trek from Northumberland, but didn't seem to bother her. She'll be here around six p.m. depending on traffic.'

'When was the last time she saw him?'

'Day before yesterday. He worked in the city centre in Newcastle, whilst they lived a few miles away. Somewhere called Ashington or something. She said he sent her a text late on Tuesday night, saying he was going to be staying over in the city due to work. Happened before, so she didn't think too much of it. Obviously, when he wasn't returning calls yesterday afternoon, she got worried. Reported him missing to local police last night.'

'I'm guessing he didn't come up in the searches we did,' Murphy said, hoping there wasn't an angle here that could be used against them.

'His name is so common, we couldn't have known.'

Murphy nodded, but still felt a little worried about the information. 'It was probably too late by then anyway.'

The phone rang on his desk, cutting the conversation short as he made his way over to it. He glanced over at DCI Stephens's office, but the blinds had been drawn since his boss had gone in there. He knew DSI Butler would have been waiting inside for her. He tried to feel guilty, but it wouldn't come.

'Murphy.'

'Time of death is approximately one to two a.m. earlier today,' the voice of Dr Houghton said over the phone without pause. 'Cause is probably something to do with his facial injuries. Blunt force trauma, as they say. Will be another day before I can tell you with what.'

'Hello to you too,' Murphy said, shaking his head at the pathologist's general lack of social graces. Strike that, he thought. It was only with him that any manners were absent. 'Forensics have a large area to look into within the warehouse. Hopefully they'll find something.'

'I deal with the bodies, David. I'll leave the rest for you to sort out.'

The line went dead, Murphy still holding onto the phone. He replaced the receiver and looked around for DC Hashem. He spied her sitting at her desk again, looking a little lost.

'Abs, come over,' he said to her across the office. She bounded over, exuding more energy than he had felt in a while. 'This other guy who supposedly committed . . .'

'Paul Wright,' DC Hashem said, standing over him with her hands behind her back.

'Right, Paul Wright. Where did he die?'

'He went back down south after graduating. Lived in Surrey, in a house owned by his parents. The cleaner found him hanging in the garage.'

'Local uniforms didn't notice anything suspicious?'

DC Hashem shook her head. 'Most open-and-shut suicide ever according to their reports.'

'Note?'

'Yeah, which makes things a bit more interesting.'

'Well, I wouldn't exactly use that word . . .'

'Oh, you know what I mean,' DC Hashem said, suddenly serious. 'I don't want you thinking I'm thinking that way. I know this is not nice at all.'

'I know, Abs,' Murphy said, pushing his chair back from his desk and stretching his legs out next to DC Hashem. 'Any chance of us seeing this note?'

'We've asked for the whole file. Hopefully it'll be over to us by the end of the day.'

Murphy checked the clock on the wall opposite, realising the end of the day was closer than he'd thought. Not that it mattered – it was likely to be another late one.

'OK, thanks, Abs,' he said, waiting for her to leave before motioning to DC Kirkham to come over. 'You found her yet?'

'Possibly,' DC Kirkham said, standing in the same place DC Hashem had just occupied. 'University didn't give us much more than a date of birth and full name. Ran that through the system and got two hits.'

'Same name and birth date?'

'Not exactly an uncommon name, Hazel Jones. Stands to reason that there'd be at least two people born on the same day with the same name. That's just in Merseyside and Cheshire as well. Before we go any further out.'

Murphy took the addresses from the outstretched hand of DC Kirkham, glancing down at them.

'It's this one,' he said to DC Kirkham, pointing at the second address on the paper. 'Laura, we're going out.'

DC Kirkham frowned, his brow furrowing as he stepped aside for Murphy to grab his coat from the peg on the wall. 'You're sure?'

'Yeah, course I am,' Murphy said, waiting for Rossi to join him at the door. 'Before you start wondering if I'm psychic, read the address again, then compare it to Tim Johnson's one.'

DC Kirkham shook his head, reading the piece of paper in his hand as if it were about to magically reveal something to him. Murphy followed Rossi out the door, not looking back to see if the young DC had worked things out yet.

'Where are we going?' Rossi said, skipping a little to keep up with Murphy's long strides out of the building.

'What do you reckon, think we'll beat the traffic if we go through the tunnel?'

'You've got that look on your face again.'

'What look?'

'That, "I've just worked something out and justified my salary for the year" look. Where are we going?'

'Tim Johnson lived on my old estate, over in Moreton. You know, when I lived over the water for that year.'

'Yeah . . .'

'Well, that's why I recognised the address,' Murphy said, almost smirking to himself. Sometimes it was nice to have a bit of a Sherlock moment. 'How much of a coincidence is it for someone with the same name and birth date as a rape victim to live next door to one of the possible rapists?'

You

There's a sense of finality within you. You know things are coming to an end. You can feel the conclusion to everything and you welcome it. It's almost as if a journey is about to come to a finish. A dark motorway, empty of other cars, small stretches of light apparent on the horizon.

You want it to stop. You're tired, the bursts of energy you once had are now few and far between. The look of horror on Matthew Williams's face as you raised that ball-peen hammer and swung it towards him, now a distant memory. Sam Byrne's limp and lifeless body a faded image in your consciousness.

The others . . . you remember less clearly.

You want to feel that power endlessly, forever, but you know it's impossible. Once the act is over, the feeling begins to weaken, tarnished by other thoughts crowding into your mind.

You wonder if you were ever normal.

When you started, you knew what the end game would look like. You knew how the closing scene would play out. You planned it perfectly, every step along the way. No one could have done it better than you. If you had continued in the way you had begun, you may never have been discovered.

You watched those two men die as they ended their own lives. The guilt too much for them, a ghost from their past revisiting enough to send them over the edge. Literally, in Chris Roberts's case. You peered into the darkness as he leaped, wondering how it would feel if you followed him over the cliff.

You think about death more often now. You wonder if there is anything afterwards. If all this has been for nothing, that there is no soul to save, no soul to diminish. You wonder how you will be judged. If your actions will be understood and forgiven.

Old Testament God will be understanding, you feel. He wasn't afraid to smite and bring death and destruction to those who erred. New Testament God, you're more worried about. He was more about turning the other cheek.

You need to stop. Take a breath, consider things and make the right decisions. You don't have time for that.

That's why Neil Letherby is currently handcuffed and bound in the boot of your car.

You don't know how you will kill him yet, but you know you will. You crave that power again. You need it, to keep going and complete your task.

You try and work out when this all began. Now it's ending, you want to track the whole process. You know it begins in 2007, when eight men met and banded together, but that's not the proper beginning. That's a prologue – a way of starting the story without really starting it.

It really began in 2010. Six years ago. That's how long it has taken you to get to this point, to finish what you started.

You think of death. You wonder if you'll welcome it once this is over.

There was no other way.

You have to believe that, otherwise everything falls apart inside you. Everything has to have meaning, it has to have an effect. What you're doing is so egregious, so outside the norm, that for it to be pointless would make all your work meaningless.

It has to change things.

You hadn't planned for something like this to happen so soon after ending Matthew Williams's life. The last place he would draw breath had been meticulously planned out. You spent time checking each warehouse on the banks of the River Mersey, to make sure you found the right one. Somewhere you could do what needed to be done in peace. Without interruption.

Now, you're driving around aimlessly, trying to find somewhere to take the bound and gagged man in the boot of your car. You know you can lead him anywhere you need to, that the sight of the replica gun currently sitting underneath your seat is enough for the man. It's finding somewhere that's key.

Thoughts cascade through your head as you struggle with tiredness, trying to find somewhere to go.

This isn't the last one. You know that. This is only number six.

You figure you have a day. Maybe two. Then, it will all be over. They are on to you, they will figure out who you are. You know this.

You don't want to leave the city.

An idea comes to you. A stretch of woods, up towards the north of the city. You don't know it well – you only

noted it down when you first started planning this all out
– but you know where it is.

It will be OK, you tell yourself. You've become so adept
at thinking on your feet that nothing can stop you.

You just need to make one stop.

You pull into the petrol station and purchase two
empty jerrycans and fill them up. You also fill the car with
petrol, so as not to arouse suspicion, and then purchase
some cigarettes and a box of matches. You make a joke
with the cashier that your attempt to stop smoking isn't
going so well.

You dump the cigarettes in the passenger-side footwell,
pocket the box of matches.

It is growing darker outside. It will be dark in those
woods.

You hope the fire won't be large enough to be seen.

You think of the warmth, the heat, and smile.

Thirty-one

The traffic through the Wallasey tunnel wasn't as bad as Murphy had feared. Within thirty minutes, they were pulling off the M53 and then down towards Moreton Cross, taking the short drive towards the Millhouse Estate. He knew the route well, having made this journey most days a few years earlier.

'Like going home, this?'

Murphy scowled at Rossi. She knew how much he'd disliked living away from his home city. 'Not at all. I break out in hives coming over here.'

'Yeah, right. You're half a Wool and you know it.'

That's the thing about Liverpudlians – leave the city for a year and you're treated like an interloper when you come back. As if at any moment you might flit off again.

'Bet you didn't say that about Cilla when she popped her clogs. She hadn't lived round here for fifty years and she was suddenly Liverpool's sweetheart again when she died.'

'Is this going to lead to another Beatles rant? Only I don't think we have the time.'

Murphy sighed, but decided to leave it for another day. He passed a parade of shops before a more suburban landscape began to reveal itself. It didn't mean there wasn't a Tesco on the corner of the road he turned into, though. 'They're bloody everywhere.'

'I heard once that they have bought a ton of plots, but can't get planning permission for most of them.'

'When there's one on every corner, that's when we can start moaning about the good ol' days.'

The road into the estate was narrow, parked cars on either side meaning he had to pull over into small spaces every now and again to let oncoming traffic pass him. Within a few minutes, he was turning off the main road through the estate and into a smaller cul-de-sac.

'Number twelve?'

'That's the one,' Rossi replied, already unbuckling her seat belt. 'We're going to have to treat this with care. Given what's happened to her, she's going to have a whole range of emotions about the fact there was never any justice.'

'I know,' Murphy said, pulling over and parking across someone's driveway for lack of anywhere else in the small street. 'Are you thinking what I'm thinking?'

'That we're close?'

Murphy didn't reply, just nodded slowly. 'She knows who is doing this.'

'Or is doing it herself. You always wanted a female serial killer.'

'Not for nothing,' Murphy said, removing his seat belt and opening the door. 'I'd rather it wasn't this one.'

The houses on the street were all small starter homes built ostensibly for families. He knew from painful experience that they were not particularly spacious. He had hurt himself on more occasions than he cared to admit, banging into door frames and walls as he tried to navigate his way around the small space. More than one child in a house this size would be ridiculous.

'We've got a twitcher,' Rossi said, nodding towards the house nearest to the one they were visiting. Murphy looked over and noticed the blinds moving on the house next door. Each home was semi-detached, but close enough to another that it made the detached part of that description almost redundant. 'Tim Johnson's house appears empty, but it looks like the other neighbour is here in case we need a welcoming committee.'

'Wonder if anyone's living in his old house,' Murphy said, giving a small wave in the direction of the twitching blinds, which promptly snapped shut. 'Did he own it?'

'No, he rented it,' Rossi replied, taking the lead and walking up the small gravel path which led to the front door. 'Lights aren't on here.'

'Could be because it's not all that dark.'

Rossi knocked, Murphy standing a few paces behind her. He looked towards the living-room window, but his view of the inside was blocked by closed blinds. He took another step back, but the upstairs windows were similarly out of view.

'Doesn't look hopeful,' Rossi said, knocking again, louder this time. 'Could be at work or something.'

'There's no one in,' a voice from the house next door said. Murphy turned to see who he presumed to be the earlier blind twitcher, standing on her doorstep with her arms folded in front of her. He placed at mid-thirties, although the hair tied up in a bun made him wonder about his first impression. Could be a decade older, given his usual accuracy. 'Hasn't been there for days. Think she's probably on holiday or something.'

'Who lives here?' Murphy said, moving across the small driveway towards the neighbour.

'Who are you first?' the woman said, brow creasing as she took in his size. 'I'm not going to give info out to just anyone, am I? You bailiffs or something?'

'No, nothing like that,' Murphy replied, fishing his ID out of his pocket and flashing her his warrant card. 'I'm Detective Inspector David Murphy and this is Detective Sergeant Laura Rossi. We're from the Major Crime Unit over in North Liverpool.'

The woman's expression changed – the usual mix of shock and intrigue. 'What's she done?'

'What's who done, Miss . . .'

'Do I have to give my name?'

Murphy looked down at his shoes for a second, taking a breath. 'No, not at the moment, but it would be easier to have something to call you by, rather than just guessing.'

'Fine, it's Julie. That's what you can call me.'

Rossi joined him at the narrow stone path which ran along each house. It was almost pointless it being there, but it grew wider near the back of the houses and the gates leading to the small gardens. Enough room for residents to wheel out a bin and put it on the street once a week. 'So, do you know who lives at the address?' Rossi said, tilting her head slightly and giving the woman a tight smile.

'I've only seen the girl, to be honest,' Julie replied, brushing a stray strand of hair from her face. The bun must have been done in a hurry, Murphy thought. 'Young, earlier twenties, if that. Could be older, though. I'm not good with guessing ages.'

You're not on your own, Murphy thought. He was now erring towards Julie being nearer fifty than the thirty he'd first imagined. 'Do you know her name?'

'Never really spoken to her. She's lived here years and never bothered to say hello. Just comes and goes as she pleases.'

Murphy rolled his eyes whilst Julie shooed a dog back into the house. 'Do you know anything about her at all?'

Julie shook her head, freeing another strand of hair from the bun on her head. 'No, not really. She has a couple of visitors every now and again, but I don't pay much attention. One of them has a blue Peugeot, if that's any help? Nice-looking guy. I assumed it was a boyfriend or something. He was always coming round. Caused murder with the parking.'

Murphy felt Rossi stiffen beside him and turned to her with a questioning look, but she was already back to normal.

'How often does he visit?' Rossi said, ignoring Murphy and keeping her eyes fixed on Julie.

'I don't know, really. Few times a month, maybe. I can't say I really take notice.'

Course you don't, Murphy thought. There was something about nosy neighbours which set his teeth on edge. The only time they came in handy was when he was at work, when they could actually be useful. 'When did you see her last?'

'Been a week, I think,' Julie said. 'What's she done? I have a right to know if she's done something bad. I have to live next door to her. It's bad enough that we had that guy who killed that woman living two doors away. If we've got someone else who's done something, I'll never sell this damn house.'

Murphy forced himself to take another breath before answering. 'We can't say at the moment. If we believe there's anything we need to inform the public of, I'm sure you will find out through the proper channels. At the moment, I'll just give you my card and you can get in touch if you see the woman who lives in the property. That would be a great help.'

'I don't think that's good enough,' Julie said. Rossi gave her a look strong enough for her to back down straight away. 'I suppose I'll keep an eye out for her.'

'Thank you,' Murphy said, giving the empty house behind them one last look before turning back to the car. 'We'll be in touch, if needs be.'

'That's it?' Julie said, raising her voice as he walked away and waited by the car for Rossi. 'You're not even going to tell me what to look out for? How am I supposed to know when to ring you?'

Murphy was by the car at that point, so he couldn't hear what Rossi was saying to the woman. He opened the car and got inside. It was another thirty seconds before Rossi joined him.

'Did you post something through Hazel's door?'

'Yeah,' Rossi replied, sitting beside him in the car and putting her seat belt on. 'She's been gone a week.'

'I know.'

'So, what do we think about that?'

Murphy turned the key in the ignition and, after performing a three-point turn, which turned into a six-point one, drove out of the cul-de-sac. 'I know what you're thinking . . .'

'Do you? Because I have a feeling you don't.'

'You think she has something to do with the murders? That's what you're thinking, right?'

Rossi shook her head, allowing a small chuckle to pass her lips. 'The blue Peugeot . . . Vincenzo drives the same car.'

Murphy took a second to make sure he'd heard her right. 'Your brother Vincenzo?'

'Do you know any other people with that name? Yes, my brother. The same idiot who has been named by two different people during this investigation.'

'It could be nothing, Laura,' Murphy said, turning to look at her as he pulled over on the side of the road leading out of the estate. He let the car idle as he turned in the seat properly. 'Just a coincidence.'

'*Merda . . . figlio di puttana . . .*'

Murphy waited for Rossi to stop swearing in a foreign language before speaking again. 'How many bloody blue Peugeots do you think there are? Come on, this means nothing.'

'I'm done,' Rossi said, turning away from Murphy, one hand on her forehead. 'I've screwed up. Royally.'

'What are you talking about?' Murphy said, feeling the air grow colder. 'There's more, isn't there?'

'I didn't think it would matter. Just another coincidence.'

'What was?' Murphy said, trying and failing to keep an edge from his voice. 'If you don't tell me, I can't help you. You know that.'

'It's too late,' Rossi said, slipping off her seat belt and opening the car door. 'I need some air.'

'Laura, what the hell is going on?'

Rossi rummaged around in the inside pocket of her jacket and found what she was looking for. Murphy shook his head as she removed the cigarette from the packet and got out of the car. He heard the snick of the lighter and then an inhale of breath.

He wasn't sure what to do, whether or not to get out of the car or wait her out. He took off his seat belt, but continued to sit there. A minute went by as he looked through the windscreen and tried to work out what was happening. Over four years they'd worked together. It hadn't always been plain sailing, but through it all, one thing was supposed to be sacred between them.

They never kept anything from each other.

He supposed he'd broken that unspoken rule first, a year earlier. He'd told her about the possibility of a missing girl being his daughter, but not before it had come to the point when it was affecting him personally at work. Plus, she'd suspected something was going on before he'd confessed.

There were moments in those four years when unspoken rules between them were ignored. It was just usually on his side rather than hers. Which made the fact she was currently smoking outside the car, hands shaking as she lifted the cigarette to her mouth, all the more worrying.

From experience, Murphy knew that people with no history of screwing up usually went for it properly when they eventually did.

'All right, here it is,' Rossi said, throwing the cigarette into the gutter and getting back into the car. 'Please, let me just get this out, then you can have a go at me.'

'I'm not going to have a go at you . . .'

'Don't make promises you can't keep, Murph. I know you.'

Murphy gave her a thin smile, but she turned away from him. Her hands were in her lap, fingers tapping against each other as she looked at the houses outside.

'He's on the CCTV,' Rossi said, voice shaking but even-toned.

'What CCTV?' Murphy replied, trying to work out exactly what she was telling him. 'From when?'

'Outside Sam Byrne's apartment, from Mount Pleasant. I spotted him when you were going through it, but didn't think it could possibly be him. I thought it was just a coincidence. How many coincidences can there be, though?'

Murphy took in a sharp intake of breath. Shit. 'What was he doing?'

'Nothing much. He walks into frame, stands around for a bit, like he's waiting for a bus or something, then walks off.'

'At what point does that happen?'

'About midnight, twelve thirty. So, an hour after the last ping from Sam's mobile phone. I should have said something, but I thought it was either someone who looked like him, or just a coincidence.'

'Have you spoken to him? About this, I mean?'

Rossi shook her head. 'I met up with him, but I didn't get past just talking to him about these men and the club. He was really defensive, which isn't like our Cenzo at all. Usually, he's straight as hell.'

'When did you see him? Yesterday?'

There was a pause, then Rossi nodded in response. She still wouldn't meet his eye. 'I've really screwed up here, haven't I? It's going to make me look like I was covering for him . . .'

'Let's not go too far,' Murphy said, reaching out and laying a hand on her shoulder; he took it away after a few seconds, knowing that would be enough. 'We have no real idea if he's involved in anything yet. You're jumping to conclusions.'

'It's the revenge theory,' Rossi said, turning towards him and meeting his gaze. 'He knows the girl. He's been either working with, or is involved with, this Hazel. They've been working on getting them all back.'

'Are you listening to what you're suggesting here, Laura?'

'It's the only thing that makes sense,' Rossi said, settling back into her seat. 'Think about it. The girl is raped, years ago, but no one believes her. Except one person. My brother. He knows these men, and what they're capable of. Over the years, her anger grows. She rents this house, next door to one of the men, probably because she wanted to see what he was like. Rather than just following him around and that, she wanted to be close to him.'

'This is a huge leap . . .'

'My brother gets involved, but maybe he's trying to help her. He's there at Sam Byrne's house to help her, maybe. I don't know.'

'You think your brother killed these men? Or that he had something to do with their deaths?'

Rossi became smaller in the seat, Murphy watching as the words she was thinking turned over in her mind.

'I don't know,' Rossi said, then threw her hand up to her mouth as if she was surprised by what she'd said. 'I can't believe I don't know.'

'I'm sure he hasn't got anything to . . .'

'How do you know that? The things we've seen over the years, how can we be sure of anything ever again? It's entirely possible that my brother has got involved in something that he has no control over. It happens.'

Murphy couldn't argue with her. It was true – the events of the past few years, his entire career, in fact, had shown him that anything was possible.

He hoped it wasn't true. That it was just another coincidence in a complete series of them.

That Rossi's brother wasn't the man they were looking for. That he wasn't a killer.

Thirty-two

It was almost ten p.m. by the time Murphy pulled his car to a stop outside his house. The drive was out of bounds, due to Sarah's car being parked there. At first, he thought that one of the neighbours had taken his usual spot directly outside the house, but then he recognised the car as belonging to Jess.

'I'm home,' Murphy said, entering the house and throwing his keys on the side. The hook seemed too far away and too much effort to use. He slipped his coat off and then did the same with his shoes. His tie had been loosened as soon as he'd got in his car earlier on. It came off entirely now, joining his coat on the banister.

'Do you have to park right outside?' he said, moving into the living room. 'It's not like you're staying over-night, and I'm not going to be arsed to move mine once you leave.'

'You lazy git,' Jess replied, moving to sit on the sofa next to Sarah. She had been sitting in his chair, but moved out of it as soon as he'd walked in the living room. That had been at least one battle he'd won. 'It's not like you have to walk that much further. You could do with the exercise anyway.'

Murphy patted his stomach, lowering himself into the chair. He started to relax, then sprang up and made his way over to Sarah. 'Hello, wife,' he said, bending over and planting a kiss on her forehead. He made his way back to his chair. 'Almost forgot.'

'What's the latest?' Sarah said, refilling her glass with the remnants of a bottle of white wine. 'Needed something to take the edge off the first week of uni,' she added, pointing to the empty bottle.

'Don't look at me,' Jess said, countering Murphy's raised eyebrow towards her. 'I had half a glass, if that. Don't be getting me into trouble for driving home.'

'Didn't say a word,' Murphy said, grinning towards them both. 'You'll be fine, Sarah. I know you'll smash it. Probably know more than the lecturers by the end of the first semester.'

'I wouldn't go that far, but thank you. I'm going over to campus tomorrow afternoon. Have a proper look around, get my bearings and that. Visit the library and pick up my cards and stuff.'

'Have a coffee in the Old Vic,' Jess said, checking her phone and then placing it on the arm of the sofa. 'There's a great café, next to the art gallery bit. They do a fantastic carrot cake. At least, they did last time I was there.'

'Sounds good,' Sarah replied, nodding at Jess. She turned back to Murphy. 'Spill the latest.'

'The latest is shit,' Murphy said, stretching his legs out in front of him. 'You don't want to know.'

'Another body this morning, right?' Sarah replied, sipping from her glass and then placing it down on the coffee table.

'Yeah, it's linked to the same case. Honestly, you don't want to know.'

'Try us,' Jess said, leaning forwards with her elbows on her knees. 'Could do with something intriguing to figure out.'

'It's difficult, Jess,' Murphy started, then thought about what to add to that sentence. 'That guy you defended recently – no body, but a murder charge?'

'I'm still pissed off about losing that one. That didn't go down well, I'll tell you. Should have been much easier than it was. Not that I was that annoyed about him being sent down. He was a smarmy get. Just don't like losing.'

'His name was Tim Johnson, wasn't it?'

Sarah looked towards Jess and then back at Murphy. 'Why do I feel like we're about to be given an aha moment.'

'What, the band?'

'No, like he's about to sweep the table cloth off and leave the plates still standing on the table.'

'What the hell are you talking about?'

Sarah giggled to herself, then winked at Murphy. 'He knows.'

He did. It was something she was always teasing him about. He never came out and just said something, it was always a production, according to her. No matter how small the discovery, it had to be done in a certain way.

He didn't think he was that bad.

'What then?' Jess said. 'Have they found the body or something?'

'No, nothing like that. He's mixed up in this case in some way.'

'The dead politician?' She waited for Murphy to nod before continuing. 'Any closer to finding out what happened to him?'

'No idea,' Murphy replied, scratching at his beard. It would need trimming at some point, but he couldn't be bothered doing it any time soon. 'Feels like we're getting close. He was in some sort of club at university.'

'The Abercromby Boys Club,' Sarah said, picking at bobbles on her slipper socks.

'Yeah, how do you know that?'

'Fellow mature student, who has been doing an access course at the university for the past year, told me about them. They have a terrible reputation and an excellent one all at the same time, apparently. Not our kind of people.'

'You're right there. That Tim Johnson was a founding member of it, along with a few others. That guy found this morning was in it as well. Along with a couple of others who are no longer with us. Could be something happening to them all.'

'Really?' Jess said, eyes widening in surprise. 'So, if someone is knocking them all off, why is Tim still alive?'

'Got me. Could be that he killed that girl before anyone had the chance to kill him. Bit more difficult to murder someone if they're behind bars.'

'Difficult, but not impossible. Have you got the others under protection orders? I think it's only right that Tim is given some sort of heads-up and taken out of general, or something.'

'All in hand,' Murphy said, covering his mouth as he yawned. 'He'll be fine. What do you know about him? Do you think he really killed that girl?'

'Evidence was pretty strong, even without the body. Forensics really did us in on that one. Hard to argue against all that blood and the DNA in his home. Also the witness statements from neighbours about arguments and other things. Didn't help that he had that whole story about a missing daughter who didn't exist. Tried to get him to drop that one, but it was no use. He was absolutely convinced she was out there. How do you deal with that?'

'Bizarre. We met with him and he's still talking about her.'

'You met him?' Jess said, settling back into the sofa. 'How's he getting on?'

'Not good from what I can tell. I assume he's appealing?'

'Yeah. I'm done with it, though. If I can't win it first time around, there's little chance I can do anything differently. I thought about it, because there's money there for the firm, but I just can't see the verdict changing. There's too much against him. Although, I don't think he did it.'

'Why do you say that?'

Jess sighed, choosing her words carefully. 'I have to imagine every one of my clients is not guilty of what they are accused of. That's just the way I work. If I think they're guilty, chances are the jury will as well. Sometimes, I know I'm kidding myself, but there you have it. In this case, it should have been like that, but I just got a feeling. I've sat across from murderers, rapists, child abusers . . . you name it. I know, deep down, when they're guilty. Tim Johnson didn't give me that feeling. I think he'd cracked a little – the whole thing with the little girl was just bizarre – but I didn't think he was a killer. He just didn't give me that feeling.'

'What's the explanation then?'

'Well, I think you know,' Jess replied, looking him straight in the eye. 'If someone wants to get back at this club or whatever, what's the best way of taking someone's life without actually killing them?'

Murphy pursed his lips and ran his tongue over his teeth and grimaced. 'Send them to prison for a crime they haven't committed.'

'Exactly. I can't think of much worse than sitting in a cell for something I hadn't done. Doesn't get much more helpless than that.'

Murphy continued to think about that long after Jess had left later that night. He lay in the darkness, his eyes growing accustomed to the lack of light permeating the room. He stared at the ceiling, able to make out the patterns there, the swirls having more of an effect in the dark.

He glanced across at the alarm clock, mentally working out how long he would sleep for if he dropped off right that second. It wasn't much, but at least it was enough to get him through the next day.

Instead, he kept staring at the ceiling. There was something keeping him awake, playing around his mind every time he closed his eyes.

Something Jess had said, just before she left that night.

There was one witness, who seemed too glad to see him in the dock. Happy for some reason. I didn't really understand it, but there was almost glee in her eyes, every time she looked at him.

'*Who was it?*'

'*Some neighbour. Think the one who lived next door. She was the closest neighbour, as she shared a wall with him. She reckoned she'd heard all kinds of stuff. Managed to get most of it struck off, but the jury still took it in. Doesn't matter if an objection is sustained – it still reso- nates. She was more than happy being there.'*

He imagined Hazel sitting in the courtroom, watching Tim being sentenced for a murder he wasn't guilty of. He could picture her, without knowing what she looked like in reality. Could imagine the feeling of justice she would have as she helped take his life away from him, as he had taken hers.

Not just that, he thought, but what if she was some- how involved in the events which led to him being there.

What if she was involved in everything.

It was a mess, Murphy thought. The whole thing. He thought about Rossi and how she had shuffled out of the office without saying anything to the rest of the team. The look she'd had on her face as she was quietly removed from the case. He had taken her into DCI Stephens's office as soon as they had returned to the station. He'd explained the situation, put his neck on the line.

He hadn't mentioned the fact she had kept the CCTV images to herself for days. Or that she had told him about the possible link earlier that day. He was protecting her, which he knew she'd be pissed off about. It wouldn't be the first time they had done that for each other, and prob- ably not the last. He was happy on one level that it was his turn this time.

Murphy turned over and closed his eyes again. Made a list in his head of things that needed to be done.

Fell asleep before he'd completed the list.

*   *   *

The incident room buzzed with tension as the early morning start caught up with Murphy. He was on his third cup of coffee, thinking about the multitude of trips to the bathroom he would have to take that day if he carried on. His bladder was similarly getting old.

'Are we really doing this?'

Murphy turned towards DC Harris's voice, rubbing a hand over his face as he did so. 'Yeah, we are. We can't find him, so do you have a better idea?'

'Not really,' DC Harris replied, making a face like he was sucking a lemon and couldn't decide if he liked it. 'Just feels wrong. What does Laura say about it?'

'Laura has nothing to do with the case now,' Murphy said, then held up a hand in apology. 'I didn't mean to snap at you. Look, this is difficult, I know, but we have to cover our arses big time here. Everything has to be done as it normally would. What would we do usually in this position?'

'Release his information,' DC Harris said, after thinking about it for a few seconds. His tone was that of a teenager giving into a parent on a point. 'Still seems wrong.'

'Of course it does. That can't have an effect on what we do, though. Once this is all over, she'll be back working with us, and she will want to know we did everything we could.'

'Unless her brother does have something to do with all this and we never see her again.'

Murphy didn't even want to consider that outcome. It would colour everything about his work. He needed Rossi, more than he'd realised in the past. 'We'll cross that bridge if and when it's built and in front of us.'

'What about the girl?'

'Hazel Jones,' Murphy said, finding himself saying what Rossi would have done in response. 'She has a name.'

'Of course she does,' DC Harris said, shaking his head a little. 'What are we supposed to do about her?'

'Finding out where she is would be a good start. There's obviously some connection, once we start looking at everything logically.'

'You know, we could only find one other man from that list so far.'

Murphy swallowed, aware of the overnight update. 'Simon Jackson. What are we doing for him?'

'We've got uniforms by his workplace, but he's eager to carry on as normal.'

'What about Neil Letherby and James Morley? Any idea if they have been found yet?'

DC Harris hesitated, which was never a good sign in Murphy's experience. 'James Morley – we've left messages with his work and at home. He lives on his own, which is a ball ache. Neil Letherby – we've got a little bit on. He has a partner, but she hasn't seen him since he left for work yesterday morning.'

Murphy bit down on his lower lip. 'Is that something that happens often?'

There didn't need to be a response from DC Harris, Murphy knew the answer before it was given. The story was too similar to Matthew Williams's one. And he was currently decomposing in the morgue.

'There's still a chance that he's out there somewhere and just hasn't let his partner know. But, no, it's not normal behaviour, apparently. We've been trying to call his phone, but it just goes straight through to voicemail. Overnight team tried him a number of times. All logged.'

'Put a trace on the last time it was on and pinged off a tower. He lives where?'

'Somewhere north of here . . . Lancaster, apparently.'

'And he had no reason to be anywhere near Liverpool yesterday? Tell me you've checked that?'

'We have,' DC Harris said, moving papers around his desk and finding his notes. 'No, we checked with his work and he called in saying he would be late. Hasn't been seen since.'

'Right,' Murphy replied, getting that familiar sinking feeling. 'So, if his mobile is anywhere near this city, that's when we start worrying. For now, let's not get ahead of ourselves.'

He was already ahead of himself, though. He was seeing where this was going.

It was going to end soon. He knew that. Mainly because there wouldn't be any more names on that list to save.

Four dead. One in prison for life. Three left to keep safe.

Thirty-three

The woods were far enough away from the main road leading up towards the northern towns of Formby and Great Altcar to feel like a foreign land. Wide open spaces of farmland, surrounded by thick, dense woodland, with an A road winding its way through it.

Traffic noise was audible, but only if you were trying to hear it. Otherwise, it was peaceful – serene. The odd bird chirping, wind rippling through the trees, the crunch of branches underfoot, as they trampled through to the small clearing ahead. Murphy stopped and stared at the tree that stood in the centre.

'It's like an altar,' DC Kirkham said from beside him. 'Like it was meant to be here for this purpose.'

Murphy chose not to speak, taking in the scene in front of him.

The browned and blackened burnt wreck of a person took up much of his attention. It hung pitifully from the tree by a chain around its waist, as if it were in the middle of touching its toes before the fire which had destroyed it took hold. The smell of burning flesh still hung in the air, mixed with smoke and petrol. There was a scorched patch of ground a few feet from the tree.

So far, only he and DC Kirkham had been able to handle looking at the body for any period of time. The sight of the charred remains had already cost them a few uniforms, and DC Hale had bolted from the clearing saying he'd check that there were no members of the public in the vicinity, but Murphy had known the truth.

'Corpse sniffer?'

Murphy turned towards DC Kirkham and nodded. 'We'd already found out that his phone was switched off in this area, so it would only have been a matter of time.'

'Is this private land?'

'Think so, but it's not exactly off-limits. There's only a few footpaths, so you can walk through here without even realising. Uniforms have already spoken to the woman.'

DC Kirkham walked away, probably to find the uniforms who had spoken to the female dog-walker who had discovered the body. Another example of the public being involved in the discovery of crimes, without having any intention of doing so. It was enough of a cliché that it put Murphy off ever wanting to own a dog. He could do without finding a dead body whilst out walking the damn thing.

'Christ . . .'

Murphy turned towards the voice behind him. Dr Houghton was standing a few steps away, taking in the scene, much as Murphy had, eyes locked on the body hanging from the tree.

'It must be bad,' Murphy said, taking a step back to allow Dr Houghton to move past him. 'Never heard you invoke His name at a crime scene before.'

'There's something about fire which always gets to me, David.'

'I know what you mean.'

Dr Houghton stood closer to the body, hands on his hips as he surveyed what was left behind. Forensic techs moved into view, none of the usual joviality and gallows humour on display. Even the scattered uniforms were keeping themselves to themselves, the eerie stillness of the area remaining undisturbed despite the increasing number of people descending on the scene.

DC Kirkham reappeared, moving to Murphy's side and looking towards the clearing without speaking.

'How is she doing?' Murphy said, leading DC Kirkham further away.

'They've called an ambulance for her,' DC Kirkham said, taking one last look behind him before trudging off in step with Murphy. 'She's in shock. It's about the last thing you'd expect to walk into. They've managed to get out of her that she usually walks the dog this way every mid-morning. She called it in straight away and didn't get too close.'

'She knew what she was looking at then?'

'I would say so,' DC Kirkham replied, shoving his hands in his pockets as they came to a stop a few more feet away. They came to a halt on a narrow path, dense woodland surrounding them, leaving little room for the two of them to stand comfortably. 'The smell probably didn't help matters.'

'She didn't see anything, I'm guessing?'

'Not that they've managed to get out of her yet. But I can't imagine anyone hanging around long after doing something like this.'

'We're isolated enough that I doubt anyone even saw the fire when it was going,' Murphy said, peering through the trees. 'I think the nearest house is over the next field.' He pointed in what he thought was the right direction, but wasn't entirely sure.

'How did the fire go out?' DC Kirkham said, joining Murphy at the top of the small bank he had ascended to get a better look at the surrounding woodland. 'Could have burned down a fair few trees, which would have made it easier to notice. Seems like it was all contained in one area.'

'Just the tree and the surrounding patch of grass . . . good question. I doubt whoever did this brought a hose with them.'

'Could just be the way it was done. I don't know. I haven't exactly come across something like this before.'

Murphy stepped back onto the path, glancing back towards the clearing, before walking away further. 'About seven or eight years ago I worked something similar. A homeless guy, beaten up and then rolled onto a bonfire. We lifted the lad who did it within a few hours. Just a kid. Teenager, who had a history of trouble. He'd run away from a foster home and met with this guy, smoked his cigarettes and shared a can with him. Then beat the shit out of him, for no reason we could find. It was bommy night, so a few people were watching this bonfire still going at about one in the morning. The homeless guy was just in the wrong place at the wrong time. We could never find out if he was still conscious when he was set on fire, but they suspected so. Always hoped the beating was enough, you know.'

'Doesn't bear thinking about,' DC Kirkham said, his voice almost a whisper. 'The one way I don't want to go.'

'I don't think we get much choice in the matter.'

DC Kirkham was about to reply, but then seemed to change his mind. He brushed a shoe across some loose soil and turned his head towards the trees. 'Two left then. What, with Tim Johnson in prison. Can't imagine it would be easy to get to him in there.'

'Get on the phone to the uniforms watching Simon Jackson. I don't care what we have to do, just get him out of that building and into safe custody. Hopefully we catch whoever it is trying to get to him.'

'Yes sir,' DC Kirkham said, snapping off his gloves.

Murphy watched the forensic techs continue to work the scene. 'James Morley – what do we know about him?'

DC Kirkham huffed out a breath. 'Not much really. He's another one who moved back down south after graduating from university here. We're struggling to find him, but there's nothing to suggest he's in the area.'

'Keep on it,' Murphy replied, pulling out his phone and checking the time. 'This feels like the end game now. Two bodies in two days means whoever we're looking for has escalated. Started to panic maybe. Means we're close.'

He waited for DC Kirkham to leave his side before reading the message from Sarah which had buzzed through just before he pulled out his phone.

Hope all is OK. Off to the uni. Will see you at home later. xx

He fired off a quick reply, then pocketed his phone and felt a little buzz of adrenaline.

It really was the end game, he thought. Four days after being told to look into the disappearance of a local prospective MP, he now had three bodies . . . the investigation had moved in ways he could never have predicted.

That was the way of things. Nothing was ever as it seemed.

He thought of the three remaining men, the last surviving founding members of the Abercromby Boys Club, and wondered if they understood what was hurtling towards them. Tim Johnson secure in prison, but the other two less safe.

He considered whether they had always suspected this would happen one day.

There was a part of him which admired the simplistic vision of revenge that was being enacted upon them. An act of vengeance they couldn't escape.

Murphy shoved his hands in his coat pockets and shook his head at the futility of it all. Wished not for the first time that he could choose who the victims were, so it made his life just a little easier.

In a way, it was no different from Jess having to defend the worst of humankind. He was currently tasked with stopping someone who was only cleaning up a mess that had been allowed to fester over the years.

If he could provide justice to only those who deserved it most, his job would be a simple one. Instead, he put his head down and trudged back to the latest crime scene and kept going.

You

You know how this began. You're beginning to see how this will all end.

You check the information again, wondering if fate is real after all. James Morley, back where it all started.

You think of him, wondering if he will know what your intentions are as soon as you walk into the room.

It doesn't matter to you really. It will almost be the end. One last name, once James Morley is no more.

You watched a man burn to death just a few hours ago. Led him to his death, tied him up to a tree, then covered him in petrol. Lay a trail to a few feet away, where you could start the fire without worrying about your own safety.

You wonder if it would have been better to have died with that man in those woods, burning alongside him.

Death scares you. You know that's normal. We all fear the only inevitable thing in our lives. You're no different. You wonder what is on the other side.

You wonder if you have made a difference.

You think of Tim Johnson, rotting in that prison cell. You wish he was dead now. You wish your list could be complete, with none of them ever breathing again. You regret not killing him. In some ways, you wish he had been found not guilty. Once he was convicted, it was done. You had no chance.

Prison is a slow death.

Tim Johnson will never accept responsibility. He will never get out.

You used to lie awake at night, trying to envisage a future where you wouldn't be plagued by nightmares as soon as you shut your eyes. You feel you might be closer now. That you will soon be able to be at peace with everything that happened. That it will no longer haunt you.

There are two names left on your battered list. Two birdies. You need just the one stone.

You have peered into windows, late at night, trying to listen to what they were doing. You have witnessed them take women back home. Stayed until the next morning, just to make sure they reappear.

You have seen them be normal.

You watched a man burn to death. Heard his screams, the pain and agony of his suffering. You saw the realisation cross his face when he understood what was going to happen to him. Heard him pleading and begging for his life.

He said your name, hoping that would help. It didn't. It only made things worse.

You wonder if you will ever forget the images which crawl through your mind. You remember Sam Byrne as you choked the life out of him. His eyes bulging as he struggled to breathe. You remember Matthew Williams and the sound of his head being pulverised by the hammer. You remember Paul Wright, desperately trying to loosen the noose around his neck. His eyes bulging, his face turning an inhuman colour. You remember the face of Chris Roberts as he fell into the darkness.

You think you will remember Neil Letherby most of all. The glow of the fire, the heat as it rose to full flame. At one point, as he burned in front of you, you could only see hell there.

You wonder if that's where you're going.

The heat from the fire returns as a memory. You had wanted to turn away, but you couldn't stop watching as the man stopped screaming and the noise of the burning took over. You had to watch as the man's skin blackened, his clothes disintegrated.

You enjoyed watching him suffer. You wanted him to.

Now, it's the end. When you discovered that James Morley would be going back to where it all began, it felt apt, somehow. It begins and ends in the same place. There is a poetry to that fact. A perfect circle being formed.

Soon, you will have finished your work. Soon, you will have what you need.

It is time.

It is time.

Now.

Thirty-four

Rossi read the news update on her phone and swore at the screen in her hand. She clicked off it and tried ringing her brother again. When the voicemail kicked in, she thought about leaving another message, but decided the other fifteen she'd left probably made the point.

She lit another cigarette, chucking the lighter back onto the coffee table. Images of the latest crime scene appeared on the muted television screen. Rossi imagined reporters scrambling to the newest place of interest within the city.

'Do you have to smoke in here?' Darren said, popping his head round the living-room door. Rossi looked up at him, giving him a quick glance before turning back to the television. He was dressed for work, but seemed to be hanging around, waiting to leave.

'I can smoke where I like,' Rossi said, trying to keep her voice level. 'If you don't like it, open a window.'

'It's not that. I just don't think it's that healthy for you. You've done so well over the last year.'

'Yeah, well, I'm having a little slip. I think it's fine in the circumstances, don't you?'

Rossi ignored the heavy sigh which came from Darren at the doorway.

'I need to get to work,' he said after a long period of silence. 'Are you going to be OK?'

'I don't need you,' Rossi said, hearing the words after she'd spoken them, realising the harshness of them. 'I mean, I'm fine.'

'I know what you meant,' Darren said, the hurt apparent in his voice. Rossi felt the need to qualify her statement further, but ignored it.

'Just leave, Darren,' she said, taking another drag from her cigarette, watching the smoke settle in the air above her. 'I'll be OK.'

'You can't keep shutting me out, you know? We're supposed to be a partnership. Whatever you're going through, I should be going through it with you. That's what I'm here for.'

'Just go,' Rossi said, shaking her head as Darren's words made her teeth clench. 'I don't need you trying to sort out my problems for me. I'm more than capable of fixing things myself.'

Another heavy sigh from the doorway. She could feel her patience wearing thin, as if it were a tangible thing.

'I'm going then,' Darren said, taking a step further into the room, before stopping and looking towards her. She could feel his eyes on her, but didn't turn in his direction. 'Speak later?'

'Have I got any choice?'

She heard the front door close a little harder than usual. Things between the pair had turned frostier as the week had progressed. Rossi had the feeling he'd been gearing up to chat about starting a family for a while and hadn't particularly liked her response. What he didn't know, was that he had instead picked the worst time to bring it up.

She turned the volume up on the television and banished Darren from her thoughts.

It was only by stepping back, having nothing else to do, that she began to realise just how much interest there was in this case. She had lived within a bubble for much of the week – not knowing that Sam Byrne's death had resonated so strongly with the wider public. The media frenzy had plainly been compounded by the other deaths that week, of which this new one was the third, but the fact that the prime minister had come out and spoken about the murder of a prospective Tory MP meant that the case was front-page news.

Rossi wondered if the PM would be so keen to comment once the full details of Sam Byrne's private life were revealed. It wouldn't be long, she thought. There was nothing like a bit of juicy gossip to keep the newspapers happy. She had already checked social media to see if anyone was making any noise, but it seemed that it was being kept quiet for now.

It wouldn't last.

She thought about Murphy, what he would be doing out in those woods now. Who would be with him and whether or not he was missing her being by his side. This would be the first time he had been out in the field without her for years. They had been with each other for so long now, she wondered if it would be weird for him.

Rossi lifted her phone again, finger hovering over the dial option, and pressed it once more. Each time, she willed the phone to ring, but instead it was the same voice again.

Welcome to the O2 messaging service …

She lifted the remote from the side of the sofa and turned up the volume even more, listening as the reporter on screen spoke about the newly discovered crime scene. The words didn't permeate her thoughts, however, as she tucked her legs beneath her and flicked ash onto the saucer she had turned into an ashtray.

What have you done?

She had been in awe of her older brothers, as they moved in and out of her young life. They seemed to exist on a different planet to her – each one bigger and more distant than the last.

Except for Vincenzo. He was closest in age to her, only a few years between them. She still looked up to him, but they at least had some things in common, which was more than she had with her older brothers. He would make time for her, in ways the others wouldn't when she was younger. Most of the time, they just complained that she had her own room and they all had to share.

She had driven around aimlessly the night before, hoping to find him. After she'd visited his home and got no reply, she'd dropped in on her parents – who hadn't seen him in a long time. She didn't know enough about him to be able to call at places he may have spent any spare time so she had taken to the roads, just hoping to find him by chance. There was a disconnect in their lives, which she'd allowed to grow over the previous few years. They all had their own things going on. That's just the way it was.

She sat forwards on the sofa, putting her cigarette out and pulling her boots back on. There was no use sitting around doing nothing but calling his number over and over, hoping for a different result. She had been out to his workplace that morning, but he wasn't there. She knew Murphy would be trying to track him down by now as well.

She wanted to get to him before he ended up in a cell.

Rossi grabbed her car keys from the coffee table and pulled her jacket on in the hallway. She ignored the mirror hanging on the wall close by, and turned towards the door.

There was someone there. A figure was standing outside her front door, making no movement. The frosted glass made it impossible to make out who was there, but the outline was enough.

She made her way towards the door, grabbing the baton she kept nearby and moving it into reach.

'Who's there?'

No answer. She wondered if her voice had carried through the PVC door. The shape of the man didn't seem familiar but it was hard to tell.

There was silence, then she jumped back as the figure raised a hand and banged on the door.

'Let me in,' a deep voice said from the outside. 'Now.'

She was still for a moment, then grabbed for the handle and pulled the door towards her.

'Fuck's sake, sis. Can you let me in?'

Rossi stood for a second, still holding onto the door, turning slightly as Vincenzo slipped past her and into the hallway.

'Are you going to close that? Only I don't really want people seeing me coming in. I had to wait until your other half left before knocking.'

Rossi shook her head and closed the door. She turned and faced her brother. 'Where the hell have you been?'

'Do you want to put that down for a start?' Vincenzo said, giving her a smile as if this was a normal meeting between them. 'I don't fancy feeling that being wrapped around my head.'

Rossi looked down and realised she was still holding onto the telescopic baton she kept near the front door. She dropped it to the floor, then bent down to pick it up and place it back in the vase where it usually lived.

'What are you doing here?'

Vincenzo turned his back on her rather than reply and made his way into the living room. She followed him, standing near the doorway and folding her arms, watching him as he sat down on the sofa.

'Looks like I might be in a bit of trouble,' Vincenzo said, leaning forwards and clasping his hands together. 'I didn't know where else to go.'

'What's happened, Cenzo?' Rossi said, still standing in the open doorway. 'Tell me what's been going on.'

'Is the kettle on?'

'It can wait. First, you tell me what you've done. I can't help you if you don't tell me everything.'

Vincenzo sighed, then moved his hands to the top of his head, smoothing down his thick, dark hair. 'I've done nothing wrong.'

'Let me be the judge of that,' Rossi replied, unfolding her arms and moving into the room. She perched on the arm of the sofa opposite to Vincenzo. 'Tell me one thing before we start ... have you got anything to do with what's happened this past week?'

There was silence as Vincenzo looked towards the ceiling, hands interlocked behind his head. 'I don't know,' he said finally, dropping his head down and looking across at Rossi.

'What do you mean, you don't know?'

'Exactly that,' Vincenzo said, hands dropping to his knees as he leaned back into the sofa. 'I don't know. Maybe.'

'Maybe?'

'Look, I'm not saying I've been going around killing people. I hope you know me better than to think that.'

'Of course,' Rossi said, hoping her voice held more conviction than she felt. 'I don't understand how you're mixed up in any of this, though.'

'To tell you the truth, neither do I.'

'Then start talking. Because I need to know exactly how far this goes.'

Vincenzo looked up towards the ceiling again. Rossi could see the effect of the previous few days on his face now. Lines creased his face, dark rings showed under puffed-up eyes. Every movement he made seemed to take more effort than it should have done.

'What have you done?'

'I was much older than most of the people at university. I was treated like a stranger there, as someone that wasn't like them. There were other mature students, but it was difficult, you know. I got talking to one guy in the first week, in the library. Sam Byrne.'

'*Mannagia* . . .'

'He seemed all right. Bit more grown up than the rest of the kids I'd met before then. We had a very interesting conversation, about history, politics, that sort of thing. Disagreed on some things, but we got on, you know? We ended up going to the pub from there and carrying on for a few more hours. He was bright, intelligent, but seemed to have something more about him than the other students. It's why he's done so well. There was always a point to everything he did. Very goal-orientated, as they say.'

Rossi kept her mouth closed as she waited for Vincenzo to speak again.

'He had this idea for a club,' Vincenzo said, bringing her attention back to him. 'He wanted to do something different. He wanted to bring a bit of class and decorum to the place, he said, but I knew there was more than just that going on. He wanted me to help him, but it didn't work out.'

'What do you mean?'

'It was about money,' Vincenzo replied, giving her a quick glance and wry smile. 'The people who joined, they were all similar to Sam. They all came from money, but another thing they had in common was that they felt they shouldn't have been there. Not at a university in Liverpool – no matter that's it's a prestigious red-brick university They thought they deserved to be somewhere different. That's where it started. You know that thing about starting out with resentment in mind?'

'Never works out well . . .'

'Exactly. They were all angry from the start and that anger bled into the club. I didn't want any part of it. I think Sam thought I'd add some kind of respectability to the group, being older and more mature, but I don't know really. He had his own reasons, I'm sure. Anyway, once I'd listened to some of the things they had in mind, I knew it probably wasn't for me. I wasn't about to spend a few grand on a suit for a kick-off.'

'What does that club have to do with what's happened now, Cenzo?' Rossi said, dropping onto the sofa.

'It grew, unbelievably to me. I thought it would just be those eight lads, getting together and drinking real ale like they were in their fifties or something. I don't know how they did it, but it became something. I would speak to Sam and a few of the others every now and again, but I still wanted no part of it. Anyway, it became something, that club. They would throw parties, which would be legendary. They had something about them. It was attractive to both men and women, even though it was a "boy's" club. No women members at all. And it wasn't just parties. There was accusations flying around all the time. That they would cheat on exams, hire people to write their essays. Then, there was the stuff they got up to at those parties. Dozens of women, all wondering what the hell they got themselves into. Dropped and discarded after they'd had their fun. Shamed.'

'Something happened in their final year,' Rossi interrupted.

'See, that's the thing,' Vincenzo said, shaking his head. 'I knew it would come out about her, but she wasn't the only one, Laura. There were many young girls over the years with similar stories. She was just the only one that tried to fight back against them. The others . . . they just accepted what happened to them as part of university life or something. I don't know. There were one or two who maybe said something, but it was quickly hushed up. Sam and his friends had power from very early on. Their parents were influential, had friends in high places, the usual bollocks.'

'Why is she different?'

Vincenzo closed his eyes for a second and looked away. 'She was the last one, I was determined about that. Turned out, I couldn't have been more wrong.'

'We know what Sam Byrne was doing.'

'He wasn't exactly discreet about it. That guy was screwed in the head. He would have killed someone eventually. I know it, you know it.'

'So, what did you do?'

There was a moment when she felt she'd gone too far. Then he spoke.

'I didn't do anything about it. That's why I'm worried about her.'

Thirty-five

Murphy could feel the shift in the mood of the incident room. It helped that he'd felt it before, on too many occasions. A sense of losing. There had been a battle going on all week and there was a feeling that they weren't winning any of it. The clock was ticking down now – that was another thing they could feel.

It was almost over.

Another photograph was added to the others already displayed on the murder board. Neil Letherby, another name to be crossed off the list.

'What do we do now?'

It was a question Murphy had heard a few times in the previous hour. He turned to DC Hashem and tried not to shrug in response.

'We keep looking,' he said, hoping he sounded more confident than he felt. 'He'll be coming to Liverpool. That's what has happened to the last three. I know there's two suicides, but maybe whoever is doing this was worried about being caught. Now, it's all zeroing in on the city.'

'I can't believe they let him get away.'

Murphy didn't respond, preferring instead to keep his thoughts on the uniforms in Manchester to himself. The call had gone in for Simon Jackson to be placed in protective custody and moved out of the building. When the uniforms had gone up to his office, he was already gone.

'Look, there was nothing we could have done . . .'

'I don't know about that . . .'

'Well, that's the way it is. We offered to take him last night, but he refused. We had people at his workplace, but we can't have eyes everywhere. This isn't over.'

'What do we do?'

Murphy ran his fingers over his head, caring little how the remaining hair on his head looked once he'd messed it up. 'We need to work out where Simon Jackson could be.'

'How do we do that?'

A few minutes later, Murphy was doing the only thing he could think of – going back to the beginning. He was downstairs in the evidence room going through everything they had collected so far.

'We're looking for anything which may give us an idea of some kind of pattern,' he said, looking over the assembled tables at the young DCs gathered there. 'I know it's a long shot, but at the moment, it's all we have.'

He waited for them to start going over the crime scenes and the evidence from them, whilst he concentrated on what had been needling him all week.

'The forensics report for each crime scene is shocking, really,' DC Hale said, sitting down with a stack of paper in front of him. 'Just nothing of any use.'

'Keep going with it,' DC Kirkham said to him, organising his own pile to go through. 'You never know what'll jump out of it.'

Murphy listened to the various conversations around him, staring at the things which had been brought from Sam Byrne's office. There was something there which had stuck in his mind, but he couldn't remember what it was.

'It strikes me that we're almost looking for a connection between them all,' DC Hashem said, walking back to the table as the door closed behind her. Murphy spied the new folders in her hand, Chris Roberts's name marked on the top file. Someone must have just delivered it, he thought.

'We already know the connection, though, don't we?' Hashem continued, stopping in the middle of the room for a second, before moving towards the table again.

'The club at university,' DC Kirkham said, the pen in his hand travelling up to his mouth.

'Exactly,' DC Hashem replied, sitting down at the table and laying the files down in front of her. 'Did we ever get any information from the university about that?'

'Nothing useful,' Murphy said, joining the conversation finally. 'They acknowledged the existence of it, but said it was unofficial and had nothing to do with the university, as such. Denied any connection whatsoever.'

'It still exists though.'

'Yes, as far as we know . . .'

'And before you ask,' DC Kirkham said, cutting in once he'd removed the pen from the corner of his mouth, 'we did try and speak to current members. No one was very helpful, though. Me and Mike went over there, but it was all very cloak-and-dagger. They barely even recognised the names we gave them. We crashed one of their meetings. They were more interested in telling us about the fact they were no longer gathering in the old pub round the corner. They have a whole meeting room thing going on now, at the Old Vic on the campus. The art gallery and museum place. Even if they did know something, I doubt we'd get any info from them without bringing them into the station and interviewing them under caution.'

'All those rich boys have a bloody good solicitor on hand, anyway,' DC Hale said, shaking his head. 'Not going to get very far there.'

'Back to the old-fashioned way then,' Murphy said, returning to the stacks of paper in front of him. 'See if something here gives us an answer instead.'

Murphy spent the next hour reading through the files garnered from Sam's office. Most contained correspondence that had no influence on the case. There were a couple of nasty letters, which he put to one side to make sure they had been followed up on. However, it seemed unlikely that this was all the work of a disgruntled member of the public. A left-wing activist who killed and dismembered rich Tory boys was probably what certain people were hoping for, but he didn't think it was going to be the answer here.

There were a number of photographs, which he stacked together. Some were framed, others loose and still in sleeves from a couple of different developers. It was odd to see them again – everyone seemed to just save their photographs on their phones or computers these days.

'Where's the report on Sam Byrne's computer?' Murphy asked no one in particular. DC Kirkham's head popped up first.

'Think it's in . . . Ah, here it is. I had a quick scan of it, but Graham was working on it. If he hasn't mentioned anything, I doubt there was anything there.'

As if on cue, the door swung backwards and DC Harris wheeled himself into the room.

'Speak of the devil . . .' Murphy said, standing up and then sitting back down quickly. He'd once tried to help DC Harris and been given down the banks for it for the following half hour. He wasn't about to repeat that mistake again. 'Just talking about Sam Byrne's computer. Anything of interest?'

'Not really,' DC Harris replied, making his way to an empty spot at the table. 'Bunch of porn, but I'm not sure that's anything out of the ordinary. A lot of "barely legal" stuff, but nothing that doesn't seem professionally put together, rather than amateur. Usually means the girls are old enough.'

'What kind of stuff?' DC Hale said, files in front of him forgotten as he leaned forwards on the table.

'Mostly nudes. The only stuff of any interest was the harder-edged images. BDSM, that sort of thing. A lot of girls tied up and that sort of thing. Never understood the fascination with that, to be honest.'

Murphy tuned out as he heard the conversation continue. He was likely to become annoyed with one of them if he carried on listening. Instead, he drew the photographs closer, going through each one in turn.

It was a minute or so before he found the photograph which had been on the edge of his memory all week. It had been lying in a drawer, rather than hung on the wall like you would expect it to.

Eight men, all in tailcoats, holding champagne flutes in front of them. Wide grins plastered across their faces.

'I've seen that picture before,' a voice from beside him said. Murphy turned to see DC Kirkham. 'It was on Simon Jackson's wall. That's what drew my attention when we were in his office and he was denying being in contact with Byrne.'

Murphy was aware that the voices inside the room had died down and everyone was listening. 'This frame,' he said, discarding the packets of photographs and leaving only the framed pictures on the table, 'it's different to all the others.'

'Older, maybe?'

Murphy hummed in response, but continued to stare at the photograph. Along the bottom edge of the photo, there was something that caught his eye.

'Pass me the box of gloves, Jack,' Murphy said, waiting for Kirkham to slide them his way and then putting a pair on. He turned the frame over and undid the clasps on the back, removing the piece of card which held the photo in place. He turned the frame back round and let the photograph fall onto the table.

'He's folded the photograph to make it fit the frame,' DC Kirkham said, leaning on the table next to him. Murphy straightened out the photograph and read what was inscribed on the section that had been hidden from view.

Where It All Began – The Abercromby Boys

'Sir.'

Murphy looked up to see DC Hashem standing on the other side of the table and pointing towards the photograph.

'There's something written on the back.'

Murphy turned the photograph, the scrawl of handwriting there now clear to see.

Sam,
Do you remember this night? End of first year, I
think. This was when you knew it was all going to
plan, wasn't it? That you had created something that
would satisfy your craven desires. This was the
beginning of the end for you.
I'm coming back.
Everyone in this photograph will pay for what they
did.
A Friend.

Murphy finished reading, remaining silent as he let everyone take in what was written on the photograph.

'That's the same handwriting that was on the note found with Matthew Williams.'

Murphy turned to nod at DC Hashem. He began to formulate a reply but didn't get a chance to.

'I think I've found out where James Morley is going to be later.'

Murphy faced DC Hale who was holding a flyer of some sort, seemingly oblivious to what was going on around him. 'What are you talking about?'

'This,' DC Hale replied, sliding the paper over towards Murphy. He picked it up, reading the simple message written on there.

THE RETURN

**ONE OF THE ORIGINAL LEADERS IS COMING BACK.
FOUNDING MEMBER GRANDMASTER MORLEY WILL BE
SPEAKING TO US ALL
3 P.M. – FRIDAY 23rd – THE OLD VIC**

'I know where that is,' DC Kirkham said. 'Do you think . . .'

'Everyone, let's go,' Murphy said, feeling the rush return. They had it.

'Where are we going?' DC Hashem asked no one in particular, looking confused as they moved towards the exit.

Murphy stopped in his tracks at the door, turning swiftly round and looking above everyone's heads. 'You know what this means, don't you?'

DC Kirkham thought for a second, then his mouth dropped open.

'He's not going to stop at just the eight men,' Murphy said, moving out of the door and starting to jog down the corridor. 'He's going to end the whole thing.'

Murphy thought of the place where the men all met up. The Old Vic, the art gallery and museum . . . the cafe downstairs where Jess had suggested to Sarah she should go that afternoon.

He started running.

Thirty-six

Rossi sat in silence, listening as her brother detailed his involvement to that point. Something changed within her as she heard his words wash over her. She knew that things would never be the same within her family after this was over. That was certain. If her parents found out what she wanted to do, that would be it. She would often shake her head at people who believed the Mafia films and their stance on *going against the family*. It wasn't as bad as all that, she would say, downplaying its importance.

It was lies.

What her brother was telling her now would send him to prison – if she chose to tell someone about it. There was no doubt about that.

If she said anything about what he was saying.

'I was trying to help her,' Vincenzo said, lost in the haze between them now. 'That's all. It's the least I could do. We spoke to the girl who Tim was interested in. She was Polish, trying to get by on her own. She'd been trafficked here or something … I wasn't sure about that part. Anyway, she was more than happy to help. She was already pregnant before she slept with him.'

'This is unbelievable …'

'Hazel talked her into the whole thing. There was a big plan. She was going to have the baby, no one would know about it, then she would disappear. Only, the fact that Tim ran away with the baby made it more difficult. We had to get the little girl back, so I . . . I helped do that.'

'Why?' Rossi said, surprised how strong her voice was. 'Why did you feel you had to?'

'I could have stopped them. The club. Back at the beginning. Told them it was a bad idea. Or, I could have joined them, brought them down from the inside . . . I don't know. I could have done more.'

'This is unbelievable,' Rossi repeated once more, running both hands through her hair, wanting to pull on it and scream.

'You have to help me,' Vincenzo said, crossing the room and sitting next to her on the sofa. 'I've screwed up, I know that. I don't know what to do.'

'You could start by telling me where she is.'

Vincenzo shook his head. 'No, I can't do that. It's not fair. There has to be something else we can do.'

'There are people dying in the city,' Rossi said, turning on her brother, stopping as he flinched backwards. 'We need to stop this.'

'It's too late,' Vincenzo said, covering his face with both hands. 'It's already over.'

'No it's not,' Rossi replied, reaching out towards him, before pulling back. 'You need to do the right thing now.'

'You know, I went to see him in Manchester.'

'Who?' Rossi said, her brow creasing as she tried to keep track of where he was going. 'Sam?'

'No, Simon,' Vincenzo replied, his hands dropping down into his lap. 'I thought he might be more willing to come forward. That he might have more of a conscience. You have to remember something here – Hazel wasn't the only one. There were other girls who suffered at their hands. Some of them didn't survive it. Simon was affected personally by what they did.'

'What are you saying?'

'They didn't kill them, but they may as well have. They contributed to at least two suicides I know of. I thought Simon might understand more, given what had happened to his sister. Hazel told me about it. Two suicides, unbelievable. One while they were still at university, another after they left. They couldn't do it any more.'

'Do what?'

'Live with the memories of what had happened, the fact that no one was there to help them afterwards. That there was no one to provide justice . . . I don't know really. When I met Hazel, she was probably at her lowest point. She was just a kid, really, just turned twenty-two, looked about sixteen. Wasting away she was.'

'You knew her before, right?'

Vincenzo was still for a second, then nodded. 'I didn't know what to do about it, though. I wanted to stop what they were doing, but there was just no way anyone would ever help me do that. They, and their families, were just too powerful.'

'You could have gone to the police. That would have been a good start.'

'And what would they do? You're one of them, you know the score.'

Rossi was about to defend her profession, then stopped herself. She had been in the company of enough police officers in the past to know what their views were, for the most part. Anything less than an open-and-shut case suddenly became a 'he said, she said' argument. 'It still would have been better than this.'

'She went to see his parents,' Vincenzo said, continuing as if she hadn't spoken. 'Hoping that they would be horrified and step in. Instead, they closed the door in her face. She was at rock bottom. She had no one. She had nothing to cling on to. With Sam being in the public eye, she thought if he and his parents knew that she wasn't going to go away, then the club could be brought down and stopped.'

'So, revenge became her reason to go on . . . great plan.'

Vincenzo exhaled, loud enough for Rossi to roll her eyes at his dramatics. 'You need to understand what happened,' he said, turning on the sofa towards her. 'He deserved what happened to him. You can see that, surely?'

'Who did? Because I'm struggling to see how anyone deserves to be cut up and put in the boot of a car. Honestly, even I'm not advocating that for rapists.'

'No, Tim,' Vincenzo said, pinching the bridge of his nose with his thumb and forefinger. 'That's all I've been a part of in all of this. He deserved to have something taken away from him, just like he'd done to her. She remembered him. His face. She thinks the others were involved as well, but she couldn't be sure. They drugged them, all the girls. His face was the only one she remembered.'

'So, you don't know where she is now?'

'I have no idea,' Vincenzo said, standing up and walking round the coffee table and stopping near the mantelpiece. 'I don't think Tim was enough. She wanted more.'

'You think it's been her doing this?'

'I don't know.'

Rossi thought for a few seconds, then remembered something. 'Why were you there that night?'

Vincenzo began to speak then stopped himself.

'Don't mess me about here . . .'

'What night?'

Rossi stood up and faced him. 'You know what night. Last Thursday, where were you?'

Vincenzo looked down at his feet. 'I don't know what you're talking about,' he said eventually, mumbling.

'What have you done? Look at me.'

Vincenzo flinched as her voice echoed around the room. 'Nothing.'

'You were there, that night. Were you *helping* her? Is that what you've been doing all along? Helping her transport a man to his death, perhaps? Cutting him up for her? What?'

There was silence. Rossi looked from her brother to where spittle had landed on the polished surface of the coffee table.

'I can't believe you think I'm capable of anything like that . . .'

'Until today, I didn't think you were *capable* of helping put someone in prison for a murder that didn't even happen.'

'OK, OK,' Vincenzo said, raising his hands up in front of him. 'I got involved in something I shouldn't have, I'll admit it. But that man was never going to change. He deserved everything he got. I promise you that. He doesn't deserve pity for where he's ended up – he should have been there a long time ago.'

Rossi simply stared at the man she thought she'd known well, wondering what had happened to drive him to this point. 'It's not right . . .'

'Right? You're telling me about right and wrong?' Vincenzo began to pace up and down the small space on the opposite side of the coffee table. 'You, of all people, should know that the world doesn't work in terms of black and white, good and evil, right and wrong. The world is grey. He should have been locked up for a long time for other things he's done, but that didn't happen. Now he is, that's the end of it.'

'No it's not . . .'

Rossi flinched as Vincenzo slammed his hand down on the mantelpiece. 'There's nothing you can do. I only came here because you're police and you're my sister. I need to know how much trouble I'm in.'

She fixed him with a stare. 'A fucking lot. As soon as they find out what you've done . . .'

'How are they going to find out?' Vincenzo said, interrupting with a laugh. 'I've only told you about this and I can't envisage Hazel suddenly spilling the beans. What physical evidence is there of me being involved?'

'I can't believe you're doing this, Cenzo.'

'I just need to know.'

Rossi closed her eyes for a few seconds, rubbing her temples with both hands. 'You need to come forward and tell them what you've done. I've got nothing to do with the investigation now – thanks to you, I've been removed from it.'

'So they know enough to throw you off the case, enough to say they want to speak to me, but . . .'

'No, don't.'

'You don't have to say anything else,' Vincenzo said, nodding his head. 'Good, good. They don't know enough, that's it, isn't it? How could they? Everything's going to be OK. Honestly. No one needs to know anything about this.'

Rossi looked up, seeing a stranger for the first time. He was her brother, yes, but he was just like everyone else. He was normal. She had looked up to her siblings – idolised them. Placed them on pedestals. They could never live up to her expectations. She knew that now.

When it came down to it, they were as fallible as everyone else.

'You're what we call a white knight, Cenzo,' she said, her voice flat and toneless. 'You think you rode into this on your big white horse, and saved the day for the stricken princess. In fact, you've made everything worse for her.'

'That's not how it is–'

'No,' Rossi said, her voice as loud as it had been earlier. 'You don't get to speak until I ask you a question. Why did you come here?'

Vincenzo stayed silent for a few seconds, staring at the floor like an insolent child. 'Because I thought you could help me,' he said finally, speaking in a low voice.

'Help you because you know they're looking for you?'

He nodded and then shrugged. Rossi gritted her teeth, watching as he shrugged again. He was three seconds from putting his hands in his pockets and going silent, like he had when he was a teenager.

'I can't help you out of this,' Rossi said. 'You've made your bed. There's nothing I can do for you. What I can do, is help stop all of this, if you tell me everything I need to know.'

'You can't leave me to deal with this. You're my sister and you're a copper . . . what's the point in having a bizzie for a sister if she doesn't help you out when it's needed?'

Rossi rolled her eyes as Vincenzo tried a smile on her. It wasn't going to work. She would deal with the consequences of her decision at another time, but for now, all she could think about was saving herself.

And maybe a couple of men she had no interest in saving. She would think about the ambiguity of it all later.

'What was her plan?'

'She didn't have one,' Vincenzo said, crossing the room and sinking into the sofa. 'Not one she told me about, anyway.'

'This all started somewhere,' Rossi said, walking across the room and taking up the position Vincenzo had just vacated. 'That's where she'll finish it. At the university.'

'If she's behind any of this.'

'Yeah, yeah, I'm sure your new girlfriend has nothing to do with any of these murders. Of course not. Just . . .' Rossi stopped talking as her brother began laughing, chuckling at first before it grew louder, then he suddenly stopped.

'What?'

'It wasn't her who called me to Sam's apartment that night,' Vincenzo said, looking up at her and widening his eyes. 'I know that much.'

'Who was it?'

Vincenzo shrugged. 'Got me. I saw them, though.'

'Saw who?' Rossi replied, feeling the air begin to suck out of the room as her brother spoke.

'The club will always exist, you know. Nothing will ever stop that, no matter how many people want to see it end. Cut off the head and two more will replace it. They're more powerful now, holed up in that new place.'

'What new place? What are you talking about?'

'The original eight leaders will be dead within a day or two. It's inevitable now. But that won't stop it happening again. The whole place would need to burn – to put them off ever trying to start up again. That's what he said.'

'Who said this?'

'It's funny, I thought he knew what had happened to her. I mean, it's not like it wasn't talked about. They crossed a line there.'

'Tell me who it was.'

Vincenzo smiled and told her the name.

You

You know this is the end. That it is time to take down the whole system. That's the only way to ensure it never happens again. You have to burn what you helped to create. That's the only chance for your salvation.

You park the car, deciding it doesn't matter where you leave it, so double yellow lines mean nothing. You remove the second jerrycan full of petrol from the car and slam the boot down. You look around at the place where you had spent so many years and say a silent goodbye.

You're not coming back from this.

You notice how little the university campus has changed since you were last there. The square is still full of students crossing back and forth to different buildings, carrying bags and their dreams along with them. There are a couple of stalls hawking day trips and advertising student support groups. The shops are quiet, but you know a few hours earlier there would have been queues outside Subway and Greggs as students on a budget looked for a cheap lunch.

Back then, you didn't ever queue up for a cheese pasty or sausage roll. You would take lunch in the old building in the centre of the square.

You stand outside it now, feeling the strain in your neck as you look up to its peak. The clock on the side is still five minutes fast, as it always was when you were a student. You wonder if anyone is looking at you as you stand outside the old gallery and museum, holding a jerrycan full of petrol and wearing a long coat. You wonder if you look suspicious enough for someone to say something. You slowly look around again, watching the young students walk past you, lost in their own worlds. Headphones in and on. Conversations unbroken by your presence.

No one notices you. No one wonders what you're doing there, or what you have planned.

You look up at the clock again, wondering if they are all sitting down now, laughing conspiratorially between themselves, excited to be there. To be a part of something. The meeting was scheduled to start ten minutes earlier, but it won't matter that you are late.

You take one last look around you, then enter the building. The security guard doesn't look up from the paper he's reading as you push through the small barrier inside. You have purpose, you're walking as if you know where you're going and have a reason to be there. That's the key for anything like this. People are trained to look out for what is the unexpected, rather than for someone who looks as if he belongs.

You learned that a long time ago.

You know where they meet. You know the large conference room they have commandeered on the first floor, the layout of it and the possible exits. You know how panic can make even the most level-headed person make the wrong choices.

You know you have to kill them all.

You know you have to finish your list and then burn the whole thing to the ground. So it will not carry on.

It's the only way.

You wonder how you'll be remembered. You wonder if anyone will grieve for you, once they know what you've done. You wonder if you'll deserve to be thought of at all, given everything you have done in the previous few months.

This was the only way.

You have to keep thinking about that. You have to make things right. You have to atone for your sins.

You stand at the door, trying to control your breathing. They're in there now, so many of them.

Dozens.

James Morley is in there. Second to last name on your list.

You grip the door handle, breathing in and out, then swing the door forwards, reaching into your coat as you do so. All in one movement.

You wait for the eyes of the men inside to swivel towards you.

Then you begin the end of it all.

Thirty-seven

Murphy was first out of the car, ignoring the screeches of the other vehicles as they pulled up on the street. He was already running, having seen something rising from one of the windows of the Old Vic.

Smoke, billowing from the top floor of the building.

'Secure the scene,' he shouted behind him, then repeated himself louder for the other arriving officers. 'Don't let anyone leave.'

He heard the alarm blaring on the periphery of his consciousness as he made his way to the entrance. People began to stream out. They were moving slowly, too used to false alarms and fire drills.

'Move,' he said, making one man jump and begin to move more quickly. Murphy tried to shove his way into the building. 'Come on, get out.'

Heads turned to see who was shouting as officers tried to shepherd people to safety. Murphy scanned the crowd, trying to see if his wife was one of those moving rapidly out of the building. There was no sign of her. He continued to try and push past the exiting people, looking for an easier way into the building. He finally spotted a better path, splitting the crowd as he pushed his way to the far side of the hallway. He vaulted over the entrance barrier and started running.

There was a moment when he had a sudden flash of clarity about the situation. Above the sound of people talking animatedly and someone crying, the fire alarm ringing overhead, a voice within him asked what the hell he thought he was doing.

He thought of Sarah and ignored it.

He wasn't going to let her be in the middle of something like this again.

Murphy looked ahead, the constant stream of people almost unending. There was a sign above him, which indicated the location of the stairwell. He made his way towards this, still battling against the crowd as he moved. He found a pocket of space and pushed forwards, keeping close to the wall. Above the noise he heard the voice of DC Kirkham, trying to direct everyone out of the building.

There was a sense of panic in the air, but the people he was moving past also stopped to see what he was doing. Who was he and why he was going a different way to all of them?

He almost fell into the open space at the back of the crowd, surprised when it suddenly thinned out. Murphy looked around, stopping for a second and catching his breath. He saw DC Kirkham and DC Hashem making their way towards him, trying to take the same route he had. Their way was more blocked, however, as the crowd of people began to push and shove to get out of the building.

He pulled out his phone, hoping that Sarah had returned his phone call or messages, but his screen was blank. He hesitated a second, then thought of what was happening above him and kept going.

Always running towards the danger. That was his job description in a nutshell.

He took the stairs two at a time, rounding the corners as it wound its way up the building. A few stragglers passed him in the opposite direction, holding onto the banister as they made their way carefully down the stairs.

One man, who could have been no more than nineteen, despite his height and thick beard, was moving more slowly, holding onto a laptop in one hand with a backpack and phone gripped in the other.

'Just leave them,' Murphy said to the man. 'Get out of the building now.'

The man looked at him, suddenly stock still. He began to stutter out a reply, but Murphy was already past him.

Priorities, Murphy had time to think, before the smell hit him.

This floor, he thought, pushing his way through double doors and into a long corridor. His instinct was right.

The screaming came from the far end of the corridor.

He was breathing hard, pain already growing in his legs as they protested against the unwanted exercise. He pushed on, almost sprinting towards the end of the corridor.

He reached the ornate double doors and pulled hard, trying to gain access to the conference room beyond, before he noticed the way in was barred.

Literally.

Something metallic and long had been shoved through the handles on the outside of the doors. At first, he thought he could slide it back through, but it was locked into place. It was as if it had been fashioned for this purpose alone, to lock the doors in place so those inside a room had no chance of getting out.

The screams were getting louder inside. He heard a mixture of voices, all panicked and full of a fear he could feel even in the safety of the corridor.

He heard doors bang behind him and a shout.

'Sir,' DC Kirkham yelled from behind him. Murphy turned, seeing DC Kirkham and DC Hashem coming towards him.

He turned back to the doors, pulling on the metal bar, feeling the thickness of the implement, the weight of it. It was stuck in place, no give in it whatsoever.

'What's going on?'

'They're going to burn to death in there unless we get this off,' Murphy said, attempting to lift the bar with two hands. Smoke drifted underneath the door as he did so, small plumes moving around their feet as he and Kirkham took an end each and tried to move it.

It wouldn't budge. Not an inch.

DC Hashem joined DC Kirkham, giving everything she had despite her small frame, Murphy ignoring the scream of effort she made in her attempt to help move it.

'Fuck this,' Murphy said, letting go of the bar. He took one step back and raised his foot, smashing his shoe into the bottom of one of the doors. Other than a slight splintering sound, the door panel made no movement. He tried again, then one more time.

DCs Kirkham and Hashem began similar attempts on the edge of the other door. Murphy decided to change tactic.

He took a few more steps back, then ran at the doors, using his shoulder as a battering ram. One of the old doors began to move on its hinges, just as a bolt of pain shot through him, down his shoulder into his chest. He ignored it, moving backwards again.

'All of us, at the same time,' Murphy said, breathing hard, sweat dripping from his forehead. 'On three.'

They lined up, the doors wide enough that there was space between each of the detectives. Murphy wondered if they would have any effect on the door at all.

'Three.'

They rushed the door, heads tucked down, shoulders in front of them. They crashed into the doors, the sound momentarily stopping the screaming behind it.

Murphy stepped back and checked to see if they had made any dent.

The top-right-hand corner, where Murphy had hit the door, was now bowed inwards. Smoke drifted out and above his head as the shouting became louder again.

'Help, get us out of here. For Christ's sake, we're going to die.'

Murphy heard DC Hashem shout back, but his ears were still ringing from the hit he'd landed on the door and his shoulder was throbbing with pain.

'One more time,' he said, turning back to the two detectives. 'On three again.'

They lined up once more.

'Three.'

This time, Murphy crashed through the right-hand side of the doors, hitting the metal bar in the middle and vaulting over it and into the room.

The smell hit him first: burning flesh, smoke and petrol.

He got to his feet, then covered his nose and mouth with the sleeve of his jacket as the smoke began to swirl around him. He peered through the fog, trying to work out what he was seeing in front of him.

There was a long table running down the middle of the large room, chairs either on fire or thrown back towards the walls. Four large windows were on one side of the room, the curtains which had once hung there were now destroyed.

The burning flesh smell was coming from one corner of the room. A figure surrounded by flames was strapped to a chair. It was already too late for him, Murphy thought, turning away from the sight.

His head cleared after a few seconds and he heard the shouting from the far end of the room. His face was already sensing the sudden increase of warmth, the heat making it feel like it was already burning.

Murphy moved slowly along the nearest wall where the fire hadn't yet reached. He tried to shout towards the group of people at the far end of the room, realising what was happening.

'Get down, we're here,' he shouted, his voice muffled by the sleeve of his coat. He felt the presence of the other two detectives beside him as they entered the room behind him.

'Come on, out,' Murphy said, his voice suddenly loud as he removed the coat from around his mouth. He continued to move towards them, reaching them within a few seconds.

They were pitiful now, all sense of entitlement gone. They were just young boys cowering from the fire devouring the room. Some were already on the window ledge, having smashed open the window in an attempt to allow air to reach the room.

Murphy began shepherding the young men out of the room, reaching across to pull back someone who was about to lift himself onto the window ledge as the flames grew closer.

'I'm not going to burn to death, I'm not going . . .'

Murphy gripped the lad's jacket and pulled him backwards. The chaos within the room was growing by the second as everyone headed for the exit, jumping over the table and fallen chairs, trying to stay away from the ever-growing fire surrounding them.

'Get out of here,' Murphy screamed, trying to get closer to the window and the one lad hovering over its edge. 'Go, go, go.'

He made it past the few remaining boys, reaching the window. 'Get back inside, you can get out.'

The lad was already out of the window, crouched on the ledge, two hands gripping the wood behind him. 'No, I can't,' he said, shaking his head, tears cascading down his face. 'I'm not coming back in.'

It struck Murphy that the boy didn't know the doors had been opened and there was now a way out. Ignoring the screams from his own muscles, he curled his right arm around the lad and pulled him back inside.

He looked down at the pavement directly below the window, hoping he wouldn't see any bodies lying there. He breathed a sigh of relief, then looked towards the crowd that had gathered on the opposite side of the street. He saw something which made him breathe an even heavier sigh of relief, even with everything else that was going on.

Sarah. She was looking directly at him, possibly without even realising. He didn't try to get her attention. Just knowing she was there was enough.

Not in danger.

Murphy turned back to face the room, the fire was getting ever closer as it raged uncontrollably in two thirds of the space. He made his way back to the door, skirting around the edge of the room as the heat began to take hold.

DC Kirkham was waiting, pulling the last lad through the opening and then extending an arm towards Murphy. He pulled him through, out into the corridor, falling onto the floor and Kirkham.

Murphy began coughing, slowly at first, then more forcefully as his insides began to protest at what they'd been put through. He tried to get to his feet, but the exertion began to catch up with him.

'Where did they go?' Murphy said, swallowing back bile growing in the back of his throat.

The lad he'd pulled from the window ledge was sitting with his back to the wall, almost balled up, hugging his legs tightly.

'Get up,' Murphy said. Then again, louder, 'Come on, we have to get you out.'

'I was going to do it,' the young man said, his face as white as the wall behind him. 'I was going to jump.'

'It doesn't matter now,' Murphy said, then paused to cough more. He lifted himself up finally, seeing DC Hashem in the distance herding the rest of the boys out of the building. DC Kirkham rose to his feet slowly beside him. 'You're out of there. Just need to get you out of the building now.'

'Was going to kill us all,' the lad said, shaking his head, his face a mess of tears, his breath coming out in rapid bursts. 'I can't believe it. Set fire to him. Right in front of us. Then locked the door so we couldn't get out. Why us?'

'Where did he go?'

'Just burst in, out of nowhere. We just wanted to hear James Morley speak to us, like the others had.'

'Listen to me. Where?' Murphy asked again, waiting for an answer.

'Said the roof,' Murphy heard the young lad say, just as DC Kirkham pulled the boy to his feet and moved him towards the exit. 'Said it was destiny.'

Murphy watched them walk away, DC Kirkham half-carrying the younger man. He stared after them, making a decision.

He looked behind him, the fire within the room burned even brighter. Heat was hitting his back now.

Murphy swallowed, coughed a little more as the smoke grew around him, then started moving.

Thirty-eight

Murphy made his way up the staircase again, slower this time as his legs screamed from the effort. He discarded his jacket, thick with the smell of smoke, dropping it to the floor and leaving it behind him. He briefly wondered what had happened to his tie, but decided it wasn't important.

The stairs grew less ornate as he climbed higher, people not usually invited to visit the upper floor. The carpet disappeared, replaced by concrete. He continued climbing, knowing he was close.

A double door announced the end of his journey. He pushed his way through it, the chipped paint and dark brown surface rough under his hands. There was another set of stairs behind the doors, steeper and more narrow. There wasn't any light in this stairwell, darkness growing around him as the doors closed behind him. The noise of the fire alarm, which had been a constant reminder to him of the situation, also dimmed as the doors closed. The sound of his own breathing was suddenly more apparent.

He climbed the stairs, taking them two at a time, before his body decided against that and slowed down. His eyes grew more used to the darkness with every step. He reached the top and pushed open the heavy fire door.

Sound whooshed out towards him as light returned. He blinked and shielded his eyes from the sun which was now blaring down on him. Murphy moved further onto the roof, slower now, hearing sirens below and in the distance.

'Nice view.'

He made his way closer to the figure standing with arms outstretched on the raised edge of the building in front of him. The person didn't turn at the sound of his voice. Murphy looked around, seeing the taller buildings of the waterfront in the distance.

'Probably an easier way of seeing the view though,' he said, continuing to move further along the roof. 'Don't you agree, Simon?'

The figure tensed up as Murphy drew closer. His arms were still stretched out, but they were struggling to stay in mid-air.

'You should have let them burn,' Simon Jackson said, Murphy only just making out the words over the noise below them. 'They deserved to die.'

'Maybe so,' Murphy replied, stopping a few feet to the side of the man in front of him. 'Not my call, though. Not yours either.'

Murphy risked another step closer, coming further into line with Jackson as he did so. He could see his face more clearly now, the way his shirt hung loose, billowing in the wind which gusted around them.

'We all deserve to die.'

Murphy breathed deep as he got closer to the edge of the roof, trying to ignore the drop below him. 'It's over,

Simon,' he said, the gravel scraping under his feet as he took another step towards Jackson. 'It's time to come down now.'

There was a soft chuckle before Simon turned his head slightly towards him. 'I've seen you before. On the television, I think.'

'Everyone has,' Murphy replied, shrugging towards Jackson. 'It's a terrible kind of celebrity. Doesn't get you anything.'

'They'll talk about me, though,' Jackson said, turning his head back to face the smaller building opposite them. 'Probably not in the same way they do you, of course.'

'Do you care about that sort of thing?'

Jackson lowered his arms a little more, then used one hand to wipe sweat from his brow as it got nearer to his eyes. 'Only in the way anyone cares about the manner in which your work is discussed.'

'Work?'

'Yes,' Jackson said, his clipped tones sounding alien in the surroundings. 'My work. I have completed my job.'

'How about helping me complete mine,' Murphy said, his breathing now under control. 'Only fair, surely?'

'Your negotiation tactics need a little work.'

Murphy held his breath as the wind picked up once more causing Jackson to sway. 'What was your job?'

'To destroy it all, of course. To rectify the mistake we made.'

'What mistake?'

Jackson turned towards him again, his eyebrows raised as he considered Murphy anew. 'I knew it was over when he came to see me.'

'Who did?'

'Wanted to talk to me about that slut who was crying rape all over campus in our final year. As if she hadn't wanted what happened. He told me what I didn't know.'

'For someone who was intent on killing everyone involved with the club because of this girl, you don't seem to be too sympathetic to her. You know, given she is the one who initiated this change of heart.'

Jackson took a step to the side, almost off the building entirely, before he found purchase again. 'It was never about her. She was nothing. She was just another one, like all the others. It was about all of them. What they made us become. They destroyed us before I even started. They turned us into something we could never be.'

'And what was that?'

'Scum,' Jackson replied, holding Murphy's stare. 'If what she, and so many others said, became known, it would never go away. They made us this way. It was girls like her that made the club the way it was.'

'That's a very black and white way of looking at things,' Murphy said, confused by the man's words. None of it made sense, the reason and motive clouded by the man's hatred of women. 'You kill men because of what they did, even though you blame the women for making them that way . . . you're going to have to help me out here.'

'They killed his sister,' a voice said from behind him. Murphy turned swiftly, stones slipping out from underneath his feet and scattering across the roof. 'Isn't that right, Simon?'

The last person Murphy had expected to appear up there with them made her way towards them.

'What are you doing here?' Murphy said, taking a step back and trying to lower his voice.

Rossi shrugged towards him. 'Had a visit from someone. A mutual friend of our man on the ledge here, isn't that right, Simon? It's the same every time. Sexist rapists, who hate women, apart from the ones they're actually related to. Of course, to some, that doesn't even matter. Except these small-minded idiot boys.'

'You don't know what you're talking about,' Jackson said, spittle flying out of his mouth and down to the street below.

'Don't I?' Rossi replied, eyes fixed on Jackson's back and not acknowledging Murphy at all now. 'You don't think I've met people like you all my life? Happy to subject women to your hatred, until it becomes someone you care about.'

'Stop talking.'

'You can't silence me, Simon,' Rossi said, coming to a stop behind Jackson, a few feet away from Murphy. 'You didn't know until my brother turned up at your office, did you? He told you the truth. About what they had done. To Ellie. You had no idea what they did to your sister. Why she killed herself.'

'I don't want to hear this . . .'

'Why not? This is your legacy. You've been trying to atone for what you helped create, by taking revenge on your fellow rapists. They took something from you and you felt responsible for what happened.'

'You don't know a thing about my life. About my work.'

'I know enough,' Rossi said, looking towards Murphy for the first time and taking a step closer. He matched her step, seeing her intentions in her eyes.

'You think you can comprehend anything? Just because they give you a suit doesn't mean a thing.'

'Because I'm a woman, is that it?' Rossi said, taking another step and removing her hands from her pocket. 'That's not going to fly here, Simon.'

'No, but I will if you keep moving towards me.'

Murphy stopped moving, now only just out of reaching distance of Jackson. Rossi took another step, before she too came to a stop.

'We need to talk this all through,' Murphy said, glancing towards Rossi and motioning with his head. 'Make sense of it all.'

'What does it matter?' Jackson said, turning around fully now. The back of his shoes were over the edge, only one movement from falling down to the pavement. 'It's done, there's nothing left to do now.'

'Tim will be released soon,' Rossi said, facing Jackson and holding his gaze. 'He didn't kill anyone. Soon, he'll be out on the streets, with nothing to answer for. Are you telling me you don't want to be the one to make sure he goes back inside?'

'You're lying,' Jackson said, but Murphy could see the hesitation on his face. 'He's never getting out.'

'Yes, he is,' Rossi replied, her voice rising above the noise below them. 'He was one of them, wasn't he?'

'She shouldn't have been there,' Jackson said, tears springing to his eyes as his feet wavered on the edge of the rooftop. 'None of this would have happened if she'd just stayed away.'

Murphy bit back a reply, hoping Rossi would do the same.

'They did to her what you all had been doing for years. To other people's sisters and daughters.'

'She wasn't like them,' Jackson said, anger on his face

now, turning redder by the second. 'She was a good girl. They took advantage . . .'

Rossi moved towards him. 'You're not going to jump off here and escape it all, Simon. You can't run away from this. You're going to face up to what you've done, make sure Tim Johnson doesn't get away with what he did. That's what you're going to do.'

Jackson wiped a sleeve across his face, looking at Murphy for a second before turning his attention back to Rossi. 'She never listened to me,' he said, a wry smile creeping across his face. 'She just wanted to be a part of whatever I was doing. She was always like that. When Vincenzo turned up at my office, I didn't know what to say. I knew, though, before then. I knew what had happened.'

'You just needed to hear it being said by someone else.'

'She never told me. She came here, for one weekend. I didn't want her at the party. I knew what they were like. Sam, Tim . . . they were the worst. They liked them young and Ellie was only seventeen. Looked even younger. I tried to keep an eye on her, but she left with them. I didn't know that, though. She sent me a message saying she'd gone back to my flat. I didn't even check to see if she was in bed or anything. She'd gone back home by the time I woke up the next morning.'

'When did she die?'

Jackson shook his head, Murphy watching the exchange without speaking. He inched a little closer, hoping Jackson wouldn't notice.

'A few months later,' Jackson said, looking up towards the sky. Murphy held his breath as he waited for him to topple backwards.

'They never said anything to you?'

Jackson shook his head. 'They would make jokes, before she died. That's all I thought they were – jokes. Banter and that. I didn't think it was actually true.'

'Vincenzo told you, though, didn't he? He told you what they did to her.'

'Yes,' Jackson replied, his head falling onto his chest, eyes closing. 'I called him a liar. Told him to keep his mouth shut, otherwise he would destroy everything. It wasn't the way things should be done. She shouldn't have been there.'

'You can't run away from this any more, Simon,' Rossi said, a couple of steps away from him now. Murphy was almost as close. Within a step or two, they would be almost on him. 'It's over.'

Jackson lifted his head, looking first at Rossi, then Murphy. He looked up towards the sky again.

'Think of your family,' Murphy said, trying to stop the inevitable. 'Are you just going to leave them to pick up the pieces?'

'It doesn't matter. They'll get by a lot better without me. I failed her,' Jackson said, lifting his arms into the air again, outstretched as if he was on an invisible cross. 'But I made it up to her. It's over all right. They'll never do it again.'

When people spoke to Murphy about these kinds of situations, they always said time slowed down. They said everything stopped and they could see everything happen in slow motion.

It didn't happen that way for him.

One second, he was reaching out towards Simon Jackson, Rossi by his side matching his movements.

The next, he was grabbing at thin air, hearing the screams from down below.

You

It doesn't matter what they say. They can never change your mind. You knew how this ended, before you even began. You knew all those years earlier, when you lowered Ellie Jackson into her early grave. The look of pain and agony on your parents' faces as they buried their daughter. You knew then, there was only one way to make up for all that you had caused.

You look at both of those strangers on the rooftop, one to the other, then lift your arms out. You hope to be welcomed home, to see her again.

To say you're sorry. To beg for forgiveness. For everything you did.

There's a second when your feet try to find purchase, then all you can feel is the wind rushing around you. You close your eyes to it all. You embrace the darkness as you fall, down and down.

You hope that the trip down ends there. That you don't keep falling afterwards. That you'll make your way back up. That you won't go to hell.

The last thing you think of before you hit the ground is her. Ellie. Your sister. The one you allowed to die. She killed herself, because she couldn't live any more.

Please forgive me.

Epilogue

It hadn't taken much to get Vincenzo Rossi to talk. He knew he was in deep trouble and that his sister wasn't going to be able to help him unless he revealed all he knew.

His information had led them to where they were now. Standing outside the anonymous door of an apartment near Sefton Park. Close to the place where Tim Johnson had lost what he thought was his daughter.

'Let them go in first,' Murphy said to Rossi. 'Clear the place just in case.'

He still wasn't sure she should be there with him, but he knew there was going to be no talking her out of it. She wanted to be there at the end, to make sure everything was done right, in case it meant even further trouble for her brother.

'Police, open the door.'

Murphy stood further back from the other uniformed officers, waiting for the door to open.

Tim Johnson was going to be released, based on Vincenzo Rossi's statement, he thought. They were currently in the process of tracking down the Polish woman he had supposedly murdered. It wouldn't take long, not with the information Vincenzo had provided.

Murphy had agreed to Rossi's request in exchange for all of this. Her brother's name would be kept out of it all. It was a risk, given that Hazel or her eventual lawyer might use that in her defence, but they could plead ignorance.

It would take time for them to get back to normal, but Murphy knew it would happen. There was just too much between them for it not to.

'We're going in.'

Murphy watched as they broke down the apartment door and quickly entered one after another. He was pretty sure they would find nothing in there.

Hazel Jones would be gone.

'What do you think will happen to them?'

Murphy turned back to Rossi, trying to figure out an answer to her question. He knew who she meant. 'I think the Abercromby Club will struggle to come back from this.'

The burnt body of James Morley, the final name on Simon Jackson's list before his own, had been returned to his family down south. With the exception of Tim Johnson, all the founding members of the club were now no more.

Already, women were coming forward with stories of the club's practices over the years. Tim may be released for a murder he didn't commit, but he wasn't going to be free for very long. There would be a number of prosecutions over the coming months and years.

'Tim Johnson won't get away with it, you know,' Murphy said, looking down at Rossi as she absent-mindedly chewed on a fingernail. 'He'll be going down for a long time.'

'Won't be enough, though, will it? It's not really justice for what he did.'

'And what Simon Jackson did was?'

Rossi waited a moment, then shrugged her shoulders. 'I suppose we can't put people in prison for being the reason someone kills themselves. We'd have to create a whole bunch of new laws for that to happen.'

'We won't tell him,' Murphy said, having found the moment he had been waiting for.

'Tell him what?'

'That the baby isn't his,' Murphy replied, peering over the heads of the officers in the hallway and seeing a shake of the head from those at the head of the pack. 'He can live his life thinking she's out there and he'll never know the truth.'

'Dangerous, don't you think?'

'In what way?'

Rossi leaned back against the wall behind her and looked up at Murphy. 'He will try to find her.'

'First, he'll be in prison for a long time. I have no doubt about that. Second, let him try and find a needle in a haystack. He has no idea what country that woman he lived with for months even went to. And we're not going to tell him. All we need from her is proof she is alive. After that, she can disappear again.'

Rossi thought for a second, then slowly nodded towards Murphy.

He hoped it was enough.

Once they had left the university, shepherded off the roof of the Old Vic and down the stairs by the firemen who had arrived behind them, Murphy heard the full story. How Hazel Jones had put her plan into place, how

Vincenzo Rossi had helped her get Irena Dubicki's daughter back to her mother. The money he had helped contribute to buy her silence. How he had aided Hazel Jones as she created a convincing crime scene.

The whole sorry tale of revenge, which had run alongside Simon Jackson's story of vengeance.

They filled in the gaps later. Vincenzo Rossi going to see Simon Jackson when Tim Johnson had been arrested for murder, and the part that had played in causing Jackson to seek his own revenge for what had happened to his sister. Jackson's need to atone for the failure to keep his sister safe from the sordid life he had created. It had driven him to end the toxic environment he had helped to create. An environment in which women were objects, things to conquer, whatever the outcome.

To kill those he blamed for her death. Including himself.

'They didn't care before,' Rossi said, back at the station that day. 'None of them did. Those women weren't like the ones they knew in their family. If what happened to Simon Jackson's sister had happened to any of their close family members, they might have reacted similarly to him. They were sexual psychopaths. All of them.'

Murphy hadn't disagreed with her. There was too much evidence coming out about the club and its activities to do so. How they created a culture at the university surrounding their activities which promoted silence and the goal of ultimate power.

Well, it would be over for that club now, Murphy thought. All it takes is a single event and a whole organisation can be brought down. Sarah had told him the atmosphere at the university was significantly different now. Everyone was falling over themselves to condemn and castigate those with any attachment to the club.

Murphy wondered if the condemnation would be matched at other universities in the country, many of which had groups of young men all doing similar things to what the Abercromby Boys Club had done.

He wondered if anything ever really changes.

'She's not here, sir,' a uniform said, joining them in the hallway. 'Evidence that she's been here recently, but there's milk on the side which has turned, so she's been gone a couple of days at least, I reckon. Left in a hurry.'

'I bet she did,' Murphy said, making his way towards the apartment, leaving Rossi where she was standing.

He was glad Hazel Jones had gone.

He hoped that she would never return.

That she would be happy, wherever she was.

Let There Be Light

The internet was slow, but eventually the *Daily Mail* website appeared. She read the main story, scrolling down and studying every word on the page. She went back to the beginning, reading it all over again. The details were slim, but there was enough information for her to take on board and digest what had happened. The sidebar of shame tried to take her attention, but she ignored it.

Simon Jackson was dead. Along with all the others. All of them, except one.

Tim Johnson remained in prison. She didn't know how long that would last, but it mattered little to her now. She had already taken what she needed from him.

She clicked onto another tab and read the message from Vincenzo again. The story they had created, which had put Tim where he belonged, was over. Soon, he would be free, but Vincenzo promised it wouldn't be for long. That he would be made to answer for everything that Boys Club had done over the years of his membership. Brave women coming forward and telling their own story. The truth.

There was more though. He would never know the truth about the little girl he called Molly. Vincenzo knew for sure.

He would never see the little girl he thought was his daughter again. And he would never know she wasn't his. She was gone, along with the baby's mother. Back to Eastern Europe, a little wealthier, a little more confused about life. She would come forward and say she wasn't dead, but that would be it. The money had been enough to buy her silence on that. The promise of more on the little girl's eighteenth birthday was the final nail in that particular coffin.

Tim Johnson would spend the rest of his pitiful life searching for a daughter who didn't exist. That was enough payback for her. First, she had taken his freedom, now she would sit back and enjoy the thought of taking his soul. He would forever be in the thrall of the lie she had created.

She enjoyed the thought of that.

She signed out of the computer, paid up for the time she had used, then left the internet cafe. She shifted the backpack, enjoying the weight of it on her back. She adjusted the cap on her head, running a hand through the short hair, trying to get used to it. It would probably take a little longer, but it was necessary. She had to be careful now. She wasn't expecting a womanhunt, but it paid to be careful.

The sun was high up in the sky as midday clicked past. She started walking, not sure of a destination yet. Just happy to have the choice to do so.

She remembered Vincenzo telling her about visiting Simon Jackson at his office the previous year. Telling him exactly what his friends had done, what they had caused. She had enjoyed that.

She had told him to visit him. She had enjoyed that feeling of power, of control. She was in charge. It had been a long time, but she finally had command of a situation.

She hadn't known what Simon Jackson would do with the information. She wasn't sure if she cared. Reading what he had been doing didn't make her feel responsible, or party to his actions.

She felt nothing.

It was another world to her now. A story with a beginning, a middle and an end. Another life. Not hers any more. They weren't around any more, but she didn't care.

She was moving past them. They were left behind her. They wouldn't trouble her any more. The nightmares would come to an end.

She hoped.

There was light in her life at last. An end to the darkness which had enveloped her. She would never forget, but she could at least live her life without looking back.

It was over.

A new chapter could begin. A new story could be told.

She allowed herself one last thought about the men who had taken that part of her away. The eight names, the eight men. They might not have all been physically guilty of what had occurred to her that night, but they all shared the blame equally in her eyes.

She wasn't sure. She could never have been, that was something she would have to live with.

She was only certain of one man's guilt.

Tim Johnson.

He deserved everything she had inflicted upon him. He deserved the harrowing life he would lead now.

That was her revenge.

She looked left and right, crossing the busy road alongside a few other people. She tuned back into the surrounding noise. The blaring of horns and shouts from the various drivers. A foreign land, a place that would soon become a footnote on her travels.

She continued walking, head held up high, looking forwards and not back.

Hazel lost herself in the crowd and became just like anyone else there.

Free of her past. Only looking to the future.

There was one last moment, when she closed her eyes and felt her fears drift away.

Then, she was gone.

Acknowledgements

Some things never change. This book may have my name on the cover, but it takes a bunch of good people to make sure it reaches your hands. Here are some names, which may not be recognisable to you, but who all contributed to the journey of publication.

Firstly, my small band of grouchy, embittered, hilarious, and warm-hearted fellow writers: Eva Dolan, Jay Stringer, and Nick Quantrill. Our continuous chats keep me on the straight and narrow. I have made friends for life in you three. Similarly, Craig Robertson, for being as much of a bastard as I am. You're stuck with me mate. England Crime Writers will beat your Scottish lot one day.

Stav Sherez, for continuing to say nice things about the series. You give me a jolt of happiness each time, given how much I admire you and your work. Thanks man.

Next, my awesome editor at Simon & Schuster, Jo Dickinson. Thank you for not panicking when I came to you two months before the deadline with a completely different story. I am so glad you reacted with excitement, rather than absolute horror. You are incredible at what you do. Never change. Also to Emma Capron, Louise

Davies, and the rest of the team at S&S. I am forever grateful for all your efforts.

My agent Phil Patterson. I cannot say enough good about this man and his continued support and presence in my life. I got very, very lucky in finding you. Also to Sandra Sawicka and Luke Speed for all you do.

Darren Dodd, who gave me an incredible amount of advice about how politics works at the local and party levels. I discarded most of it, as no one would find it believable, but what I did use came from that conversation. Thank you sir. All mistakes are my own and intentional. As always.

Sarah Hughes and all at Waterstones Liverpool One, Karen Sullivan, Bob Stone and all at Write Blend, Pete Sortwell, Liz Barnsley, Jo N and all at Tandragee Library, Paul D. Brazill, Tracy Mearns, THE Book Club on Facebook, Anne Cater, Steph Broadribb, Vicky-Leigh Sayer aka The Welsh Librarian, "Eloquar", and "Book Addict" Shaun. Thank you for all the support you give me and the books on and offline. Couldn't appreciate it more.

Thank you to Emma Palmer, who won an auction to have a character named after herself. Supporting that particular charity is massively appreciated. Hope you enjoy seeing your name in amongst this unsavoury bunch of characters.

To my parents, siblings, grandparents, uncles, aunties, cousins, and in-laws. You're all fantastic, as always.

Gina Kirkham, for your unending help and drive. Hope to continue to make you proud.

Finally, the best for last. My wife Emma and daughters Abigail and Megan. Abs and Migs – you know the score now. Instead of me saying something nice which makes you roll your eyes, how about this . . . tidy up your rooms, do your homework, stop arguing, and eat all your tea. Like good girls. Only joking! Well, not really, but here's something nice as well. You make me so proud every day. You're both incredibly talented, funny, and clever. Thank you for being my daughters. To Emma – I can't imagine a life in which I don't have you supporting me every step of the way. You make my life easier. You're my partner, and other half, in every sense. There are no books without you. In fact, without you, I would be covered in bees constantly. *Ti amo, bella*. Thank you.

Missed out on Luca Veste's last book?

Turn the page for chapter one of

Bloodstream

Available in paperback and eBook

Chloe and Joe

She watched him die.

She did nothing, as the man she supposedly loved took his final breath. Knowing that she would have to live with that inaction for whatever time she had left.

She told herself there wasn't much she could have done anyway. She could only watch as the realisation hit him, filmy eyes locking with hers. A single word dropping from his mouth, before it dissolved into nothingness and he began to fade away.

She had simply stared at him, soft tears rolling down her cheeks as she watched him convulse. Saw him fight with a diminishing strength, his muscular, fit body amounting to little in the end. A growing horror building inside her as the final gurgles of breath left his body. The effort of keeping her eyes open exhausting her.

She didn't try to move, to try to help him. The desire to do so obliterated by his words.

The knowledge that she had wanted this was driven to the back of her mind. Only the thought of what was going to happen next. Whether she would die or be let go.

She was glad he went first.

She was glad he had died looking her in the eye, knowing she had wanted it to happen.

She was glad that he'd died knowing that she was happy that he was gone.

It hadn't started out like that.

They were famous, away from that room. Celebrities. Everything she'd ever wanted to be. Chloe Morrison. Famous for no reason other than for being famous.

Chloe was taken second, after Joe, and only because of what she had been shown. Joe, tied to a chair, beaten and bloodied. She hadn't thought of herself or her family. Only him and the danger he was in.

She knew what people thought of her – that she had an elevated sense of self-worth. She had a reputation for getting what she wanted, when she wanted it. That she believed she deserved the attention, based purely on who she was.

It wasn't completely true. Not all of it.

Joe had been central to her life. It didn't matter if she spent hours making herself look 'right', presenting the flawless version of herself to the world. The spray tans and endless hair and make-up sessions. The rumours of plastic surgery to explain the way her body looked in tight-fitting clothes. To Chloe, that was all just part of the celebrity game. One she had wilfully taken a role in.

She had sought fame. She had a need to be famous. To be noticed. Without the talent or skill for it to be in music or sports, or even a vile personality. There was only one way.

Reality TV.

Chloe had thought the only way to get on one of those programmes was to either turn posh and move to Chelsea, or pretend to be from Newcastle and become more willing to piss the bed in front of a camera. That was until she saw the advert on Twitter, asking for girls from Liverpool to audition for a new reality show that was being made. She'd slept in her rollers and turned up along with hundreds of others a few weeks later, prepared to be as glam and gorgeous as possible, knowing that she had to be more *real* to stand out in the crowd.

The first time they'd met was at the auditions. She'd thought he was good-looking, if a bit full of himself. It was clear the producers on the show had plans, pairing them off a few times before filming began. It had made them comfortable together, giving them better on-screen chemistry. She'd found out Joe played for a lower division football team she'd heard of in passing. Played on her side of the water, on the Wirral. Not that she was pretending to be anything other than a proper Scouser at that point.

That had been almost two years ago. Since then, her life had changed in every single way she could have dreamed of. She was *known*. People stopped her in the street, asking for a selfie – the new autograph. She'd become the queen of the fake smile. People would tell her how funny she was, how *real* she was. How they'd known from day one that she and Joe would end up together. How happy they were that Chloe and Joe had fallen in love. How they just knew ChloJoe were going to be together forever.

On the show, cameras had followed every move they'd made. The 'first' meeting in the house they'd all had to share. The first date. The first kiss. The first time they'd said the words 'I love you' to each other. Granted, that had been in the middle of a nightclub, shouted over music, which wasn't all that romantic. They'd had to go back and dub it over, so it could be heard properly on TV. Saying it over and over in a sound booth into a microphone had kind of stripped away the romance of it, but she'd tried her best. Even if it was the weirdest thing she'd ever done.

The sex was awful, but she had all the time in the world to make that better. The proposal episode of the show had millions of viewers. She'd known beforehand, of course, but had to act as if it was all a surprise to her. It wouldn't matter. She was going to be a bride.

Then, just like that, she was bound to a chair, on what had, at first, been just a normal Friday. Darkness and the smell of rotting wood. A room in a boarded-up house, somewhere she didn't know. Joe was opposite her, breathing in short bursts as he sobbed quietly. A man almost blending into the black, his voice a whisper in her ear.

'Secrets and lies. That's why we're here. They're wrong. Everyone knows that. So many relationships have these secrets and lies going on within them. And now here you both are. The ultimate celebrity couple ... until another one comes along to replace you. Even the two of you can't escape what is real. The veneer of celebrity, everyone looking up to you. All these impressionable young minds you pollute with your lies. I'm talking real lies. Real secrets. You disgust me.'

Chloe heard the words through a fog of confusion, aware of the voice speaking directly to her and Joe. She wasn't able to focus on form or being. Just the words and the puzzling mix of them.

'Say we have a relationship as public as yours. One that is in the news all the time, in every glossy magazine, every tabloid, every celebrity blog ... one would think there could be no secrets. No lies. Everything out in the open, for us all to enjoy.'

The man moved closer to Chloe. 'But we know that's not true, don't we?'

Chloe shook her head, slowly, the room spinning as she did so. She tried to speak, before remembering the duct tape plastered across her mouth.

'Don't worry, I'll be removing it soon,' the man said. 'This would be no fun if you couldn't speak to each other.'

Chloe looked across at Joe as his head slumped forward onto his chest. Tried to catch his eye, but he wasn't moving.

'Chloe,' the man said after a few more seconds of silence. 'I want you to tell each other everything. All the secrets you have kept from each other. Then we'll see how I feel. Do you understand?'

She began to feel a little more clear-headed; the mist lifted and her focus returned. She rocked her head side to side, almost losing it again.

'Oh, Chloe. From what little I know about you, I don't think you could hide a single thought in that thick little brain of yours. No, I'm guessing you're an open book with little old Joe here. I bet he knows everything you're about to say before you've said it. Probably because it'll be about shopping or exposing yourself in some magazine.'

Chloe could feel herself shaking, the duct tape binding her hands together straining against her wrists.

'Chloe, you have to listen now. Do you understand? I think Joe has something he wants to tell you.'

It wasn't quick in coming.

When it did, she had stopped shaking through fear. Forgotten about the man in the room, what he'd done to make Joe tell her the truth. There was only her and Joe.

And anger. For everything he'd said. Everything he'd done to her.

A few minutes later, she watched him die. Watched as the man curled a piece of rope around Joe's neck, and choked him to death.

Chloe had wanted it to happen.

She was pleased that it had. That he'd got what he deserved.

'Now, Chloe,' the man said, coming down to his haunches as he got close to her. She could feel his hot breath on her neck, as he whispered in her ear. 'It's time for you to go to sleep.'

@scousemum38
Have you heard about that Chloe and
Joe from that shit Liverpool show?

@kezza11990
Yeah. Just read it. Bet they've just
gone off on holiday somewhere.

@EchoNews
BREAKING – 'ChloJoe' missing. More
information here – bit.ly/576fb5 #ChloJoe

@Gizmod87
Waits for 'exclusive' beach pictures

@Insert_Name_Here_22
Ugh. I hope they are found in ditch
somewhere #realitytvisshit

@ScouseanProud_8
They give us a bad name anyway.
Hope they don't come back.

@ScouseanProud_8
Both wools anyway. Sod 'em.

@Fayz20
I reckon they've gone off and got
married. #fairytale #newshow

@HELsBELs98
Shes a slag anyway. Hope hes found
someone better. #Joeishot

Chapter One

He hadn't seen anything like this for a long time. An authentic confession to murder. No ifs and buts. No *I didn't really mean it, it was all just a terrible accident.* Simply a total and utter acceptance of the facts and what seemed like genuine remorse.

Detective Inspector David Murphy let his size thirteen shoes slide off his feet a little and scratched at the closely shorn beard on his face.

'I don't believe you.'

The man sitting in front of him didn't gasp in shock, but moved back in his chair a little.

'Wh . . . what do you mean? I'm telling you I killed her. Stabbed her right in the chest, here,' the man said, hitting his heart for effect.

'I'm not buying it,' Murphy said, letting his eyes drift round interview room two. It needed a new paint job. The white walls where now a faded, almost grey colour.

'I'm just trying to be helpful here,' the man said, almost pleading. 'I'm doing the right thing, aren't I? I mean, it must have been me who did it. It has to be. I hear her voice sometimes and I have to tell someone what I did so she'll stop. That's the right thing to do, isn't it?'

'Oh, it would be. If a word of it was true,' Murphy replied. 'The problem is I don't think any of what you've told us since you sat down in here is the truth. Is it, Keith?'

A long sigh came from beside Murphy. DS Laura Rossi becoming bored of the exchange, he guessed. 'Tell us again.'

Keith took a deep breath and began to speak.

'We were seeing each other, me and Amy. We're like boyfriend and girlfriend. We talk about everything. Spend loads of time with each other. Have been for a few months . . .'

'See, that's the first problem, Keith,' Murphy said, attempting to keep a smile from his face. 'Boyfriend and girlfriend?'

'That's right.'

Murphy shook his head and tried to hold the laughter in. That this guy could have any chance with Amy was ridiculous. Amy was just about to turn nineteen, a fresh-faced beauty with her pick of men. Keith was in his forties, with a pock-marked face scarred by teenage acne that had yet to disappear. The grease from his hair alone was enough to keep the local chippy in business for a good few weeks. That was before you considered other 'issues'.

'Go on,' Murphy said with a wave of his hand.

'We must have got into an argument, like, and I had hold of a knife. I did it. Stuck it right in her chest. Sometimes people argue with me and they won't stop. They just go on and on, so I have to stop them somehow. I see knives and I put them in their chest and they go away for a bit. Then they come back some time later and start up with me again. So, that'll be how it happened. I can see it, all in here.' He paused a second, but then pointed to his head.

'Go back a minute,' Rossi said, writing down notes as Keith spoke. 'Slower this time. You've been seeing Amy for a few months, right?'

'Yeah. I have, honest. I know it sounds weird, right, but she liked me. Always speaking to me nicely, smiling and saying sweet things to me.'

Murphy made a noise, somewhere between a snort and a laugh. Rossi ignored him and continued talking.

'Why do you think no one close to Amy would mention you, Keith? Because this is the first time we've heard your name mentioned.'

Keith looked off to his left. 'I . . . I don't know. Maybe she never told anyone about us.'

'You've been together for a few months in your words and she doesn't tell anyone?'

'Must be.'

Murphy pictured Amy walking hand in hand round town with this guy, laughing with him, gazing into his eyes . . . it was ridiculous.

'How did you meet her?'

'I went into the shop where she worked. It's over the road from my flat. It's on the ground floor, so I'm level with the street. I like that. I used to go in every morning for the paper and other stuff. Then, I'd wait until she was definitely on shift. Got to know her pattern and that. We hit it off straight away, honest. She was so nice to me. Always smiled as soon as I went in there. Then, I practised at home asking her out. Over and over again and she always said yes. So . . . so, I did it. I asked her. I definitely did. I think I did.'

Murphy shook his head and looked away. Muttered 'Christ' under his breath and checked the time.

'What happened after you say you stabbed her?'

Keith glanced at Rossi before averting his eyes from her stare. Murphy watched him, trying to work out why he thought he had done something like this.

'Well, when you stab someone, they bleed a lot. I've seen it on telly and that. In films, they stab people and there's blood everywhere. So, I wou . . . couldn't stop the bleeding, but she wouldn't be breathing anyway by then. If you stab someone in the chest, they die really quickly. It happens in loads of films and TV programmes. I have bin bags in my house, so I must've wrapped her up. I would have done it nicely though. Then I took her home. Carried her there all by myself. From the shop. There must have been a lot of blood there, so can you say sorry for me? I don't remember cleaning it up, so it must have been all over the place. I don't know. I haven't been in there since.'

'When was this?'

'About ten in the morning, I think on a Friday. Or a Tuesday. Few weeks ago. Or two. It was quiet, so no one saw me. She didn't weigh that much, so I could do it on my own all right.'

Murphy motioned with his hand to continue.

'After that, I reckon I took her out to the front past Speke Airport. Garston way, down by the docks there. Put her in the Mersey and watched her float away. That's what I probably did.'

'You didn't do anything to her other than wrap bin bags round her and just dump her in the river?'

Keith looked at Murphy and gave him a shrug of the shoulders.

Murphy allowed the snort from his nostrils to escape. Bodies didn't float down the Mersey for very long without being seen, even those at the tail end of the river where there were fewer tourists. Further up, near the Albert Dock, it wouldn't have lasted five minutes before being seen. It ... she ... would have been found by now.

That was just the practical element. There was also the fact that Keith seemed to have mental health issues, which made everything he was saying about what he may have done to Amy questionable to say the least.

Part of Murphy was thinking 'poor guy' ... the other part was complaining about the time that was being wasted.

'Are you ready to give us your surname yet, Keith?' Murphy said, attempting to be more professional and not the irritable detective he had been for the previous hour. 'So we can check into you, things like that?'

Keith didn't respond. Just stared at the table, finding the grooves scratched into its grey surface of unyielding interest.

Amy Maguire had been missing for over three weeks. Vanished, one Thursday night. Into thin air and everything that went with it. Murphy and Rossi had been helping the short-staffed F Division in Liverpool South investigate Amy's disappearance. Their division in North Liverpool had been almost overstaffed at that point. The newly created Major Crime Unit now in existence, following a few years of increasingly high-profile cases. Higher command hadn't spread resources widely or anything as logical as that. Instead, they had simply bulked up the numbers in Liverpool North.

The Amy Maguire case might have fallen through the cracks if it wasn't for the fact nothing major had come through their doors in almost a month. Liverpool South had a multitude of other cases to deal with, so the investigation had been shifted north and Murphy was about to hand it off to a detective constable to handle, when he'd seen something in the file which piqued his interest.

Amy's mother, Stacey. A name and an address he remembered well.

A few days after she had disappeared, Murphy and Rossi had gone down to the shop where she'd worked. Rain had been coming in bursts, threatening to soak the ground and anyone in its way. Rossi had struggled to hold an umbrella over them both while Murphy looked towards the shuttered-up shop as they stood in the last place CCTV had caught Amy's image. The camera only caught the area immediately outside the shop entrance. Amy had left the edge of the frame and disappeared into darkness. Police tape strewn almost randomly across the street, as uniformed constables struggled to keep order. A small number of angry voices with nothing better to do, snarling at the plain-clothed detectives, screaming for a justice the country didn't provide.

Murphy blinked and was back in the interview room.

'Interview terminated at ten fifteen a.m.'

Amy Maguire was still alive. She had to be.

Murphy walked ahead of Rossi as they left the quiet of the room and stepped out into the corridor. He pushed through into the stretch of corridor that led towards the main incident room, making an effort to keep the door open for Rossi, before letting it swing shut behind him. Calm to cacophony in a single walk.

'How long have we worked together for now? And don't you dare say "too long".'

'Must be over three years. Why?'

'Have we ever had someone come in and confess to a murder they haven't committed?'

'A few times. Usually they don't get this far though. Uniforms downstairs tend to see them coming. Obviously slipped through the cracks this time.'

'It's not like I'm averse to people confessing crimes to me – I've heard enough of them in the past – but it doesn't half piss me off when someone confesses to something that hasn't happened.'

'Wait up, will you . . . *Mannaggia*.'

Murphy slowed a little to allow Rossi to match his step, then carried on towards the new office near the back of the building. Their old incident room was now used by the Matrix team who focused on drugs and gangs, leaving domestic violence, trafficking and the occasional murder for Murphy and his team. He wasn't sure which was worse.

He threw open the door and walked to his desk at the back of the room past the array of staff now technically under his supervision. In his peripheral vision he saw his boss through the glass of her internal office, but he kept his gaze forward, unwilling to be beckoned within just yet.

Murphy slammed his fist into the back of his chair, instantly regretting it as it spun away and into the wall.

'I've told you not to hit it so hard,' Rossi said, sitting down at the desk opposite Murphy's. 'You'll end up breaking a bone. We'll have to get you a punchbag in here or something, if you're going to spit your dummy out every time you don't get your own way.'

Murphy made some sort of guttural noise at her and dragged his chair back. He sat down, shaking his right hand to rid himself of the low throb which had already set in.

'Why don't you start up boxing again,' Rossi said, leaning across the desk.

'Because I'm too old for all that now. Been almost twenty years since I was in a ring. I'd get flattened in a second. Plus, the pain in my hand says I've forgotten how to throw a punch properly.'

Rossi hummed and sat back in her chair. 'Who does that?'

'Does what?' Murphy replied, as he began to calm himself. 'Punch chairs? At least it wasn't a wall . . .'

'I meant confess to a murder which sounds not only improbable, but of which there is no evidence that it has actually happened.'

Murphy swept open palms across his cheeks. 'Attention seeker? Mental health patient . . . God knows. We know it's not true . . .'

'Possibly . . .'

Murphy went on as if Rossi hadn't spoken. 'We're still treating this as a missing person, not a murder enquiry. So, we send a report and see if there's anything anyone wants to do with Keith. That's not our problem.'

Rossi nodded slowly. 'Don't think we should dismiss it entirely though. It's not like he was confessing to killing JFK or something. It's possible that he could be telling the truth.'

'It was Amy on the video. Walking from the shop at eleven at night, not at nine in the morning like he said. Her mum was still awake at one in the morning and it's only a ten-minute walk from there. Amy would've been home well before then.'

Murphy had spoken a little harsher than he'd meant so wasn't exactly surprised when Rossi didn't answer at first, instead giving him a silent moment of contemplation.

'People don't just disappear ...' Rossi replied after allowing the silence to drag on for a few moments longer than was comfortable.

That was the only problem with trying to dismiss the thought that something had happened to Amy. Almost three weeks with no word. Nothing to say that she had run off of her own accord. Murphy scratched the back of his head and pulled himself closer to his desk. 'Sometimes, you just have a feeling, okay? Remember that girl we pulled out of that basement a few years back?'

'How could I forget? That was the first proper case we worked together on. It's burned on my memory. It was about that time I started seeing more lines on my face in the morning.'

'Well, I bet everyone thought she was dead or on some island somewhere. Turned out to be wrong, didn't it?'

'I think that was probably a one-off. I'm not sure how many people want to take young girls off the street then keep them alive in a dark basement for a year. Just for some kind of experiment. We have to be realistic here.'

'Yeah, well, maybe it's something else this time.'

'I'm all for positive thinking, Murph, but even I'm struggling with this one. Kick it back to Liverpool South and let them deal with it. Nothing more we can do now. We've spoken to all her friends, done the press thing, all that. Not a single lead, other than a possible mental health patient, confessing to a murder that we have no evidence for.'

Murphy didn't answer. He was remembering Stacey Maguire as she had been years earlier. Seventeen, almost the same age as Amy was now. Mid-nineties haircut and pale skin. He smiled without thinking.

He was broken from his thoughts by DC Michael Hale appearing next to his desk. 'Boss is calling us in.'

Murphy raised an eyebrow at Rossi before following her and DC Hale, catching up to them as they entered the boss's office. The boss being DCI Stephens, head of their not-so-little corner of E Division.

'I'll get straight to the point,' Stephens said. Murphy closed the door behind him, not for the first time bristling at the fact that there was enough room for four people to work comfortably in this room whereas everyone else was tripping over themselves.

'We've got a situation developing at the moment near Anfield . . .'

'At the stadium? Someone nicked a footballer's car or something?' Hale said. Murphy gave him a withering look, which made Hale stiffen and turn away.

Stephens deigned to look at him for a second before switching her attention back to Murphy and Rossi. 'If you'll allow me to finish my sentence . . . no, not at the stadium. Although not far from it. Two bodies found in a house in Anfield.' She rattled off an address which Murphy was pleased to see both Rossi and Hale noted down.

'Suspicious?' Murphy said, noting a harried look in Stephens's eyes and wondering what had caused it.

'Very. And that's not all. Early reports are that we've found our missing celebs. And that it's bad. Very fuc—'

Stephens stopped herself short. 'Let's just say if what I'm hearing is right, we're about to have a lot more company than usual.'

Murphy nodded and turned round, not waiting for Rossi and Hale to follow.

It always begins with a body. Or bodies, in this instance. Murphy thought of the cases over the years – the bodies he had seen in their last moments – and carried on walking.

That was what he was paid to do. To keep walking towards the bodies.